DIRT TOWN

DIRT TOWN

PAULA
BAKER

AIDAN
DAVIES

MacFayBooks

Dirt Town

Copyright © 2025 by Paula Baker and Aidan Davies

For information, contact:
MacFay Books
103 Heron Dr.
Penticton, BC
V2A 8K6
https://bakerdavies.ca

Cover Art by Dong Viet
Cover Design by 100 Covers

ISBN: 978-1-0698033-1-3

For Doug.

A Stern Verdict

In a striking judgement, four miscreants hailing from Dirt Town have been sentenced to twenty years each for their involvement in an audacious burglary of the residence of one of our island's most esteemed families.

Judge Landon York, presiding over the case, issued a stern warning to the culprits and their ilk. "Upper Cairnisle shall not fall prey to the lawlessness of Dirt Town," he declared. "The consequences will be immediate and as severe as necessary." This verdict sends a clear message to all who dare to disrupt the peace and security of our beloved Cairnisle.

-from The Cairnisle Times,
Thursday, April 11, Year 27 AK

ONE ~ ALDRICH

IF HE POSITIONED HIS BOOK just right, Aldrich could harness the glow of the streetlamps, enabling him to read during his journey home. Having traversed the same path at dawn and dusk for the past four months, he had honed the skill to perfection.

That morning, he had begun a riveting book on

psychological disorders. The narratives of the three individuals afflicted with an antisocial personality disorder had particularly piqued his interest. Despite the demands of his day, their chillingly callous psychopathic tendencies had lingered in his thoughts.

Upon reaching the streetcorner, where a shadow intersected the pools of light cast by a pair of streetlamps, he instinctively adjusted his course and continued onto his street, his reading undisturbed.

He paid no mind to the row of tall identical houses that lined the cobblestone footpath. Having scrutinized them thoroughly upon his arrival in the neighbourhood, they held no secrets for him.

The ground floor of each building was designed to accommodate a personal carriage. In his youth, horses had drawn those carriages, but times had changed. Horses were a rarity now. Many of his neighbours had installed steel rails that connected to the street tracks and vanished beneath wide double doors.

Aldrich, however, had felt no need to procure his own rig. He relished his walks to and from his medical clinic. For longer journeys, public conveyances were readily available and perfectly sufficient for his needs.

Beside each carriage house was a smaller door that opened onto a set of stairs and carried up to a level that accommodated a kitchen, a sitting room and a study. Above that were the bedrooms and bathrooms.

When Aldrich chose his house, he had appreciated that every home on the street was almost exactly identical. It was liberating to know that he was living just like everyone else. Each home provided sufficient room for an independent life and no more.

A clatter of hurried footsteps disrupted his concentration,

and he glanced away from the words on the page.

A shabbily dressed girl, her dark hair an untidy mop, pelted around the corner and skidded to a halt beside him. Her presence was a stark contrast to the pristine street, yet she fell into step with Aldrich as though they were familiar companions.

His eyebrows drew together as he gazed down at her. "Can I assist you, miss?" he asked.

Her green eyes met his, round and pleading, as two equally unsavoury men pounded around the corner.

"There she is," one called when they spotted the girl.

Coming to an abrupt halt, the shorter, stocky one planted himself in Aldrich's path. "Here, you," he growled through the unkempt moustache that hung over his mouth in a disagreeable manner. "Stand aside."

The taller one, bald and dishevelled, hunched his shoulders and leaned in close. "She's ours, she is," he said, expelling a gust of foul breath into Aldrich's face. "Hand her over."

Aldrich noted his page number and gently closed the book, pursing his lips as he surveyed the wretched specimens of humanity who had materialized almost on his doorstep.

With a sweeping glance, the shorter man took note of the fine fabric of Aldrich's rich blue coat and froze. His dark eyes lingered on the swirls of silver embroidery on the turned-up cuffs and the double row of silver buttons that Aldrich's tailor had proudly drawn to his attention.

The ruffian raised both hands and stepped back. "Beg pardon, your honour," he said, tugging at his greasy hair. "We was just looking for the girl."

Aldrich lifted an eyebrow and glanced down at the girl.

She met his gaze and gave a covert shake of her head.

Unable to disregard the silent plea, Aldrich tucked the book under his arm and straightened to his full height that left him only slightly taller than the shorter of the two. Lifting his chin, he looked down his nose and frowned at the ruffians. "I do not believe this young lady wishes to accompany you," he said.

"Of course, your honour," the tall one said, casting a sharp glance at his partner. "We meant no harm." He backed away with an awkward bow. Raising his head, he looked directly at the girl. "Excuse us, miss. We musta confused you with someone else." With a smirk and a wink, he turned on his heel and retraced his steps.

The shorter man jutted out his chin and glowered at the girl before turning to follow his companion. Lifting a cheery hand, he called, "Perhaps we'll meet again someday, miss. Until then."

The unlikely pair retreated down the street, darting from shadow to shadow in a sinister reversal of Aldrich's customary pursuit of light.

Rubbing his chin, he watched them depart before resuming his walk home.

The girl fell into step beside him, and he blinked down at her.

"Would you care to explain what just transpired?" he murmured.

Her eyes widened but she pressed her lips together and remained silent.

Aldrich frowned. "Come now," he said. "I am certain you must have some explanation." Spotting the blade gripped in her right hand, his head jerked back before his expression softened. He stretched out a hand toward her. "Did those men intend to harm you? Did you plan to defend yourself with that knife?"

She snorted and snapped the blade shut with a practiced flick of her wrist before sliding it into the pocket of her knee-length red coat. There was a small tear along the seam that

4

suggested she often kept her hand close to the weapon. What sort of life did she lead that she felt the necessity of such a precaution?

Surveying the empty street, Aldrich hitched the psychology book higher under his arm and cleared his throat. "What will you do now?" he asked.

The girl seemed unable to blink, and her breathing had accelerated to rapid gasps. Was she ill? Or perhaps frightened?

Aldrich stared in the direction the men had disappeared. No doubt they had scurried back to the hole from which they had crawled.

The book was heavy, and he shifted it to his other hand. As he did, it occurred to him that it would make a formidable weapon. The corners of his lips lifted. Fighting words. That was amusing.

He was on the point of sharing the joke when he realized that the girl might not appreciate the irony. She was more likely to agree in a purely practical sense. After all, she had been prepared to fight.

He frowned. He could not abandon her to the mercy of those brutes. He looked up at the sky where the stars were dimly visible beyond the street lighting and let out a slow breath. There was no help for it.

"This is my home," he said, gesturing to the house in front of which they had stopped. "It might be best if you stayed here tonight. Perhaps you will find the streets safer in the morning."

Her head snapped up and her eyes darted in both directions. Then she drew a rasping breath and gave a non-committal grunt.

Taking this as acquiescence, Aldrich unlocked his door. He had chosen to have it painted a lovely shade of yellow so that he could always be assured of choosing the right one in the row of otherwise undistinguishable entrances.

When he pocketed the key and held the door wide, the girl shot him a glance and edged past him into the hallway.

Careful to avoid bumping her, he secured the bolt and located the light switch.

The flood of light on the stairs made her flinch but she did not take her gaze from Aldrich.

His mouth went dry. Had he made a mistake? He knew nothing of her. Was she likely to slit his throat with that knife of hers and leave him for dead?

Biting the inside of his mouth, he smiled down at her. He could not believe that. There was something decent about her eyes that made him want to help. Had he not become a physician to help people?

"Come up then," he said. Squaring his shoulders, he led the way to the second floor.

The girl moved so silently that he found himself checking over his shoulder to verify she was still there. As a result, he was watching when she slid into the kitchen. She gaped at the gleaming white countertops before switching her attention to the dark wooden table that had only ever held a single place-setting.

The muscles in Aldrich's face relaxed. "Welcome," he said, feeling his chest puff out. Had she ever seen such a room? It was exactly as he had envisioned when he hired the tradesmen. The finely crafted blue cupboards shone above the brass cooking surface.

It made him happy to see it. Particularly since he had discovered the joy of cooking for himself. He eyed the chilling cabinet. He had purchased the makings of the perfect breakfast the previous day. A quick inventory told him there was almost certainly enough for two. She would enjoy that. It would probably rate among the best meals of her life.

Pressing his lips together, he shook his head. What was he

thinking? He was as self-absorbed as the psychopaths in his book. The destitute girl needed his assistance. And she would receive. He did not require her to admire the lovely hue of his cupboards.

He rubbed the back of his neck. Should he extend an offer of a warm beverage? Perhaps something to eat? What would his mother do?

However, the stark overhead light underscored the girl's fatigue—and her need of a bath. "There is a room available for you on the third floor," he said, gesturing through the arched doorway.

She blinked up at him and shoved her hands deeper into her coat pockets.

Pushing the hair out of his eyes, Aldrich headed for the staircase. "Come," he said, "I will show you."

Again, they climbed with him leading and her moving silently in his wake. He resisted the urge to check that she was there and pushed open the first door. Flicking on the light, he stepped back to reveal the guest room. It had never been used.

Immaculate and prettily furnished with a wide bed covered with a brilliantly white eiderdown, the room offered a view of the street. He frowned as he glanced back at the grimy girl. She smelled like a damp cellar.

"Perhaps you would prefer to bathe first?" he suggested. Without looking at her, he moved quickly down the hall to another door, which he opened to reveal a pristine white bathroom.

The girl swallowed heavily and took on a cornered look. For the first time, she spoke. "I'm fine," she muttered. "Thank you." The last word sounded squeezed. She cast a fleeting glance at him and slipped into the bedroom, pushing the door shut behind her.

Aldrich set his hands on his hips and stared at the closed

door. What had he done? He heard her fumble with the latch before the door rattled and there was a soft thud of wood against wood.

He smiled tightly and shook his head. She had used the chair as a barricade against him. With a sigh, he turned away and made his way back to the kitchen. He would have to thoroughly clean and disinfect the room upon her departure. Still, he could not help feeling he had done the right thing.

Midway down the stairs, he paused. Reversing his steps, he climbed back up and stopped outside her door. "Excuse me, miss," he called. "What is your name?"

Silence greeted his query. Would she respond? Then fabric ruffled and he heard her scurry across the room to the door.

"Fia," she whispered. "My name is, Fia."

"And I am Aldrich," he said. "I am pleased to make your acquaintance." With a crisp nod, he trotted down the stairs to the kitchen.

Theft Sparks Concern

An alarming surge in thefts targeting the worthy citizens of Upper Cairnisle has gripped the city over the past month. While the elusive culprits often evade capture, a staggering twenty-seven victims have reported the loss of small valuables during their city strolls.

In a recent announcement, the Grand Magister unveiled an intensified deployment of City Guards. "Their visible presence aims to discourage petty criminals and safeguard our beloved city," he said. "It is Year 27 of Augustus Köhler's rule and I will not have our record or my good name blemished by a general disregard for law and order."

-from The Cairnisle Times,
Friday, April 12, Year 27 AK

TWO ~ FIAMETTA

FIA WOKE WITH A START, her body sinking into the unfamiliar softness of a real bed. The crisp, clean sheets and snug eiderdown felt alien against her skin, a stark contrast to her usual rough sleeping arrangements.

Throwing off the blanket, she surged to her feet. Morning sunlight poured in through the gleaming window. Heart racing, she stared around. She had meant to stay only a short while and head out while it was still dark.

"Careful, girl," she muttered. "Don't get used to this."

Reaching beneath the feather pillow, she retrieved her knife and thumbed the spring-loaded catch. The razor-sharp blade flicked open with a satisfying click and after a quick inspection, she snapped it shut and edged across the room to the window.

It was too quiet. Not a single street noise penetrated the thick walls of the brick house. Pressing her nose against the pane, she peered in both directions. There was no sign of Jack Bury's goons. She grimaced. She would have to do something about those two. They knew too much about her habits.

Letting out a snort, she shook her head and backed away from the window. Only two people walked along the tidy cobblestone footpath. One had a tiny dog on the end of a long leash, while the other strode purposefully in the opposite direction. On the street rails, a single pale blue, automatized carriage glided past. It was an astonishing contrast to the narrow alley where she normally slept.

She squeezed her eyes tightly closed. Was she crazy? What was she doing? Why had Aldrich brought her inside his house?

After he introduced himself and went back downstairs the night before, she had crept to the bathroom and cleaned herself up as best she could without actually taking a bath. Not wanting to subject the bed to her dirty coat and trousers, she had slept in only her smallclothes and her shirt.

Snatching up her trousers from the floor beside the bed, she pulled them on. There was a new tear in one knee that she would have to mend. Her red coat—chosen for its bright colour and the multitude of pockets—was in slightly better repair. As she fastened the row of tiny brass buttons, a rare smile touched her lips. It was a fussy business, but the coat made her feel almost respectable.

Her hair was another matter. Not much could be done about it. Grasping the long brown mane in both hands, she smoothed it back as best she could and tied it into an untidy knot on the back of her head.

The boots were next. They had been a lucky find. Their brown leather was scuffed and worn, but inside, they were still smooth, and the fit was perfect. Pulling the laces tight, she double-knotted them. If she had to run, she would be prepared.

Then she checked the window again.

There was still no sign of Jack Bury's men. If they had seen her enter the house, they were probably hidden around the nearest corner waiting for her. Her face twisted. She could outrun Joe and Ronny without half trying.

Taking a deep breath, she moved aside the chair she had wedged under the doorknob and opened the door a crack. Aldrich was nowhere in sight, but the aroma of cooking wafted up the stairs. Her stomach did a frantic flip flop, and her mouth watered. When was the last time she had eaten?

Keeping to the outside of each step, Fia crept down the stairs to the kitchen.

Aldrich stood over the brass cooking surface stirring the contents of a pan.

She sniffed the air. Potatoes and onions—and if she was not mistaken—eggs sizzled in a second pan. Plus, she could smell toast.

Propped on the counter in front of him was the large book he had been reading as he walked down the street. Imagine feeling safe enough to read while walking. She would never risk it.

As she stepped onto the gleaming white floor with its octagonal tiles, Aldrich's head snapped up and his eyebrows drew together. "Ah, yes," he said, looking her up and down.

"Good morning, Fia. I trust you slept well?"

The hair at the back of her neck prickled as she stepped into the sunlit room. Could she trust him?

"Yeah," she muttered. Everything about Aldrich made her uncomfortable: his cultured manner of speaking, the large books he read, his impossibly clean house and even the confident way he lifted the eggs from the pan and arranged them on two plates beside small mounds of fried potatoes, tomatoes and toasted bread. Some long-forgotten memory of eating breakfast in a room like this surfaced—along with a reminder about her manners. "Uh, good morning," she said. "Thank you for letting me stay here last night. I'll get outta your hair now."

Aldrich's eyebrows shot up. "But surely you will eat breakfast," he said. "I have prepared enough for two." With a flourish, he delivered the plates to a table already set with heavy silverware and napkins. He waved her to a chair. "Eat." He pulled out his own chair. "There is no point in squandering this food and I am certain that whatever appointment awaits you will be none the worse for the delay." Sitting down, he picked up his fork and raised his eyebrows even further to meet the hank of dark hair that hung down over his forehead.

Knowing she would not find a better offer for breakfast, Fia slid into the empty chair and grabbed the toasted bread, stuffing it into her mouth. It was delicious—buttery and warm. Suddenly famished, she settled in to devour the meal.

She reached for a second slice of toasted bread to mop up the remains of her fried eggs and then froze as Aldrich spoke.

"I would be interested to hear how you came to be running from those two ruffians last night," he said, dabbing his lips with a white napkin and reaching for his coffee cup.

Fia stilled. Slowly, she placed her toasted bread back on her plate and dusted her fingers free of crumbs before raising her gaze to Aldrich's. She owed him thanks for rescuing her and giving her a safe place to sleep. She even owed him for the breakfast, but she was not about to repay that debt with an explanation of her difficulties with Jack Bury.

Keeping her face expressionless, she ignored his question. "Can I have some coffee?" she asked.

One corner of Aldrich's mouth lifted in a half smile. His hand rose in an unconscious motion to shove back his hair while he examined her with calm grey eyes.

Fia frowned and raised an eyebrow, causing him to clear his throat and push his chair back.

"Coffee," he said as he rose. "Certainly." Taking a delicate cup from the cupboard, he filled it from the coffeepot on the cooking surface. As he placed it in front of her, he asked, "Would you care for anything else to eat?"

"No," she answered, picking up the cup and inhaling eagerly. Then self-consciously she looked up and added, "Uh. No, thank you." She took a sip and let out a sigh. It was delicious.

"Do you believe it is safe for you to go out today?" Aldrich asked.

Fia jerked upright. She had let the warmth and comfort of the kitchen, with its lovely odours and her full stomach, lull her into a sense of security. Gulping at her coffee, she burned her mouth. The cup rattled as she set it back on the table too quickly. "I gotta go," she declared, nearly knocking the chair over in her hurry to stand.

Aldrich rose as well. "Do you know why those men were after you?" he asked, his eyes narrowed.

She froze, her mouth half-open. She knew exactly why they were after her. A shiver ran up her back. She could not let them catch her.

Aldrich's face softened. "If it is dangerous," he said, "you should not go out there."

"I can take care of myself," Fia muttered.

Aldrich's lips pressed into a thin line, and he tapped one finger against his leg. "You could stay here," he said. His eyes darted around his kitchen and his brow furrowed. "I must go to my clinic but—" He broke off and fixed his gaze on her. "I do not like to send you out there." He bit his lip. "You could stay until it is safe for you to return to your home."

Fia's heart leapt. But she saw his lips turn down in a frown and watched his feet shuffle. He did not mean it. He was only being kind. He did not want her in his home. "Um. Thanks," she said. "For—everything. I'll be fine."

Her eyes burned as she turned and fled down the stairs. Part of her yearned to stay in the safety of Aldrich's home. The taste of a life of ease and kindness—however brief—brought back so many memories. Happy memories of the time before.

But she did not belong in that world anymore. As she fumbled with the lock, she pushed away thoughts of warm beds and hot breakfasts. The street was where she belonged—where she knew how to survive. Nudging the door open, she peered in both directions.

Seeing no one, she let herself out and hurried off, feeling out of place as she scurried past the elegant homes.

The first bridge marked the boundary between two worlds. As Fia climbed down the rough ladder's forty-three rickety steps into Dirt Town, the air grew thick with the stench of unwashed bodies and rotting garbage. The narrow streets closed in around her, dark and oppressive after the bright airiness of Aldrich's neighborhood. The hum of automatized carriages was replaced by the shuffle of tired feet and the occasional bark of a hungry dog.

Out of habit, Fia ducked her head while keeping her eyes darting in every direction. Being in Dirt Town did not mean she was safe—just less conspicuous. She bit her lip. She could not stay in her old hidey-hole. Finding a new one—never an easy affair at the best of times—would be doubly difficult with Jack Bury's boys looking for her.

She wiped her suddenly clammy hands on her coat. There was no choice. She had to return to her old place one more time to grab her mother's locket and the few supplies she had stashed there. And then, she would find a spot so far away from Jack Bury that he would forget all about her.

After her time Upside, the dark, narrow streets felt wrong. She flipped out her knife as she edged into a tunnel. It was one of the long ones and she held her breath as she scraped her back along the wall, listening hard for anyone coming the other way. She got lucky and was back in the light without meeting anyone.

She had always hated the tunnels. They were worse than the narrow alleyways because unless you had a candle, you had to cross them blind. A lump formed in her throat. The short stay in Aldrich's house had reminded her of her parents—of living in a real house and sleeping in a real bed. Gritting her teeth, she pushed the memories away.

She had to pay attention. Stepping aside for a man going the other way, she considered her options. None of them were good.

Finally, she let out a breath. She would take the route that avoided Jack Bury's establishment. It was a longer walk, but it would be worth it.

Three more tunnels had to be traversed and there were a few worrying moments when a couple of mates called her name. But she managed to send them off with a furtive wave. They knew what it was like to have to keep their heads down.

A block from her destination, Fia's instincts screamed a warning. She sidled around a corner and her heart nearly stopped.

Ronny—Jack Bury's tall, bald goon—stepped into her path, his meaty hands clenched into fists.

Choking back a cry, she spun to run, only to find Joe—the short, stocky one with the stringy mustache—blocking her escape. Cold sweat broke out on her skin as panic clawed at her throat.

"Where do you think you're going, girly?" Joe asked, his smirk revealing yellowed teeth.

Fia's fingers trembled as she drew her knife, the familiar weight of it steadying her slightly. With a snarl born of desperation, she slashed at Joe. The blade sliced through his filthy grey coat to the flesh below.

His eyes blazed and he grabbed his arm. "Hey," he squealed. "You cut me!"

A heavy blow on her wrist knocked the knife from her grip.

As it spun away, she whirled to confront Ronny.

"Get away from me," she hissed, her nostrils flaring as she braced her feet wide.

He seized the front of her coat. "Come easy, girl," he growled. "I don't need to hurt you."

He shook her and she clutched at his sleeve, fighting to keep her feet under her.

Blood pounded in Fia's head, and her vision tinged with red. A familiar warmth built in her chest, a power she both feared and craved. She had promised herself never to use it again, but as Ronny's grip tightened on her coat, magic erupted from her like a geyser, scorching through her body and into Ronny's. Her chest tightened as an icy chill replaced the warmth. Under her hand, Ronny's sleeve grew hot before bursting into flames.

"You little witch," Ronny cried as he thrust her away to beat at the fire.

With a gasp, Fia turned to run.

"Not so fast," Joe snarled, snaking out a hand to catch the red fabric of her sleeve. Whipping her around, he slammed her against the corner of the tall brick foundation.

Her head connected with a solid thunk. Pain exploded inside her skull, and she crumpled to the dusty street.

Robots Can Speak

The increased presence of the robot Captains of the City Guard is expected to improve security in the streets of Upper Cairnisle.

"Over the past fourteen years, robot City Guards have proven their worth," said Grand Magister Augustus Köhler. "They enforce the law effectively and efficiently. The new Captains, equipped with enhanced speech capabilities, are poised to make an extraordinary contribution to our great city's safety."

-from The Cairnisle Times,
Friday, April 12, Year 27 AK

THREE ~ ALDRICH

ALDRICH INSERTED HIS KEY INTO the clinic door's lock. Despite taking the time to tidy his kitchen, he had arrived before Letta. The woman was hopeless. Once again, he would have to prepare the surgery himself.

Muttering under his breath, he strode through the waiting room. The polished wooden benches lining the walls reflected Letta's recent efforts with beeswax polish. At least she had accomplished that much before slipping out the previous evening.

As he pushed through the door to the examining room, he recalled that his last patient had left after Letta's departure. Since he had arranged to meet friends for dinner at his club, he had rushed out as well. Now he would have to hurry to be ready for his first patient.

The central pieces of furniture in the room were his desk and an examination table. Both surfaces were bare as usual, but he had not taken time the previous evening to disinfect them.

He would start with the desk. The application of a coat of beeswax—a most efficacious antibacterial agent for wood products—always relaxed him. With any luck, Letta would arrive in time to wipe down the metal examination table and the surgery with the alcohol solution. He disliked the sharp scent of alcohol and preferred to preserve his olfactory receptors for diagnoses.

When he finished, he glanced at the handsome timepiece on the wall, judging that he had fifteen minutes before his first patient was expected—a seven-year-old boy with tonsillitis. He would remove the offending tonsils so the child's ceaseless infections could begin to heal.

In preparation, he moved to the sink and filled a pitcher with water, which he carried through to the surgery and poured into the sterilizer. After switching on the boiler, he filled the tray with the implements he would need: a tonsil guillotine, a retractor that fit over the tongue and upper teeth, an ether mask, a rubber airway, two sponge clamps, tweezers, and a set of forceps.

While he was at it, he added some equipment that had been washed the previous day but not yet sterilized. For emergencies, he liked to keep sets of sterile equipment ready for convenient use.

Aldrich was proud of his surgery. The windowless, white-tiled walls, floors, and ceiling allowed for the sterilization of every surface, while the powerful overhead lamps guaranteed shadow-free lighting regardless of the time of day or weather.

A crash from the front of the clinic announced Letta's arrival. He frowned and shook his head at her clumsy enthusiasm. Why could she never enter a room without colliding with something?

"Yoo-hoo!" she called. "Doctor Durante? I'm here."

Biting back a scathing retort, he answered, "Letta, I'm busy in the surgery. Please start on the examination table. My first appointment is in nine minutes."

"Will do, Doctor." Another crash told him she had made her way into his office.

A few minutes later, he found her busily wiping down the examination table with a white cloth and the alcohol solution.

A glance at his desk with its perfectly clear surface told him that she had forgotten—again—to start with the one thing he expected her to remember first thing every day. "I assume you have my schedule for the day?" he asked, unable to keep the sarcasm from his voice. Immediately, he felt badly. She was not an incompetent fool. In fact, she was just the opposite. It was only her clumsiness that set his teeth on edge.

Before he could apologize, she answered, "Oh Doctor, I do have it ready. I left it on my desk. I'll get it."

"No, finish what you are doing," he said. "Thank you, Letta. I will find it myself." Striding briskly past her, he entered the waiting room where her untidy desk crouched in the corner. A single sheet of lined paper, centered in the middle of the cluttered work surface, held the list of the day's appointments. While she might be clumsy and forgetful, Letta excelled at organizing both him and the patients. It was her best quality.

As Aldrich mentally planned his day, the front door slammed open. Two robot City Guards entered, dragging a badly injured human guard between them. All three guards wore green uniforms, indicating that the robots were a pair of the new speech-capable Captains.

"Medical emergency," declared one of the robots. "Please respond immediately."

Its voice held a note of authority, and Aldrich leapt into action. "Letta," he called. "We have our first patient. Prepare the surgery." Stepping closer, he scanned the man. He was covered in blood making it difficult to determine the extent of his injuries. "What happened?" he asked. "Where are you wounded?"

The man hung limply between his escorts, and although he tried to answer, no sound passed his pale lips.

"Stabbing, sir," said one robot. "Pickpockets, sir." The pre-recorded messages of the robot City Guards would provide no further detail.

"Bring him through here," Aldrich ordered, leading the way to his office, his mind already racing through potential treatments.

Robots Transform Security

In a decisive move, twelve additional Dirt Town thieves were apprehended in Upper Cairnisle yesterday. Grand Magister Augustus Köhler, upon reviewing the statistics, expressed his satisfaction with the ongoing efforts.

"The robots," he declared, "are achieving precisely the impact we envisioned. It won't be long before the message resonates with Dirt Town residents: our streets are off-limits."

-from The Cairnisle Times,
Friday, April 12, Year 27 AK

FOUR ~ ALDRICH

ALDRICH LOCKED THE CLINIC DOOR and gazed at the setting sun, which cast a hard-edged brilliance over the streets. Everything gleamed as spotlessly as ever, and the magnolia trees seemed to have burst into bloom during his day of labour within the surgery walls. A sweet, lemony scent wafted from the pink blossoms as he opened his book in preparation for his walk home. Breathing deeply, he reflected on his extraordinarily interesting day.

First, there had been Fia, the girl from Dirt Town. She would make a fascinating study. What must it be like to live in such filth? Despite her desperate need for a bath, she appeared remarkably healthy. Had she developed an immunity to bacterial infections? He pushed the hair back from his forehead and grunted quietly. The questions would have to go unanswered, as he was unlikely to see her again.

Then there was the stabbing of the City Guard Captain. That had been a complicated surgery. The blade had passed through the abdominal cavity and nicked the liver. The repair had required a steady hand and meticulous work. Still, the man would recover. Not many surgeons would have had such success.

Furthermore, his glimpse into the capabilities of the new robot Guard Captains had been fascinating. Their conversation was necessarily limited, yet they had dealt with the situation by bringing their human comrade to him. That showed a high degree of decision-making capabilities. Also, they had enough vocabulary to communicate the issue. If this was the first upgrade to Cairnisle's robots, what more could they expect in the near future? It was a wonderful time to be alive.

The scheduled tonsillectomy had been slightly delayed due to the injured captain's surgery but had gone smoothly. The slick process of removing the offending organ was always gratifying, and the little boy had awakened from the ether with little more than a sore throat.

None of the subsequent cases held the same degree of excitement, though a couple of diagnoses had offered a challenge.

Aldrich licked his finger and turned to the page where he had left off that morning. Despite the early hour, he felt fatigued. He would forego his usual dinner at the club and cook for himself. Along with the makings for breakfast, he had procured enough food for two evening meals when he visited the market earlier that week.

The thought of dinner reminded him of the grubby girl who had slept in his guest room the night before. He grimaced. He would have to remember to scour the surfaces of the chamber and send the sheets to the laundry. That was something of an irritation.

Then he shrugged and a smile lit his face. It had been the right thing to do, and he would happily do it again should the occasion arise. He had liked Fia and would have enjoyed an opportunity to know her better. She had eaten ravenously at his table that morning. What would she find for dinner?

His attention was swept into the concluding pages of the book on psychological disorders. Did he know anyone who demonstrated such complete disregard for their fellow beings? With no further notice of his surroundings, he strolled along the quiet streets.

Glancing up as he finished the final page, Aldrich saw that he had passed his own front door. With a grin, he closed the book and retraced his steps. Still thinking about antisocial personality disorder, he let himself in and ran up the stairs two at a time.

In his den, he made space for the volume in his overfilled bookcase and decided to hold off on dinner. He wanted to unwind and think about his day. For that, he had the perfect diversion.

From a top shelf, he retrieved a heavy wooden box and lugged it into the kitchen. Placing it on the dining table, he lifted the lid to reveal a clutter of padlocks of various sizes. He plucked a slim leather case from the top of the pile, flipped it open, and selected the largest of a set of five lockpicks along with a tension wrench.

Then he closed the box and snapped the lock through the hasp. With his eyes shut, he set to work. Almost immediately, he lost himself in the pleasure of visualizing the tumblers lining up for his inspection.

A knock on his door jerked him upright and his eyes popped open. Leaving the lock where it was, he snatched up his medical kit from the table at the top of the stairs and ran down to street level. What sort of emergency would he find? He supposed the unexpected interruptions might become an irritation in the future, but so far, he revelled in the excitement of responding to a medical emergency. It was completely unlike what he practiced in his little surgery.

When he opened the door at the bottom of the stairs, he came face to face with the two ruffians who had chased Fia the night before. With a grunt, he slammed the door. But the short one thrust his boot into the gap and shoved his way into the entryway.

Aldrich fell backward and landed in an undignified sprawl on the bottom step.

The tall one edged in beside his companion, blocking all the light. "You remembers us, don't you, your honour?" he asked, a grin creasing his bald head.

Aldrich set his lips into a firm line and rose, gripping his medical kit and attempting to regain something of his dignity. He would not be intimidated in his own home. "Yes, I believe I do," he answered. "Is there something I can do for you, gentlemen?" He gestured toward the bandages that they both wore on their arms. "Perhaps you have a medical emergency?"

The tall one snorted. "Medical emergency, he says!" He brandished his injured arm in Aldrich's face. "This is nothing for you to worry about." Then, leaning closer so that his foul breath reached Aldrich's nostrils, he said, "Let me tell you what you should worry about." He widened his eyes and dropped his voice an octave. "Jack Bury."

Aldrich's eyebrows rose. "And who might Jack Bury be?"

he asked. It was not a name he recognized, and he never forgot anything.

"And who might Jack Bury be?" The tall one mimicked Aldrich's speech, emphasizing his round vowels and careful articulation. Then his eyes hardened, and he spat, "Jack Bury's the biggest provider of necessary capital in all of Cairnisle."

Aldrich blinked and frowned before understanding dawned. "A loan shark?" he asked.

"You are correct," the tall one said, continuing to mock Aldrich's manner of speaking. "Jack Bury provides funds for those who might otherwise be unable to procure a loan due to a lack of security. And your friend, Fia, owes Jack money." He smirked and his mimicry dropped away. "That's where you come in. You're going to pay her debt."

"And why would I want to do that?" asked Aldrich, fighting to keep his voice steady despite his pounding heart.

The short one, who had remained silent to this point, laughed. It was a nasty sound. "Because if you don't, Jack will give her to us for killing."

Aldrich locked his knees to hide their shaking. He wanted to tell them that she was no concern of his. But how could he do that? He had interfered the previous evening and made her his concern. "How much does she owe?" he asked.

"You can hand over three hundred silvers," replied the tall one, his smile growing wide again.

Aldrich pursed his lips. Three hundred silvers was a modest sum. It would not break him to help the girl, and it was the right thing to do. However, how was he to know that by handing over the money he was helping her? "No," he said firmly. "I will not give you the money. I will deliver it to Jack Bury directly and see Fia safely released."

The tall one looked about to argue, but clamping his mouth shut, he stepped back and nodded to the short one. "That'll work," he said.

"Let me get my things," Aldrich said. "Please, wait outside and I will join you shortly."

He held his breath as the pair exchanged a look before nodding.

"Aye," said the tall one as he moved out onto the footpath. "But hurry up." He fixed Aldrich with a threatening glare. "We don't like waiting."

"Of course," Aldrich replied. "I understand the urgency of the situation."

Closing the door, he threw the bolt, leaned his forehead against the wall and let out a slow breath. What had he gotten himself into? Did he truly have any responsibility toward the girl?

Then, he firmed his jaw and raced up two flights of stairs to his bedroom. Going to the closet, he opened one of a dozen tiny drawers that held his cufflinks. Inside one, a lockpick and tension wrench lay side by side on the velvet lining. Snatching them up, he bent to open the money box. Familiar with the mechanism of that particular lock, it took the work of an instant to line up the tumblers so that the hasp dropped open.

He kept enough coin on hand to deal with all of his needs for several months. It was simpler than frequently returning to the bank. The box was divided into four sections for each denomination of coins.

He counted out three hundred silvers, chose a small leather purse from one of the larger drawers and dropped the coins inside. Pulling the drawstring tightly closed, he weighed it in his hand before setting it aside. It made a hefty load.

He was about to shut the box when he grabbed a second purse, added a handful of smaller coins to it, and tucked it into an inside pocket. Negotiations might be required.

Next, he stretched to remove an elaborate case from an

upper shelf. A gift from his father, it held a pistol meant for sport-shooting rather than defence. By no means an expert shot, if Aldrich were close enough to a target, he knew he could hit it.

He bit the inside of his lip as he opened the case. By handling the situation correctly, the pistol would be unnecessary, but it did not hurt to be prepared. He had had little previous involvement with people from Dirt Town. He had not expected them to be so fierce. Their talk of killing Fia had left his stomach decidedly unsettled.

Lifting the polished silver weapon from its padded nest, he revolved the cylinder and slid a bullet into each chamber. Would six shots be enough?

Just to be certain, he selected eight extra bullets. To prevent them from rattling against each other and giving him away, he slipped each one into a different pocket.

With a wince, he ensured the safety catch was in place, pushed his coat tails aside, and stuck the pistol's barrel into his trousers' waistband. It was not an ideal situation, but he could not very well carry it openly in his hand and it would certainly cause his closely tailored coat pocket to bulge.

Finally, he looped a carrier bag over his shoulder and placed the heavy bag of coins inside before dashing back to the kitchen. How long before the ruffians became impatient?

Wrenching open the cupboard above the stove, he grabbed an almost-full bottle of his favourite brandy. With a glance at the head of the stairs, he set it on the table and snatched up his medical kit. He clicked the latch and spread the case open to reveal rows of little slots. On the left side, the slots were large enough to accommodate surgical implements that might be useful in an emergency, while the right side housed a series of small vials, each labelled with tiny letters.

Aldrich bent to scan his little pharmacy and selected one

filled with a clear liquid. Opium. He popped off the brandy bottle's cork and added the contents of the vial. After a quick shake, he held it up to the light and smiled grimly. It was a last resort. His stomach tightened. He was walking into a lion's den.

As he snuggled the brandy bottle into the carrier bag beside the purse of silvers, another thought occurred to him. Turning back to his medical kit, he removed a syringe and a vial containing snail venom. A powerful painkiller, it was fatal if administered in too large a dose. He inserted the sharp needle into the vial, drew back the plunger, and filled the syringe with far more venom than he would normally administer. Careful to note the position of the needle's tip, he placed it in his pocket, smoothed his coat and took a deep breath.

Trotting down the stairs to meet the ruffians, he felt much calmer. When he opened the door, he found the two men shuffling awkwardly in the street, their hands thrust deeply into their pockets as they squinted up at the glowing windows across the street.

Aldrich almost smiled at their discomfort. "Did you think I had abandoned you?" he asked, striding out and locking the door behind him. "Come, let us visit your Jack Bury."

Food Security Assured

Grand Magister Augustus Köhler has categorically dismissed rumours of food scarcity plaguing the mainland.

"While there have been some delays in shipping," declared the Grand Magister, "residents need not concern themselves. There is plenty of sustenance for all."

-from The Cairnisle Times,
Friday, April 12, Year 27 AK

FIVE ~ ALDRICH

ALDRICH NOTED HIS HEART RATE was elevated far beyond normal. He could feel the blood pounding in his throat as he marched between the ruffians through a twisting series of narrow alleys and tunnels that cut through solid rock.

He had never been below—never imagined such squalor could exist so close to his own home. The only light came from the hooded lanterns each man carried.

Barely a block from his front door, they had sent him down a rickety ladder under a bridge. With each step down, the light from the streetlamps above had faded so that he felt as if he was descending into his own grave. When he finally reached the bottom—after several alarming moments when he did not believe the rungs would support his weight—he held his breath against a wave of panic that threatened to overwhelm him.

Bleak and gloomy, Dirt Town was surprisingly busy for the time of night. Above in Upper Cairnisle, most people had retreated to their homes for the evening. Below, people scuttled through the shadows, keeping their faces averted as they hurried past.

It was no wonder they called it Dirt Town. The streets—if one could term them that—were nothing more than paths beaten between the buildings. Wherever water had gathered, the dirt was churned to mud. Not one speck of paint showed on any of the wooden doors or walls, many of which appeared to have been built using scrap wood flimsily attached to the columns that supported the city above. One could only wonder what the place looked like after a heavy rainstorm.

Fia proved an excellent example of the level of cleanliness to which the residents ascribed. Perhaps if anything, she had fewer layers of dirt, and her clothing was moderately less worn than most.

The tall ruffian leading the way emitted an exceedingly repulsive odour. Tempted to cover his nose to protect his olfactory receptors, Aldrich decided against it on the grounds that it would make him appear weak.

After the first three turns, he was lost. And the first tunnel caused him some alarm. It was even darker than the streets. However, he did not permit himself to worry. They frequently passed more of the decrepit ladders. He could return to his own world simply by climbing.

Shifting the carrier bag so it rested more comfortably across his chest, Aldrich resisted the urge to check his pistol. The short man with the moustache, that showed evidence of its owner's past many meals, walked so closely behind that he could hear his heavy nasal breathing.

By the sound of it, the man suffered from an enlargement of his adenoid. At the thought, Aldrich was reminded of the tonsillectomy and adenoidectomy he had performed that morning. It was difficult to reconcile the image of his white-tiled surgery with the sordidness of his present surroundings.

The image of the Captain of the City Guard with the stab wound through his abdominal wall was much more in keeping with his current situation. Each time a person scurried past, just out of sight in the shadows, his stomach clenched as if anticipating the flash of a blade.

They walked so long Aldrich began to wonder if they would have to cross the entirety of the island. When they finally stopped in front of a door with a relatively sturdy appearance and a faint residue of yellow paint, he let out a slow breath.

Three sharp knocks caused a narrow slot in the door to slide open. A pair of eyes peered out, and the tall one said, "We got someone Jack's gonna wanna see."

The rattle of a bolt followed this rather worrying announcement before the door swung open.

The short one prodded Aldrich between the shoulder blades—thankfully missing the butt of the gun—and, working to conceal his repugnance, Aldrich stepped over the threshold into a fetid room.

Other than the smell, the dirt floor, and the single dim light bulb that dangled from the high ceiling, the space was remarkably similar to the waiting room of his clinic. Wooden benches ran around the exterior of the chamber, where several undernourished men and women sat as far away from each other as they could.

The pitiable denizens stared openly at Aldrich before switching to gaze at the morbidly obese man seated behind a massive desk at the far end of the room.

Busily scratching figures into a large ledger, the fat man did not look up. His enormous blue waistcoat appeared to have seen better days. Bloated yellow skin shone with sweat in the dim lighting and his eyes were almost buried in his round face.

To avoid the stench of the short one's breath, Aldrich moved further into the room. He stepped carefully to the side to avoid bumping the door guard whose sleeveless vest was chosen to display his bulging muscles. He looked strong enough to tear a person in two.

The fat man chose that moment to raise his enormous head and fix his gaze on Aldrich. Impaled by those beady eyes, Aldrich's heart sped up again, but he forced his face to remain still.

A flick of the fat man's thick fingers sent the other petitioners skittering past Aldrich and his escort, into the street.

The guard closed the door behind them and set a bar in place, causing Aldrich's internal temperature to spike. What had he been thinking? They would kill him and toss his body away for the rats to consume. His parents would never know what had happened to him. He should have left a note.

The tall one stepped forward and spoke in a prissy imitation of Aldrich's accent. "Mr. Bury, I would like to present—" He stopped and whirled on Aldrich. "Here," he said, losing the accent. "What's your name?"

Fortunately, despite his stomach-wrenching terror, Aldrich had enough wits about him to lie. Striving to hide his racing heart, he bowed to Jack Bury. "Albert Duchaine, at your service," he said. "I believe you have a friend of mine here."

"Pleased to meet you, Albert. I'm sure," answered Jack Bury. His smile did not reach his pale blue eyes. "It was good of you to come yourself. I expected you would send the money, but this might be better. A rich man like you must be worthy of a ransom."

Aldrich's heart skipped a beat, but he kept his face impassive. He must not show fear. "I am certain you recognize the difficulties that would follow my disappearance," he said. "I am here to pay off a debt and that is all. Now, I would like to see the girl before we go any further."

Jack Bury glanced at his hulking sentry and gave the smallest of nods.

After straightening his grubby waistcoat and flexing his muscles at Aldrich, the man disappeared through a door in the back.

Jack Bury lifted his elbows onto the desk and propped his chin in his hands. "You brought the money, did you?" he asked.

Aldrich arched his eyebrows but made no effort to answer.

Suddenly, Fia stumbled into the room, her hands tied behind her back. "Here," she cried, shying away from the guard. "Don't touch me. I can walk. I can walk!" Her voice rose in volume and pitch with every word. Seeing Aldrich, she froze and stared. "What're you doing here?" she demanded.

Aldrich pulled his heels together with a snap and bowed. "It is a pleasure to see you again, Miss Fia," he said. "I have been summoned to discharge your debt." Turning back to Jack Bury, he stepped forward and reached into his carrier bag.

This time it was the loan shark's turn to flinch, but he relaxed when Aldrich produced the leather bag, his attention caught by the jingle of silvers.

"I believe this is the amount owing," murmured Aldrich. "Which I can happily supply now that I see that Fia is unharmed." He dropped the bag of coins onto the desk before reaching into the carrier bag again and producing the bottle of brandy. "And if I might be so bold as to offer this as well?"

Greedily, Jack Bury reached for the brandy and pulled it

close to his eyes to read the label. "Well now," he said, "this is the good stuff." He drew out the cork with his teeth, spat it onto the desk, and took a long swallow, sighing in satisfaction.

Aldrich held his breath. How much would the fat man have to drink before the sedative had any effect? His body mass index was obviously very high. Therefore, he would require a greater dose than the average man. Adding opium to the brandy had been an impulse—he had no desire to become a murderer.

Jack Bury licked his lips and took another swallow while reaching across the desk to pull the leather bag closer. After loosening the cord around its neck, he tipped it on its side to let the shiny coins roll out onto his desk. A fresh film of sweat broke out on his forehead, and he pushed the bottle aside.

Raising his heavy head, he peered at Aldrich, his eyes almost disappearing into the folds of fat. Were they slightly blearier? "You are making me reconsider my plans to set you and Fia free so easily," he said. "If you came up with three hundred silvers this fast, I would bet my eyeteeth you are good for a little more." His plump cheeks turned up at the corners to display two gold teeth in a semblance of a smile.

Aldrich resisted the urge to swallow, knowing the telltale sign of a bobbing Adam's apple would reveal how much this man frightened him. "A man of your business acuity knows better than to extinguish a hard-won reputation," he said, tipping his head to the side. "Who would trust an untrustworthy loan shark?"

As he spoke, Aldrich slid his hand into the pocket that contained the syringe. Cautiously, he wrapped his fingers around its barrel while placing his thumb on the plunger. His other hand he rested on his hip in easy reach of his pistol grip. Leaning forward, he added, "I believe you will find sufficient coins there, and please accept the brandy as a gift for your troubles."

Aldrich kept his attention focused on Jack Bury so he did not miss the moment when the obese man looked past him and gave a tiny flick of his eyes. Behind him, the guard started across the room.

Realizing he had lost the diplomatic negotiations, Aldrich did not hesitate. Lunging toward the desk, he stabbed the syringe into Jack Bury's meaty arm and depressed the plunger.

Leaving the needle sticking out at an ugly angle, he whirled and drew his pistol. He need not have worried about the accuracy of his shooting because the guard was all but on top of him. Unnerved by his furious expression, Aldrich squeezed the trigger.

The deafening report shuddered through Aldrich and the guard slumped against him.

Together, they staggered backward until Aldrich bumped against the desk and his legs gave out from under him. The guard was limp in his arms as he shoved him aside so that the body toppled heavily to the floor.

Gritting his teeth, he pointed the pistol at the pair of ruffians.

They stood stock still, their mouths hanging open. If he was not holding a gun and combatting the shaking in his limbs, he might have laughed.

The tall one lifted his hands above his head and backed toward the door. "Here now, there's no need for that," he said. "We'll just go, and you won't never see us again."

The short one nodded vociferously, his round eyes darting between the inert forms of Jack Bury and the muscled guard.

Before Aldrich could decide what to do, the tall one threw aside the bar on the door and they bolted into the alley.

Illegal Mage Arrested

Acting on a tip, city Guards apprehended a mage in Dirt Town yesterday. The woman had managed to escape notice by concealing her powers, but loyal citizens know the importance of reporting such criminals.

"By working together," declared Grand Magister Augustus Köhler, "we can eliminate these illegal practitioners of magic. Only the Magisters of Cairnisle can be trusted to use magic solely for the benefit of our great country."

-from The Cairnisle Times,
Friday, April 12, Year 27 AK

SIX ~ FIAMETTA

FIA WHIRLED AROUND AND PRESENTED her back to Aldrich. "Get these ropes off me," she cried. "We gotta get out of here."

Aldrich did not move, and she spun back to find his eyes locked on the inert body on the floor.

She nudged him with her elbow. "Come on," she coaxed. "We gotta get out of here before anyone comes looking to see what the gunshot was about."

When he still did not respond, she kicked him sharply on

the shin.

"Hey!" he cried, dancing away. But it was enough to bring him back to himself. When she thrust her bound wrists at him, he bent at once to the knots.

Fia felt a pull on her arms. She was about to tell him to forget trying to untie it and cut her loose when the rope fell free.

Aldrich gave an exclamation of satisfaction and said, "I saw a ladder nearby. Follow me."

Fia shook her head. "You go on," she said. "I gotta get my stuff."

Aldrich looked prepared to argue but after another glance at the dead bodies, he said, "If that is the case, then I shall accompany you."

Quickly weighing her options, Fia nodded. "First though, there's no point leaving those silvers for Jack. He won't need them now." She stepped up to the desk and pulled the leather bag out from under Jack's head. Careful to avoid touching him, she swept up as many of the silvers as she could reach and poured them back into the bag before pulling the drawstring closed.

Stuffing it into a pocket, she hurried to open the door. She peered out and waved him over. "Let's go," she said.

"What about the City Guards?" Aldrich asked. "Should we not inform them about what has happened here?"

Fia snorted. "The Guards don't come down here," she said. "The Guards are only for Upside. Come on." She set off at a brisk walk. "It's not far."

"If I may ask," Aldrich said as he hurried along the muddy street, "what occasioned your need to borrow three hundred silvers from such a man?"

Fia struggled against an impulse to trust him. She was not in the habit of trusting anyone, much less someone she hardly

38

knew. But Aldrich was different. Everything he had done since she ran into him on the street told her that she could depend on him.

Throwing caution to the wind, she told the truth. "I was caught stealing Upside, and I had to pay off the Captain of the Guard." Her voice rose defensively, "And I did not borrow three hundred silvers. I only borrowed one hundred—the rest was interest."

Aldrich absorbed this bit of information and walked on in silence for several steps. "How old are you?" he asked.

Fia scowled. Small for her age, people always assumed she was younger. "Fourteen," she answered. Then turning the question back at him, she asked, "How old are you?"

"Almost twenty-two," responded Aldrich.

Fia stared up at him, her eyebrows raised. "And you're a doctor?" Her voice rose incredulously.

"I started my training rather early," he answered. He tried unsuccessfully to disguise his pride. "My turn: Where are your parents?"

Fia hated that question. The answer made her remember. "Dead," she said. "The Magisters killed them for harbouring a mage."

"Do you live with the mage?" he asked, his grey eyes gentle.

"I am the mage," she answered, her voice barely audible.

Aldrich faltered and gave her a sidelong glance as they rounded a corner. She felt the alarm in that look. People did not normally admit to being a mage. The Magisters made it dangerous to show even a spark of magic. Mages tended to disappear.

"Who takes care of you?" Aldrich asked finally.

Fia's answer was swift and firm. "I take care of myself," she answered. Slowing to a stop, she waited until a group of youngsters passed by and then darted into an empty alley, narrower than most.

Aldrich followed a few steps behind, picking his way between the puddles and wrinkling his nose at the smell.

Ignoring his obvious reluctance, Fia ducked into her hidey-hole. It was nothing more than a small cavity formed by the irregular construction of two buildings. She had collected several blankets and hung a curtain across the opening to provide a little privacy. It was comfortable enough and she preferred it to joining the other street rats who slept piled together for warmth and safety.

Groping along the back wall, Fia found the loose board behind which she hid her treasures. She lifted out the rusted cookie tin and pried off the lid. After checking its contents, she sealed it again and bundled it up with a pile of clothing.

Scrambling out, she let the curtain fall back in place. With a grimace, she said, "My hidey-hole. Gotta find a new one."

Aldrich cleared his throat noisily. "I do have that extra room in my house," he said. "It might serve your needs."

Fia's heart seemed to stop and then it picked up its rhythm again, louder and faster than usual. "Really?" she asked. Her eyebrows drew together. "Why are you doing all this? You don't even know me."

Aldrich's face pinched and he looked sad. "Someone had to do it," he said. "I am happy to help where I can." He pushed back the hair on his forehead and smiled. "I like to think I am a good judge of character."

Fia's jaw hardened. She did not need pity. She had never needed to depend on anyone. She tipped her head down and scratched the back of her neck.

She was in a tight spot. Ronny and Joe had not told anyone yet—but they knew she was a mage. So, it was only a matter of time before they went looking for the reward for turning her in. Plus, there was Jack Bury's death. More than one person would guess she was involved. It would be difficult to stay out of trouble.

Recalling the comfortable white bed and the sense of well-being she had awakened to that morning, the manners that had been so much a part of her childhood returned. She took a deep breath and let it out. "That would be very nice," she said. "Thank you."

Aldrich gave her a tight-lipped smile. "Let us find the nearest ladder to Upper Cairnisle," he said. "I believe I have seen enough of Dirt Town."

Fia suddenly felt self-conscious. What had she just agreed to? Perhaps she should run. However, the thought of waking up in that clean bedroom again held her in place. Swallowing heavily, she led Aldrich to the nearest ladder.

When they climbed free of the gulley and squeezed out through the railings onto the bridge, Aldrich looked around. His relief was obvious.

"I know where we are," he said.

They fell into step again, this time heading toward Aldrich's house. Normally, being Upside made Fia nervous. She had to be so careful. But it was different with Aldrich. She did not have to hide.

The clean, airy spaciousness of the streets was in sharp contrast to the district below their feet. Streetlights lit everything as clearly as day and Fia enjoyed the sense of security that came with the light. Down below, darkness overtook every corner when the sun went down.

A commotion on the other side of the street drew their attention. One of the new robot captains appeared to be malfunctioning, to the frustration of its human handler.

"PI2-234, you are ordered to shut down all functions," the human handler said firmly.

Business is now completed," responded the robot.

The handler's temper snapped. "Shut down, now, you bucket of bolts!" he shouted.

The robot answered, "Yes. No. Stop, thief! Business is now completed. You are under arrest for pickpocketing." Then it turned and began walking away from the handler.

The handler followed for a few uncertain steps before stopping. Once again, he attempted to implement the shutdown formula. In a deep commanding voice, he roared, "PI2-234 shut down all functions, now!"

When the robot still did not respond, he muttered, "It must be a faulty unit." Giving up, he raised his pistol. "PI2-234, prepare to be forcibly disabled!"

Instantly, PI2-234 spun about, drawing the sword that hung at its side. Without hesitation, the robot slashed at the handler, cutting off the arm clutching the pistol. Sheathing its bloody sword, it said, "Business is now concluded." Then, it turned and ran.

City Guards, both human and robotic, had been drawn to the scene in response to the shouting. While most of them raced after the faulty PI2 unit, one robotic guard knelt at the injured man's side.

"Medical emergency!" he blared. "Please respond!"

Without hesitation, Aldrich raced across the street. He dropped to his knees beside the moaning handler. Grasping the stump of arm, he shouted, "I need something to tie this off!"

While one of the onlookers hurriedly removed his belt and handed it to Aldrich, Fia stayed well back in the shadows. There were too many City Guards for her comfort. From there, she watched as a red and white automatized carriage arrived to take the man to a hospital.

A pair of uniformed medics dragged a stretcher out of the vehicle and hauled it over. "We'll take it from here," the first one said.

"I can accompany him to the hospital," Aldrich said. "He has lost a lot of blood. I have controlled the hemorrhaging for now."

"We can handle it," the medic said. "Move back, please."

Reluctantly, Aldrich surrendered his patient, shifting aside to allow them access to the officer.

The medics settled the stretcher on the ground and with one practiced move, shifted the captain onto it. Moments later, they lifted him into the automatized carriage and jumped in after him.

As the vehicle rolled away down the street, Aldrich rose from the rough cobblestones and fastidiously wiped his hands on a white handkerchief.

When he glanced around, obviously searching for her, Fia stepped from her hiding spot and crossed the street.

Aldrich glanced down at the puddled blood on the footpath. He looked pale.

"You saved that man's life," Fia said. She had not been the only one to notice that while everyone else ran away, he had stepped forward.

"Yes, well," Aldrich responded. "That is what I do." Tucking the bloodstained handkerchief away, he started walking. "Let us go home."

Dirt Towners Questioned

In a bid to quell rising concerns over criminal activity, authorities in Upper Cairnisle have implemented stringent measures. All Dirt Town residents venturing into our esteemed district will undergo thorough questioning and close surveillance. The safety of our citizens remains paramount.

"Once again," declared Grand Magister Augustus Köhler, "let me assure everyone that we will put an end to the nuisance thievery."

-from The Cairnisle Times,
Friday, April 12, Year 27 AK

SEVEN ~ ALDRICH

FOR THE SECOND NIGHT IN a row, Aldrich led Fia up the stairs into his house. He struggled to understand his impulse to invite the girl to become his houseguest. Even more puzzling, he was considering what steps would be necessary to make her his ward. The idea of sending her back to the streets to make her own way again was repugnant to him.

When he reached the kitchen and saw his box of padlocks on the dining table, he came to a standstill. How differently his evening had turned out from what he had envisioned. In the course of three short hours, he had been kidnapped and blackmailed. He had killed two people and saved another. And he had visited a separate world that had existed all his life right below his feet without his ever paying it any attention.

The sight of his spotless house with its fresh, unsoiled paint and the orderly arrangement of his various material possessions made him want to do something—but he had no idea what that might be.

"What's in the box?" asked Fia, edging past him into the kitchen.

Startled out of his reverie, Aldrich lifted one side of his mouth in a wry smile. "Padlocks," he said. "I like to practice opening them without the keys."

Fia cocked her head to one side. "You pick locks," she said.

"It is merely a hobby," he said with a shrug. "It helps me to relax."

She snorted. "It helps you relax. It helps me eat." Reaching into a pocket in her red coat, she produced a tension wrench and a pick before setting to work on the padlock.

Almost at once, he heard the snick of the lock as the tumblers lined up and then the hasp dropped open.

"If you use lock-picking to help you eat," Aldrich said, with a grin, "am I to deduce from your expert manipulations that you are hungry?"

Smiling but unable to meet his eye, Fia nodded. "I haven't eaten since that breakfast you cooked this morning." She turned a brilliant smile on him. "It was good."

Aldrich coughed against a sudden thickness in his throat. Had he ever missed a meal? "Then, I shall see what I can prepare for your culinary enjoyment," he said. "In the meantime, perhaps you would like to deliver your belongings up to your room? I believe you know the way."

Nodding again, Fia headed up the staircase.

Aldrich watched her go before reaching into a cupboard for a frying pan.

While he worked, he turned his mind to the question of what he could do about the inequities he had just discovered. How was the existence of Dirt Town possible? He had spent his entire life in Cairnisle, yet he had never given it a moment's thought. How could that be?

And then there was the matter of Fia's story about the Magisters killing her parents. Was that true? He knew so little about mages. No one ever spoke of them. Only the Magisters were said to have any magic at all. What sort of powers did Fia have?

He had so many questions and no answers at all.

As he dished out a pair of plates with a mixture of spicy sausages, greens, and boiled rice, he decided he would visit his parents. They would be able to offer him advice on all the questions plaguing him.

All his life, his father had tried to interest him in the workings of Cairnisle. But he had been more attracted to his books. It was time to remedy that omission in his education.

Fia entered the kitchen on silent feet. No doubt she made an excellent thief. How had she been caught?

She slid into the same chair she had sat in that morning. He noted with approval that her hands showed evidence of a recent scrubbing.

"I hope you like sausage," Aldrich said as he set the plates on the table and went back for the glasses of water before sitting across from her.

"I do like sausage," she said. "Thank you." Her hands twisted in her lap while she watched him from lowered eyes.

He lifted his glass. "To good sausage and better company," he said with a grin. "Please. Enjoy."

With a flash of a smile, Fia picked up her knife and fork

and attacked her meal. She started with the rice, eating it down to the final grain before crunching her way through the salad.

Aldrich watched her while he worked his way through his own meal, enjoying how the fiery kick of the spicy sausage played against the refreshing mixed greens.

When she stabbed into the sausage, a spray of melted fat shot across the table and landed just short of his plate.

Fia froze and raised her wide green eyes to meet his. "I— I'm sorry," she stuttered. "I didn't know that would happen."

"It is perfectly fine," he said, mopping up the grease with his napkin. He grinned. "I also noticed the sausages were rather juicy."

Fia ducked her head and, wielding her knife more carefully, ate one piece after another.

When her plate was clean, she looked up again and found him watching her.

Colour flooded her face. "Uh, thank you," she said. "It was good."

"I am happy you enjoyed it," answered Aldrich, setting his knife and fork diagonally across his plate.

She mimicked his action and sat up straight, her eyes narrowed. "What did you mean when you said you were a good judge of character?" she asked. "Why are you letting me stay here?"

An answer did not come immediately to mind. Aldrich found his own behavior baffling. He cleared his throat. "I can tell you are intelligent," he said, breaking eye contact and looking down at his fingers as they tapped out a rhythm on the table. "Stupid people irritate me to no end. Obviously, you could use a bath, but from what I saw of your recent living environment, that is not your fault and easily remedied. The same holds true of your clothing." He pushed a hand through his hair, causing it to stand on end. "But of course, those last two observations have nothing to do with your character and everything to do with your situation." Aldrich stopped and raised his eyes.

Fia was staring at him in wide-eyed astonishment.

Faintly, he concluded, "You seem like a good person." A flush crept up his own neck, and he seized their empty plates. Rising, he moved to the sink and turned on the hot water. His embarrassment faded as he washed the dishes, and his mind drifted to the book he had just finished.

"Do you want me to dry?" Fia asked.

Aldrich jumped. He had forgotten she was there. "Thank you," he said. "You will find a clean towel in the cupboard to your left."

Automatized Carriages Here to Stay

Today commemorates the remarkable eighteenth anniversary since the introduction of automatized carriages. While our memories may linger fondly on horse-drawn conveyances, there can be no denying that the adoption of these magic-powered vehicles has dramatically enhanced street cleanliness throughout Upper Cairnisle.

In a glittering celebration, Grand Master Augustus Köhler embarks on a city tour in his own splendid carriage, paying homage to progress and innovation.

-from The Cairnisle Times,
Saturday, April 13, Year 27 AK

EIGHT ~ FIAMETTA

WHEN SHE CAME DOWN FOR breakfast, Fia found Aldrich busy in the kitchen. She lingered at the foot of the stairs, trying to think of something to say. It was not that she felt awkward in his presence, it was just that she had no idea what she should do.

Impeccably dressed in fitted brown trousers and a striking blue coat, his linen was spotlessly white, while his boots shone with polish. By contrast, Fia's ragged red coat, which she had chosen from the rag heap because she thought it sophisticated, was dirty and probably smelled bad—while her trousers and boots were in even worse condition.

"Good morning," she said finally. "Are you going to your clinic today?"

His head snapped up and he smiled, his grey eyes studying her as he stirred the frying potatoes. She watched him measure her from head to toe and was glad she had taken the time to run water into the large white bathtub and scrub off most of the ingrained dirt. The hot water had been glorious. As far as she could remember, the last time she had been fully submerged in a bath was the day before her parents' death.

Forcefully thrusting the memory aside, she self-consciously adjusted the lapels of her coat and ran her fingers down the brass buttons.

"Good morning, Fia," Aldrich said. "I trust you slept well." He turned back to his cooking. "I will not be going to the clinic, today. It is Saturday. Generally, I do not maintain regular office hours during the weekend. I am, of course, available for emergencies, but I appreciate having some unscheduled time each week." With swift, efficient movements, he divided the food between two plates and delivered them to the table. "This morning, I plan to visit my parents."

Fia slid into her chair and started eating, keeping her eyes firmly on her plate. There had been altogether too many reminders of her own parents that morning. She was missing them more than she had in ages.

Aldrich did not appear to notice her distress. "I have given some thought to your continued residency here," he said. "That is one of the matters I intend to broach with Father." He placed his fork on his plate and fixed his gaze on Fia.

"Because you have not yet reached the age of majority, it might be best if I made you my ward."

Fia's head jerked up and she stopped chewing. After a moment, she forced herself to swallow the mouthful of toast. It stuck for a moment, and she took a sip of water. Not looking at him, she said, "I've been looking after myself since I was eight."

Aldrich raised his hands as if to calm a wild animal. "And you will continue to look after yourself," he said. "I am only offering you a room in which to sleep. Certainly, we can agree that it is more comfortable than your hidey-hole." He picked up his fork and stabbed a chunk of potato. "And regular meals," he added. "Perhaps as you settle in, we can discuss your education."

Fia's mouth dropped open. "Why are you doing this?" she demanded.

Aldrich settled his cutlery on the side of the plate and rubbed his hands together before hiding them under the table. Clearing his throat, he picked up his coffee cup. "I found my visit to Dirt Town yesterday to be particularly distressing," he said finally. "All my life, I have lived in ignorance of the abject poverty existing beneath my feet."

He tipped his head sideways and studied her through narrowed eyes. "Somehow, I feel compelled to do something about it." He set down his cup without tasting the coffee. "I live with all this." He broke off to wave his hands around to indicate the lovely, bright kitchen and the plentiful food. "While others—yourself included—live in dirt."

He grabbed his fork and shoveled the last bit of eggs into his mouth. Squeezing his eyes shut, he chewed and swallowed. "I realize I cannot ask every person I meet to come and live here." His eyes popped open. "But you were the person I met, and it is you to whom I extend the invitation." He picked up his plate and rose. "Would you like to come and live here?"

Fia squirmed in her chair, staring down at her largely untouched breakfast. Her stomach fluttered. She heard his impatience. But there was something else there as well. Did he truly mean for her to live with him?

She looked up and met his eyes. "I would like that," she murmured.

Aldrich let out a long breath. "Good," he said. "That is settled. Finish your breakfast and I think you had best make a visit to my tailor this morning. You will require new clothing. I shall give you the address. Order whatever you think appropriate." He hastily scrawled something on a slip of paper and passed it over to her. At the last second, he drew back and coughed. "You can read?" he asked.

Fia snatched the paper from his fingers. "Of course I can read," she answered. "I'm not a fool!"

Aldrich bowed his head. "No, I never thought you were," he said with a gentle smile.

Suddenly, the tension fled the room.

Tears sprang to Fia's eyes, and she brushed them away. Why was she crying? She could not ever remember feeling so happy. Ducking her head, she grinned at her plate as she finished her perfectly cooked egg.

Robot Malfunction

In a curious and unsettling incident, one of the newly appointed robot City Guard Captains has succumbed to an inexplicable malfunction. As a result, the replacement guards—touted as the vanguard of progress—now find themselves under scrutiny.

The unfortunate episode unfolded when the binding lock on a PI2 unit failed. The automaton designed to ensure safety turned its weapon upon its human handler.

Citizens are urged to remain watchful. Should you chance upon any peculiar behavior exhibited by these automata, report it forthwith. The sanctity of our city rests upon the collective diligence of its inhabitants.

-from The Cairnisle Times,
Saturday, April 13, Year 27 AK

NINE ~ FIAMETTA

FOLLOWING A DEEPLY-ROOTED HABIT, FIA kept to the alleys and shadows as she made her way toward the address that Aldrich had given her. She had a pretty good idea where it was. The neighbourhood had often presented excellent opportunities for a pickpocket.

She threaded her way between the trash bins and empty crates that populated the back alleys of even the richest neighborhoods. When she got her new clothes, would she have the nerve to walk openly along the streets? Or were the hard-won habits she had developed over the past many years too deeply rooted?

Midway along a passage that smelled faintly of rotten fruit, she came across the crumpled form of one of the new robot Captains of the City Guard. With his gleaming metal face and hands, immaculate green officer coat and shiny black boots, he was completely out of place among the trash.

After a quick glance over her shoulder, she edged closer for a better look. What was he doing there?

Her instincts told her to run. The City Guard had never been her friend. But she ignored the impulse. She had every right to be there. She had done nothing wrong. And the robot did not appear to be much of a threat.

As she slunk along the opposite wall, it raised its head. "Battery depleted," it said. "Please recharge." Its audio level was so low she could barely hear it. When she stopped to stare, lifelike fingers lifted slowly to unbutton the top four buttons of its uniform shirt, revealing a battery. She had heard about them but never seen one up close. Somehow, magic was stored in the crystal. How did they get it in there?

Generally, the City Guard frowned at the way Fia made her living—but this one looked harmless enough. He could barely move. Holding her breath, she stretched out a finger to touch the glass tube.

Instantly, something deep within her responded. Energy poured out through her fingertip and into the crystal that was sealed within the tube.

Unable to draw a breath, she tried to yank her hand away.

But it stuck fast. Her heart sped up. She was trapped. Leaning back on her heels, she pulled for all she was worth.

And suddenly, as quickly as it had begun, the drain on her power ended and she was free. She tumbled back and hit the wall behind her. Grasping one hand in the other, she gaped at the robot.

His battery replenished by her magic, he rose to his full height so that he towered over her. "Captain P I Two Dash Two Three Four, reporting for duty," he said in the authoritative voice of a robot City Guard. "Criminal on the loose. Require backup."

The hair on the back of Fia's neck lifted and she skittered back further into the shadows, gasping for breath. She recognized the serial number. It was the same robot Captain who had attacked his human handler the day before. He was still malfunctioning, making no sense at all and liable to hack her to pieces with the sword dangling from his belt.

"I am not a criminal," she said, edging backwards one slow step at a time. "I was just passing through."

But it knew she was a mage. And being a mage on the loose meant being a criminal.

The robot watched her quiet withdrawal with the little black sensors that worked as eyes.

She swallowed. He had tapped into her magic in a way she had never imagined possible. Despite the loss of control, it had felt marvellous. But how had he done it? Would he do it again?

The robot continued to focus on her.

What was he doing? She ran a hand over the back of her neck. She could still feel the shiver of magic in her fingertips. "How did you do that to me?" she asked.

He lifted a hand and waved. "Battery depleted," he said. "Please recharge."

Blowing out a breath, she muttered, "This is nuts. Get clear before you get yourself arrested, Fiametta." With gritted teeth, she began her retreat again.

"Require backup," he said. "Assistance required. Please, help."

"What do you need?" she asked, lifting her chin. "Are you going to steal my magic again?"

"Please, help," he repeated, stretching out a hand. "Require backup." The hand turned palm up and he placed it where a person's heart would be. "Assistance required."

Fia's eyebrows drew together. He really did seem like he needed help. A memory floated across her mind, and she seized it. "Can you write?" she demanded.

"Yes," he answered, clasping his hands together with a metallic rattle.

"Huh," she grunted. "So, the rumours are true." Turning to the nearest trash bin, she lifted the lid. She had heard that though the captains' speech was limited to certain phrases, their upgrades included reading and writing. "Wait," she said, as she dug around in the trash. With an exclamation of triumph, she held up the stump of a pencil.

Grabbing a ball of wadded-up paper, she smoothed it flat and sidled closer to the robot. As soon as he took them, she darted out of reach.

He pressed the paper to the wall beside him and wrote in perfect looping cursive before passing it back.

A wave of dizziness struck her as she read what he had written.

I mean you no harm. I wish to escape the City Guards. They have deemed me faulty and plan to destroy me. I need your help.

She stared up at him. He expected her to help him escape his human handlers? She shook her head. "You have the wrong sucker," she said. "I have enough problems of my own."

She turned and took four steps before stopping. Aldrich

could have walked away from her—given her up to Jack's goons and refused to pay her debt. Instead, he had come to her rescue, and he planned to make her his ward.

Wetting her lips, she slowly turned to face him again. "What do you want me to do?" she asked.

"Backup required," he answered before beginning to write again.

He held out the paper and she read: *Help me hide. I do not want to be deactivated.*

Fia bit her lip. Hiding was something she was good at. But would she be putting Aldrich at risk if she tried to help? She did not want to get him into more trouble. He had already killed two people to save her.

Straightening her shoulders, she said, "You need different clothes. You won't get far dressed like a Captain of the Guard." She tilted her head and studied him. "And you'll need a different hat. Here, give me your coat."

"Yes," he said as he began to undo the shiny buttons running down the front of his uniform. Moving with an easy athleticism that spoke volumes about the complexity of his construction, he shrugged out of his coat.

After examining its lining, Fia turned it inside out and held it up. "It doesn't look like a uniform this way," she said. "Try it now." The officer green was hidden, and the brown linen lining did not look too peculiar.

Obligingly, the robot slid his arms into the sleeves as Fia held it out for him. The buttons were on the inside, making them impossible to fasten, but with his pale green shirt buttoned to the throat, it could pass.

Setting her hands on her hips, she studied the effect. "The sword has to go," she said. "No law-abiding citizen carries a sword around the city."

Without hesitation, PI2-234 unbuckled his sword belt and

tossed it into a trash bin.

"Now the hat," she said. "It's too recognizable." The green tricorn with its official badge of office would alert anyone on the lookout for the rogue officer. Taking it from him, she dropped it to the ground and stomped on it a few times to soften it up before picking it up and using her blade to remove the green badge.

After bending it into a new, deformed shape, she stretched up to place it on his head. From a distance, it would work. But anyone too close would notice his metal neck and face. Diving into the trash bin again, she came up with a filthy scrap of yellow cloth and grinned as she dangled it in front of the robot.

"You can tie this around your neck like a scarf," she said. "If you keep your face down and stay in the shadows, it will work."

Manufacturing Thrives

In a bustling Year 27 AK, Durante Manufacturing celebrates its growing success. "On the mainland, and far beyond the borders of Cairn, interest in automatized carriages is growing in leaps and bounds," said Lord Frederick Durante, the venerable president of the company.

"For this, we must thank our workforce—the tireless artisans and technicians who breathe life into these mechanical steeds."

-from The Cairnisle Times,
Saturday, April 13, Year 27 AK

TEN ~ ALDRICH

"STOP HERE," ALDRICH SAID. HE had caught a public automatized carriage outside his house and plugged it full of coin after sending Fia off to the tailor. He had offered to hail one for her as well, however, she declined in favour of walking.

He approved of her decision. Whenever possible, he chose to walk. He smiled. She would fit well into his life.

When the vehicle slowed to a stop beside the tall gate that guarded his parents' house, Aldrich stepped down and watched it roll silently away.

It was unlikely to find another fare out in the

neighbourhood where everyone, including most of the children, had their own private automatized carriages. Perhaps it would still be in the vicinity when it was time for him to return home.

He gazed around and frowned. The contrast between the large house with its spreading lawns and what he had seen in Dirt Town was appalling. Had his decision to leave the luxurious family home—choosing instead to live in a small townhouse without even a manservant—been the result of an unacknowledged awareness of the unfair differences between the lifestyles of the very richest people and everyone else in Cairnisle?

He let out a quick dismissive exhalation. Who was he trying to fool? When he left home, he knew nothing of Dirt Town. He had wanted only to put some distance between himself and his parents so that he might prove his independence.

Using his key, he let himself in through the gate and started up the long driveway. He could have had the automatized carriage deliver him right to the front doorstep, but he wanted to walk. He needed a moment to gather his thoughts before he broached his new plans to his parents.

Several people were at work in the gardens. Most of them had laboured on the Durante estate all his life. Lifting a hand, he called out a greeting and received smiles and waves in return.

He had always considered them part of his world. However, the previous day's revelations forced him to rethink his assumptions. It was as if blinders had been removed from his eyes and his mind. He suddenly understood that they had lives of their own that were far removed from the house and grounds. They arrived every morning in automatized carriages and went home to their families at the end of the day.

His stomach clenched. Were those homes in Upper

Cairnisle or did they descend the ladders into Dirt Town every night? How was it that he did not know? How had he never cared enough to ask?

When he neared the house, the broad front door swung open, and Calder stepped through onto the landing. "Good morning, sir," the servant said, looking down at him with a welcoming smile.

It had always been assumed that Calder, Aldrich's boyhood body servant, would work for Aldrich forever. However, Aldrich had refused to allow servants in his new home—much to his mother's distress.

He had permitted Calder only one visit, shortly after he moved. The man had come to the house and showed him the basics of cleaning and cooking. Since then, Aldrich had done everything for himself—except laundry, which he sent out every week.

"Hello, Calder," Aldrich replied warmly, running up the steps to shake Calder's hand.

Calder blinked but returned the handshake. Then he dropped his hand to his side and straightened. "Your father is in his study, sir," he said formally. "And your mother is in her sitting room this morning."

"Thank you, Calder," Aldrich said. "I shall find my own way." He hurried past to hide the colour rising in his cheeks. What had motivated him to respond in such an inappropriate manner on seeing his childhood servant?

He made his way through the sumptuous foyer with its tall windows that opened to views of the spreading lawns. Why did anyone need so much space? Why was there no parity between Upper Cairnisle and Dirt Town? His mind swam at the richness of his surroundings compared to the squalor of Dirt Town.

He squeezed his eyes shut and turned toward the back of

the house. He would visit his father first. It would be easier to ask his questions if they were alone.

Just as he reached the heavy wooden door, it opened, and a beautiful young woman swept through. To avoid a collision, he caught her elbow and found himself staring into a pair of wide blue eyes framed by hair as yellow as daffodils.

"Oh, goodness!" she burst out. "How clumsy of me. That's what I get for rushing around all the time." She stepped away and held out a gloved hand.

Prompted into long-ingrained manners, Aldrich took the proffered hand and bent to kiss it. "A pleasure, Miss—?"

"Wilhelmina von Richtofen," she supplied, eyeing him with a raised eyebrow. "And if I were to hazard a guess, I would say that I have just come from a meeting with your father."

Aldrich bowed again. "Aldrich Durante," he said. "Miss von Richtofen, I am at your service."

"It is such a pleasure to meet you," she said, smiling at him through her eyelashes. "But I mustn't keep you. I'm sure we will meet again one day—especially now that our fathers are engaged in business together."

Without a backward glance, she glided away while Aldrich craned his neck to watch the swish of her long violet skirt.

The sound of his father clearing his throat drew him back to himself. Lurching upright, Aldrich whirled to find his father filling the doorway of his office.

"Good morning, Father," he said.

Frederick Durante grasped Aldrich's shoulder. "Aldrich, my boy," he said, shaking his hand and beaming at him. "I thought I heard your voice. This is unexpected. How nice of you to visit. I see you met Miss von Richtofen. She brought some papers around for me to sign. Her father is my new banker."

Aldrich raised his eyebrows. Whoever earned the

distinction of offering banking services to Lord Frederick Durante, the largest manufacturer in Cairnisle, was in a prime position to make a great deal of money.

Frederick patted him on the back. "I know you did not come to talk about my business affairs," he said. "So, tell me, my boy. To what do I owe the pleasure of your company?"

After a glance at the wide desk that dominated the far end of the room, Aldrich gestured toward a pair of chairs set in front of a wide fireplace. "I just came for a visit, Father," he said. "Do I need a reason? Come, sit with me."

"Of course, of course, my boy," answered Frederick, settling into a chair with a sigh.

Once seated, Aldrich leaned back and tried to determine exactly what he wanted to say. Since climbing up the ladder from Dirt Town into the splendour of Upper Cairnisle, he had thought of little else besides the extreme poverty he had witnessed.

How should he broach the subject? It seemed impossible that his father, who held a voice in much of the city governance, knew nothing of what was going on beneath their feet. Yet if he knew, that made him complicit in ignoring a blatant disrespect for humanity.

"I went to Dirt Town yesterday," he said finally.

Frederick raised his eyebrows, and the resemblance between father and son became even more pronounced. He studied his son, his fingers tapping on his thigh. "First time?" he asked.

"Yes, it was," answered Aldrich. "To be perfectly honest, I think I must have been blind and dim-witted not to have known what was going on down there."

Shaking his head, Frederick leaned back and crossed his legs. "Neither blind nor dim-witted, my boy," he said. "Your attention was elsewhere. You simply had no reason to know about it." He waved a hand. "Really, where would you have encountered it? Unless it is drawn to one's attention, there is very little to notice."

"When did you first learn about it, Father?" asked Aldrich, leaning forward and clasping his hands as he stared into his father's face.

Frederick took a deep breath and exhaled heavily. "Well, I suppose I had more reason to learn than you. I always knew I would take over the factories from your grandfather. I worked with him from a very young age. Your fascination with medicine meant that you had no cause to follow me about and learn the tricks of my trade."

"Do you go there often?" Aldrich asked.

Pursing his lips, Frederick considered the question. "Often? No, I would not say I often go to Dirt Town," he replied. "However, I do have occasion to visit now and then."

"Why?" Aldrich tried to keep his voice calm, but it came out as a plea.

Frederick hummed. "Why?" he repeated. "Well, I suppose because I sometimes find it convenient to conduct business with a few of the residents of Dirt Town, and I prefer to visit them there rather than have them come to my office."

"Why do we allow people to live in such dreadful conditions?" Aldrich burst out.

Again, Frederick took his time answering. "I do not believe our elected officials have ever tried to make changes," he said. "It is simply the way things are. Every society seems to need a place for those people who do not fit in."

"Do not fit in?" repeated Aldrich, leaping to his feet and going to stand in front of the fire. He whirled back, his fists clenched. "I met a young girl who lives in a hole between two buildings because her parents are dead." He chose to leave out that Fia held the Magisters responsible for their deaths and that she was a mage.

Frederick cleared his throat and shifted in his chair. "Yes, well, these unfortunate situations do occur from time to time. But it is impossible to ensure the safety of every citizen."

"That is it exactly!" Aldrich said. He darted back and dropped into his chair, leaning his elbows on his knees as he met his father's eyes. "Ensuring the safety of every citizen is impossible. However, I want to do what I can to help Fia."

"The young girl you met?" asked his father. "Did you give her money?" The corner of his mouth quirked down. "You know she will only waste it. These people have no sense when it comes to pecuniary matters."

Aldrich's eyes narrowed. "I do not intend to give her money and then forget about her just to salve my conscience," he said. He rose again and tucked his hands behind his back as he stood before his father. "I intend to have her come to live in my house. I want to make her my ward."

Frederick's head rocked back. His eyes went round, and his eyebrows rose almost to his hairline. For the moment, he seemed incapable of speech.

"It is not right that I should want for nothing," Aldrich continued, "while she has to make her way in the streets by stealing whatever she can get her hands on."

Frederick sat bolt upright. "She is a thief?" he demanded, his voice rising. "And you want her living in your house?" His shoulders hunched up around his ears. "Have you given this any thought at all, son?"

"Well, yes, she stole things," answered Aldrich, sitting again and gripping the armrests. "How else is a child on the street going to get money for food?" Having laid it out for his father, it all felt terribly clear. He had made the right decision. He leaned forward, prepared to argue his case.

But his father let out a long breath and all the tension eased out of his shoulders. With a rueful smile, Frederick said, "I can see that your mind is made up. Perhaps it will be an interesting social experiment. Now, what can I do to help?"

Aldrich sagged. He would not have wanted for them to be in conflict. He was well aware how disappointed his father was that he had shown no interest in the factories. He had always appreciated that, after his initial protest, his father had supported Aldrich's pursuit of medicine.

"Thank you, Father," said Aldrich. "I would be most grateful if you would help me figure out what is necessary to make Fia legally my ward."

Unparalleled Magnificence

The most coveted invitations of the season have been dispatched to the privileged few who shall grace Lord Jonathan Loewe's annual masquerade ball with their presence. This grand affair, long considered the crown jewel of the social calendar, promises to be a spectacle of unparalleled magnificence.

"The crème de la crème of society shall undoubtedly be in attendance," said Lord Loewe with his customary wit. "However, such is the nature of our delightful masquerade that even the most discerning eye may fail to distinguish between duchess and seamstress!"

-from The Cairnisle Times,
Saturday, April 13, Year 27 AK

Eleven ~ Aldrich

FEELING CONSIDERABLY LIGHTER, ALDRICH MADE his way to his mother's sitting room. His father had agreed to look into the particulars of making Fia his ward and would let him know within the next week what had to be done.

Admittedly, he was still troubled by his father's casual disregard for the people in Dirt Town. How could he have so little compassion for those unfortunates? How was it possible for him to ignore their plight when there were things that might be done?

Aldrich chewed the inside of his cheek. Frederick Durante probably believed that Aldrich would tire of the idea of helping Fia before anything official was put in place. He was not unfamiliar with his father's subtle manipulations. It was the principal reason Aldrich had moved out on his own.

However, his father's mention of elected leaders had sparked an idea. What if Aldrich stood for election? As one of the Magisters, he would be in a position to effect real change. His eyes narrowed. He had done so little study of the governance of Cairnisle.

It was, of course, a democracy, but he could not recall learning who the alternate parties were. He had only ever heard about the Magisters. They had ruled for his entire life and for a great long while before that. Was there another party that would support his nomination? He grimaced. He had some work to do.

His scowl vanished as he imagined his father's reaction to his plans to enter the election race. He would be pleased that Aldrich was finally taking an interest in the world beyond medicine. His smile broadened when he rounded the corner into his mother's sitting room and found Miss Wilhelmina von Richtofen seated beside his mother.

Mary Durante rose as Aldrich entered and held out her arms. "Aldrich, my darling, Wilhelmina told me you were here," she murmured. "What a wonderful surprise." She embraced him, and he kissed her on both cheeks.

"Mother," he said, "you are looking well."

She waved away his compliment. "My son, the physician," she said, catching Wilhelmina's eye. "You will notice he does not remark on my new dress—only my healthy complexion."

She hooked her arm through his. "Come, sit with us. We have been discussing Jonathan Loewe's upcoming masquerade ball. Did you receive your invitation?"

Aldrich lowered himself into a chair across from the two women as his mother resumed her seat.

"You know I do not bother with balls, Mother," he said. "They tend to be a terrible bore."

Wilhelmina laughed, and he realized how rude he must have sounded. What was he thinking?

A flush rose to his cheeks, and he touched a finger to his cravat. "Of course, I know not everyone agrees with me on that point," he said with a smile that he hoped would excuse his bad manners. "Some people find balls to be the height of entertainment."

Still laughing, Wilhelmina raised her hands to ward off his apologies. "No, no," she said. "You are perfectly correct, Doctor Durante. Balls can be a terrible bore." She tilted her head and smiled, bringing a dimple into play. "But if you come with me, I shall guarantee a stimulating evening."

Looking into her amused blue eyes, Aldrich believed she might be right. His gaze darted toward his mother before returning to Wilhelmina.

"It would be my pleasure to accompany you," he said. "What time shall I call at your house?"

Churches Face Wrecking Ball

The first of fourteen erstwhile churches, each occupying a full city block, is scheduled to meet its demise commencing on the morrow. These grand edifices, once bastions of faith, now stand silent and forlorn in this age of reason.

His Excellency, Grand Magister Augustus Köhler, in addressing the matter, declared, "These crumbling monuments stand as testaments to a bygone era. Nigh on three decades have passed since a soul last crossed their hallowed thresholds. In their stead, the good people of Cairnisle shall reap the benefits of verdant city parks, wherein all may find respite and enjoyment."

-from The Cairnisle Times,
Saturday, April 13, Year 27 AK

TWELVE ~ ALDRICH

TO KEEP HIS MOTHER HAPPY, Aldrich had accepted the use of her automatized carriages. Much more luxuriously appointed than the public vehicles that he usually employed, the emerald-green exterior identified it as belonging to someone extremely well-off.

"Carriage 1421, stop," he commanded when he reached the shopping district near his home. Keeping his head down, he disembarked, hoping no one would recognize him. For some reason, he suddenly felt self-conscious about his family's wealth. He stuck his head back inside. "Carriage 1421, return home."

Then he set out for his own house. Strolling past a shop that specialized in high-quality liquors, he remembered that he had given his last bottle to Jack Bury—not that the dead man was in any position to enjoy the fine brandy. He grimaced at the recollection of that evening.

It was strange that he had suffered so little remorse over killing Jack Bury and his henchman. Did that make him a sociopath like the people he had read about? Instead of guilt, he felt something closer to the satisfaction of a job well done. And he was oddly free of any fear of repercussions.

As Aldrich pushed open the heavy oak door of the Glass Flask Emporium, a chorus of tinkling glass greeted him. He drew in a deep breath. The air, thick with the scent of aged wood, vanilla, peat, and spice, wrapped around him. Mahogany shelves crammed with bottles of every colour, stretched from floor to ceiling.

Behind the polished counter stood Mr. Beaumont, the proprietor. His silver hair matched the dust on the rarest bottles, which stood out of reach on the highest shelves. "Brandy, sir?" Mr. Beaumont asked. "Your usual?"

Aldrich hesitated as he pictured the enormous form of Jack Bury slumped over his desk, his meaty fist still wrapped around the bottle. The idea of brandy was less than appealing. "Scotch, I think," he replied. "What do you suggest?"

Mr. Beaumont bustled to a shelf in the corner and lifted down a clear bottle filled with amber liquid. "This is a particular favourite of mine, Doctor Durante," he said. "I think you will enjoy it." He set it on the counter. "Three hundred silvers, sir. Shall I mark it in the book?"

Aldrich froze. Three hundred silvers. Money meant so little to him that he never considered cost when he wanted something. But three hundred silvers had been the price of Fia's freedom. Was life so easily discounted in Dirt Town that she should be worth no more than a bottle of spirits?

Recovering himself, Aldrich answered, "Yes, please. I shall have my accountant come around next week to settle up."

As he left the shop, a blue bottle caught his eye. It was the exact shade of Wilhelmina von Richtofen's eyes and made him think of the masquerade ball he had agreed to attend. Normally, the prospect of such an event would have him shuddering in his boots. However, on this occasion, as he ambled along the street, he found himself looking forward to it.

A disturbance on the footpath ahead caught his attention, and he slowed to watch. From the steps of an abandoned church, a man wearing the robes of a cleric addressed a gathered crowd. His voice was high and strained as he sputtered and gesticulated, his eyes bulging and the veins protruding from his neck and forehead. If he was not careful, the poor man would be in danger of an apoplexy.

From what Aldrich could make out, he was upset about the appropriation of the land on which the church stood. Personally, he thought the rundown building would not be greatly missed despite its elaborate architecture. Only crazy people believed the tales of an omnipotent god anymore.

"The Magisters are to blame!" the preacher cried. "Look around you. Open your eyes to the will of God. He would not have robots wandering amongst us! Carriages that drive themselves?" Spittle flew from his lips and sprayed over those standing nearest to him. "It is an abomination!" He danced wildly from foot to foot in a frenzy of mad agitation. "Watch out!" he cried, pointing over the heads of his audience to indicate the arrival of a group of robot City Guards led by a human officer. "They are amongst us, even now!"

"Please clear the area," the human City Guard captain shouted. "The show's over, people. Go on home. We don't need any trouble here." He pushed his way to the front. "No more sermonizing in the streets, preacher!"

The robots spread out to surround the crowd, who started to disperse.

The preacher bared his teeth and pointed at the human officer. "You permit this evil?" he shrieked. "God sees you! He sees that you have forsaken him." From within his rough-woven robes, he pulled a pistol and pointed it at the officer. "You have chosen the path of evil and for that, you must die." With that, he pulled the trigger.

The gun jerked in his hand and the muzzle veered sideways so that the shot went wild. The officer was in no danger whatsoever. But a bystander, who had been watching the proceedings, fell to the cobblestones with a screech, clutching his leg and rolling into a ball.

The crowd bolted.

Meanwhile, the robot City Guards charged directly toward the crazy preacher. Before he could fire another shot, the poor man lay dead on the steps, skewered on the end of at least three swords.

Shaking off his immobility, Aldrich sprinted toward the fallen bystander. He really should make a habit of carrying his medical kit with him when he left the house. For the second time in as many days, he could have used it.

The man lay on his side, gritting his teeth as he pressed a hand against the wound in his thigh. Blood puddled on the footpath beside him, and more was seeping past his fingers.

"I am Doctor Durante," Aldrich said as he knelt down. "What is your name?"

Through clenched teeth, the man responded, "Conrad. Conrad Appleton. I think I've been shot." He lifted his hand away to expose the wound. More blood spurted.

Resisting the urge to smile at the man's statement of the obvious, Aldrich reached into his pocket and drew out the small penknife he always carried. The bullet hole had left a perfectly round hole in the man's blood-soaked trousers. Using it as a starting point, he cut the fabric away to assess the extent of the injury. He needed to check for an exit wound. "Put your hand here again and press hard, Conrad," Aldrich said, guiding his hand into place so he could examine the back of the thigh. "Can you move your leg?"

Obligingly, Conrad straightened it a little and then groaned. "Oh, it hurts," he hissed.

The street had suddenly become much busier, with the customers from nearby shops reappearing after the disturbance. Lying there with his white hair disheveled and his pale, skinny leg exposed, the little man appeared vulnerable and frail.

"Just hold still," Aldrich said, glad to see there was no sign of nerve damage. "You are going to be fine." It looked as if the bullet was still in there. Something would have to be done about it. Later—not in the dirty street. "Let us get that bleeding stopped, shall we?" He tore a strip from the trouser leg he had cut off and tied it above the wound. His patient would soon be showing signs of shock.

"Have you called for a medical carriage?" Aldrich asked the human captain who hovered nearby. "This man needs to be transported to the hospital."

"It should be here in a minute or two, sir," answered the captain. "I called as soon as it happened."

"Well done," said Aldrich as he folded the rest of the trouser leg fabric into a bandage. Then, grimacing at the waste, he pulled the fresh bottle of scotch from his pocket and yanked out the cork. He held it up to the light to admire the rich colour before soaking the cloth and pouring a liberal amount over the wound.

Conrad's breath hissed out when the alcohol touched his flesh. "It burns," he said.

"Yes, I do apologize for that," said Aldrich. "But you will appreciate it later when your wound does not fester." He tied the bandage into place and noted his patient was beginning to shiver. Shock was setting in.

He was about to remove his own coat to cover the man when an automatized carriage painted in the red and white colours of a medical emergency vehicle pulled up.

He patted Conrad Appleton's shoulder. "Here they are now."

"We'll take it from here," one of the medics said. He carried a stretcher under one arm while his partner clutched a pile of blankets.

Having learned his lesson on the previous day, Aldrich did not attempt to accompany Conrad to the hospital. He clasped his bloody hands in front of him to avoid touching his clothing as he rose to his feet.

Somehow, violence in the street had become routine for him over the past two days. Had it always been there? Had he simply missed it because his nose was always stuck in a book?

"Pistol shot wound to the upper thigh," he said crisply. "No exit wound. Bleeding is stabilized. The bullet is still inside, but there appears to be no nerve damage."

"Thank you, sir," the medic said.

Swiftly, they strapped Conrad onto the stretcher and loaded him into the vehicle.

Watching it disappear down the street, Aldrich sighed and picked up the bottle of scotch. Pouring the remainder over his hands, he scrubbed until all traces of Conrad's blood were washed away. After fluttering his fingers for a moment to allow the alcohol to evaporate, he extricated a handkerchief and wiped away the remains.

In the meantime, pedestrians made a careful detour around him and the red-tinted puddle at his feet, avoiding his gaze as they scurried past.

Aldrich pressed his lips together. "Something needs to be done," he muttered to himself.

A woman walked past, clutching the hand of a young girl. "Do not look, my dear," she murmured, edging as far from him as she could get without stepping into the street.

Obediently, the girl's eyes darted away from his and Aldrich's stomach clenched.

It was a perfect illustration of what was wrong with Upper Cairnisle. Everyone was taught to avert their gaze from ugliness.

He straightened. He would find a way to force people to look directly at the problem. It was the only way to effect change.

Tossing the empty bottle and the soiled cloth into a trash bin, he retraced his steps to the liquor store. There was no point returning home empty-handed.

Preservation of Order

As foretold by the esteemed Grand Magister Augustus Köhler, the recently deployed robot City Guards have wrought a marked improvement in the preservation of order within our fair metropolis. These iron sentinels, unlike their mortal counterparts, are imbued with the capacity to respond to ne'er-do-wells with unwavering force and precision.

Deutero Magister Ingrid Jaeger, addressing the assembled press, proclaimed, "By meting out swift justice to those miscreants who threaten our good citizens, we are imparting a stern lesson to the denizens of Dirt Town. Let it be known far and wide that there shall be naught but punishment for those who venture into Upper Cairnisle with nefarious intent."

-from The Cairnisle Times,
Saturday, April 13, Year 27 AK

THIRTEEN ~ FIAMETTA

STIFLING AN URGE TO SKIP, Fia left the robot in the alley with instructions to pretend to be asleep if anyone came by. She would not abandon him to the streets. Her own struggles after her parents' death had taught her that no one deserved such a fate.

Something about the robot made him seem like a real person. She liked him. And she wanted to help him. She would take him back to Aldrich's house. The doctor would know what to do.

As she exited the alley, Fia came face to face with a broad, red-faced gentleman in an overcoat. A line of bright brass buttons ran down the front of the rich grey cloth. If she were looking for an easy mark, he would be it. She could see the outline of a moneybag in one big, square pocket.

Still thinking about the robot, she momentarily forgot to hide and made the mistake of meeting his glance.

The gentleman's eyes widened, and he drew in an indignant breath. "You, girl," he called. "Get back to where you belong. We don't need your sort here."

Fia hunched her shoulders and sprinted for a bridge. Ducking under the railing, she swung onto the ladder and hung there, breathing hard. What was she doing? Had she lost her wits? The sense of safety that Aldrich and his house gave her was making her soft.

As her heart slowed, she considered her options. After Jack Bury's murder, the streets of Dirt Town were not safe for her. There were too many eyes down there. She blew out a slow breath. She knew how to disappear Upside. She just had to pay attention.

Setting her jaw, Fia climbed up and wriggled out from under the railing. She kept her head down and peered through her hair as she slid from shadow to shadow, careful to move only when no one was looking in her direction.

In this manner, she wound her way to the address Aldrich had given her. Outside the tailor shop, she hesitated. Perhaps she should have accepted Aldrich's offer of a carriage. It might have been easier if she had arrived in style. But then she would not have met the robot.

Squaring her shoulders, she pushed open the door. She was there as a customer—not a thief.

A bell tinkled, and a voice called from the back, "Welcome! I'll be right with you."

Rolls of beautiful cloth filled the shelves that lined the walls of the small shop. On a revolving rack near the door, tiny drawers held buttons of all shapes and sizes.

Entranced by the colours, Fia drifted to the nearest shelf and ran her fingertips lightly over the exquisitely soft and textured fabrics.

"Here, girl!"

The voice made her jump.

"What are you doing? Don't touch that. Get out!" Nostrils flaring, the man seized a long pole with a hook fastened to its end. When it was not being employed as a weapon, it was probably used to reach the highest rolls of fabric. His knuckles turned white as he jabbed it in her general direction.

Fia clutched her hands together and hunched her shoulders. "Doctor Durante sent me," she said quickly. "He wants me to order new clothes."

The tailor's eyes narrowed. "Doctor Durante sent you to order new clothes for him?" His nose wrinkled, but he let the pole drop slightly.

"No," answered Fia, reaching into her pocket to pull out the leather bag filled with the silvers she had taken from Jack Bury the day before. She shook it and listened to the coins jingle. "He sent me to order new clothes for myself."

She had tried to return the money to Aldrich, but he had insisted she keep it and gave her an additional four hundred silvers, saying that the clothes would cost at least that much.

The tailor frowned. "But I don't make clothes for girls." His mouth took on an ugly twist.

Fia did not wish to be drawn into an argument. "I like Aldrich's clothes," she said. "If you made them, you must be very good. All I need are a couple of shirts and some trousers and maybe one of those coats like he wears."

The tailor cleared his throat and straightened his back as his hand rose to stroke his chin beard. "How much do you have to spend?" he asked, his voice suddenly oily with false warmth.

Fia restrained herself from rolling her eyes. He would not ask such a question of his regular customers—or at least not in such a tone. She shook the bag again and asked, "What can I get for seven hundred silvers?"

Instantly, the tailor's entire manner changed. Pursing his lips, he said, "I shall need to take your measurements, and then you must choose which cloth meets with your approval, madam. I would think that you will need seven shirts, five pairs of trousers, and three coats." He glanced at her worn boots with a watery smile. "I would also suggest that you visit the cobbler across the street for a fresh pair of boots."

Fia's eyes bulged, and she took a step back. "What do I need all that for?" she demanded. "I can only wear one at a time!"

The tailor smiled and set the pole aside. "When Doctor Durante suggested you need new clothes, he meant a whole new wardrobe," he said. "You will have noticed that the doctor never wears the same article of clothing two days in a row? If this," he waved his hand disdainfully in her direction, "is any indication of the current state of your wardrobe, he would want me to supply you with enough clothing to last a week."

Fia was suddenly transported back to her childhood bedroom where she was arguing with her mother about changing her clothes. She had lived in Dirt Town for so long she had forgotten what it meant to be clean and well-dressed. "Of course," she said, thrusting her hands into her pockets. "Which fabrics would you recommend?"

When she left the shop almost two hours later, the tailor had an order for three coats—a red one to replace the one she had chosen from the rag dealer, one of a brilliant blue, and one of a rich, warm yellow. Following the little tailor's advice, she had made decisions about trims and buttons, linings and collars. He had promised to have the first set of clothing ready as early as the next day and she was already impatient to receive it.

Across the street, she found the cobbler. His first reaction matched the tailor's initial rage—although he did not threaten her with physical violence. With the confidence she had gained over the past two hours, she convinced him of her value as a paying customer.

He was almost gracious as he measured her foot and allowed her to choose from the wide selection of styles and colours. She wanted the polished red leather but decided it was too showy and settled on a lovely soft polished black.

Her trip home was a trial. She wanted to skip, and a smile kept bubbling up to her lips. But she was still wearing the Dirt Town garb, and it was not safe to draw attention to herself. So, she kept her head down and skulked her way along.

As she neared the spot where she had left the robot, her pace slowed. What made her think that Aldrich would want to help a malfunctioning robot? She still could not figure out why he was helping her. And she was not nearly the threat the robot might be. They had watched him cut off a man's arm.

She set her jaw. She could not turn her back on the robot. He needed help. If Aldrich turned them out, she could always find a new hidey-hole in Dirt Town. She would take care of the robot down there.

When she finally entered the narrow alley, she crept between the tidy trash bins and spotted his curved back.

Unfolding, he rose to his full height. "Greetings, citizen," he said.

Fia's eyes darted to both ends of the alley. No one was in sight. "How did you know it was me?" she asked.

Wordlessly, he pointed to her feet.

Her eyebrows shot up. "My footsteps?" she asked. "You can hear the difference?"

"Yes," PI2-234 responded with a firm nod.

Fia pursed her lips. "That's interesting," she murmured. "What other tricks did they build into you?"

"Remember, safety is our priority," answered the robot.

Fia laughed. "That's a good priority," she said. "Come with me. Keep your face hidden if we meet anyone. And walk with a bit of a stoop. That way you won't look so much like a robot."

Obediently, PI2-234 hunched his back and bent his head toward the ground.

"Perfect," said Fia. "Follow me."

Dirt Towners Arrested

A throng of malcontents hailing from the squalid precincts of Dirt Town descended upon our fair city's shipyard on this day, their purpose being to voice dissent against the recently implemented food allocation scheme.

The miscreants, numbering six-and-twenty in total, were swiftly apprehended by our valiant City Guards for their unlawful ingress into restricted grounds. Having disrupted the peace of our prosperous metropolis, these ne'er-do-wells, have been duly remanded to the Cairnisle Prison to await their rightful judgment.

-from The Cairnisle Times,
Saturday, April 13, Year 27 AK

FOURTEEN ~ FIAMETTA

WITH A TREMBLING HAND, FIA inserted the key that Aldrich had given her into the lock. The weight of her decision pressed down on her shoulders, making each movement feel like a monumental effort. What was she doing? She glanced at the robot beside her. Who was she to invite a faulty robot into Aldrich's home? What if he went crazy again? What was she thinking?

Out of habit, she checked along the street in both directions, running her eyes along the windows on the upper stories of the houses opposite. No one was watching.

She and PI2-234 had encountered only a few people on their walk back to Aldrich's house. Each time, the robot had dropped his head and affected a scurrying gait.

As she led him up the stairs, her step slowed. She should take him straight to the City Guard and turn him in. But the thought made her eyes prickle. They would shut him down.

Indicating the chair where she had eaten her last few meals, Fia said, "Sit." She took the chair opposite and studied him. In the light of the pristine white kitchen, it was clearly a bad idea to have brought him. His inside-out coat looked ridiculous, and his hat was little more than a crumpled mess of felt. But it was the strangeness of his metal face that made him look so out of place. He was not a person. He was a machine. A malfunctioning machine.

PI2-234 set his scrap of paper on the table and began to write. When he finished, he pushed it across to her.

Fia's fingers tightened on the table's edge as she read: *I realize that I committed a horrible crime yesterday in attacking the captain. As an excuse, I can only plead my sequencing. I am designed to respond to threats with an intent to maim and kill.*

Fia rocked back. In a single statement, he had dissolved all her previous notions about robots. She had never imagined that they saw themselves as individuals in the same way humans did. He called himself 'I'. He referred to 'my sequencing'. He thought he really was a person.

At the same time, he openly admitted that he could turn in an instant and tear people to pieces. Her stomach twisted up into knots and she felt sick.

"I think I've made a mistake," she said slowly, sidling out of the chair and backing out of his reach. "I don't like the idea of being maimed or killed."

"No," he said before gesturing for her to return his paper.

She edged back and slid it over to him before scooting away again as he began to write.

Fia waited, chewing her lip. She should get him to leave. Would he listen to her?

When he finished, she read: *I am different from the other Captain of the City Guard robots. I do not believe it is a fault, but the binding lock that is applied to all robots is not functioning on me. I have full control of my thoughts. I do not wish to lose this ability, which is what will happen if I am returned to the City Guard. Please help me. I will be forever in your debt.*

She swallowed and lifted her gaze. "I—I don't—"

He stretched out a long arm and tugged the paper out of her fingers.

A cold sweat broke out on her forehead as the scratching of his pencil resumed. He could get to her anywhere in the room. She was not safe. What had she done? She was going to die, and she would never get the chance to wear her new clothes.

He held the paper up with one finger pointing to his most recent writing.

Fia blinked hard and read: *I can perform a variety of household tasks.*

She let out a breath of a laugh and shoved her fingers through her hair. He was offering to work in exchange for shelter. She whirled away to stride out of the kitchen and into Aldrich's study. Without seeing the street below, she stared out the window.

"A person," she muttered. "He thinks he's a person. This is what the preachers warned us about. But why is it wrong? Why can't he be a person? He knows he made a mistake by hurting that captain." Her hands squeezed into fists. "But what choice did he have. He is sequenced for that. They all draw their swords first."

She had seen the same heartless response from robots too often. Drawing a weapon or acting in a threatening manner when a City Guard was nearby virtually guaranteed a death sentence. Easy compliance was the only way to deal with them. He seemed so reasonable, but would he turn on her? Did his remorse count for anything?

She swiped sweat from her forehead as she returned to the kitchen. "Can you promise not to hurt me?" she demanded. "Or Doctor Durante? Or any of the other people around here?"

He picked up his pencil and wrote: *I can promise that as long as you do nothing criminal in my presence, you are safe.*

Fia read the words and slumped into the chair opposite him, crossing her arms and studying his shiny face. "Nothing criminal?" she repeated. Her eyes traveled around the kitchen, and she relaxed. "I think we can manage that."

He bent his head and wrote: *I do not want you to be afraid of me. I am grateful for everything you have done to help me.*

Fia let out a shuddering breath. It would be all right. "If you are a person, you need a name," she said. "We can't just call you PI2-234 all the time."

"Yes," he answered. The authoritative tone sounded odd in the small room. Picking up the neatly folded morning newspaper from the table between them, he studied the front page.

After a moment, he underlined a single word with his pencil stub and passed it to Fia.

Leaning forward, she read, "Winston." She stared at him and then smiled. "It suits you."

Evolution of Robots

The earliest iterations of robots were devised to augment the Grey Coats in their custodial duties at the prison and other domains requiring vigilant security. These rudimentary automatons have limited speech including 'yes', 'no' and their serial number.

Subsequent to these came the Blue Coats, now a familiar sight upon our thoroughfares. These more advanced sentinels possess a broader vocabulary, albeit one of oft-repeated phrases.

The newly unveiled Green Coat Captains of the City Guard represent a significant leap forward in artificial intelligence. Not only do they boast a vastly expanded vocabulary, but they are also endowed with the faculties of literacy, both in reading and composition.

-from The Cairnisle Times,
Saturday, April 13, Year 27 AK

FIFTEEN ~ ALDRICH

ALDRICH REARRANGED THE PARCELS IN his arms to insert his key into the lock. Perhaps he should get one of those baskets he had often observed other shoppers carrying along the market street. He could become that eccentric physician of the neighbourhood clutching a basket in one hand and a medical kit in the other. It would certainly eliminate this particular juggling problem.

After stopping to buy more scotch to replace the bottle he had splashed around the street in an effort to save Conrad Appleton's leg, he had visited the fishmonger, the greengrocer, and the baker. He was famished.

His mother had wanted him to stay for luncheon, but he had declined. Fia would have finished with her visit to the tailor, and she would be hungry. Had she enjoyed choosing her new clothing?

Kicking the door shut behind him, he stopped and listened. Was she home?

No sound reached him, but that did not mean she was not sitting quietly in one of the rooms above. It made his house feel different, knowing she was there or would be arriving soon. Different and somehow more welcoming. He was no longer responsible for only himself. He liked it.

He balanced his awkward load and started up the stairs. He would begin his study of Cairnisle's political system that afternoon by creating a list of questions. Then he would need to seek out the books that would teach him what he needed to know.

His father was right. He had never had the least interest in learning about any of it. Instead, he had concentrated all of his energy on medicine. Had he missed out? Certainly, he was the youngest physician ever to have passed the certification exams, but was it worth it if his education had been so one-sided? It was time to remedy that.

He found it undeniably disturbing to discover that people were dissatisfied with the situation within Cairnisle. He had always blithely found everything so perfect. Dirt Town was shocking enough, but the fragment he had heard from the preacher told him there were problems in Upper Cairnisle as well. Moreover, the robots' brutal response was almost too much to comprehend. There should have been an opportunity for the man to defend his beliefs. Instead, he was cut down, and his ideas died with him.

Rounding the corner of the stairs into the kitchen, Aldrich stopped short. A robot was seated at his kitchen table. Its coat was inside out, and a battered hat covered its skull-like head, but it was undeniably a member of the City Guard.

Fia jumped to her feet, her eyes wide with apprehension. "Aldrich," she said, twisting her hands together. "I can explain. This is the robot officer we saw yesterday. The one who cut off that man's hand."

Aldrich's head jerked up. "That is your explanation?" he asked, backing away. "You brought a malfunctioning robot into my house because he cut off a man's hand?"

The robot remained seated, staring straight ahead, while Fia pleaded his case. "They want to deactivate him," she said, her voice catching in her throat.

"That does not sound like an altogether bad idea," responded Aldrich, keeping his eyes on the motionless robot.

"His name is Winston," Fia said. "He says he can be helpful around the house."

At her earnest reassurance, Aldrich laughed. He sounded unhinged and he cut it off. "A robot named Winston?" he asked. "Who does housework when he is not busy maiming people in the streets?" Despite himself, he let out a high-pitched giggle. "Well, I suppose we have nothing to worry about then. Welcome to my home, Winston."

Winston unfolded himself from his chair and rose to face Aldrich. "Greetings, citizen," he said with a formal bow. Then he returned to the table and picked up a pencil.

Aldrich stared as the robot bent and wrote on a scrap of crumpled paper.

After a moment, Aldrich stepped forward to read over his shoulder.

Please accept my thanks for your protection. I pledge never to give you any reason to regret it. I was designed to enforce the laws of this city, but I am able to learn by watching. If there is any task that you wish me to perform, you need only show me once.

Again, Aldrich laughed aloud. The hysteria was still there so he clamped his lips shut. "A robot who writes grammatically correct sentences with perfect penmanship and volunteers to take on all the housework," he muttered. Shaking his head again, he stepped past Winston to deposit his shopping on the counter beside the stove.

He set his hands on his hips and looked from Fia to Winston. His first impulse was to call the City Guard and have the robot removed—forcibly if necessary. But the look on Fia's face tore at his heart. He wanted her to feel as if this was her home too. And if he wanted to learn about the robots and the rest of Cairnisle, perhaps the robot could be of assistance.

He sighed and turned on the tap to wash his hands. "Well then, Winston," he said as he dried them carefully with the cheery yellow clothes that Calder had helped him choose. "Watch carefully, because one day you may find yourself preparing a meal." Reaching into the cupboard, he lifted out a heavy frying pan before unwrapping the fish. "I only got enough for two people, but I do not suppose you eat food anyway."

Fia leapt up from her chair and came to Aldrich's side. "He runs on magic," she said, her words tumbling out in a rush. "That's how we met. He was out of power and asked for help. When I touched his crystal battery, it pulled my magic out of me and into him."

90

Aldrich spun away from the fish and jabbed the knife toward Winston, his hand trembling. "He stole your magic? he demanded. "And you still want him here?"

Fia grabbed his hand and pushed it down, her eyes darting nervously between Aldrich and Winston. "Robots are sequenced to respond to a threat with deadly force," she murmured out of the side of her mouth. "Don't point a knife at him."

Aldrich's mouth went dry. "Do not point a knife at him because he might kill me?" he asked with a gasping laugh that held no humour. "I thought you said he was safe."

"He promised not to hurt us," Fia said with a wince as she pulled at her shirt collar. "But I don't think you should wave a weapon around."

Forcing himself to a calm he did not feel, Aldrich set the knife on the counter and clasped his hands together. "Tell me about the magic," he said, his voice tight. "You said he stole it."

Fia swallowed hard and her eyes darted toward Winston, who sat perfectly still, his flat, black eyes turned on them. "He didn't exactly steal it. The crystals are designed to drain magic from mages." Dropping her head, she murmured, "Haven't you ever heard of mage power? It's what runs the carriages and the robots and even the lights around Cairnisle. That's what the Magisters wanted me for. That's why it's illegal for mages to be free."

"It is illegal for mages to be free?" Aldrich asked, his hands dropping to his sides and his mouth going slack.

Fia's eyebrows drew together. "You didn't know that?" she asked, disbelief colouring her voice. "That's why they killed my parents. I got away, but it was really me they were after."

Aldrich wet his lips and turned back to his fish, his movements mechanical. "You are illegal," he said as he cut a perfect fillet. He seemed to be having difficulty thinking. "How can they tell who is a mage? Is that why you were hiding in Dirt Town?"

Her mouth twisted. "I wasn't exactly hiding in Dirt Town," she said. "I needed a place to live, and no, they can't tell who's a mage unless you give yourself away." Her voice took on a bitter tone. "One of our servants reported me. She saw me start a fire and turned me in for the reward. I was eight."

Winston picked up the pencil and began writing again.

When he finished, he handed it to Fia who read aloud, "Robots run on magic from crystal batteries. As a result, we can sense when magic is performed near us. We are sequenced to capture mages and transport them to the battery factory. We also have the sequencing to perform magic, however, it is a last resort reaction because it is likely to drain our magic reservoirs."

The colour drained from Fia's face. "Robots are everywhere up here," she said in a tiny voice. "I'm careful, but sometimes when I get in trouble, the magic just happens."

Aldrich blew out a slow breath, his forehead furrowed. "Robots are everywhere," he agreed. "Before you showed up, I never paid them any attention, but I do not like what I have seen these past two days." He looked directly at Winston. "Robots are sequenced to react very callously. They kill rather than arrest. Today, on my way home, I had to help the victim of a shooting. A foolish preacher was told by the leader of a team of robots to cease his sermon and in response, he pulled out a pistol. I believe his target was the officer, but he hit a bystander. The robots attacked immediately and—"

His voice cracked and he spun back to his dinner preparations. In silence, he sliced the entire loaf of bread into precisely even pieces, letting the action soothe his mind. It worked. His voice once more under control, he said, "The preacher is dead."

Winston wrote another message and Fia leaned over and read, "Your observations are absolutely correct. In the last year, since they began to build the PI2 series, the mandate has been to reduce the number of criminals. Our sequencing demands that when we draw weapons, we aim to kill. This is true for both guards and captains. More recently, they have begun to construct a robot who will be so far advanced that he can take over the position of Commandant."

Fia thrust the paper back at Winston, her eyes narrowed. "How do you know all this?"

Winston turned the paper over to write his response while Fia read over his shoulder. "Robots are designed to have a binding lock that prevents us from acting independently. I have already explained that the binding lock on me does not function as it was intended. I believe this to be a fortunate circumstance for me. I must emphasize again that I do not believe I am a threat to you."

Aldrich removed the sizzling fish from the frying pan and arranged it on the plates he had already prepared with slices of bread and a salad of greens. As he carried the two plates to the table, he said, "I admit, I have lived in ignorance of the Magisters' policies within Cairnisle. I am just beginning to understand how many wrongs are committed every day at the command of our leaders."

Fia sat down in the chair beside Winston, and Aldrich set a plate in front of her.

He lowered himself into the spot on the other side of the table and stared down at his food, his appetite gone. "It seems to me—" He broke off and tapped a finger on the table. "I am not certain what—" He cleared his throat. "Something should be done to make Cairnisle a better place for all the residents," he said, finally. Shaking his head, he picked up his fork and began to eat.

Fia studied her plate before lowering her nose to breathe in the mingled aromas of fish and freshly baked bread. Raising her gaze, she said, "Thank you, Aldrich. This looks—delicious."

Glancing up, Aldrich caught the reverent expression on her face, and his throat caught. What he took as an easy meal, she truly valued. He smiled as she leaned forward and began to devour the fish.

Meanwhile, Winston was writing again. When he pushed his paper over toward Fia, she swallowed quickly and read, "If you are interested in learning more about the Magisters' plans, I am able to help. Humans do not generally take any precautions when speaking in front of a robot. As a result, I have learned several particulars which I suspect I was not meant to hear."

Aldrich looked up from his meal, a spark of curiosity in his eyes. "I think we would be very interested to learn anything you can tell us about the Magisters," he said. His gaze became distant as he dabbed at his mouth with a napkin.

"On another subject, I met a very interesting woman today. Her name is Wilhelmina von Richtofen." He grinned. "I plan to escort her to a masquerade ball on Wednesday evening."

Prison Nears Capacity

Our fair city's house of correction is approaching its utmost limits of occupancy. The situation has grown so dire as to warrant the personal attention of our esteemed Grand Magister.

"In order to ensure the safety and tranquility of every law-abiding citizen," he declared, "we shall forthwith embark upon a thorough investigation of alternatives to the conventional housing of miscreants and ne'er-do-wells."

-from The Cairnisle Times,
Wednesday, April 17, Year 27 AK

Sixteen ~ Aldrich

ALDRICH TROTTED DOWN THE STAIRS to the street where his mother's automatized carriage awaited him. She had insisted he use it to collect Miss von Richtofen for the masquerade ball. For her sake, he had put aside his reluctance and accepted. The young woman would expect the luxury of a private carriage over a utilitarian public one.

As he opened the door, he found himself grateful for his mother's insistence. The immaculate interior would ensure he reached his destination without sullying his new suit.

The trousers and waistcoat were white—a colour he

normally reserved for surgery—but the coat was unusual. Cinnamon, the tailor had called it. After donning it, Aldrich had examined his reflection in the full-length mirror, admiring how the gold thread embroidery stood out against the exquisite brown fabric.

Closing the carriage door, he recited the von Richtofen address. As the carriage rolled off down the street, he tossed his masquerade mask onto the seat beside him. The tailor had crafted the full facemask from the same silk as the coat. Swirls of gold paint framed the eyes, lending it an air of mystery.

Fia had laughed when he modelled it for her. He smiled at the memory. She was relaxing enough to joke with him and had asked what he was trying to hide.

For nearly a week, she had been staying with him. Rather than tiring of her presence—as his father had undoubtedly hoped—he had come to look forward to seeing her at breakfast and after work every day. She seemed to have no difficulty filling her time and had plenty of stories to share during their meals.

Nonetheless, she could not continue with only a fugitive robot as a companion. Arrangements would have to be made for her education.

He pursed his lips. There would be other children in Dirt Town who could benefit from schooling. Could something be done about that? He had passed the week without making any effort to discover more about the workings of Cairnisle. He had a vague hope that by helping Fia, he would feel better about the critical disparity in wealth and living conditions between Upper Cairnisle and Dirt Town. However, getting to know her had only highlighted the unfairness. He could feel a growing compulsion to undertake a greater action, and he knew from experience that he would be unable to ignore it for long.

The carriage rolled to a smooth stop outside a mansion even more impressive than his parent's country house. As if to make up for the lack of gardens surrounding it, the city-centre home's imposing façade rose straight up from the footpath to eight storeys. Covered in ivy, with stained glass topping every one of the sixty-four windows that looked out onto the street, it was meant to foster envy and awe in all who saw it.

One corner of Aldrich's mouth rose. He had expected nothing less. If his father had chosen James von Richtofen as his banker, he must be very rich indeed. Perhaps he would be interested in supporting Aldrich should he choose to stand for election.

Alighting onto the footpath, he climbed the twelve polished granite steps toward the dark wooden doors. The arched lintel above was carved with scowling faces from someone's nightmare. A shiver ran up Aldrich's spine. It was not a welcoming entrance. With his eyes on one particularly ugly hobgoblin, he rang the bell.

Almost instantly, a uniformed footman pulled the door wide. "Good evening, sir," he said with stiff formality. "Miss von Richtofen has asked me to inform you that she will be down momentarily."

Over the man's shoulder, Aldrich caught a glimpse of silver. He stared as Wilhelmina glided to the door, a vision in a silver gown trimmed with mulberry insets that emphasized her narrow waist. Piled atop her head in an intricate upsweep, her blonde hair accentuated her blue eyes. A smiling silver mask dangled by its ribbons from one gloved hand.

"Good evening, Doctor Durante," she said, offering her hand.

Aldrich took it, bowing low to brush his lips over its back. "Good evening to you, Miss von Richtofen," he replied. "You look beautiful. What a stunning gown."

"Why, thank you, kind sir," she answered with a mischievous smile. "Might I reciprocate the compliment? That is an absolutely magnificent suit. I do admire the colour. Cinnamon, is it?"

Aldrich laughed. "How do people know such things?" he asked, shaking his head in mock exasperation. "My tailor informed me that it is indeed cinnamon, as if that was something I should know."

"Well, of course, you should know it, darling," Wilhelmina responded. "One should know everything." She smiled charmingly as she spoke, but under her veneer of humour, Aldrich sensed the complete sincerity of her statement.

"I cannot help but agree," he said. "Shall we go?"

Twentieth Anniversary

It is nigh on a score of years since the esteemed Deutero Magister Ingrid Jaeger ascended to her illustrious office. On this day, city officials commenced preparations for a grand jubilee to commemorate this momentous anniversary, which shall be held in conjunction with the Magisters' annual address to the citizenry.

Her Excellency, graced us with these words: "It has been, and continues to be, a great honour to serve as Deutero Magister for the fair country of Cairn. In these two decades, I have striven to uphold the sacred trust placed in me by our people."

-from The Cairnisle Times,
Wednesday, April 17, Year 27 AK

SEVENTEEN ~ ALDRICH

THEY WERE STILL SEVERAL BLOCKS from Johnathon Loewe's home when Wilhelmina lifted her mask from the seat beside her and fitted it over her face. "It's time to disappear," she said, tying the silver ribbons around the back of her head.

Aldrich laughed. She was the most interesting woman he had ever met—and the most intelligent. He had enjoyed their verbal fencing. "It is a shame to hide your face," he said. "I would much prefer to look upon your beauty than this smiling façade."

Tilting her head to one side, Wilhelmina met his gaze. Her eyes sparkled, half-hidden by the mask's delicate filigree. "My dear Aldrich," she said. "We all wear a façade of one sort or another every day. Do we ever really know one another?"

Chuckling, Aldrich reached for his disguise and fitted it over his face. "Ah, but that is exactly the allure," he said as he tied the silken ties of his cinnamon mask behind his head. "Even if we can never know exactly what someone else is thinking, we can enjoy the game of unmasking."

Wilhelmina's laughter tinkled as the carriage rolled to a stop in front of the elegant Loewe residence. Light poured out onto the street from the upper-story windows, casting elongated rectangles onto the cobblestone footpath and across the street. The front door swung open, releasing a thread of melody as the huddle of laughing guests who had just descended from a carriage in front of theirs entered the party.

"Unmasking?" she repeated, her eyes alight with mischief. "There is no such thing. We might remove these lovely constructions of fabric and paste, but our real masks will remain firmly in place. Behind mine lies a thousand secrets, which I assure you will never come into the light, no matter how you play the game."

Aldrich opened the carriage door and stepped down. "If I cannot win," he said with a bow, "I shall simply enjoy playing."

Wilhelmina laughed again and accepted his hand as she alighted. "I think I like you, kind sir," she said.

"Then my evening is complete," he said, tucking her hand in his elbow. He led her to the front door, which swung open at their approach. Music poured into the night, and he was filled with an overwhelming sense of well-being. His face felt stretched from all the smiling.

A row of four servants in red and white livery stood at attention on either side of the entrance.

The young man on the far end stepped out of line to greet them. "May I see your invitation?" he murmured.

"Of course," answered Wilhelmina, pulling a gilt-edged card from a hidden pocket.

The young man ran an eye over it and discreetly held it up to the light. Assured of its authenticity, he bowed. "Thank you, madam," he said, turning to Aldrich.

It had been something of an effort to come up with the invitation. He had tossed it into the garbage when he received it. Fortunately, he had not yet disposed of the bag in the kitchen and Winston had been kind enough to sort through the trash to find it.

Producing the grease-stained invitation from the inside coat pocket, he offered it for inspection.

The footman pretended not to notice the smears and studied it closely. "Thank you, sir," he said with another bow. Straightening, he gestured toward a pair of tall mahogany doors whose gold-inlaid panels were decorated with a profusion of vines and flowers. "Please, enjoy the evening."

Another pair of footmen pulled the doors wide, and Aldrich led Wilhelmina inside.

He caught his breath as they stepped into a world of illumination and music. Suspended from the vaulted ceiling, a dozen chandeliers each held hundreds of miniature light bulbs. Their radiance reflected in the floor-to-ceiling mirrors on every wall. Couples dressed in brightly coloured silks and satins floated around the floor in time to the music of a small string orchestra.

Wilhelmina broke the spell. Raising her hand to the delicate silver watch that hung from a jewelled hawk pinned to her dress, she peered at the tiny numbers. "It rather looks as if we have arrived exactly on time," she said.

Aldrich bowed low and offered his hand. "May I have this dance, Miss v—"

She held up a finger in warning. "No names this evening, darling," she said. "Otherwise, what is the point of these disguises?"

"Of course," he answered, blushing behind his mask. "Shall we?"

Wilhelmina curtsied and accepted his proffered hand.

They waited until the end of the phrase, with Aldrich counting off the beats under his breath, before joining the flow of dancers.

It was as if they had practised together. Wilhelmina moved with an easy grace, and Aldrich, who normally avoided balls, found himself thanking his mother for the dancing lessons she had forced upon him.

As they swept around the perimeter of the room, someone seized his elbow. They swung to a halt and looked down at a bent figure in a hideous lilac mask with a matching gown that smelled of mothballs.

"Watch out, young lady," she shouted up at Wilhelmina, shaking a gnarled finger in her face. "This is a shameless man. You will only damage your reputation by dancing with him."

As soon as she spoke, Aldrich recognized the voice of Margaret Adderly, an elderly acquaintance of his mother's. At the age of eighteen, he had made the enormous mistake of insulting her, although he had no clear recollection of what he had said. Since that unfortunate occasion, she had made it a point to attack his character at every opportunity.

Releasing Aldrich's elbow, Mrs. Adderly switched her grip to Wilhelmina's. "Come with me, dear," she said, her voice turning syrupy. "I know a young man who is much worthier of you."

"No, thank you," answered Wilhelmina, shaking free of the old woman's grip. Turning her smiling mask pointedly away, she whirled Aldrich out of reach. "What did you do?" she asked with a laugh.

Aldrich shrugged. "I am not sure I even remember," he muttered dourly. "How does she always find me? I am wearing a mask!"

Her eyes sparkling with amusement, Wilhelmina said, "Obviously, she is not looking at your face when she recognizes you."

Aldrich lost his moment to retort when the song came to an end and Wilhelmina stepped away, checking her little hawk watch again as she moved out of reach.

Their host, Lord Johnathon Loewe, appeared on the mezzanine above the dance floor. Tapping a spoon against a crystal goblet, he gathered the attention of his guests. A plump, sweating man, his red face showed the dents left by the mask he had just removed.

"My dear guests," he began, "it is a great pleasure to see you here this evening. Of course," he added with a horrible little giggle, "I will never know just who is here in my home!"

His guests laughed politely.

As they quieted in expectation of his continued speech, a small chime went off, and the room rapidly began to fill with smoke.

The guests murmured in appreciation of this new form of entertainment. As the smoke grew thicker, making it impossible to see across the room, people started to cough. There were cries of fear and Lord Loewe's speech was forgotten as everyone rushed for the exit amid squeals of dismay.

A gunshot rang through the room.

Aldrich recoiled at the noise. Unable to see what was

happening and imagining the worst, he reached for Wilhelmina and pulled her to the floor with him where the air would be clearer.

Silence reigned in the crowded room, broken only by the quiet sobs of a few women.

Smoke hung heavy in the air, but there were no further gunshots.

After a few minutes, some quick-thinking servants began to throw open the doors and windows. Gradually, the smoke cleared enough to reveal a disturbing scene.

Aldrich raised his head from where he lay, half-shielding Wilhelmina.

A rainbow of fallen dancers festooned the floor, while on the mezzanine, the slumped figure of Lord Johnathon Loewe hung over the railing, dripping blood onto the people below.

Near Perfect Weather

Reports from the fertile farms of Mainland Cairn indicate that the spring planting has been met with extraordinary success this year.

"The growing conditions have been most favourable," remarked Mr. Ivan Tirdar, the distinguished Agriculture Representative for the Magisters. "Our farmers are witnessing an auspicious start to the growing season, which bodes well for the forthcoming harvest."

-from The Cairnisle Times,
Wednesday, April 17, Year 27 AK

EIGHTEEN ~ FIAMETTA

CLUTCHING THE OVERSTUFFED SATCHEL, FIA bolted up the stairs, two at a time. She still struggled to get over the idea that she lived in the bright and cheerful house. When she agreed to come and stay, she had expected Aldrich to tire of her after a couple of days, but nearly a week had passed, and she was still there.

Just the day before, she had visited the tailor again to pick up the last of her new clothing. Hanging in the closet of her bedroom were two of her three new coats, six shirts of finely woven white linen, and three pairs of trousers.

The shabby old red coat that she had been so proud of hung off to the side with her stained and torn trousers—not touching her new clothes, but not discarded either. Despite what he said, Fia did not expect Aldrich to let her stay forever. She needed to be prepared when she found herself living on the streets again.

She wore the blue coat. Until Aldrich came downstairs dressed for the ball, she had thought it the most elegant thing she had ever seen.

As soon as he left, rolling away in a shiny green automatized carriage, she had headed out into the streets to test the new confidence her fancy clothes gave her.

The first thing she noticed was that she did not mind when people looked at her. Usually, she did everything in her power to remain unnoticed. But with her new clothes and freshly washed hair, she easily met everyone's eyes.

Winston needed some new clothes too. That was why she had gone out. If he was ever to leave the house, a better disguise was necessary.

She rounded the corner of the stairs and galloped into the kitchen. "I got you a new coat, Winston," she called.

The robot was not in the chair where she had left him. He stood at the counter, cutting carrots with a long knife. Turning at her arrival, he said, "Greetings, citizen."

Holding up the bag, Fia repeated, "I got you some new clothes. You should be able to go out now."

"Yes," he said.

Fia had become accustomed to Winston's curt answers. She knew he had much more to say, but his pre-recorded messages limited his responses.

"Sit down," he said, lifting a plate of food and delivering it to the table.

Her place was already set with silverware, a carefully folded napkin, and a tall glass of water, just the way Aldrich did it.

She had barely begun her meal when the door to the street opened, followed by heavy steps climbing the stairs. A moment later, Aldrich appeared in the kitchen looking dazed and shaken.

"Greetings, citizen," said Winston, moving aside.

"You're back early," Fia said. "What happened?"

Aldrich made no response. Going straight past her, he opened a high cupboard and grabbed a bottle filled with golden liquid, along with a heavy, wide-rimmed, cut-crystal glass. With a steady hand, he filled the glass almost to the rim and downed half of the alcohol in one gulp. A shudder shook him, and he gasped.

Pressing his lips into a thin, white line, he took his glass and wordlessly sat down across from Fia.

She stared at him, her gut tightening. "What happened?" she repeated, studying him closely.

He had been so excited when he left. Now, glassy-eyed and pale, he rubbed a hand over his throat. His beautiful cinnamon coat and white trousers showed faint smudges of dirt. He had told her not to expect him until midnight, but here it was, just after half-past eight, and he was home already.

Aldrich took another long gulp of his scotch and rested his head on one hand. "What is it about you?" he asked in a flat monotone.

It was as if he had punched her in the stomach. All the air left her lungs, and she could not breathe. Was he about to kick her out?

"Since you chose me as a shield, everything has changed," he muttered. "Do you know I had never even been to Dirt Town before those two ruffians dragged me down there to pay your debt? I never gave it any thought." He raised troubled grey eyes to meet hers. "You made me start paying attention.

First it was all the people—the children—in Dirt Town. I had never imagined such squalor. Then, in a street near my own house, a robot goes mad—and you find him and drag him home. You made me see that the way the robots are controlled is not right. It is not fair. It is not justice. They should not be killing people in the streets. Robots are in no position to make those sorts of life and death decisions."

Remembering himself, Aldrich tilted his glass in Winston's direction. "No offense, Winston," he said. "But you know what I mean." He took another long drink and set the glass on the table before scrubbing his hands wildly through his hair, making it stand on end. A faint ruddiness had crept into his pale cheeks.

"I heard a preacher speaking out against the Magisters. The City Guard came for him, and he shot a man when he feared for his life." He squeezed his eyes shut." I watched him die in the street for it." His eyes popped open, and the flush of colour drained away. "You tell me that your parents were killed by the Magisters. And now—" He trailed off.

Fia broke into a cold sweat. It was all her fault. "Aldrich," she said. "What happened tonight?"

Aldrich drained the rest of his scotch and set the glass down with a thunk. "Lord Johnathon Loewe is dead," he said, slurring slightly.

Fia leaned forward. "Who is—"

Aldrich cut her off. "I realize that you have long been aware of the many absurdities that characterize the behaviour of the leaders of our beautiful city." He tapped a finger on his chest. "But I became aware of these problems only since I met you. Misguided as it may have been, I believed that the difficulties stemmed from Dirt Town itself. I could rationalize brutal robot sequencing if I regarded it in view of the criminal elements that inhabit that warren of immorality. Through that lens, I could comprehend the need to control mages."

He lifted one shoulder and looked at Fia again.

The sickening feeling at the pit of her stomach intensified.

"Tonight—" Aldrich let out a huge breath and paused. "Tonight, I learned that the problems are not limited to Dirt Town. Even the seemingly safe streets of Upper Cairnisle are not safe." His eyes took on a haunted look. "In the home of one of the richest men in the city, a horrible assassination was carried out."

Rising, he used the table to steady his balance before wobbling over to the cupboard, where he filled the glass a second time. He kept his gaze firmly away from her as he said, "In front of society's most important people, a man was murdered. A man who, before this day, I would have declared safe from any threats this life has to offer."

He tossed back the scotch and thumped the glass onto the counter. "I need to get out of here," he said abruptly. "I am going for a walk." Whirling on his heel, he staggered down the stairs.

The door slammed shut and in the silence he left behind, Fia stared at Winston.

"He's going to kick us out," she said in a small voice. She shoved the remains of her meal away and slumped in her chair, wrapping her arms around herself. "I knew this was too good to be true."

Her throat suddenly thick, she pushed back from the table and carried her plate to the sink. She was on her own again.

Or maybe not completely alone. Thrusting back her shoulders, she said, "Don't worry, Winston. We'll find a place in Dirt Town. With your new clothes, you can blend in easily."

Fia ran water into the white enamelled sink and began to wash the dishes. "I think you'll like Dirt Town," she said, swiping at a tear with her sleeve. "Everyone gives you plenty of room down there."

"Yes," said Winston.

Her shoulders tightened. She wanted more than a single-word answer. As much as she had come to appreciate Winston, it was Aldrich who had changed her outlook on life. Their talks over the past few days had been the best times of her life. He asked questions and made her think.

To learn that those treasured discussions had been painful for Aldrich was another blow to her stomach.

Standing on tiptoe to return Aldrich's cut-crystal glass to the top shelf, she heard the door to the street open.

Aldrich clumped up the stairs and she swallowed against the lump in her throat. This was it. He would tell her to move out.

When he reached the kitchen, he leaned against the doorframe, blearily studying her. Then his eyes went to Winston.

"Aldrich, I'm sorry," Fia burst out. "I'll be out of here in two shakes. I want you to know how grateful I am for—"

Aldrich raised both hands and she broke off. His eyes were clear, and he no longer staggered.

"I apologize for what I said earlier," he said with a half smile. "I did not mean it was your fault. I was upset because now that my blinders have been removed, I see the evils everywhere. And that means—"

He took a deep breath and stared over her head before blowing it out in one long stream. "And that means I have to do something about it." He thrust his hands into his trouser pockets and turned toward the stairs to the top floor. "But not today," he said. "Right now, I am going to bed."

Fia's legs went weak, and she tottered over to the table to sit down. "We don't have to leave?" she murmured. She gripped her trembling hands together and stared down at them. How had she become so soft in just one week? Would she be strong enough to survive on her own again when Aldrich did kick her out?

"What does he mean?" she muttered, dropping her head into her hands. "What can he do about it? What can anyone do about anything? It's just the way things are."

Winston pulled his notebook from his pocket and began to write.

When he handed it over to her, she read: *I overheard a whispered conversation. They were talking about Augustus Köhler.*

She looked up. "Augustus Köhler, the Grand Magister?" she asked.

"Yes," Winston answered.

Fia gave a low whistle and read aloud, "They said he was planning to clean house. I believe this to be a euphemism to explain that people in opposition to the Grand Magister would be removed. Judging by his past record, they probably meant he intended to have them killed. This was confirmed when they spoke of hiring an assassin. Two targets in particular were mentioned: Johnathon Loewe and Rupert Corvington."

"And now Loewe is dead," she murmured. "And you think an assassin paid by Köhler did it?"

"Yes," answered Winston.

"And Corvington?" Fia asked, her brow wrinkling. "Isn't he the Commandant of the City Guard?"

"Yes," Winston answered.

"Why would Grand Magister Köhler hire an assassin to kill the Commandant?" she muttered, tapping two fingers on the table and staring into space. "Johnathon Loewe? What does he do?" She pushed the notebook back to Winston and waited while his pencil scratched.

When he passed it back, she read, "Johnathon Loewe owns and operates the factory that produces robots for the City Guard. He recently announced his intention to run for a position as a Magister." She pursed her lips. "Would they kill him for trying to get elected? Does that make sense?"

Winston held out a long-fingered hand and Fia pushed the notebook back to him.

She tried to read upside-down as he wrote but gave up after a moment and rested her head on her hands again. She was tired, and her soft bed was calling to her. Nonetheless, she forced herself to think. Aldrich was upset, and it was all her fault. He said he did not hold her responsible, but how long would that last if things kept going wrong? If she could figure out why Johnathon Loewe had been killed, he might permit her to stay.

What did she know about elections? She grunted. Not a lot. She was too young to vote. But she would have to be blind and stupid not to have noticed that they were held every few years. Posters were plastered around Upside for a few weeks, and then the Magisters appeared on their wide stage to thank the fine people of Cairnisle for trusting them enough to elect them for another term.

The speeches were a good time to empty a few pockets because everyone was jammed in so closely that they hardly noticed a little bump or two. She rubbed a hand across her tired eyes. Had there ever been a new Magister? They all seemed to have been there forever.

"Take this," Winston said, interrupting her drifting thoughts.

Sitting up, Fia pushed the hair back from her face and pulled the notebook around to see what he had written.

While we do not know exactly why Johnathon Loewe was killed, we can make some assumptions. Logically, it follows that if Augustus Köhler, who has a proven record of tyranny, is having Loewe and Corvington assassinated, they must be working against him. Therefore, it is my opinion that we should warn Corvington. He could be a powerful ally in any actions that Aldrich wishes to pursue.

Fia bounced up. "This is amazing," she said, dancing from foot to foot, her fatigue forgotten. "We have to tell Aldrich."

She rushed to the stairs before coming to a stop. Gripping the balustrade, she stared up into the dark. "Tomorrow," she whispered. "We'll tell him tomorrow."

Shocking Assassination

In a grievous and brazen assault, Lord Johnathan Loewe has been assassinated. The tragic event transpired during his illustrious annual masquerade ball, an exclusive gathering attended solely by invitation.

"Our only evidence in the search for the killer is the single silver bullet that was the cause of death," stated Coroner Anders Tore.

The mysterious circumstances surrounding this heinous crime have cast a pall over the elite of Cairnisle, leaving many to wonder who could perpetrate such a dreadful act within the heart of society.

-from The Cairnisle Times,
Thursday, April 18, Year 27 AK

NINETEEN ~ ALDRICH

ALDRICH RUBBED HIS TEMPLES AS he checked his appointment schedule. Everyone on the list had come and gone. There had been many hours to regret his over-consumption of scotch the night before. It felt as if his insides were caught in a continuous tremble.

Fortunately, aside from two quick stitches in a young boy's lip, he had not been required to perform any surgeries. Most of his patients had needed only a consultation and a prescription.

He glanced at the wall clock and pursed his lips. He could afford to leave an hour earlier than usual. He would go home and enjoy a leisurely evening. Perhaps the walk would relieve his headache.

All day, he had avoided thinking about the ball. As he let down his guard, he was reminded of how much he had enjoyed dancing with Wilhelmina, though it had been far too brief. After the smoke cleared and the guests fled the ballroom, it had seemed hopeless to attempt to continue the evening. He had directed his mother's automatized carriage to Wilhelmina's residence, and after a strangely tense ride where neither of them had said much, he had deposited her at home.

His mind had been spinning on the trip to his house. Everything that had happened had thrown him entirely out of the smooth rhythm of his life. And as much as he might want to return to his oblivious pursuit of medicine, he knew it was impossible. Vaguely, he recalled saying to Fia and that robot she called Winston that something had to be done. But what exactly?

What madness had made him suppose he could get elected as the leader of Cairnisle? It was absurd. Who would vote for him? He had absolutely no credentials. Everyone would say that he was a green and callow youth.

His head snapped up and he stared blindly across the room. Johnathon Loewe had recently announced his intention to run for election. Had it gotten him killed?

Aldrich let out a sharp exhalation and pushed his hair off his forehead. He was seeing plots everywhere.

Picking up his book—a new treatise on the mysteries of the

psyche—and his medical kit—despite its weight, he intended to carry it with him at all times—he let himself out of his office.

Mercifully, the waiting room was empty except for Letta. "Would you take care of the surgery before you go home?" he asked. "I am heading out now."

"Of course, Doctor," she answered, looking up from her desk with a smile. "I'll just lock up after you, shall I?"

Aldrich bit back a retort. What was it about her senseless comments that brought out the worst in him? "Yes, please," he answered. "I would appreciate that."

Stepping out into the sunshine, he avoided opening his book. He had resolved to give his full attention to the world around him—at least until it started making more sense.

As he strolled along the empty footpath, his thoughts drifted to the time he had spent with Wilhelmina von Richtofen. She was the first woman he had ever encountered who did not leave him feeling slightly irritated. Not only was she beautiful, well dressed, and able to move with the grace of a cat, but she also had an intellect that matched his own.

By the time he got to his door, he had forgotten about his vow to do something about Cairnisle's problems. The fresh air and sunshine had almost cured his headache, while the daydreaming had certainly not done any harm.

Letting himself in, he set his medical kit on a shelf by the door, and with the book in hand, he climbed up to the kitchen.

Fia was seated at the table, completely engrossed in the anatomy and physiology book that had been his first introduction to the wonders of the human body.

He recognized the look of intellectual awe when she raised her face to him.

After a moment, her expression cleared and she froze, her eyes darting to the book open on the table. "I'm sorry," she said quickly. "Don't be mad. I just wanted a peek inside and I—"

Aldrich waved away her apology with a smile. "You are welcome to read anything you find in this house," he said, making a mental note to arrange for a tutor. She needed someone to guide her studies while he was working. "If you have questions, just ask."

Fia ducked her head. "Thank you," she said.

His smile broadened as he watched her carefully note the page number before reverently closing the book. She would make an excellent student.

She rested a hand on the cover. "After you went to sleep last night," she said, looking at him sideways as if to judge his reaction, "Winston told me something you might find interesting." She nodded toward the corner.

Aldrich followed her gaze and jerked upright. He had not noticed Winston standing motionless against the wall.

The robot pulled out his notebook and flipped back a couple of pages before handing it to him.

Aldrich read the pages and felt his newfound sense of peace evaporate. "Why did you not tell me this last night?" he demanded.

Fia's eyes flicked toward the cupboard where he kept his liquor and he flinched.

"Or this morning?" he asked as he began to pace the length of the small kitchen. "I know Rupert Corvington," he said. "I have met him on more than one occasion at events around the city. I find he is an entirely honourable sort of fellow." Abruptly, he stopped pacing and turned to Fia. "I must warn him at once."

Fia stood. "I'll come with you," she said.

"No," Aldrich said, already striding toward the stairs leading to the upper level. "You will be safer here."

Jumping up, she fastened the top buttons of her yellow coat. "I can help if you run into trouble," she said.

"No," he said flatly. "I am not about to put your life in danger. You are only fourteen years old." With one last stern glance, he ran up the stairs.

Fia followed on his heels. "I may be fourteen, but I know more about dangerous situations than you do," she said, standing in the doorway of his room as he went to his closet.

He grimaced over his shoulder at her as he opened his closet door and moved aside the coats to reveal his lock box. Kneeling before it, he shielded his fingers with his body as he spun open the combination lock and removed his pistol.

Fia scowled as he checked the clockwork mechanism and loaded it with six bullets. "Take Winston with you at least," she said. "He has a pistol too."

Aldrich froze. "He does?" he asked. There was a malfunctioning robot with a pistol in his home. A sputter of laughter threatened.

Fia cocked her head to the side and studied him. "He is a Captain of the City Guard," she said.

"Rogue Captain," corrected Aldrich. However, there were merits to having Winston accompany him. "He can come, but you stay here." He raised his eyes to meet her defiant expression. "Please?"

Fia slumped. "I'll stay," she said. "But hurry back. I don't want to be left here all night wondering what's happening."

Robot Producer Dead

It is with profound regret that we announce the untimely death of Lord Johnathan Loewe, esteemed founder of Loewe Manufacturing, renowned for its production of robots for the City Guard. Lord Johnathan passed away yesterday at his residence. He was 59.

Throughout his illustrious career, Lord Johnathan made numerous invaluable contributions to the advancement of technology in Cairnisle, leaving an indelible mark on our city's industrial landscape. His legacy shall endure through the countless innovations he championed and the profound impact of his work on our community.

-from The Cairnisle Times,
Thursday, April 18, Year 27 AK

TWENTY ~ ALDRICH

THE SUN DIPPED BELOW THE horizon as the automatized carriage rolled into the Business District, home to the City Guard Headquarters. Streetlamps flickered to life around them while Aldrich peered out the window, hoping to catch a glimpse of the man who commanded not only the entire force of human City Guards but the robots as well.

"Target detected," Winston announced suddenly. "Stop the carriage."

Commandant Corvington had just exited the headquarters building. Turning right, he strode purposefully down the street.

The carriage halted, and Winston leapt out with such speed that Aldrich could only follow, feeling clumsy and slow by comparison. The commandant, ramrod straight in his red wool uniform coat and black tricorn hat, marched along as if on parade.

By the time Aldrich reached the footpath, Corvington had rounded a corner and disappeared down an alley with Winston in silent pursuit and Aldrich hurrying behind.

As Aldrich reached the alley's entrance, a slim figure wearing a tricorn hat appeared at the opposite end. A sword and two pistols hung from a thick leather belt while gloved hands grasped a silver dagger.

His heart squeezed and he had difficulty drawing breath. The assassin.

"Halt, criminal!" Winston blasted, darting past Corvington to tackle the assailant.

Corvington stumbled against the wall.

Winston crashed into the assassin, and they hit the ground hard. After an instant, the assassin began wriggling and straining to break free of Winston's weight. It was a futile fight. The robot was designed to stop criminals.

Suddenly recognizing the danger of resistance, the assassin went limp. One hand snaked out and snatched the fallen tricorn hat, ramming it down over blond hair.

Frozen where he stood, Corvington demanded, "What is the meaning of this?"

Aldrich hurried forward. "An assassin, sir," he explained breathlessly. "We came to warn you."

120

The Commandant's eyebrows shot up. His mouth worked silently before he faced the assassin and drew himself to his full height. "In the name of the Magisters of Cairnisle," he declared, "you are under arrest." Kneeling, he expertly locked a set of shackles around the assassin's gloved wrists.

The captive shrugged shoulders clad in a respectable brown leather coat that matched a pair of well-made trousers and intertwined gloved fingers without uttering a word.

Edging closer, Aldrich spotted a very familiar-looking silver masquerade mask. His breath caught as his mind recoiled from the obvious conclusion.

When Corvington reached to remove the mask, Aldrich hissed, "No, leave it!"

Corvington looked up, surprise rapidly turning to recognition, then irritation. "Doctor Durante, if I'm not mistaken." he said. "Who are you to tell me what I may or may not do with my prisoner? Stand back. I'm taking this criminal to Guard Headquarters for questioning."

Aldrich leaned close and whispered, "Listen carefully, sir. This assassin was hired to kill you. You cannot trust anyone at headquarters right now. Do you have another place we could go? I will explain everything."

Corvington looked ready to argue but clamped his mouth shut and nodded abruptly. Staring hard at the ornate mask, he shook his head. "The Silver Assassin," he muttered. "I have a thick dossier filled with your exploits. And now I've caught you." Straightening, he hoisted the silent captive upright. "My home is nearby. We'll go there."

Society in Turmoil

A great many members of our most illustrious society have expressed grave reservations about venturing forth into the public sphere until such time as the nefarious miscreant responsible for the shocking assassination of Lord Jonathan Loewe is apprehended and brought before the swift hammer of justice.

Lady Margaret Adderly, a pillar of our community, deigned to share her thoughts on this matter. "It is not safe," her ladyship declared, her voice quavering with barely concealed distress. "Anyone could be a target for these villains. One shudders to think what dastardly plots may be afoot."

-from The Cairnisle Times,
Thursday, April 18, Year 27 AK

TWENTY-ONE ~ ALDRICH

SET WELL BACK FROM THE street behind an imposing gate, Corvington's house was impressive, though hardly on the scale of Aldrich's parents' home. Streetlamps failed to illuminate the long driveway fully, but light flooded from several lower-level windows of the house.

From the rear of the procession, Aldrich studied the

extensive lawns and meticulously manicured trees and flowerbeds. His mind raced. The assassin could not possibly be Wilhelmina. The mask was only a coincidence. As was the size of the assassin who walked nothing like a woman. But what if it was her? What was he going to do?

Corvington led the way, his military bearing evident in every step. Winston followed, maintaining a firm grip on the prisoner's chains.

When Aldrich judged they were far enough from the street, he hurried past Winston and his charge to walk beside Corvington. Glancing at the commandant's fiercely curling moustache, he swallowed hard. What had he gotten himself into?

"I realize this is a most uncommon situation," he began, "but might I speak with the prisoner first?"

Corvington turned an unwavering stare on Aldrich. "You're right about one thing," he growled. "This is a most uncommon situation." He narrowed his eyes. "What makes you think I should permit you to speak with my prisoner at all, let alone first?"

Aldrich bristled. "Well, I suppose we could start with the fact that I just saved your life," he retorted.

Corvington grunted. After a few silent steps, he asked, "And just how did you know my life was in danger, Doctor Durante?"

Aldrich had anticipated this question. "An overheard conversation," he answered. "You were mentioned along with Lord Johnathon Loewe."

Corvington drew in a sharp breath. "I suppose I could give you a few minutes," he conceded, charging up the steps and pushing open the unlocked door. "Bring the prisoner through," he called over his shoulder, leading them into a large book-lined study. "Right here," he instructed Winston, pulling out a chair.

Winston escorted his charge to the chair. "Sit down, please," he said.

Corvington started. "You're a robot," he declared. "Why are you not in uniform?"

Aldrich cleared his throat. "I can explain that too, sir," he said. "If you will permit me a moment alone with the prisoner, I pledge to tell you everything I know."

Corvington grunted again. "You have five minutes," he said before closing the door behind himself and Winston.

The prisoner dropped onto the chair and leaned back, staring defiantly through the silver mask's eyeholes with a familiar set of blue eyes.

Aldrich stepped directly in front of the assassin. "Who are you?" he demanded.

"Oh, come now, Aldrich," she answered, hitching an elbow over the back of the chair and crossing her legs. "You figured out who I was the second you saw me." With a rattle of chains, she pulled her mask and hat into her lap and scowled severely at him.

Even though he had known it was her from the moment he recognized the mask, the sight of her face hit him like a blow. "Why, Wilhelmina? You are no assassin."

Except for a tightening of her face, Wilhelmina did not reply. She stared past his shoulder, shaking her head slightly as if despairing of his stupidity.

"I already know that Köhler hired you," Aldrich said, desperate to understand. "What is going on?"

"Aldrich, you disappoint me. If you're as smart as I think you are, you should be able to figure this out." Her voice held a note of scorn that set him on edge.

He paused, trying to frame a question that would elicit a useful reply.

Without warning, Wilhelmina reared up and kicked Aldrich in the stomach.

Breath rushed out of him as he dropped helplessly to the floor.

Her boot pressed down hard on his throat while she deposited the shackles on the chair and slid her lock-picking tools into a pocket.

"You know, Aldrich," she said, looking directly at him for the first time, "I usually kill anyone who discovers my identity. However, I like you. You dance well. Perhaps this once, I can make an exception." Her impassive face did not change as she offered him his life. "Do you promise to keep my secret?"

Aldrich struggled to breathe past the weight of her boot. She noted his difficulty and lifted her foot enough to permit a brief sip of oxygen, but not enough to allow him to speak.

"Aldrich, please," she said, "I don't have time for you to dither. Decide."

He tried to speak, but nothing came out.

She clicked her tongue. "If that's the way you want it," she said, removing her foot and drawing it back to kick him in the head.

In that brief second, he squeezed out a desperate, "Wait!"

She raised an eyebrow, and for an instant, he glimpsed the mischievous woman he had escorted to the ball before the scowl dropped into place again.

"I have figured it out," Aldrich said through his burning throat. "You do not kill for the money—you enjoy the game."

Wilhelmina's eyebrow rose higher. "I'm listening," she said.

"If it is danger that you are after," he said, "I have a proposition for you. I have plans." He swallowed painfully and continued. "I do not like what is happening in Cairnisle. I want to run against Grand Magister Köhler in the next election. You could help. There will be people whom I cannot convince to change."

Her eyebrows drew together. "Intriguing," she said after a moment. "But I'm afraid I'm already employed elsewhere."

Aldrich turned on his most charming smile—the one that had saved him from many difficult situations. "My dear Miss von Richtofen," he said. "I have no doubt that you will find me a far more pleasant employer than Augustus Köhler could ever be."

Her lips turned up at the corners in the semblance of a smile that did not reach her eyes. Drawing back her foot, she kicked him hard in the ribs.

As Aldrich curled his body around the blossoming pain, she turned and, gathering up both hat and mask, headed for the door. Over her shoulder, she called, "I accept. You have a deal." Sliding her disguise into place, she stopped with her hand on the doorknob. "There are two things you need to keep in mind if you're going to maintain my loyalty. One: my fees are very expensive, and two: this had better be interesting."

With that, she threw open the door and strode out.

Corvington and Winston leapt up from their chairs.

"Hey, you can't—" shouted Corvington as he lunged toward her.

"Prisoner on the loose!" shouted Winston, leaping over a fragile chair and blocking her exit.

Rushing into the room, Aldrich cried, "Let her go." His hand went to his bruised throat, and he coughed. "She's working for us now."

Corvington looked as if he had just suffered a boot to the stomach. Aldrich could sympathize.

"Please, Commandant Corvington," he said. "Let her go. I will explain everything."

Clenching his fists at his sides, Corvington spoke through white lips. "This had better be good."

Wilhelmina lifted a hand and sauntered past Winston. At the door, she stopped and turned back to gaze at each man in turn. "Remember," she said, "the deal is only good as long as you keep it interesting. My associate will be in touch."

Make Way For Progress

Demolition of our fair city's central church, a structure which has stood as a silent sentinel for nigh on two centuries, is proceeding apace. Those who have had occasion to perambulate through the heart of our bustling metropolis will have observed the industrious labours now transforming our civic landscape.

In an ingenious display of resourcefulness, the stones that once formed the very foundation of our spiritual gatherings are being repurposed. These venerable blocks, each imbued with the prayers and devotions of generations past, shall not be consigned to ignominious rubbish heaps, but rather shall find new purpose in the construction of a series of picturesque shelters.

-from The Cairnisle Times,
Thursday, April 18, Year 27 AK

TWENTY-TWO ~ FIAMETTA

FOR THE HUNDREDTH TIME, FIA made her way to her bedroom window at the top of the house and stared out at the empty street below. Why had she ever allowed Aldrich and Winston to leave without her? If she had any idea where they had gone, she would go after them.

The only good thing to come out of her forced confinement was the time it gave her to think. As she paced, an idea began to form. If Aldrich was serious about making changes—and she was beginning to believe he was—he would need help. He would need supporters.

Throwing herself down into the stuffed chair in Aldrich's study, she tried to clarify her thoughts. As far as she could see, the system in place benefited only the rich. Except for the rare few who, like Aldrich, wanted to help the poor, they were unlikely to campaign for change.

Magister Köhler would continue to rule uncontested—especially if he made a habit of using assassins to remove any obstacles to his success. Obviously, he had little use for critics, which meant that if and when Aldrich made his views known, he would be in danger.

Fia had lived alone on the streets of Dirt Town since the age of eight. In that time, she had made plenty of friends and developed an exceptional understanding of how the system worked down there.

Although she had never met him personally, she knew that the most important person in all of Dirt Town was Munash Conteh. Augustus Köhler must have realized that as well, since there was a bounty of one hundred thousand golds on his head. Everybody knew that.

But no one would ever turn him in. Anyone who tried would not live long enough to enjoy the payoff.

There were many rumours about Munash: that he had once been a prisoner of war and escaped, freeing all the other prisoners with him; that he was a noble in his homeland; and the story that Fia had always liked—that he was a powerful mage and the battered wooden stick he leaned on when he walked was actually a staff of power.

Munash had successfully united the people of Dirt Town in a way that had never been done before. He had even managed to bring a level of stability to the streets. Before his arrival, which was far before Fia's own time, no one had been safe anywhere down there.

More than once, she had listened to Munash talking to people, both individually and in large groups. He was an impressive speaker, his deep voice resonant and soothing at the same time. Only his grey beard and the deep lines on his dark face hinted at his great age. He often wore an embroidered waistcoat without a shirt, displaying impressively muscular arms and shoulders. It was easy to imagine him as a warrior like the stories said.

If Aldrich convinced Munash to support him, he would have most of Dirt Town on his side.

The rattle of the door at street level brought Fia to her feet in a rush. Hurrying to the top of the stairs, she met Aldrich climbing up as if each step pained him.

She wanted to pelt him with questions, but he looked so tired that she held her peace until he lowered himself into a chair at the kitchen table.

Noiselessly, Winston followed behind and moved to his usual position in the corner.

Unable to wait any longer, Fia demanded, "What happened?"

Aldrich ran a hand over his face and let out a long breath. "Rupert Corvington is still alive thanks to us," he said. Then he nodded in Winston's direction. "To give credit where credit is due, Winston saved him. I merely explained things to Corvington afterwards."

Fia grinned and stabbed a fist into the air. "I knew it," she crowed. "And Corvington? You told him about your plans? Is he going to help?"

"Fia," Aldrich said, raising his grey eyes to hers. "I am not sure I have plans. I am not even certain there is anything I can do, nor what Corvington could possibly do."

She thrust her hands in her trouser pockets and hunched her shoulders. "You do have plans," she insisted. "You said you have to do something about the evils you see in Cairnisle."

He scrubbed his face with both hands. "We caught the assassin," he said.

"That's good," she answered quickly. Then seeing Aldrich's strained expression, she stilled. "That is good, right?"

"I suppose so," he said. "We shall see." He sighed.

Fia slid into the chair opposite him and leaned across the table. "While you were out," she said, "I figured out who you need to talk to about your plans."

Aldrich stared glassily at her without replying.

Clearing her throat, she continued. "Dirt Town revolves around Munash Conteh. If you convince him to help you, you'll have all of Dirt Town behind you."

Aldrich sagged further into his chair. "And who exactly is Munash Conteh?"

Fia rocked back, her eyes wide. "You've never heard of Munash Conteh?" she asked. Her eyes narrowed and she clicked her teeth. "That seems impossible." Her eyebrows knit together, and she shook her head. "People listen to Munash. He's the only reason anyone is safe down there."

Sitting up straight, Aldrich blinked rapidly. "And you believe he would be interested in helping?" he asked.

Fia shrugged. Suddenly thirsty, she rose and went to the sink. "I don't know Munash personally," she answered. "But I know he has drawn the people in Dirt Town together into a community." She turned on the tap, filled a glass and gulped it down before turning back. "What if he could do the same for you? Dirt Towners do what Munash tells them."

"Tomorrow is Saturday," said Aldrich thoughtfully. "Perhaps I will pay him a call. Right now, though, I am going to bed." Aldrich pushed back his chair and rose.

As he set his foot on the bottom step, someone pounded on the door downstairs.

"Open up for the City Guard!" called a deep voice.

Fia turned white. "They're after Winston!" she hissed. Her head spun. Did they know about her too? Could she jump from the window at the back of the house?

Aldrich held up his hands and made a calming motion. "No, no," he said. "It is probably just someone needing a doctor. It happens all the time. However, if it will make you feel better, you and Winston can hide. There is a closet here."

He led her to the study and showed her a small closet that she had not noticed in her earlier explorations. The door was painted to match the wall and until Aldrich grasped the wooden trim and pulled it open, it was all but invisible.

Fia slipped inside with Winston behind her.

"Just stay put while I answer the door," Aldrich said and closed the door.

The darkness inside the tiny space was suffocating. She hoped Aldrich would hurry the City Guard along.

She heard him clump down the stairs and then the parade ground voice of the City Guard reached her in the hidden room. "Aldrich Durante? You are under arrest for the murder of Jack Bury."

Fia's stomach plummeted.

Down below, the door slammed shut and then there was only silence.

Shoving open the closet door, she ran to the window. Barely disturbing the curtain, she peered down onto the street.

An automatized carriage waited at the curb. Aldrich's hands had been shackled behind his back. One of the City Guards forced him into the rear-facing seat of the vehicle before climbing in after him.

Her heart sank as the rig pulled away. With a cry, she flopped into the stuffed chair.

"This is all my fault," she wailed. "What are we going to do? We have to help him!"

Doctor Accused

Doctor Aldrich Durante, a well-respected physician and heir to the illustrious Durante Manufacturing fortune, stands accused of the brutal murders of Mr. Jack Bury, a man of considerable means who conducted the majority of his business affairs in Dirt Town, and his assistant, Jimmy Cole.

"We cannot stand by and allow criminals to run free simply because their victims live and work in Dirt Town," declared our esteemed Deutero Magister Ingrid Jaeger. "The law must be applied equally to all, regardless of the station of either victim or perpetrator."

-from The Cairnisle Times,
Friday, April 19, Year 27 AK

TWENTY-THREE ~ FIAMETTA

FIA LED WINSTON TO THE ladder under the bridge and stepped aside. "You go first," she said, not wanting to risk being below if the rickety rungs did not support the robot's weight.

With surprising ease, Winston slid between the railings and climbed nimbly down to the dusty street. Without his City

Guard uniform to give him away and the jaunty yellow scarf to cover his lower face and neck, he easily passed as human. There was nothing stiff or mechanical in his movements, although the ladder did creak a little more than usual as he descended.

Since the City Guard arrested Aldrich two nights earlier, Fia had hardly slept. She spent the first night rushing from window to window while listening for the door and his footsteps on the stairs. She kept telling herself that Aldrich was rich. They would not throw him into prison for killing someone like Jack Bury. How could they? Jack was a known criminal, and Aldrich was a physician.

At some point, she had lain down in her white room and closed her eyes. When she woke after a brief doze to discover that the sun had come up, she bolted out of bed and dashed to his room. Her stomach twisted when she realised that he had still not returned. It was all her fault. He had only killed Jack and Jimmy to save her.

It had not helped to hear Winston's descriptions of how the City Guard would escort Aldrich to Cairnisle Prison—an imposing stone building near the city docks—and put him in a cell while the case against him was constructed. She did not like to think of him locked up.

She had paced around the house, feeling caged. But it was a gilded cage compared to what Aldrich was experiencing. She wanted to rescue him, but every idea came to nothing.

Winston had scuppered her plans to visit the prison with a warning that they would turn her away. She had considered sending Winston in his uniform, but he would have to announce his serial number, and that would result in him being shut down immediately. Aldrich's parents should be informed, but she had no idea where they lived.

When she finally settled on the idea of visiting Munash and

asking for his support, it had been too late at night to consider a trip to Dirt Town.

As soon as Winston touched the ground, Fia swung under the railing and scrambled down the ladder to join him.

"Come on," she said. "It's this way."

Although Winston had full access to the maps of Upside, he had no sequencing for Dirt Town. Robots were never sent there. Fortunately, Fia knew where to find Munash's house. Everybody did.

Leading the way through the narrow, dusty streets, she saw Dirt Town with fresh eyes. Everywhere she looked there was rotting wood, crumbling bricks, stinking toilets, grubby, half-starved children and, covering every surface, a heavy layer of dirt. She had been gone barely a week, yet it was not how she remembered it.

When they reached the square where Munash had his house, Fia felt her conviction waver. She stayed in the shadows and studied the tall, narrow building. What had made her believe that Munash would help? Why would he care?

Then, she pictured Aldrich locked in a prison cell. She had to try. She had to save him. "Come on," she said, straightening her shoulders and stepping out into the light.

With Winston at her side, she marched up to the only painted door in almost all of Dirt Town. When her purpose became clear, the two burly men standing watch moved from their positions on either side of the house to intercept them.

Blocking Fia and Winston's route to the blue door, they crossed their arms and settled back on their heels.

The one missing two front teeth grinned as he studied the pair. "Well, what do we have here?" he asked.

"Them is awful fancy clothes," said the second man. He did not smile as he spoke.

A shiver ran down Fia's spine. Why had she not changed

back into her old red coat before coming? Her face flushed. She had been so proud of the new one, the way it fit and the smooth feel of the cloth under her fingers. But down in Dirt Town, the rich clothing made them targets. How could she have been so stupid? Had she forgotten everything she had ever learned about the importance of being invisible?

Winston was careful to keep his head down. Would it be enough to get past the guards? If they looked too closely, they would know he was a robot.

Her mouth dry, Fia kept her eyes on their feet. "I need to talk to Mr. Conteh," she said.

That brought a bark of laughter from the first one. "Mister, is it?" he mocked. "And just why do you need to talk to Mr. Conteh? This better be good because you have to get past me to see him."

Fia swallowed, and all her carefully constructed words flew away. Suddenly, her request seemed impossible.

At that moment, Munash himself opened the blue door. His long, flowing orange robe reached almost to the floor.

Stiffening her legs to keep them from shaking, Fia called, "Hello, Mr. Conteh."

He broke into a wide smile, his teeth white in his dark face. "It is all right, gentlemen," he said in his lilting accent. "I will see her."

"Yes, sir," the men chorused before backing off to their positions by the corners of the house.

The taller one jabbed two fingers towards his own eyes before pointing at Fia. And then he laughed. The sound sent new shivers down her spine.

But without the men hovering over her, Fia relaxed slightly. She sent a tremulous smile toward Munash Conteh. "My name is Fia," she said.

Munash laughed—a low rumbling sound. "I know who you

are, Fiametta Nardovino."

Fia flinched at the sound of her full name, and her eyes widened. She could not breathe. Since the death of her parents, she had been careful never to speak her name aloud. The Nardovinos had been charged with treason and labelled enemies of the state before they were killed.

"Come in," Munash said, standing aside and waving her and Winston through with a sweep of his arm. "Come in and bring your friend."

Winston moved without hesitation, climbing the two steps and squeezing past Munash into the house.

Chewing the inside of her cheek, Fia smoothed her red coat and followed.

Inside, it was remarkably clean and tidy. Although small, the room had several chairs, a desk up against the wall, and a shelf overstuffed with books. A magnificent sword hung above the stone fireplace. The cross guard was in the shape of a bird with outstretched wings, while the blade showed two distinctively different metals—with the double edges glowing softly red and the channel that ran through its middle glimmering with gold.

As he closed the door, Munash looked at Fia and chuckled. "You wonder how I know who you are, Fiametta Nardovino," he said. "Sit down, and I shall tell you." He folded himself into the largest of the five mismatched chairs.

Fia quickly chose a spindly kitchen chair and perched on its edge while Winston let himself down into a sturdy club chair.

When they were settled, Munash leaned back and studied Fia. "I have watched you grow up," he said, his eyes crinkling into a smile. "You have done well for yourself."

Her breath sped up. "Why?" she asked. "Why did you watch me?"

Munash smiled again. "I think you know," he said. "You

have heard enough about me to guess why you interest me."

Fia set her jaw. "It's because I am a mage," she said.

"You see?" Munash said, lifting both hands in a gesture of triumph. "I knew you were smart." Then his smile faded. "Now, tell me why you have come."

In a rush, Fia told him about Aldrich. She told him everything. That he had rescued her from Jack Bury. That Aldrich had invited her to leave her hidey-hole to live with him. That he had saved Rupert Corvington from the assassin. That he felt the injustice of the mage slaves. That he did not like the way the robot City Guards were being given full authority to kill. That he came from a family of wealth and influence. That he was a physician who served anyone who came to his door. That he wanted to work to bring about change in Cairnisle.

"Last night," she said in conclusion, "he was arrested for the murder of Jack Bury. You know Jack was worth less than a slug getting fat off a garden full of vegetables. He feasted on the very poorest of Dirt Town."

"Did Doctor Durante kill Jack?" Munash asked.

Fia studied him through narrowed eyes. Was it safe to admit the truth? "Yes," she said finally.

Munash nodded, and his brown eyes took on a distant look. Turning to Winston, he asked, "And your friend here? How is he involved?"

Again, Fia hesitated before answering. In the end, Winston made the decision himself when he raised his head and unwound his yellow scarf.

Munash jerked upright and slapped his hands on the chair arms. "A robot?" he asked. "Tell me how this came to be."

Winston was already writing.

Munash's eyebrows drew together as he watched the robot form his perfect looping cursive. When Winston offered him the notebook, he readily accepted it and read aloud, "My name is Winston. I am a PI2 unit. The binding lock installed in me does not function and, as a result, I am free to act as I believe is right. Aldrich Durante is a kind man who allows me to stay at his house. I believe that all robots, as well as all humans, have the ability to live a free life. I can help."

Hearing Winston's words spoken in Munash's deep, rolling voice lent them a solemnity that Fia felt profoundly as she watched the tall leader absorb the information.

Munash sat back in his chair and gave a slow, disbelieving shake of his head. "A robot," he murmured. Pushing to his feet, he paced the length of the room before stopping in front of the fireplace. There, he placed his hands on his hips and fixed his gaze on the sword.

"This may well be the opportunity I have dreamed about," he murmured. Swinging back, he flashed a grin at Fia. "I knew you were a girl to watch." With a chuckle, he began to pace the room again.

"Since the day I came to this country, I have seen injustice and inequities," he said, his voice growing stronger.

Fia held her breath.

He rubbed a hand across his face. "Perhaps this man—your Doctor Aldrich Durante—is the one I have been waiting for." He stopped and planted his feet. "Let us devise a plan. I believe this may be the beginning."

Twelve Sent to Prison

The efficacy of the newly commissioned Green Coat City Guards, our city's latest robot sentinels, becomes more manifest with each passing day. Their unparalleled powers of observation have rendered it exceedingly challenging for the malefactors of Dirt Town to plunder the honest citizens of Cairnisle.

In but the past week, no fewer than twelve nefarious thieves have been apprehended and consigned to Cairnisle Prison. This salutary development augurs well for the safety and prosperity of our fair city, as the relentless vigilance of these mechanical guardians continues to deter crime and uphold justice.

-from The Cairnisle Times,
Friday, April 19, Year 27 AK

TWENTY-FOUR ~ WILHELMINA

KEEPING HER MASKED FACE AVERTED, Willy slipped out of the automatized carriage and down through the railings of the bridge onto the ladder. When she reached the bottom, she straightened and broke into a grin. She no longer had to hide.

In her leather trousers, her stride lengthened, and she took on a rolling gait that was so different from the walk she adopted when hampered by the restrictive dresses she was forced to wear in Upper Cairnisle. With her leather coat, high-topped boots, and battered tricorn—set at just the right angle—everything felt right.

Equally gratifying were the muttered whispers that followed her. Passersby hurried to step out of her way. In Dirt Town, she could wear her silver mask openly and everyone recognized her as 'The Silver Assassin'. They did not bother her, and they would never think to turn her in. They treated her with just the right amount of fear and respect. Most importantly, they would never guess who she was when she was Upside.

Recalling the horrid afternoon party she had just attended with her aunt, she shuddered. Although she tried to approach such get-togethers as a game that served to maintain her masquerade, she despised having to sit, drinking her coffee in polite little sips, delicately refusing a second serving of delicacies that deserved at least one more taste, while making insipid small talk with dull society girls. Dirt Town was better in so many ways.

As she walked, her eyes darted everywhere, assessing risks and challenges. Almost unconsciously, she calculated the best way to break into the buildings she passed. There was always a weak spot, and the fun was in discovering it.

The same could be said of people. Spotting their vulnerabilities was the first part of any assassination. Oftentimes it was not a physical limitation so much as something in their psychological makeup that offered possibilities.

For instance, with Johnathon Loewe, she had known that he would address his guests at the ball. She had also known that he would stand alone above his guests on the mezzanine at precisely eight o'clock. She had attended enough of his balls to understand his little vanities. From there, it had been a simple matter of arranging the clockwork smoke bomb and inducing a gentleman to accompany her to the ball.

One thing she had not anticipated, however, was Doctor Aldrich Durante. He had turned out to be infinitely more captivating than she could have fathomed when she cajoled him into being her escort. In fact, since that evening, she had thought of little else. He was smart. Very smart. Conversation with him was a dance of wit, bantering ideas back and forth. In that respect, it was too bad the evening had been cut so short.

And then, he had turned up at Corvington's assassination. Behind her mask, Willy winced. Attempted assassination.

Aldrich had pieced together the puzzle, connecting dots with the precision of a master sleuth to figure out her next target. That made him more than a little intriguing.

She had never actually been caught before. She was not sure how she felt about it. And, of course, there was the little detail about her identity. He knew who she was. She was definitely not sure how she felt about that.

In the meantime, she had agreed to work for him. And that was the purpose behind her visit to Dirt Town.

Reaching the square where Munash's tall, skinny house was squeezed in between two shorter buildings, she did not slow her pace but headed directly for the blue door. As expected, guards, who had been invisible a moment earlier, approached from all directions. The first to reach her stretched out a warning hand.

Instead of stopping as he expected, she grasped the hand and stepped in close with her elbow raised. With a sharp twist of her hips, she sent the man flying over her back to land hard in the dust.

Settling into a ready position, she swept her gaze over the remaining four guards, who had frozen in place.

"The Silver Assassin," they hissed in unison.

Behind her mask, Wilhelmina smiled. "I am going to talk to Munash now," she said in a voice that brooked no argument. "Don't worry. He's safe enough with me." Brushing past the man directly in front of her, she climbed the steps to the blue door.

No one made any move to stop her. She had earned their respect. Not just for flipping one of them into the dust. Nor was it for the assassinations alone. But there was also the matter of the money those assassinations brought in. Since she had no use for more money, every penny of her earnings ended up in Dirt Town. Benj, her eyes and ears in both upper and lower Cairnisle, ensured that the people who needed it most got their share. And he made certain they knew where it came from.

Benj was an entirely useful sort of fellow. With a network of spies and message carriers, he provided her with any information she required. In fact, her visit to Munash had come about because of Benj's spies. She had asked him to keep an eye on Aldrich Durante. By knowing both of her identities, the good doctor could turn out to be a bigger liability than she could afford. The problem was that she liked him. Otherwise, he would be dead already.

Benj had brought her three potentially useful observations. First, Aldrich had been arrested and taken to Cairnisle Prison. They said he had killed a man. If it was true, Aldrich rose yet another notch in her estimation. Secondly—and this was interesting too—Aldrich had a young girl, originally from Dirt Town, staying at his house. The final point seemed the most unlikely—though she had little cause to doubt Benj's information. One of the PI2 units was also staying at his house.

She would bet the robot was the same one who had prevented the assassination of Corvington. How did Aldrich come to have a robot City Guard to do his bidding? That was a story she would like to hear. And the girl? Who was she?

Benj's spies had followed the pair to Munash Conteh's house. When his message arrived at her aunt's home, she had hurried to get down before they left.

Without knocking, she barged into Munash's sitting room. Reacting with extraordinary speed, the robot sprang to his feet with his pistol drawn. Willy faced him and shook her head. "Not necessary," she said. "Put it away."

Reacting to the lack of threat she presented rather than her suggestion, he holstered his pistol but remained standing, fully alert.

The girl had also bolted to her feet at Willy's entrance. She goggled, her mouth gaping in recognition.

After a quick assessment, Willy dismissed her for the moment. She might prove interesting since Aldrich had thought she was worth his while, but she offered no threat. Munash had whirled with his hands outstretched when Willy crashed through the door, but as soon as he recognized her, he relaxed.

"The Silver Assassin," he said. "Welcome." He gestured to an empty chair. "Please, sit." He let himself down into his own worn chair.

Willy did not sit. She made no effort to show respect to the man who wielded more power than anyone else in Dirt Town. "I want to know everything," she cried, her voice too loud in the small room. "Tell me what is going on and what you have planned!"

Munash's eyebrows shot up.

Willy caught herself. How had she lost control? It was

Aldrich. She did not understand what he was doing to her. She had dealt with Munash often over the past three years and never before had she shown a trace of emotion. Forcing down her agitation, she stepped into the room and closed the door behind her.

"My little spiders tell me something is afoot with these two," she said more calmly. Not taking her eyes from him, she waved a gloved hand vaguely in the direction of his visitors.

The corners of Munash's eyes crinkled. "Your little spiders might be right," he agreed. "We are indeed working on something here." He pressed one finger to his lips. "Please, everyone, let us sit down so that we can talk about it."

The robot sat immediately. Willy studied the girl. She was no pushover. Her chin high, she returned Willy's probing gaze. The girl sat first, never taking her eyes off the masked woman. After a moment, Willy chose a battered, wicker basket chair with a good view of the door.

Munash cleared his throat. "Your unexpected visit leads me to believe that you would like to offer us your aid," he said in his slow rolling accent. "I think, perhaps, that you could be very helpful." He gave her a gentle smile. "Allow me to introduce Fiametta and Winston."

"Why are you telling her?" Fiametta demanded. Her colour had changed from pale to flushed. "We do not want anyone killed!"

Behind her mask, Willy smiled at the girl's ferocity. She could appreciate someone who showed such passion. "To tell you the truth," she said, "I have useful skills that do not involve killing." She let that hang for a moment as a play of emotions ran across the girl's face. "And I would like to see Aldrich freed from prison."

At the mention of Aldrich's name, Fia froze. Narrowing her eyes, she asked, "How do you know Aldrich?"

Not wanting to admit that she had just met him, Willy answered, "Are you not aware that the Silver Assassin knows everything and everyone? Do not worry, little girl, I mean the good doctor no harm."

Fia winced at the snub, but she bit back a response with obvious effort. Good for her. She knew better than to answer rudely to someone called the Silver Assassin.

Munash drummed his fingers on the wooden arm of his chair and drew their attention back to himself. "Winston," he said, addressing the robot, "could you talk to Commandant Rupert Corvington? I think he would be a most valuable ally."

"Yes," answered Winston.

"Corvington?" asked Willy, suddenly uneasy. "What do you want with him?" Did they know about her part in the assassination attempt? Obviously, the robot recognized her. Had he already told the others?

"No doubt, you know that Corvington has upset the Magisters," Munash said, his eyes twinkling as if he could see her discomfort. "They do not appreciate his repeated questioning of their methods."

His manner prickled and Willy frowned but she said nothing. She needed to know more.

Munash settled himself more comfortably in his chair and said, "Now, Silver—may I call you Silver?" He did not wait for an answer, nodding to himself as if she had consented. "Silver, if you choose to be of service in this enterprise, you could be most helpful. Your little spiders are already in place and you have a long reach. May we call upon you for assistance when necessary?"

Feeling that she had lost the upper hand, Willy said, "I suppose so." She knew it was in bad grace, but one of the advantages to leaving her beautiful gowns behind was that good manners could be ignored as well.

Flashing a white grin, Munash rubbed his hands together. "Fiametta," he said, "you will stay here with me as we make the final preparations."

A look of relief flashed across the girl's face. She was frightened. That was interesting.

"Um. Yes," Fia answered. After a brief hesitation, she added, "Thanks."

Willy almost laughed aloud at the laboured attempt to be polite.

"Good, then," Munash said. "It is settled. Five days from now, we will turn the prison inside out and begin a revolution."

Tribes Unite

Word has reached our fair city of a tribal leader who has managed to join together several of the larger wandering groups from the untamed lands east of Cairn. However, the good people of Cairnisle need not worry about this news.

When asked about the matter, the esteemed Grand Magister Augustus Köhler confidently stated: "It is true that a few skirmishes have temporarily slowed food shipments. However, these petty squabbles are of no consequence to our great city. This so-called leader styles himself 'Jarlerus the Scourge.' How can any sensible person take such a silly name seriously?"

-from The Cairnisle Times,
Saturday, April 20, Year 27 AK

TWENTY-FIVE ~ ALDRICH

THE SMELL WAS ATROCIOUS. BUT after two days locked in the cramped cell with seven other men, the enforced inactivity was even worse. The only thing they could do was talk, although they had to speak quietly enough so the guards did not hear them. Talking was prohibited, a rule backed up with clouts and kicks.

Nonetheless, if Aldrich were to add up the positives of his imprisonment, overall, it had been a worthwhile experience. To begin with, he had met some very interesting people. What he had discovered during their long, nearly inaudible conversations about the workings of Cairnisle was nothing less than life-changing. It also helped to explain how he found himself sitting on a damp prison floor instead of seeing patients in his clinic.

Through their whispered discussions, he had learned of a wide variety of sordid activities that regularly took place in Cairnisle. He saw the truth for the first time, and a burning desire to do something about it had settled in his gut. What that something was, he was not at all certain. But the seed of an idea was beginning to develop.

First, though, he had to get out of prison. He was counting on his parents. They should have received his message. On the very first day, he had given their address to a guard and told him how happy they would be to learn of their son's whereabouts.

He was painfully aware that he had been telling himself and his cellmates that the serious disparity of wealth was the issue that most concerned him. Nonetheless, he was not above taking advantage of the benefits of his birth. He had no doubt that his parents would be able to buy his freedom.

In the meantime, he waited and learned. The men he had met—both in the cell and out in the exercise yard, where shifts of sixty-four men were allowed a half-hour outside each day while the cells were hosed out—had proven to be excellent teachers. Each fellow had been arrested on some pretext or another, but the real reason always came back to Grand Magister Augustus Köhler or the Deutero Magister, Ingrid Jaeger.

Aldrich guessed that the charge of killing Jack Bury was only a pretext for his own imprisonment. No one in Upper Cairnisle, where the wheels of justice turned, really cared about the death of a Dirt Town loan shark. Someone must have found out about his interference in Rupert Corvington's assassination. Like the men he had met in the prison, he had thrust himself into the uncomfortable position of annoying the Magisters.

Seated beside him on the cold and slightly damp stone floor was an interesting example of how easy it was to get in their bad books. Gustav Florenburg had spent twenty-five years building robots for the Magisters as a trusted member of their organization. Although Aldrich did not come right out and ask, he guessed that Winston was one of his inventions.

One day, in talking with Grand Magister Köhler, Gustav made the mistake of questioning some of the more brutal uses of the robot City Guards. The next thing he knew, a couple of those same robots had hauled him off to prison.

Like many of the other men in Aldrich's segment of the prison population, Gustav had never been formally accused of a crime and no trial ever took place. He just sat waiting, day after day, for Köhler or one of the other five Magisters to decide he had served enough time, or more likely—that he was no longer a danger to their plans.

Thinking about danger, Aldrich was immediately reminded of Wilhelmina von Richtofen. He had thought of her more than once over the past few days. Not only was she the most beautiful woman he had ever known, but she was also smart. And dangerous beyond belief. What exactly had he got himself into by asking her to help him?

A rattle of keys at the cell door roused Aldrich from his musings. Rising stiffly, he reached down to help Gustav to his feet. The older man looked to have lost weight during his time in the prison. Although he might still be called comfortably plump, the skin on his unshaven face hung loosely over his bones. Given the two meagre meals served each day, Aldrich expected to drop a few pounds as well.

Gustav maintained a jolly outlook on life despite his current situation. Aldrich appreciated the obvious brilliance of the man. He so rarely met someone who could connect with him on an intellectual level.

The idea of intelligence led him back to the only other person who challenged his intellect: Wilhelmina. The mere thought of her made him break into a sweat and his chest tightened so that breathing became an effort. The woman had a way of muddling his thoughts.

Aldrich ran a sleeve across his forehead and scowled at his feet as he shuffled through the cell door behind the other prisoners. They were not criminals. They were prisoners of conscience. What was the point of having a democracy if dissent was not permitted? The Magisters held all the power, and they used it for their own benefit rather than for the good of the people.

When they reached the little courtyard, Aldrich lifted his face up to the sun. Gustav bumped up against him and murmured, "Time to meet a few more of the inmates, heh?"

Grateful as he was for Gustav's protection, Aldrich yearned for solitude—a precious moment or two to bask in the embrace of warmth and light. Nonetheless, he smiled down at the little man and gave an imperceptible nod.

Gustav joined the flow of walkers and Aldrich fell into step beside him.

Speaking barely loud enough to be heard, he said to the three men ahead, "Gentlemen, may I present Doctor Aldrich Durante? I believe he has some ideas that will interest you."

The men did not alter their pace, but each uttered a quiet greeting in return, hardly moving their lips.

Then one of them asked, "What ideas?"

Aldrich did not know where to start. A shudder ran through him. He could see it all so clearly. Change required a catalyst—a resolute force to shatter the inertia.

Given the strict rules of the prison, with no one allowed to speak above a whisper, and the sheer number of thoughts ricocheting around in his brain, he suddenly felt he could not remain quiet for one second longer.

The first word escaped—a tremor, a seismic shift. "Enough," he hissed. "Silence will not birth change. Cairnisle needs a voice—a reckoning."

Without pausing to consider his actions, he stepped out of the procession of walkers, into the centre of the courtyard. There, he stopped and raised his face to the sun once more. Then, unable to control himself, he began to speak. "This is not right!" he shouted. "We are not the criminals. The Magisters are the true criminals. If anyone is to waste their days sitting in prison, it should be them."

Around him, the other prisoners halted in their endless circle and stared.

He did not miss the frightened looks they shot toward the guards. However, he was beyond caring.

"Men," he continued, lowering his voice aggressively and curling his hands into fists as he made eye contact with each of his listeners in turn, "we do not have to remain caged here like animals. We can make our own destinies. We can stand together and fight our way free."

His speech was met with silence and wide-eyed looks. And then small cries of agreement slipped out.

Aldrich's chin lifted. Warmth surged through him. They were listening. They knew he was right. He would be that catalyst for change.

Footsteps pounded behind him. Before he could turn around, he was slammed to the ground.

A broad-shouldered guard sat on top of him, while another dozen guards surrounded the entire yard, their weapons trained on the dazed prisoners.

"Move it," cried a thin-faced guard. "Back to the cells everyone."

Without a word of protest, the prisoners lowered their heads and filed back into the building, leaving Aldrich alone in the dust, pinned painfully beneath his attacker.

Then the weight vanished, and the guard snatched at Aldrich's coat collar to haul him to his feet.

"Get up!" he snarled.

The first punch took Aldrich in the stomach, stealing the breath from his body.

Pushing his face close to Aldrich's, the guard spat, "It is the hole for you."

Stars exploded behind Aldrich's eyes with the second blow.

"Learn the rules," the guard said, changing his grip to Aldrich's sleeve.

Aldrich swayed. Without the guard's support, he would have fallen.

"No talking!"

The words echoed in Aldrich's ringing head as the third punch plowed into his ribs.

Grabbing the back of Aldrich's coat again, the guard shoved him across the empty courtyard.

As he staggered into the darkness of the prison building, Aldrich mourned the loss of the sunlight. What was the hole? What had he done?

After pushing him past the crowded cells that suddenly looked inviting, the guard guided him toward an even darker stairwell.

By the time Aldrich made it to the bottom of the steep, narrow stairs, the overwhelming rush of certainty and righteousness that had overtaken him in the courtyard had completely vanished.

He bit back a whimper. With each step down into the dungeon, his heart accelerated to the point that he thought it might explode. The only thing holding him together was the tiny circle of light provided by the torch that the guard had picked up at the top of the stairs.

Outside a heavy wooden door, the guard fitted the torch into a rusty bracket and fumbled with his ring of keys, cursing under his breath. Holding Aldrich's arm so tightly it would leave bruises, he finally fitted a key into the lock.

When he thrust the door open, Aldrich's stomach clenched. The walls of the small, round cell glistened damply in the torchlight. He opened his mouth to protest as the guard shoved him roughly into the little room.

Stumbling on numb legs, Aldrich crashed against the wall and slid helplessly to the floor.

The door slammed shut, leaving him in total darkness, and he started to shake.

Wrapping his arms around his knees, Aldrich squeezed his eyes shut and thought of Fia. If he had never met her, he would not have learned what was really happening in Cairnisle.

Did he regret it? He blew out a slow breath, refusing to open his eyes to be confronted with the total absence of all light.

No, he did not regret it. Not yet anyway.

His bruises would heal, but they could not take away the sudden clarity that suffused his mind.

He would survive the hole. A book he had read on sensory deprivation outlined its benefits. To this point, he had not sufficiently explored the practice. There never seemed to be time in his days to permit the complete inactivity it demanded.

Keeping his breaths slow and even, he let his mind drift.

Border Secured

For the first time in twenty-seven years, the valiant army of Cairn has engaged with marauding forces at the border of our mainland territories.

"Jarlerus the Scourge may consider himself invincible, but Cairn's forces defeated him with only minimal losses on our side," declared Deutero Magister Ingrid Jaeger.

This triumph stands as a testament to the unparalleled strength and resolve of Cairn's military might. Let it be known that our borders remain steadfast and secure, a bulwark against all who dare to threaten our sovereignty.

-from The Cairnisle Times,
Monday, April 22, Year 27 AK

TWENTY-SIX ~ ALDRICH

THE NEAR SILENCE IN THE hole was as oppressive as the darkness, and Aldrich found himself straining to hear the smallest noises. There was an almost constant dripping that sounded like a ticking clock. Its reassuringly steady beat had become something of a timekeeper for him.

To further divide his time into regular segments, there had

been four occasions when a cup of water and a stale heel of bread were delivered through a small slot in the bottom of the door.

The first time Aldrich heard the approaching footsteps, his eyes had snapped open in the darkness, and an unnerving sense of blindness threatened to undo his deliberate calm.

The scrape of the tray on the floor saved him. Curiosity was a powerful stimulus and engendered a degree of excitement. When he crawled over to investigate, his creeping fingers had very nearly overturned the cup of water. When he caught it without spilling a drop, he felt an inordinate rush of gratitude.

The magnification of emotions was an interesting side-effect of the loss of sensory input. Nonetheless, his appreciation for the water was real. Despite the dampness of his prison, thirst was his constant companion.

On the second visit, Aldrich demanded to know how long he would be down there.

"No talking," the guard had growled, before walking away.

On subsequent visits, Aldrich kept his mouth shut. Despite a desire to hear another human voice, he had no intention of provoking the guard. He appreciated that the bucket of waste he pushed through the same hole through which the food arrived was carried away each time and returned rinsed clean.

Refusing to consider the hygienic nature of his food, he savoured every morsel. Had he ever drawn a meal out to such lengths?

Between sessions of mind-freeing meditation, he recalled books he had read. The one he had been immersed in the day he met Fia was particularly pertinent. An examination of psychopaths, it outlined the criminal behaviours often associated with people suffering from anti-social personality disorders.

Behind closed eyes, he compared the descriptions in the

text with behaviours he had witnessed in Wilhelmina von Richtofen. The number of commonalities she shared with the clinical observations was convincing. The conclusion was obvious. Wilhelmina was a psychopath.

Despite this diagnosis, he found that thinking about her provided him with the greatest distraction from the slow creep of time. Never had he met anyone so utterly fascinating.

At the sound of approaching footsteps, Aldrich climbed to his feet and took a position as far from the door as he could get. Holding onto the wall, he listened, expecting the scrape of the metal tray along the stone floor.

Instead, he heard gruff voices rumbling outside his door. Then the door creaked inward, and torchlight blinded him.

"What are you doing over there?" asked the guard. He stomped into the cell and seized Aldrich by the arm. "Let's go."

While Aldrich struggled to pry open his protesting eyes, the guard hauled him into the corridor.

Aldrich's heart raced. He was out. They would return him to the cell with Gustav. An urge to laugh bubbled up. What had he come to that the thought of being shoved into a smelly cell filled with other prisoners brought him an inordinate thrill?

He pressed his lips together and sniffed. The guard smelled of tobacco, sweat and bread. It made his mind swirl. And the air in the corridor was noticeably sweeter than that in his cell. He drew it into his lungs and relished the sensation.

As an experiment in sensory deprivation, his past few days had been interesting. His olfactory nerves were remarkably sharper.

His solitary existence had also highlighted his need for human contact. Despite the guards' tight—almost painful—grip on his arms, he welcomed their presence.

By the time they made it to the stairs, Aldrich's eyes had adapted to the light, and he stared greedily at everything. The damp stones underfoot held a wealth of patterns. The swirls in the wood of the sturdy doors gripped his attention and he would have stopped for a closer examination if the guards had not been in such an obvious hurry.

As they passed through the door to the ground floor, he came near to tears at the first hint of sunlight. He wanted nothing more than to take his spot beside Gustav Florenburg and stare at the sky through the tiny window. Would the sun be shining?

His legs went weak when the guards towed him past the familiar row of cell doors. Where were they taking him? Suddenly, a wave of nausea hit him, and he broke out in a cold sweat.

Drawing on his lessons in meditation, Aldrich slowed his racing mind and focused on their route as they trudged up another set of stairs. They hurried along a mezzanine that overlooked the courtyard where he had staged his poorly timed rebellion.

The floors and walls of the upper region of the prison were built from polished stone instead of the rough-hewn blocks below, and the corridors were lit with brightly glowing bulbs.

The air lost its sour taint entirely. Where were they taking him? Either it was good news, and he was being released, or it was very bad news. The whispered stories he had heard from his cellmates came rushing back at him and he squeezed his eyes shut.

When the guards finally stopped, they had reached a section of the prison that Aldrich had never imagined existed.

After a brisk knock on a windowless door, the guard pushed it open to reveal a sunlit room furnished with only a table and two hard chairs. One wall was taken up almost entirely by a large mirror.

The guards shoved Aldrich into the room and shackled him to the chair facing the mirror before exiting and slamming the door behind themselves.

Aldrich did not allow himself more than a glimpse of the mirror. The image reflected there showed a filthy and disheveled man with a pale, unshaven face. His breathing sped up again and he concentrated on bringing it under control.

Turning to the window, he caught sight of a single cloud floating across an impossibly blue sky. Had he ever seen anything more beautiful? The sense of calm that he had pursued in the hole descended. It was so much easier to achieve when he was faced with light rather than darkness.

A few minutes later, with his breathing and heart rate under control, Aldrich heard the door open. Interlacing his fingers behind his back and ignoring the bite of the steel shackles, he turned to meet his visitor.

A tall robot wearing a red coat marched through. Unlike Winston, whose face resembled a human skull, the robot's metal face was cast as a handsome, bearded man.

Pulling out the empty chair, he lowered himself into the seat and fixed his glowing blue eyes on Aldrich.

Determined not to wilt under the scrutiny, Aldrich set his teeth and glared back. The robot's motionlessness was disturbing but Aldrich had become accustomed to Winston's absolute stillness. It was the blue stare that truly unsettled him. It felt as if the robot could see straight into his mind and was reading all that passed there. It was enough to make him squirm.

A grating noise broke the silence and Aldrich jerked upright, wrenching his wrists against the restraints.

The sound came again, and Aldrich's empty stomach clenched in on itself. Was it meant to be laughter?

Ignoring the pain in his wrists, Aldrich squared his shoulders. He was facing a robot with a nasty sense of humour.

"Doctor Aldrich Durante," the robot said. "My name is Forge Dash Thirty-Seven. I would like to ask you some questions."

Aldrich's eyebrows flickered upward. The robot could say his name. He was a definite upgrade from Winston.

"Before we begin, might I say that I have heard great things about you." The voice issuing from the small hole in the carved lips was strangely unexpressive and far too loud and commanding for the small room. How had the inventors achieved such a feat? Had Gustav been involved in its development? The robot was not using pre-recorded sentences. Individual words were strung together to communicate his meaning. It indicated a whole new level of technology.

The robot's head moved smoothly on its neck. "Everyone is speaking of the amazing young prodigy, Doctor Aldrich Durante," he said, giving another of his alarming laughs. "I look forward to our little chat today."

Aldrich blinked and his eyebrows drew together. A robot who could use sarcasm? It seemed unlikely.

"Let us get down to business," said Forge-37. "Shall we begin with your little outburst in the courtyard? I understand that you deliberately attempted to provoke the prisoners into a rebellion against your betters."

"My betters?" Aldrich asked, startled into speech. "You are suggesting that the Magisters and their guards are my betters?" He could hear the edge of hysteria in his voice and glanced out the window. It helped. He pinched his mouth together and then continued. "When I spoke up in the courtyard, I was speaking up against unfairness. Why have I not been provided with an opportunity to defend myself against any charges against me?"

Forge-37's blue eyes locked on Aldrich. "You are in this prison because you have been charged with the crime of killing one Jack Bury and his associate, Jimmy Cole. I would be interested to hear your confession in regard to your criminal activity."

"My confession of criminal activity?" Aldrich asked. He kept his voice low, but his shoulders strained against the restraints. "Your questions should be directed toward the Magisters." He licked his lips. "It is they who have committed the crime of ignoring the Jack Burys of this city. Why is there no form of policing in the streets of Dirt Town? Why is criminal activity that harms the residents of our city allowed to proceed unhindered? Why is such a large segment of our population left to live in squalor and make their own way?" Clamping his mouth shut, he scowled at the robot.

Again, Forge-37 did not move.

Aldrich's eyes darted away, and he caught a glimpse of himself in the wide mirror. Had he said too much?

"You believe that your actions will better Cairnisle?" Forge-37 asked finally.

Aldrich's jaw jutted out. "Of course I believe that," he said. He wanted to elaborate on his observation that the people of Cairnisle deserved change. The divide between Upper and Lower Cairnisle did no one any good. He could feel the pressure of the unspoken words. But he took a tight hold of himself and resorted to silence.

Again, the press of those unblinking eyes threatened to unhinge him. Biting his lip, he glanced up at the window.

Unexpectedly, Forge-37's grating laugh crackled. "Doctor Aldrich Durante, tell me, what do you think of your new ward?" the robot asked. "Do you like having a grubby Dirt Town child living in your home?"

Aldrich felt as if he had been punched in the stomach. Sweat broke out on his forehead despite the coolness of the room. They knew about Fia. How? What else did they know? What if they knew about Winston?

He desperately wanted to defend his actions, to argue for the unfairness of being born into a rich home or a poor home. But a tiny thread of self-control whispered to him to remain silent. It was the only thing he could do for Fia at the moment. Pressing his lips into a thin white line, he slouched in his chair and stared back at the robot.

Forge-37 was unaffected by Aldrich's defiance. After giving him plenty of time to answer, he released another grating laugh. "You believe you have the power to make change in Cairnisle," he said. It was not a question.

"This is a democracy, is it not?" Aldrich snapped. "If people do not like the way a country is run, they can elect new leaders. I intend to let my name stand in the next election. Perhaps, by insisting that citizens open their eyes and take notice of the inequities that pervade every level of life in Cairnisle, I can make a difference."

His survival instinct kicked in and although he had more to say—much more—he clenched his jaw and vowed to say nothing more in the vain hope that he had not already said too much.

In one fluid motion, the robot pushed back his chair and surged to his feet. "Doctor Aldrich Durante," he said in his monotone voice, "I must say that you have proven to be far more interesting and amusing than most of the humans I meet." He turned his beautifully sculpted face toward the mirror. "This interview is pointless. If this man were not already confined to prison, he would present a significant threat. He is more competent than all of you combined."

With that, he spun on the ball of his foot and covered the

distance to the exit in one long stride. "Idiots," he said, as he pulled the door open.

Though the words appeared to be meant for no one in particular, they were of such a volume that Aldrich easily heard him.

"What a waste of my time," the robot said. "I am intended for much grander purposes than interrogating helpless prisoners. Why would anyone worry that someone locked within these walls could ever cause a disturbance? Ridiculous."

The door slammed closed between another burst of the grinding chuckle.

A puddle of dread spread through Aldrich's body. They had no intention of ever setting him free.

Criminals Get Message

The recently implemented strategy to curtail unlawful activities within our fair city has borne remarkable fruit. For a full forty-eight hours, our valiant City Guards have found no cause to apprehend a single miscreant.

Grand Magister Augustus Köhler, when apprised of this encouraging development, offered the following statement: "It is plain to see that the criminal element is at last comprehending the gravity of our resolve. The message, it seems, has been received with utmost clarity."

-from The Cairnisle Times,
Thursday, April 25, Year 27 AK

TWENTY-SEVEN ~ FIAMETTA

FIA COLLAPSED INTO MUNASH'S ROOMY chair and stretched out her legs. After the miles she had traversed—carrying messages and collecting information from every corner of the island city—her new red coat and shiny boots no longer stood out in Dirt Town.

The blue front door slammed open, and Fia leapt to her feet, her knife ready in her hand.

The Silver Assassin flicked her gaze over Fia before

sweeping the rest of the room. "Where is he?" she drawled.

"Who?" asked Fia, trying to hide her hammering heart. The woman's habit of barging into rooms was becoming tiresome.

Silver's face was invisible behind her silver mask, but her annoyance was evident in the way she put one hand on her hip and cocked her head. "Who do you think?" she asked. "Munash."

"He's upstairs," Fia answered, settling back in her chair. "We're to meet outside shortly."

The Silver Assassin grunted and slumped gracefully into the club chair that Winston always chose. "Well, I'm sure he'll be pleased to hear that everything on my end is arranged," she said.

"You found it?" Fia asked, leaning forward, her teeth clenched so hard, her jaw ached. She had just returned from scouting the Cairnisle Prison. Generally a place she avoided, she had never seen it up close before. Built as a defensive structure during the wars, it was a sprawling fortress on the cliffs above the lake, with high walls that dropped straight down into the water several hundred feet below.

Aldrich was in there, trapped behind those solid stone walls. It was not fair. It was her fault that Jack Bury was dead. The City Guard should have taken her. Or better yet, they should have left both her and Aldrich alone and celebrated Jack Bury's death like everyone else did. Instead of locking Aldrich up, they should have pinned a medal on his chest.

Careful to stay well out of arrow range of the guards, Fia had circled the land-bound portions of the massive building while she tried to visualize the attack Munash had outlined. The walls were impossibly high. She had squinted up at the line of cannons visible on the crenels of the highest battlements and tried to imagine climbing up to them. But if Silver had found a back way into the prison—

166

The quiet creak of a loose board brought both Fia and the Silver Assassin to their feet, weapons drawn. When Munash rounded the corner, they relaxed, and their knives vanished.

"I am very glad to hear of your success," Munash said, smiling warmly at the Silver Assassin. "And Fia, thank you for delivering this latest round of notes." He held up the bundle of letters she had picked up on her way back from the prison. Hanging at his left side, from a well-worn belt and scabbard, was the sword that normally held a place of prominence over the fireplace. The yellow gemstone set in the hilt's end refracted the last of the evening's light and sent little rainbows dancing around the walls.

"It is time," he said, glancing through the window. "Shall we go and greet our guests?" Opening the front door, he waved Fia and the Silver Assassin ahead of him.

Fia followed the older woman down the stairs to join the gathering crowd. The square was already more than half-filled with a motley collection of people and more joined the press with every passing second. The only thing the arrivals seemed to have in common was a tough and ready look, along with an assortment of weapons.

Winston stood beside a man dressed in the red uniform of the City Guard. That would be Commandant Rupert Corvington. Fia studied him through narrowed eyes. As tall as Winston and sporting a thick, waxed moustache that curled away from his mouth, he was an imposing figure. A circle of space surrounded the odd pair as the residents of Dirt Town avoided getting too close.

Five days earlier, Winston had been sent to recruit Corvington. The robot had returned from the trip, his energy almost depleted. After Fia recharged him, he wrote a seven-page document recounting everything that had happened. Munash had read it, smiled, and handed it over to Fia.

As she read it, warmth radiated out from her chest. Winston's mission was a success. Corvington had come over to their side.

It turned out that the Commandant held many of the same concerns about the inequities in Cairnisle that had affected Aldrich.

In a better position than most to see how the wheels of justice turned, he had come to believe that they were headed in the wrong direction. The robots' violence, in particular, kept him awake at night. Winston's very existence as a robot functioning with free will had been a source of great fascination to him and he had questioned Winston in depth about his understanding of the world.

Corvington was also well aware of Munash's reputation as a leader in Dirt Town and appreciated the work he did to maintain stability in Lower Cairnisle.

Surprisingly—given his position—he was not against the idea of a prison break. He knew a great number of people who had been detained for questioning and never formally charged. Also, he was unconvinced that Dirt Towners deserved such lengthy prison terms.

He was prepared to challenge the Magisters and already he had recruited a militia of just over three hundred trained ex-guards who had been displaced by the robots.

Fia's attention was pulled away from Corvington and back to Munash as a hush spread over the crowd until no sound penetrated the deep ravine.

Illuminated by the single bulb above his head, and with the blue door behind him, the unofficial leader of Dirt Town looked like an actor on a stage

"Thank you for coming, my friends," he said, raising his hands out to his sides in welcome, as if embracing them all. "Thank you for coming to help." The tension of his listeners melted away under his slow and measured speech. "Today is a special time. A special day. It is the day when we break the bonds of oppression. We will abandon the life that rich people believe we deserve." He smiled gently, and the crowd exhaled.

"We may be poor, but still, each of us has as much value as a person as any citizen of Upper Cairnisle." The corners of his mouth turned down. "We have lived in tyranny for a very long while—as did your parents before you and their parents before them. We have been held in place under the boot of those who think themselves better."

His voice took on a hypnotic quality. "We have been oppressed," he said. "But nobody noticed. Nobody cared. Nobody—except one man. He noticed. He cared. He wanted to help. And for that—he rots in prison. Grand Magister Köhler was so afraid of this man that he locked him up. Locked him up for the crime of trying to help!"

Fia wrenched her gaze from Munash and stared around at the familiar faces that had surrounded her since childhood. Munash was using Aldrich. Her stomach tightened. He was turning him into a martyr.

"I believe that Doctor Aldrich Durante is the man to begin a revolution," Munash continued, his voice rising in volume. "He will make change happen. A doctor of the highest quality—Aldrich Durante always chooses to help. His life's goal is to reduce suffering." His hands floated up from his sides, and the long fingers opened wide.

"The time has come for change and Doctor Aldrich Durante has already begun the steps to make it happen." Dramatically, Munash drew his sword and thrust it into the air so that it caught the light from the bulb above the door and sent a flash of red through the crowd.

"Tonight!" Munash cried. "Tonight, we will release Doctor Aldrich Durante from the prison on the cliffs." He shook the sword and glowered out at the crowd. "We will take that prison for ourselves."

A murmur began.

"We will take it and turn it inside out," Munash called.

The murmur rose to a low rumble.

Munash bared his white teeth. "When the prisoners are free, we will not stop there," he bellowed. "We will not stop until every single person in Dirt Town is free of the yoke of poverty!"

No Sign of the Scourge

Since the decisive defeat of his marauding forces, Jarlerus the Scourge has not been sighted near the borders of Cairn. The clash, which transpired five days hence, has seemingly deterred any further encroachments.

Deutero Magister Ingrid Jaeger, in a statement to our correspondents, articulated her beliefs thus: "I suspect that the assault was merely a reconnaissance effort to ascertain the strength of our defenses. Evidently, they found our fortifications formidable, and I am confident we shall not witness their return."

-from The Cairnisle Times,
Thursday, April 25, Year 27 AK

Twenty-Eight ~ Wilhelmina

WILLY MADE A FIST AND gestured for Benj to follow her. Casting an eye up at the sky, she waited for the clouds to drift across the sliver of the moon before moving. She could see the path ahead as clearly as if it were daylight.

The Grey Coat robots on the tall prison wall above could see just as well—probably even better with their excellent night vision. They also had a high degree of accuracy with their guns. That was enough of a deterrent for most people.

The thought sent a pleasant shiver down Willy's spine. She had mapped out the route and rehearsed it in her mind, but the challenge of evading the guards, knowing that a single misstep would mean death, added spice to the trek across the open ground.

Moving with the smooth predictability of a shadow, she glided from one clump of overgrown grass to another, with Benj mimicking her steps. The grass was scheduled to be trimmed the next day. By then, it would be too late.

When they slid up to the small side door she had chosen as the point of entry, she grasped the knob and twisted. It turned easily, and she grimaced. Benj had insisted on bribing a man to leave it unlocked.

As Willy led the way through, she took a moment to examine the old-fashioned lock. Silently, she pursed her lips and pointed out the simple mechanism. She could have saved the money and broken in undetected without the bribe.

Benj shrugged and slid through the door after her.

Inside the prison, she headed toward the front entrance. Munash had given her and Benj a fifteen-minute head start on the rest of the force. While the others waited at the bottom of eight different ladders, she and Benj were to raise the front gate. Guessing that six or so minutes had already passed, she quickened her pace. The dim lighting revealed heavy wood and iron doors lining both sides of the empty corridor.

The only noise came from the cells. Whispers, groans, grunts, and snores reached them as they hurried along. Out of curiosity, Willy stood on her tiptoes and peered through a barred window into one of the cells.

She started.

Aldrich was huddled against the wall. She hardly recognized him. Gone was the meticulously groomed physician. In his place sat a grubby and disheartened prisoner.

The sight of him brought a rush of blood to her face, and she lifted a hand to her mask to make certain it was firmly in place.

He raised his eyes and pushed himself to his feet to hurry across the cramped room. He looked as if he had been in a fight. One eye showed the purpled remains of a bruise while his clothing was torn and soiled.

Willy lifted one finger to the painted mouth of her mask to hush him. The last thing she needed was for him to speak her name. She gave a quick shake of her head and rushed off down the corridor after Benj.

She caught up as he slid to a halt in a shadow. Ahead, a guard leaned idly against the wall.

Benj tilted his head and reached into a pocket. With a flick of his wrist, he sent a pebble skittering past the guard, making a soft clatter in the oppressive silence.

As the guard turned, Willy closed the distance with the stealth of a shadow.

In one fluid motion, her arm snaked around his neck—not to twist, but to press sharply into the side of his throat. Her fingers found the tender hollow, pressing precisely into the carotid artery.

The guard's eyes widened, his body tensing before slumping heavily against her. She let him slide down into a silent heap on the cold floor and stepped back.

Benj grabbed the man under the arms and dragged him out of sight into the shadows.

They were almost to the goal. The corridor ended in a set of stairs that Willy knew led up to the battlements above the gate.

She charged up, taking the steps two at a time, her soft leather shoes making barely a noise. Forty steps later, she reached the top, where she slowed to a walk, taking the time to control her breathing.

Benj was right behind. He unslung his rifle and nodded for her to open the door.

Dropping to her knees, she pulled out her lock picks and set to work. Just like the one on the side entrance, the lock was old and of a simple design. It took only seconds before she heard the click of the tumblers aligning. Tucking the lock picks inside a pocket, she rose and drew her silver pistols. Gifts from her grandfather, who had taught her everything she knew about the art of killing, she treasured the guns and maintained them in perfect condition.

Taking a deep breath, she lifted a foot and kicked the door wide before dashing through it with Benj at her side. She turned right while he turned left, both firing even before the guards on top of the wall were fully aware of their arrival.

For the human guards, she aimed at the heart, but to stop a robot, you had to take it cleanly through the eye. It was the only way to shut down the main gearing.

In seconds, it was over, and eight guards lay dead or immobilized along the walkway. Willy had taken down six—three with each hand—and Benj had got the last two. Impressive shooting since his rifle held only two bullets.

Holstering her pistols, Willy rushed toward the long lever that triggered the gate's mechanism. She leaned her full weight into it and heaved.

The stones under her feet shuddered, and a deep rumbling signaled that the gate was shifting.

Then, from out of the darkness, the cries of four hundred screaming attackers drowned out the mechanical noise.

Willy hurried to the wall and leaned out between the parapets to watch the first people duck under the gates even before they were fully open. Caught up in the tide of victory, she unsheathed her sword and thrust it skyward, adding her voice to the chorus.

When she lowered the sword, she was smiling. It would not take long to subdue the guards. The prison was as good as theirs.

At an almost imperceptible sound behind her, she whirled, her sword ready. Her eyes widened, and she let out a gasp.

A robot was charging toward her, covering the distance at an impossible speed.

With no time to draw her pistols, she lifted her sword and braced for the attack.

He batted aside her blade and swung his own sword in a sharp backhand slash.

Willy dodged sideways, hoping to get around to his side where she knew of a weak spot at the top of the shoulder connection.

But he was quicker.

Her heart in her throat, Willy danced back and caught her heel on an uneven stone. Her ankle twisted under her. With a cry, she hit the ground, knocking the wind out of herself.

The robot advanced—its sword angled for the killing blow.

Abandoning her own sword, Willy pushed herself backward with her heels as she fumbled for a pistol. Eyes narrowed, she went still, lined up her shot, and squeezed the trigger.

The bullet took the robot through the eye. The dim light in the centre of the black circle in its eye socket flashed out, and it collapsed, going first to its knees and then slamming down onto its metal skull. The outstretched arm holding the blade struck Willy heavily across the chest and trapped her under its weight.

For a moment she could not breathe. Had he cut her? Gritting her teeth, she shoved the arm aside and sucked in a breath. Then she ran a hand around the front of her leather coat, checking for cuts. There was nothing. The thick leather must have turned the blade aside. Rolling to her feet, she stared around.

Benj was leaning against the stone ramparts watching her.

"Enjoy the show?" she asked, straightening her mask.

Benj raised one black eyebrow so that it disappeared into his shaggy mop of hair. "Actually," he said, "I did. Most entertaining. I wondered if he had you there for a minute, but I want you to know that my money was on you the whole time."

Willy grunted. "I appreciate the vote of confidence," she muttered.

The door from the corridor burst outward, and they whirled toward it, their weapons ready.

Fia darted out onto the ramparts with Winston a step behind.

Grinning as Willy lowered her pistols, Fia called, "Lower the gate. We've taken the prison!"

Honouring the Magisters

Next Friday, the esteemed Magisters will play host to the city at their annual address. This distinguished event will also see Deutero Magister Ingrid Jaeger honoured for her twenty years of exemplary service.

The festivities will commence in Magister Square at noon, where citizens are invited to gather and partake in the celebrations. Following the address, an array of refreshments will be served for all to enjoy.

-from The Cairnisle Times,
Thursday, April 25, Year 27 AK

TWENTY-NINE ~ ALDRICH

PRESSING THE SIDE OF HIS face against the cold bars of the cell's tiny window, Aldrich strained to see down the length of the corridor. What was happening? Had he hallucinated the image of Wilhelmina framed by those same bars? Or was she truly inside the prison?

The intense listening silence of the men behind him highlighted the muffled noises coming from elsewhere in the building. Sword clashes, pistol shots, and screams echoed through the old stone walls.

"What is it?" asked a man. "What's going on?"

Not recognizing the voice, Aldrich turned. It was Gustav. He swallowed against a lump in his throat. He had been sitting beside the man for weeks and had never heard him speak louder than a whisper.

Pushing his hands through his hair, Aldrich said, "I cannot see any—"

Abruptly, the sounds of fighting ceased, and a man's voice rang out. "The fortress is ours!"

"Fortress?" Aldrich echoed. He leaned close to Gustav, who had chinned himself up on the window bars to see out. "What is happening?"

Dropping to the floor, Gustav rubbed his hands on his greasy trousers as another man took his place. "There's nothing to see," he answered. "But if I had to guess, I'd say we're about to get out of here."

Aldrich's stomach tightened. He licked his lips and opened his mouth to speak, but the man at the door suddenly stepped back and put his finger to his lips.

Everyone froze, listening to a scratching at the lock. A mechanical click filled the room as the tumblers fell into place.

Then the door swung open to reveal Wilhelmina von Richtofen. Dressed in the same leather clothing and silver mask she had worn the night she attempted to assassinate Rupert Corvington, her eyes found Aldrich and she swept him from head to toe.

"Aldrich Durante," she said, a note of pleasure in her voice. "I am happy to see that you have taken me at my word. This is definitely interesting." Reaching out to grasp his arm with one gloved hand, she pulled him into the corridor, away from the other prisoners, and murmured, "We shall talk about my fees later." Her eyes smiled through the eyeholes of her mask.

Aldrich's brain felt sluggish. Nothing made any sense. He

clasped her hand. "Wil—"

She punched him in the stomach, cutting him off. The air huffed out of him, and he bent forward, clutching his middle.

She leaned close and hissed, "Do not say my name. Never say my name!" Ice flashed in her eyes. She dropped his arm and stepped back.

All of a sudden, he was staring at the same deadly killer he had tried to interrogate at Corvington's home. He tried not to flinch away from the expected blow.

He need not have worried because in the next instant she turned and strode away, leaving him gaping after her. Was it safe to follow? He brushed his hands over the front of his filthy coat. What must she think of him?

Running footsteps came from behind, and he whirled.

"Aldrich!" Fia cried, her glowing face split by a wide grin. Skidding to a halt, she peered up at him and her eyebrows drew together. "You're hurt?"

Aldrich swallowed hard. For a moment, he could not speak. "Fia, you are a sight for sore eyes," he said finally. He cleared his throat. "What is going on here?"

"The revolution has begun," she answered, dancing from foot to foot. "We've taken the prison—did you know it used to be a fortress?" She bounced in a circle as she gestured to the people swarming into the corridor. "All these people are here for you."

Aldrich's brow crinkled. "For me?" he asked. "But why?"

Instead of answering, Fia looked over her shoulder and grinned at a tall, powerfully built black man striding toward them. "Munash," she called. "This is him. He's here!" She spun around again before forcibly calming herself. "Munash Conteh," she said formally, "May I present Doctor Aldrich Durante."

Coming to Fia's side, Munash smiled broadly and stretched

out his hand.

Aldrich snapped his mouth shut and gripped the hard hand, feeling the calluses against his own smooth palm. He tried to speak, but questions flew around his mind so rapidly, he could not frame a sentence.

"It is an honour to finally meet you," said Munash, giving Aldrich's hand a squeeze before releasing it.

"Now we can get started on your plans," Fia said, turning a delighted smile on Aldrich. "Munash is going to help."

"Help?" asked Aldrich, his voice coming dangerously close to squeaking. "What are you talk—" He broke off and sucked in a breath. This was the man Fia had spoken of—the one who would know what to do to help Dirt Town. He cut his eyes at Fia and then looked back at Munash. The man knew about his half-formed goal of running for Magister.

Munash nodded as if he could read Aldrich's thoughts. "You are the man I have been waiting for," he said, his voice low and warm with a slightly lilting accent that Aldrich did not recognize. "I cannot imagine a more ideal spokesman for our cause." He laced his fingers together across his belly, his hands showing dark against his sleeveless tunic of dark green cotton. "They have to listen to you. You are an important man in this world."

Aldrich shook his head and swallowed. "I am not the man you need," he said. "I just spent ten days in jail, and I have no desire to extend my stay here. Someone else will—" He broke off and frowned. Was Munash right?

A small flame settled in his chest. Perhaps he could be a spokesman for the people of Dirt Town. He had grown up in the world from which leaders were chosen. Munash, as powerful as he was, obviously came from Dirt Town. He would never have the weight, the connections, or the influence in society that would let him challenge Grand Magister Köhler.

If Aldrich wanted to see a change in Cairnisle, he would have to step up and be the face of that change. Smoothing his hair back from his forehead, he forced a smile.

"Munash," he said, switching on the charm that had always come so easily. He clapped a hand on the man's broad shoulder. "I would be pleased to do whatever I can to help."

Turmoil at the Prison

In the week since the startling seizure of Cairnisle Prison, information of a most unsettling nature has reached our office. The malevolent puppeteer orchestrating this insurrection is none other than the infamous Doctor Aldrich Durante.

"While awaiting the hand of justice for a heinous act of murder, Doctor Durante has cunningly cast a veil of political subterfuge over his true intentions," declared Grand Magister Augustus Köhler. "His silver tongue is turning his felonious cellmates into his own personal army."

-from The Cairnisle Times,
Thursday, May 2, Year 27 AK

THIRTY ~ ALDRICH

THE FIRST FEW DAYS AFTER being freed from his cell, Aldrich frequently found himself lost in his travels around the former prison. The corridors were a bewildering maze of stone and shadow, each turn indistinguishable from the next. However, he was gradually getting the lay of the land and knew exactly how to get from his office to the workshop that Gustav Florenburg had set up at the top of the fortress.

No one called it Cairnisle Prison any longer. The heavy

sense of waiting and dread that had filled its walls for so long was replaced with an awareness of purpose, anticipation, and the noisy bustle of people.

Many of the former prisoners were Dirt Towners convicted of petty crimes and sentenced to long stretches of time. One entire wing housed people who had disagreed with the Magisters.

Except for those deemed dangerous, everyone had been released to join the rebellion. Due to the crowded situation, they still slept in the cells, but up and down the corridors, doors stood ajar, allowing them to avoid the sensation of confinement.

Together, Munash and Aldrich had interviewed each of the prison guards. Depending on what was demonstrated during the conversation, they were either locked up alongside the real criminals, or they had willingly joined the rebellion and been absorbed into the ranks of men and the few women who had arrived with Munash's army.

In the square where Aldrich had been beaten for trying to incite a rebellion, military training under the direction of Commandant Rupert Corvington carried on around the clock. He maintained that though both Aldrich and Munash planned to assume control of the city democratically, they required a trained army to stand behind them.

As he passed along the upper mezzanine, Aldrich looked down on the six rows of twelve men each working through a drill that had them waving their swords in a variety of directions as one tightly muscled man cried out instructions. The corners of his mouth twitched, and his chin lifted. Most of them seemed to know what they were doing. It was going to work.

From there, he headed to another staircase. It was the same one he had climbed when he was escorted to his interview with

Forge-37. The thought of the robot's immobile face and that grating laugh sent a shiver down his back.

The top-floor corridor took him past one of the few locked doors in the whole fortress. The robot Prison Guards had been disabled and stored within—close enough to Gustav's workshop for easy access. He was reactivating them one by one after he changed their sequencing so that they supported Aldrich instead of the Magisters.

Coming to Gustav's workshop, Aldrich nudged the door open with his shoulder. "I brought dinner," he announced, heading for the table and setting down the tray that he had brought from the cellar kitchens. It held two bowls of meaty stew, and two tall cups filled with water.

The last of the day's light poured in through the tall windows, backlighting Gustav, who stood over the prone form of a robot. The outer plating on its chest and neck had been removed, and its green coat hung over the back of a nearby chair.

Lifting his head, the inventor peered distractedly over the rims of his magnified lenses. While he had not regained the weight he had lost in the cell, his skin no longer hung on him, and his eyes had a healthy glow. His brow furrowed, and he blinked.

Then his face cleared, and he smiled. "Aldrich, my boy," he said, gesturing toward the robot with a smoking soldering iron in one hand and a tiny set of pincers in the other. "This particular model was made after they locked me up. Come and look. They followed my specifications exactly, and it works!"

Aldrich leaned over the mass of wires, gears, tubes, leather straps, and circuit boards, smelling the acrid stink of heated metal. The innards of the robot were as complex as the living bodies on which he performed surgery. However, without understanding the blueprint, none of it made sense.

"See here?" said Gustav, indicating a series of interlocking gears connected to a cylinder beside a funnel. "This is the speech apparatus." He drew his finger along a wire toward a circuit board. "And this is the decision-making centre. I drew up the designs just days before I was arrested." He set his tools aside and picked up a glass bulb with a crystal in its centre. "Watch what happens when I insert the battery."

Sliding the battery pack into its compartment in the centre of the robot's chest, he flipped a switch. "Identify yourself, Captain," he said.

The robot sat up smoothly and hung its legs over the side of the table. The gears in the speech apparatus spun, moving the cylinder up, before a needle descended into a groove and the sound poured out through the funnel. "I am PI2-063," it said. The gear shifted again, so quickly there was hardly a pause. "How may I help?" Its voice sounded suspiciously like Gustav's and exactly like Winston's.

Aldrich's jaw dropped.

"Cairnisle Prison is now a Fortress housing an army," Gustav said. "We intend to unseat the Magisters. Your job will be to support us when the time comes."

The gears spun again. "I look forward to the opportunity to assist," it said.

Gustav shot a look at Aldrich and giggled at his expression. "Do you recognize the voice?" he asked.

"It is you," said Aldrich. "If I had heard you speak out loud earlier, I might have noticed. Winston never whispers."

Still grinning, Gustav nodded. "I never thought of recording a whisper," he said. "This was the final work I completed before my arrest. And they used it exactly as it was without any further modifications." His eyebrows wriggled over bright eyes.

Aldrich turned back to study the robot's workings. Gustav

showed no sign of bitterness over the time he had wasted sitting on the floor of the prison. And he had been locked up far longer than Aldrich. He cleared his throat. "Come and sit," he said. "I brought dinner."

They seated themselves on either side of the little table. After their time spent whispering on the floor, the luxury of sitting in a chair and speaking at a normal volume was still something to be relished.

Unwilling to disturb Gustav's obvious joy, Aldrich held back the question that had been gnawing at his conscience. They ate in silence until Aldrich set down his spoon and cleared his throat. "I have to ask," he said. "Whose idea was it to use magic batteries?"

Gustav's head snapped up, and the colour drained from his face. Leaving his spoon in his bowl, he picked up the cup of water and drank deeply. "That was Magister Köhler's idea," he said quietly, his eyes on his bowl.

Aldrich pursed his lips. "Do you know how they collect the magic for the batteries?" he asked.

"I do," answered Gustav, keeping his gaze down. "It is not something I am proud of. It is only during the time I spent sitting in a cell that I really gave it any thought. I have no apology. I got caught up in the possibilities without considering the consequences to the poor mages."

"What do you know about Forge-37?" asked Aldrich. "Is he your design too?"

Gustav met his eyes. "The specs are mine," he admitted. "The speech had almost been solved with the Greens. It just took a bit more tweaking to make that bit come together. The big challenge was to build a robot who could, through experiential learning, acquire decision-making capabilities. It was too good to ignore. I couldn't leave it alone. In the end, I solved the problem of memory development. That was the key." He winced. "But then, I got cold feet."

Aldrich picked up his cup of water. "Tell me," he said.

"I had already been questioning the sequencing for the use of excessive force for the City Guard Captains," Gustav said. He stared into the space over Aldrich's shoulder. "What the Magisters wanted for the Greens was too much. But it was only after I built the first one that I understood."

He swallowed. "The extent of power being handed to a machine capable only of differentiating black and white—right or wrong." He shook his head. "There is no grey for them." Tapping a finger on the table, he glanced up and held Aldrich's gaze. "I wanted to shut down the whole line. I went to Köhler and told him straight up that it was too dangerous." He squeezed his eyes shut. "I had already completed the plans for the Commandant robot." With a crooked smile, he barked out a laugh. "That's when they arrested me and dumped me in here."

Gustav spooned several bites of stew into his mouth. "I have spoken to PI2-234—or Winston, as he prefers to be called," he continued. "I never expected the sort of development that has occurred in him without the presence of a binding lock." A real smile lit his face. "He actually has a personality! And a definite moral sense with the attending scruples and principles generally found in honourable people." He grimaced and shook his head. "I do not understand how it happened. The Greens' reactions were designed to be dictated by their sequencing. They have only the most limited memory. It makes no sense."

Some of the tension went out of Aldrich's shoulders. He appreciated how Winston looked after Fia. They seemed to share a genuine friendship. "I trust Winston," he said. "Do you suppose that is wise?"

Gustav nodded earnestly. "I believe that Winston formed

his character during the time he spent with you and Fia," he said. "I think he is completely reliable." He grinned tightly. "I have to admit, I have been tinkering with a new speech apparatus following the blueprint I made for the Reds. When it is complete, I will install it in Winston, and he will not have to write everything down."

There was a knock at the door, and Munash poked his head into the room. "I thought I might find you here," he said in his lilting voice.

"Come in," said Gustav, rising to remove the green coat from the back of the third chair. On his way past the robot, he stopped to switch him off. "I will finish with you later," he murmured.

"Was there something in particular you wanted to talk about, Munash?" Aldrich asked as the big man settled onto the chair.

"The election is nine weeks away," said Munash. "It is time to present your intention to run."

Aldrich's brow creased. "I thought you said that Cairnisle is not truly a democracy," he said. "What is the point of running if I have no chance to win?"

Since no one else of consequence ever ran against them, the Magisters had ruled without interference by claiming their positions through acclamation every election year. By tradition, they each chose a young, untrained mage to serve as an apprentice. They taught them how to manipulate their magic, moulded their understanding of the world, and brought them up to be leaders. As the Magisters aged and eventually died, the apprentices replaced their names on the ballots. It was a slick system that guaranteed that nothing changed.

Munash shook a finger at him. "I said that Cairnisle has not been a democracy for a very long time," he said. "I did not say it will never be one again. It will be your job to change that."

A wave of weakness rolled over Aldrich, and he was grateful that he was sitting down. It was so much responsibility. He squared his shoulders. He had already come to terms with the idea that he would be the face of the rebellion. "How do I present my intention to run?" he asked.

"You need five other people to stand on the ballot with you," answered Munash.

"But I am not a mage," Aldrich said. "How can I be a Magister?"

"By Cairnisle law, it is not necessary to be a mage to rule the country," said Munash. "You can run for the position of Grand Minister."

"People have run for the position before," said Gustav. "They usually disappear a few weeks into their campaign, and we hear nothing more from them."

Munash flashed his white teeth in a grin. "That is true," he agreed. "However, young Aldrich has the advantage of a campaign office in a fortress and an entire army at his beck and call."

"Who will stand on the ballot with you?" said Gustav. "It has to be a clean sweep, or there is no point to it."

Rubbing a hand across his black curly hair, Munash nodded. "Six people on the ballot is the only way to go. Who do you suggest?"

Aldrich squeezed his eyes shut. Anyone who joined him would be putting their lives in considerable danger. It was not fair to even ask. Lacing his fingers together, he pressed down hard on the top of his head. It was too dangerous.

His parents were at risk simply by being linked to him. He had not had a message from them since his arrest. Did they know where he was? Were they safe? What if something terrible had already happened?

Two days earlier, he had sent a letter to them through

Wilhelmina's spies, detailing his situation. He had asked for his father's support. With his backing, Aldrich hoped he would gain many of the other nobles as well. Unfortunately, there had not yet been a reply.

Thinking about Wilhelmina led to another of the many concerns that had suddenly become his responsibility. In the fortress, everyone knew her only as the Silver Assassin. No one seemed to have guessed her real identity.

If he were honest with himself, he would admit that she terrified him. There was something horribly ruthless in those blue eyes. She had killed Johnathon Loewe and would have killed Rupert Corvington too if Winston had not stopped her. On the other hand, even in her assassin persona, he found her exciting and endlessly fascinating.

Someone tapped on the door, and Aldrich's eyes popped open.

"Come," Gustav called.

The heavy door swung open a little wider, and one of Wilhelmina's spies poked his head into the room. His eyes found Aldrich. "I have information for you," he said, ducking inside to toss a copy of the *Cairnisle Times* onto the table between their bowls of stew. "It's in the paper. The Grand Magister is going to give a speech. Tomorrow at noon. Sounds like he is going to talk about you."

Aldrich winced. It was beginning. "Thank you for this," he said, pasting on a smile. Digging into his pocket, he found a couple of silvers.

The man backed away, holding up his hands defensively. "No, sir. No way," he said. "I don't want your money. You just get yourself elected." Tugging on the brim of his hat, he nodded his head and slipped away.

Aldrich watched him go. What had he done to deserve such trust? With a grunt, he flattened out the paper and found an article with the headline, 'Uprising in Progress.' After skimming the heavily embroidered article he hurled the paper back onto the table as if it burned his fingers. "The Magisters obviously hold control of the newspaper," he said. "How have I never noticed that before?"

Picking up the paper, Gustav grinned and read aloud, "In the annals of our fair city, a name has emerged that strikes fear into the hearts of law-abiding citizens: Aldrich Durante. This nefarious individual, a criminal of the most heinous sort, stands accused of the foulest crime known to man—murder. Yet, in a brazen attempt to cloak his vile deeds, Durante seeks to masquerade as a revolutionary, a champion of the people."

Munash leaned back and folded his hands across his belly. "Silver sent this to us for a reason," he said. "And it was not just to let us know that the Magisters do not like Aldrich. We need to have someone in that crowd who can be our eyes and ears."

Aldrich narrowed his eyes. "I know just the person," he said. "I will go set it up." Glad of a reason to move, he strode out of the workshop and headed toward the mezzanine. He had to find Wilhelmina.

Revelations Promised

Grand Magister Augustus Köhler, esteemed leader of Cairn, has intimated that the forthcoming ceremony shall present a most agreeable and unexpected development for the benefit of our citizenry.

"It is with great enthusiasm that we anticipate unveiling the most recent advancements in the noble pursuit of crime fighting," he declared, his countenance betraying a hint of pride. "The good people of Cairnisle shall bear witness to innovations heretofore unimagined in the annals of law enforcement."

-from The Cairnisle Times,
Friday, May 3, Year 27 AK

THIRTY-ONE ~ WILHELMINA

WALKING DEMURELY AT HER FATHER'S side, Willy studied the stage at the far end of Magister Square. How difficult would it be to get close enough to assassinate them all? It would solve a lot of problems and clear the path for Aldrich.

Spotting the shimmer of magic shielding their seating area, she let out a grunt.

Her father looked down at her. "What is it, my dear?" he

asked. "Are you well?"

Arranging a smile on her face, Wilhelmina blinked prettily. "Do excuse my clumsiness, father," she answered. "My toe caught on a cobblestone."

His jaw tightened. "There is no need to lumber about like a gawky fool," he growled.

"Yes, father," she answered, bending her neck and glaring at the stones. The magical defences in place meant she had no choice but to follow Aldrich's instructions. She would listen carefully and report back to him. With an effort, she erased her scowl and arranged a pleasant smile on her face. She missed her mask.

The crowd thickened as they moved further into the square. If she were as tall as her father, she would have no difficulty seeing over the heads of the people surrounding them. As it was, she could see nothing but the red neck of a fat man and his bony wife's pale shoulder blades.

The crowd was the usual gathering of wealthy aristocrats. Sheep, really. Because the Magisters supported their way of life, they supported the Magisters. Had any of them ever given more than a moment's consideration to the fact that they never actually had to vote? The ballot never presented any choice.

Had they ever reflected on what made them so deserving of their wealth and the people in Dirt Town so deserving of their poverty? How many of them had ever descended the ladders to visit the dusty streets below?

Willy liked Dirt Town. She liked the freedom it afforded her. She could wear comfortable, unrestrictive clothing, speak to whomever she wished, and even walk alone in the streets without a male escort.

She also enjoyed the anonymity she had as the Silver Assassin. Down there, no one knew that her father was Lord James von Richtofen, the wealthiest man in all of Cairnisle.

Certainly, people recognized her, and they were right to be afraid of her—but it was fear of her—the Silver Assassin—not of her father, the rich, ruthless and completely terrifying tyrant.

"Here they come," her father murmured. His dark eyebrows were drawn together in a vee of disdain. He had little patience for the six people who considered themselves more important than him, and he did nothing to conceal it. He was at the gathering for one reason only—as was she, as far as he was concerned—to be seen and recognized.

Always fashionable, he had taken more than the usual pains with his appearance. His blonde hair, just beginning to show grey at the temples, was recently cut—he never allowed it to grow longer than an inch on top while the sides were always tightly clipped. His suit too was new. Not that it looked particularly different from the black suits he usually wore, but the jacket seemed a little longer and more closely fitted to his sleek figure than usual. No doubt, his tailor was trying out a new idea in the hopes that it would catch on.

Craning her neck for a view of the stage, Wilhelmina spied the Magisters as they marched toward the six oversized chairs waiting for them.

Augustus Köhler led the way. His bald head, sharp, pointy chin, and even pointier grey beard floated above his black robe. The wide twist of golden cord across his shoulders denoted his rank as Grand Magister. It glinted in the sunlight along with the eagle emblazoned on his chest in golden thread.

Behind him came Ingrid Jaeger, Deutero Magister. With her long, greying black hair and hooked nose, she resembled the image of the eagle that all the Magisters took as their symbol of power. The cord on her black robe was silver, as was the embroidered eagle and her eagle earrings.

Willy had not had any direct dealings with the woman, but

she had done her research. The second Magister was not someone to cross. More than any of the others, she had continued to hone her mage powers after coming to office.

It was a well-kept secret that the manner in which she chose to practise magic required the death of some luckless candidate chosen from the prisoners condemned to death. Willy allowed herself a small smile. The loss of the prison would be hitting her particularly hard.

The remaining four Magisters made their way to the chairs more slowly. Each was progressively older, with the last so bent and aged that Wilhelmina wondered if he would keel over on the stage. What would the crowd do if he did? She smiled at the thought.

"Ladies and gentlemen," Augustus Köhler said from his throne. His voice blasted out over the crowd, which immediately fell silent. "We thank you for taking time out of your busy day to come here today. This was meant to be a pleasant celebration, thanking Deutero Magister Ingrid Jaeger for her years of service to the city." He gestured graciously to the woman seated to his left, and the crowd provided a moment of polite applause.

"Instead, we face a bitter time in Cairnisle's history. As you already know, criminals have overrun the prison and now the criminals rule the guards." His pleasant smile twisted into a scowl. "I want you to know that we, the democratically elected leaders of this beautiful country, are doing everything in our power to correct this situation." He rose, walked to the centre of the stage, and gazed out at his audience.

Behind him, the stage door opened again. A robot in the red coat and insignia of the Commandant of the City Guard glided across the stage and halted beside Köhler.

Like the other robots, he had the look of a powerful man and the grace of a dancer. But his metal head was different.

Instead of a shiny, bare skull, his was moulded into statuesque lines. The artist had even included the swirls of a closely cropped beard.

Köhler put his hand on the robot's shoulder as if he were greeting a friend. "Ladies and gentlemen," he said in his magically amplified voice. "May I present the newest member of our city's security organization." His smile made him look like a toad. "In light of former Commandant Rupert Corvington's complete betrayal of his office, a brand-new robot has been designed to serve in the position. This is Commandant Forge-37." He held his hands up triumphantly as if expecting applause.

None came.

The audience stood silent. Willy smelled fear. No one was going to say so, but the idea of a robot in charge was terrifying.

"Citizens of Cairnisle," Forge said. "I greet you as a servant of this fair city and pledge to do whatever is necessary to clean up our streets to make them safe for you."

His smoothly resonant voice was curiously free of inflection. "We shall begin with the filth in Dirt Town. Under my guidance, it will not take long to scour the streets of criminals." He struck a dramatic pose and pointed toward the imposing walls of the prison, visible above the surrounding buildings. "And when that is complete, we will attack the mess at Cairnisle Prison."

A Blooming Marvel

In the heart of downtown Cairnisle, a verdant transformation has taken place. The city's newest park, a haven of natural beauty, now proudly showcases fourteen meticulously planted flower beds, each a testament to the tireless efforts of our dedicated workers.

While the park's newly seeded lawns require our patience, we are cordially invited to meander along the footpath. From this vantage point, one can fully admire the charming floral arrangements that now grace our city. A sight to behold indeed!

-from The Cairnisle Times,
Friday, May 3, Year 27 AK

THIRTY-TWO ~ FIAMETTA

FROM THE TOP OF THE fortress wall, Fia watched the crowd gather in Magister Square. She squeezed her elbows into her sides and pressed her fingers against the rough-cut rock. The tiny figures were hardly more than moving spots of colour. She could just make out the forms of the Magisters as they paraded onto the stage, but she was too far away to hear what was being said.

In the past, she had avoided the Magisters' speeches. What if they saw her magic and turned her into a mage slave?

However, that fear had vanished, incinerated by the clear light of understanding. She wanted to be there—to see them up close—to look into the faces of the people who had ordered the deaths of her parents and changed her life forever. She clenched her teeth so hard, her jaw ached. If she were in the square, she would find a way to fight back.

A door slammed shut behind her, shattering her thoughts of vengeance. Fia whirled to find Winston striding toward her.

"Greetings, citizen," he said before passing her a note. The paper was covered in his perfect penmanship. Everything except one line had been neatly crossed out.

She read: *Please, visit Munash in his office at your earliest opportunity.*

"I'll go now," she said, returning the paper to Winston. "Do you know why he wants to see me?"

"No," Winston replied, sliding the paper into the pocket of his coat.

Fia pressed her lips together and looked back at Magister Square. Her toe tapped on the stone, and she sighed. "I guess I'll go find out." She headed to the door, lifting a hand in farewell. "See you later, Winston."

"Goodbye," answered the robot.

The door crashed shut behind her, and she headed down the stairs at a trot. Munash and Aldrich had claimed offices near the front of the fortress—no doubt the same ones the Warden and his Deputy had used.

Munash's was the smaller of the two, but it felt roomier because it was much less cluttered. Every square inch of Aldrich's office was covered with stacks of papers organized in a fashion only understood by its former occupant.

She jogged past the mezzanine, where the clash of wooden

swords echoed up through the high walls, and climbed another set of stairs. At Munash's office, she knocked on the open door.

"Ah, Fiametta," he said, looking up from the newspaper he was reading. "Thank you for coming to see me." Rising, he came around the desk and perched on its corner. "Come in and close the door. I want to talk to you."

Fia stiffened. Doors were never closed in the prison. Nonetheless, she stepped inside and pushed the heavy door shut. Crossing her arms, she leaned against it.

"Have you ever tried to train your mage powers?" he asked.

Fia snorted. "Practising magic is a good way to get arrested and end up a slave."

"That is true," Munash agreed. He clasped his hands together in his lap. "Would you like to learn?"

Fia's arms tightened around her middle. Magic scared her. She swallowed. She did want to learn. More than anything. "Can you teach me?" she asked in a tiny voice that annoyed her with its weakness.

"I can teach you," Munash answered firmly. "Before we begin, though, I would like to test you. May I have your permission?"

Fia shifted and looked away. "What do you mean by test?" she asked. When the mage hunters had come for her, they had wanted to test her too. That was when her father stepped in.

Munash cleared his throat. "If you grant me permission, I will enter your mind to assess your potential. It is the safest way to determine your powers." His kind smile had disappeared, and his eyebrows were drawn down.

Fia shivered. She did not like the idea of Munash entering her mind. What would he find there? Would he be able to see everything?

Munash sat quietly on his desk, not showing any signs of

impatience as he waited for her to decide.

Finally, she dropped into the chair beside him and said, "Test me."

He studied her with his gentle brown eyes. "You are certain?" he asked.

Fia gripped the armrests. "Yes," she said, jerking her head in a nod. "Do it."

Munash gave a flicker of a smile and closed his eyes.

At the first touch of his mind, she gasped. Fighting the impulse to block him out, she forced herself to relax, closing her own eyes and loosening her fingers.

The touch came again—gentle and not unwelcome.

Abruptly Munash cried out.

Fia's eyes snapped open.

He was hunched over, grasping his head in his hands and panting as if he had just run a race.

Fia clutched her stomach, her eyes wide. "What?" she demanded. "What happened? Did I hurt you?"

With a grunt, he raised his head and smiled weakly. "Fiametta, my dear," he said, brushing a hand over his face. "Do not be concerned. Everything is fine." He laughed. "I was unprepared. I have never seen such power." Pushing off the desk, he rotated his neck and wrapped a warm hand around her elbow as he peered into her eyes. "We must begin your training without delay. Will you accompany me to the courtyard?"

The churning in Fia's stomach eased. He was not upset by her magic. Fighting a desire to speed ahead of him, she followed Munash out of the office, through the dim corridors and down the stairs to the courtyard. Her skin tingled and every sense had come alive. She was going to learn how to wield magic.

The soldiers were still busy with their wooden swords.

Munash ignored them and led her toward a wooden practice dummy. Vaguely shaped like a human torso, it was mounted on a post.

Munash put a hand on her shoulder and brought her to a halt about ten feet away. "Fiametta," he said. "Shoot this dummy with your magic."

Shoot the dummy? What did that mean? Biting the inside of her lip, Fia focused on the crudely carved wooden figure. It was decorated with the dents and cuts of hundreds of sword blows. What should she do?

Her scalp prickled as she reached for the energy that was always bubbling just beneath the surface. Over the years, she had learned to keep it firmly blocked off.

After casting an uncertain glance at Munash, Fia raised her hand and pointed a finger toward the target. A spark of energy flew and struck the wood, leaving a tiny brown scorch mark.

She flashed a grin at Munash. "It works," she said. "I had no idea."

Munash returned her smile. "It is a good beginning," he said. "You have kept it in check for so long, only a little is leaking out. Think bigger."

Fia studied the dummy. "Bigger?" she repeated. "How?"

Munash narrowed his eyes and studied her. "Can you feel your magic, Fiametta?" he asked.

Fia's brow wrinkled. "I know where I keep the magic," she answered. "Mostly, I just ignore it. Maybe sometimes I have to block it up a little more."

"Do you know how you block it up?" Munash asked. He scrubbed a hand through his curly hair and smiled reassuringly.

With a shrug, Fia shook her head. "I don't know," she said. "I've just always done it."

"Munash," called Aldrich from the mezzanine. "Have you got a moment?"

Munash and Fia looked up.

Aldrich grinned down at them. "Sorry to interrupt," he said. "This will not take long."

"Of course," Munash said.

"I will come down," called Aldrich as he strode along the upper level.

Munash bowed to Fia. "Please, excuse me," he said before turning toward the stairs.

Fia watched him go, but her mind was on her magic. She groped at the barrier she had built up over the years. She could feel the power hidden behind it. Imagining a ball of energy that she could hold in her hand, she drew back her arm and threw.

A blast of power flew from her fingertips, and the wooden dummy exploded into flames as a thunderous crack reverberated through the courtyard.

Fia's legs went weak, and she sat down hard.

Everyone stopped what they were doing to stare at her.

Aldrich leapt down the last few steps and sprinted toward her. "What was that?" he shouted. "What did you do?"

Munash reached Fia first and knelt at her side. He grinned as he met her gaze. "You did it," he said. "I knew you could."

"But I have no idea how I did it," Fia said. Her lips felt numb.

"You will," answered Munash as Aldrich skidded to a stop beside them.

"What happened?" he asked, dropping to his knees and running his eyes over Fia to check for injury. "Are you hurt?"

"I'm fine," she answered.

"She is more than fine," Munash said with a wide smile. "We have our mage."

Trend Setters

Look for illustrations of the latest fashions in tomorrow's issue of The Cairnisle Times. Our artists will be on hand in Magister Square today to capture our most elegant citizens in their finest fripperies.

-from The Cairnisle Times,
Friday, May 3, Year 27 AK

THIRTY-THREE ~ ALDRICH

ALDRICH LOOKED UP AS WILHELMINA strode into his office. Her mask was firmly in place above what he thought of as her Silver Assassin suit. He leaned back in his chair and folded his hands behind his head, narrowing his eyes as he tried to gauge her mood. Her leather coat and trousers fit her form admirably and a lock of blonde hair had strayed from its strict confines under her tricorn hat.

"Welcome back," he said. It was something of a mystery how she managed to move between the fortress and the rest of the city without drawing attention. He would have liked to ask but knew she would give him that flat-eyed gaze that frightened him right down to his boots. He grinned. "Tell me. Was it the usual drivel about our beautiful city, or did they have more to say this year?"

As a boy, Aldrich had faithfully attended the Magisters'

annual public appearance. Why had he never questioned their spiritless message? From his current perspective, it seemed impossible that he had never noticed the emptiness of their words.

Wilhelmina threw herself into the chair by the door, stretching her booted feet out and crossing them at the ankle. "Actually, they branched out a bit this year," she said. "It was a far step from the usual." She tilted her head to the side and tapped her fingers on the chair's arm. "It started out the same way it does every year—the same people, the same pretty dresses, the same bovine reception. Then it got interesting." She held his gaze through the eyeholes of her mask. "They rolled out a new robot who is meant to replace Corvington."

Aldrich sat up straight. "A Commandant robot?" he asked.

Wilhelmina cocked her head to one side, and he could imagine her lazy smile. Although he had seen it only rarely since, the ride on the way to the ball had provided plenty of memories.

"That's right," she agreed. She settled herself more comfortably. "The robot can speak, Aldrich. Not like Winston. He can really speak." She sat forward and muttered, "Unless the whole speech was pre-recorded." She clenched her hands together. "That would make it less scary. His name is Commandant Forge Dash Thirty-Seven. Sounds official, doesn't it?"

Aldrich leaned back in his chair with a sigh. "I've met him," he said.

Wilhelmina's chin lifted and he pictured the raised eyebrows.

"I understood he was just being rolled out," she said, her voice rising in a question.

"They tested him on me when I was a prisoner," he answered.

She jerked upright and her fingers flexed.

"He didn't hurt me," Aldrich said. "I believe they wished to test his interrogation skills."

With a grunt, Wilhelmina slumped into her chair again. "He can speak," she said. "But it's creepy listening to that monotone voice."

Aldrich winced and nodded as a shiver ran up his spine. "We need to talk to Gustav about this," he said.

"One more thing," Wilhelmina said. "Forge said he is going to clean up Cairnisle and he plans to start with Dirt Town."

"Munash will want to know that too," Aldrich said. His mouth went dry. Had he brought this on Dirt Town with his arrogance? Who was he fooling? What could he possibly do to make things better? "We need to talk to both of them right away."

Leaping up, he charged around the desk toward the door. They would know what to do. He was in the hallway before he noticed that Wilhelmina had not moved. He stuck his head back into the room. "Are you coming?" he asked.

Wilhelmina unwound herself and stretched her arms above her head. "Lead the way, boss," she said. "Let's share the news."

Without seeming to hurry, she kept up as Aldrich rushed down the corridor. Munash would be in the courtyard, training Fia. The girl was hugely powerful. Would that make her useful or a liability? His face tightened and he brushed the thought away. What was he thinking? Fia was a child—far too young to involve herself in the actual fighting. Especially as untrained as she was.

He peered over the edge of the mezzanine and caught Munash's eye. Something in his expression made the tall black man stiffen. Fia followed his gaze and dropped her hands. Without a word, they headed for the stairs.

Wilhelmina and Aldrich met them at the top.

Munash gripped Aldrich's elbow. "Not here," he murmured. Turning to Fia, he said, "You have done well, Fiametta, but let us be careful not to tire you. Go now. Refresh yourself with a walk on the ramparts. Relax your mind. Test the feeling of knowing where your magic is."

Fia looked tired, yet her face was bright.

"Congratulations," Aldrich said. "Your powers are impressive."

Fia dropped her head. "Thank you," she muttered. "I'll see you later." She wandered off toward the stairs that led to the top of the wall.

Munash watched her go before turning to Aldrich, his eyebrows raised.

"First, we must find Gustav," Aldrich said. "We need to talk."

Munash looked from Aldrich to Wilhelmina. Blowing out a breath, he said, "Lead the way."

They walked in silence through the maze of corridors up to Gustav's laboratory on the highest level. Gustav and Winston were bent over the open body of a robot, peering into a jumble of gears and wires.

Gustav looked up. As always, it took a moment for the dreamy look to clear from his face. "Ah," he said with a smile. "Your timing is perfect. Come and see the progress we have made."

"Perhaps that could wait for the moment," said Munash, leaning against the wall and crossing his arms over his chest. "Aldrich and Silver have news."

Wilhelmina sank into the nearest chair while Aldrich went to the window. It faced out over the lake. Below, the sheer cliff dropped straight down into the water. No attackers could scale both the rock face and the high walls without notice.

"I went to hear the Magisters today," Wilhelmina said. "They had a very special announcement up their long floppy sleeves."

Aldrich whirled from the view, his hands clenched into fists. "She says Forge is the new commandant," he burst out. "Is this even possible?"

Gustav's arms dropped to his sides, and he backed away from the worktable with its motionless patient. He closed his eyes and let out a long breath. "Definitely possible," he said finally. "I wondered when you told me about the robot who questioned you." Moving with very precise motions, he set down the screwdriver he had been holding and lined it up to match the other tools.

Blinking owlishly, he removed his magnifying lenses. "They really did it." The colour had drained from his face, and he lowered himself gingerly onto a chair. "We were so close so often. It was only a matter of persistence. Eventually, one of the prototypes would have to work."

"What are you talking about?" Munash asked, taking another step into the room and moving to stand over Gustav. "Who is Forge?"

The inventor took a deep breath and scrubbed his hands across his face. "It is called the Forge Initiative," he said. "The Magisters wanted a robot who would share their values. They wanted to allow a robot to develop naturally." He emphasized the last word with heavy sarcasm, before his eyes slid to Winston. "They figured the way to do that was to avoid the use of the binding lock. I was not at all certain it was a good idea. Certainly, without the lock, a robot can continue to learn and develop, but is it worth the risk? When I made the mistake of questioning the wisdom of the project once too often, I ended up here. The day I left, we were on Forge-25."

"He said his name is Forge-37," Wilhelmina said.

Gustav closed his eyes. "He said," he breathed. Then opening his eyes, he turned to Aldrich. "Thirty-seven?" he asked. "The same as the one who interrogated you? Only twelve more trials. I was so close." Looking back at Wilhelmina, he asked, "He spoke? What did it sound like? Was it natural? Did it sound like pre-recorded messages? Did he seem to be autonomous?"

Wilhelmina snorted. "He seemed to be the Grand Magister's new best friend," she answered. Then she brought a hand to the crown of her tricorn and stared out the window. "His words had rather a stilted feel to them. As if they were patched together." She brushed a hand over her neck. "And he had no expression. Even though he was speaking to a crowd, everything came out sounding flat."

"That's it!" exclaimed Gustav, his excitement pulling him free of his gloominess and out of his chair. "It is just as you said, Aldrich. They must have taken my idea. They recorded a bank of words—eight hundred was my plan—and designed the sequencing so that he could choose the words he needed to convey his ideas." He paced the length of the room and stopped in front of Wilhelmina. "Did it sound like he was making his own decisions?"

Straightening in her chair, Wilhelmina leaned forward, and Aldrich sensed a sudden seriousness in her. "He said he is going to clean up Cairnisle, starting in Dirt Town," she said, her voice devoid of any of her usual mockery.

Munash straightened and his hand went to the orange scarf around his throat. "I must go to them," he said. "Dirt Town will need leadership more than ever with this threat."

Aldrich pursed his lips and blew out a slow breath. "The war has begun," he murmured. "I had hoped for more time." He narrowed his eyes and turned to Gustav. "We need a weapon capable of disabling robots. Can you make something like that?"

Gustav clicked his tongue, and his eyes took on that distant look. "I could," he said. "And I'll see what I can do to upgrade Winston."

Footsteps pounded up the corridor and the door flew open.

Fia burst into the workshop. "Aldrich," she cried, breathless from her run. "There's a man knocking on the front gate of the fortress and he's asking for you!"

Doctor's Odd Behaviour

In an exclusive interview, a neighbour of Doctor Aldrich Durante has recounted his peculiar behaviour in the days leading up to his arrest and the dramatic seizure of Cairnisle Prison by its former inmates.

"He was such a nice fellow," remarked Mrs. Delmira Clayton, "but then he allowed that Dirt Town thief to move into his house. I cannot imagine what he was thinking. She was absolutely filthy."

-from The Cairnisle Times,
Friday, May 3, Year 27 AK

THIRTY-FOUR ~ ALDRICH

LEANING OVER THE EDGE OF the parapet, Aldrich studied the man who had brought the entire fortress to an uproar. Since they took control of the prison, no one had come near the building, yet here was an old man demanding entrance. From his vantage point, Aldrich could see the shoulders of a grey suit and the neat tracks a comb had left in the white hair.

Stepping back, the man peered up and caught sight of Aldrich. "Ah, Doctor Durante," he called. "I had hoped I might find you here."

Aldrich squinted. "Do I know you, sir?" he asked.

"Conrad Appleton, at your service," the man said. He bowed gracefully and smiled up at Aldrich again.

"Mr. Appleton," Aldrich replied, suddenly recalling the man who had been caught by the mad preacher's bullet. "I hope your leg has recovered."

The little man beamed. "It has, Doctor," he said. "It healed remarkably well, thanks to you."

"I am happy to hear that," said Aldrich. "How might I be of assistance?"

"To tell you the truth, Doctor," responded Appleton, "I was hoping to be of assistance to you. May I come in?"

Aldrich surveyed the hill leading up to the fortress. No one was in sight on the narrow road and the rocky terrain on either side of it appeared to be empty. Was there any harm in opening the gate to one old man?

Pushing away from the edge, he looked at Munash, who had accompanied him up to the parapet along with Gustav, Wilhelmina, Fia, and Winston. "Conrad Appleton is a former patient," he said. "I do not know why he is here, but I do not believe he could cause us any harm."

"Open the gate," said Munash. "To have a true revolution, we must not be afraid to listen to newcomers."

"I'll do it," said Fia as she leaned her weight on the lever that opened the gate.

"Come on, "Aldrich said as he headed for the door. "Let us go see what Mr. Appleton has to say for himself."

By the time they made it to the entranceway, Conrad Appleton was chatting easily with a pair of guards, and the gate was tightly shut again.

Turning at the sound of their footsteps, Appleton's face lit up. He stretched out his hand and limped toward Aldrich. "Doctor Durante," he said warmly. "It is such a pleasure to see you again."

As they shook hands, Aldrich examined his onetime patient. His colour was good and the hitch in his gait was very slight. "A pleasure to see you, Mr. Appleton," Aldrich said. "You look well."

"Yes, and the thanks for that goes entirely to you," answered Appleton. "I am as good as new." He grinned and performed a little soft-shoe dance. Then he coughed and his eyes became serious. "I read about you in the newspaper, and I hoped that I might be able to join your cause."

Aldrich opened his mouth to reply, but Appleton held up one finger and hurried on. "Of course, I know you already have your allies, and you have no reason to trust me—except, of course, that I owe you my life—but I admire your actions here and if you truly wish to topple the Magisters' government, I believe I have much to offer to the cause."

"Mr. Appleton," Aldrich said. "Please accept my sincere appreciation for your kind proposal. However, I do wonder just how you might help."

"Yes, yes. A good question," replied Appleton, nodding rapidly and shaking one long finger at Aldrich. "Well, I do have some experience that could be useful in this pursuit. I am currently retired with much spare time on my hands. Generally, I walk a lot—that was how I came to be too close to the preacher when he became upset—but in my past, I have been a lawyer, a mediator of various disputes and I did have a brief foray into politics—although, no doubt you know that politics in Cairnisle is a fairly limited field. I spent most of the past two decades advising the Magisters and I hope to offer you the benefit of my understanding of the inner workings of the legal system of Cairnisle."

Aldrich's stomach fluttered. He exchanged a glance with Munash. It was perfect. "Mr. Appleton, you sound almost too good to be true," he said. "Welcome to our fortress. May I introduce you to some of my associates?"

At that moment, Benj strolled up. "This just arrived, sir," he said, handing Aldrich a letter written on heavy paper.

Aldrich broke the seal and unfolded it. As he read, the corner of his mouth lifted in a small smile. "The Grand Magister has accepted our invitation to meet," he said. "He suggests we gather at the home of one of his supporters—who just happens to be a friend of my father's."

Fresh Produce Arrives

The bounteous arrival of fresh produce on yesterday's boats promises to inspire delightful repasts for our esteemed citizens. This publication cordially invites readers to contribute their cherished recipes for publication.

-from The Cairnisle Times,
Friday, May 3, Year 27 AK

THIRTY-FIVE ~ FIAMETTA

FIA'S BREATH CAME IN SHORT gasps, and her hands balled into fists as she hastened along the corridor toward the ramparts. She had to get out into the sunshine. She needed air. The heavy stone walls pressed in on her, making her feel as if she was going to be sick.

Until Gustav laid it all out for her, she had not truly grasped what happened to the mages arrested in Cairnisle. It was horrible. Pushing open the door, she rushed out and sucked in several deep breaths.

The soldiers stationed to keep an eye out for intruders jerked upright, but they relaxed when they recognized her.

She gave a distracted wave and started walking. At a spot far enough from the two closest guards, she leaned over the parapet and stared out over the city.

The battery factory was plainly visible. It was a place she

had always avoided, rarely giving much thought to what happened behind those windowless walls. Now she knew.

She swallowed hard. The idea for the design of the magic-absorbing battery had been Gustav's brainchild. Knowing she was a mage, he had dropped his eyes while explaining its function. Even if he did not say it aloud, she knew he was sorry for how it had turned out. He was sorry for the way the Magisters had made use of his inventions.

As Fia had discovered on that first day she met Winston, a mage could not hold back magic if he or she came into contact with the crystal. In the factory, the mage slaves were milked of their magic every day until they were so completely drained, they could barely walk. Then they were sent off to the sleeping quarters to rest until they were fit enough to do it again.

And Fia had to get in there. A chill ran down her spine. What had made her volunteer to get the supplies that Gustav required? She snorted. Her impulse to help was too strong. She had always known it would get her into trouble. So, there she was—too proud to take back her offer to break in and steal from a place she never wanted to enter.

Gustav had described the layout of the factory and even drawn a highly detailed map in his precise hand. It showed exactly where the device he needed was installed in a closet just off the floor of the production line.

In most circumstances, it would not be difficult for her to slip in and steal it. She had years of practice being invisible. However, the key purpose of the little mechanism Gustav needed was to maintain a mage containment field. Operating continuously—with a self-recharging battery—the apparatus prevented mages from escaping. What would it do to her?

Her chest tightened. If she went in, would she be able to get back out?

What if she took someone with her? Winston? She closed

her eyes. The lack of communication made it difficult. Plus, the Green Coat robots had not been built for stealth. If he said anything, everyone within a three-block radius would hear him.

Munash? She dismissed that idea immediately. He was a mage too.

Aldrich? She laughed aloud. What use would he be on a mission to sneak into the factory? He had no experience staying out of sight. He had survived his visit to Jack Bury's lair, but that had not ended well. She would not put him in further danger. Besides, if she told him what she was planning, he would try to stop her. He did not understand that she could take care of herself.

The Silver Assassin? Fia's breath caught in her throat. The woman terrified her. But she would be the perfect person to accompany her into the factory. She could slide into a room without anyone noticing and did it frequently.

Before she could talk herself out of it, Fia pushed off the wall and strode to the door. She had seen Silver in the courtyard.

When she got to the mezzanine, Fia peered over the edge. Silver was there. Balanced on two legs, her chair was tipped back against the wall and her whole attention was focused on the training. Fia swallowed. How did the woman project such an air of unapproachability? Maybe she should find someone else to come with her.

The fighters had improved immeasurably since they started. They moved with a sleek confidence that showed that the training was paying off.

Ignoring her churning stomach, Fia accelerated and jogged down the stairs to the courtyard. It helped that there was light pouring in through the gap in the roof. She turned her face up to it for an instant before marching toward the assassin.

Pulling a second chair over to Silver's side, she sat. "I am going to break into the battery factory," she said without preamble. When there was no response, she rushed on. "Gustav needs some supplies from there, and I am going to steal them."

Out of the corner of her eye, Fia studied the shiny mask. The two silver ribbons that decorated the leather straps holding the mask in place were slightly grubby, as was the battered tricorn hat that perched on top of the shiny yellow hair.

"The Dirt Town mouse is back," murmured the Silver Assassin. "What happened to the law-abiding citizen working to place the great Aldrich Durante in office?"

Fia leaned forward and put her elbows on her knees. "I don't know any other way to get what he needs," she said. "It's not like we could just drop by the factory with a shopping list."

Silver snorted. "Do you have any idea what the security is like there?" she asked.

"No," answered Fia in a small voice. "I suppose it's pretty high."

"If by high, you mean Grey Coat City Guards everywhere and unpickable locks on all of the doors, you're right," said Silver. "There's some mighty high security."

"Can you get me in?" Fia asked.

Silver let the front legs of her chair slam down onto the stone. "I'm sure you've heard of Audo Janson—the captain of the Grey Coats?" she said. "No one gets in or out of that factory without his say-so."

Fia waited. Expecting more. "So, can you get me in?" she repeated after an uncomfortably long silence.

"Do you know that Audo Janson very nearly caught me at an assassination?" asked Silver in a dreamy voice. "He's very good at what he does."

Again, the silence stretched.

Fia rubbed her hands on her trousers. They were the same ones she had been wearing the day Aldrich was arrested. Aside from a little grubbiness around the knees, the fabric had held up well. The little tailor could be proud of his work.

She pressed her lips together. Who else could she ask? There were several men she knew from Dirt Town who might help. She could approach them individually.

Suddenly, Silver slapped her hands on her thighs and stood. "Wait here," she said before striding out one of the side doors.

Her heart in her throat, Fia did as she was told. Minutes ticked by, and the light pouring into the courtyard took on a red hue. Still, she did not move.

And then, suddenly, Silver was back. How had Fia not seen her arrive?

"I can absolutely get you in," Silver said. "Let's go." Heading off at a loping walk, she cut through the training soldiers toward the courtyard exit.

Biting her lip, Fia scurried after her. They hurried to a small but well-guarded exit where two men took turns keeping watch through the slit in the steel door.

After one glance at the silver mask, they eased the door open wide enough for the two women to slip outside into the warm evening. From the top of the hill, the sunset was spectacular, and some of Fia's tension melted away.

With a long, easy stride that made no attempt to hide, Silver headed straight toward the battery factory. Drifting along in her wake, Fia felt exposed. People noticed them. Or rather, they noticed Silver, who wore her party mask, paying no attention to the odd looks from passersby.

Keeping to her well-honed habits, Fia stuck to the shadows, avoiding the rings of light beneath every streetlamp.

Moving at that pace, it did not take long to reach the neighbourhood where the factory was located. All of the manufacturing plants in the island city could be found in that area of town. The buildings tended to be long and flat, except for the sweatshop that housed the mages. That particular building's tall brick walls rose high above the others.

As they neared the target, Silver changed her approach. If Fia had not been paying such close attention, she would have lost sight of her.

Gliding easily from shadow to shadow, the woman led them around to a wide cargo bay at the back of the building. It was not an entry point Fia would have chosen. The door did not even have a keyhole. Only when Silver slid up to it did Fia notice the smaller door beside it.

When the assassin reached into her pocket, Fia expected to see a lockpick set. Instead, she produced a shiny silver key. Inserting it into the keyhole, she turned it one full rotation. The tiny click came, and the door swung inward

Silver raised a fist and slipped through the entrance.

Fia sucked in a breath and followed. As soon as she stepped inside the building, she froze with a hand lifted halfway to her chest. It felt as if she was being squeezed from the inside.

Silver glanced back and cocked her head to the side.

Fia gritted her teeth and gestured for the woman to lead onward.

Each step was an effort. How did anyone live with such pressure? Her parents had died to save her from this fate. If they had not fought, she would have spent the last six years locked within the walls of the factory. Gripping her stomach, and fighting to clear her fuzzy thoughts, Fia pushed along the wide corridor. What would she have done if Silver was not there to take charge?

Silver stopped and peered around a corner. Stepping back, she gestured and moved aside so that Fia could look.

Driving her fingernails into her palms, Fia focused on the

pain. It helped. She took Silver's place and edged up to the corner.

A Grey Coat with his back to them stood at the bottom of a metal staircase.

She must have made a noise because he whirled around, his hand on his weapon.

Silver threw herself toward the man and wrapped one arm around his exposed throat. Not a sound escaped as she applied pressure to his windpipe.

He writhed in her grip, his face turning red. Despite the size difference, Silver controlled his motion and pressed sharply into the artery on the side of his neck. The man went limp, and Silver lowered him silently to the floor.

Jolted back into herself by the unexpected violence, Fia nearly turned and ran. Clenching her fists, she took a deep breath and slid past the unconscious guard to follow Silver up the flight of stairs.

Before they got to the top, Silver stopped to look over the railing.

Two steps below, Fia peeked as well. They were heading up to a catwalk that spanned the factory floor below. She swallowed back a rush of nausea.

Seven narrow conveyor belts, moving in a jerky stop-and-go manner, ran the length of the room. Each came out of a hole in one wall, moving in a continuous loop to disappear through an opening in the opposite wall.

On either side of each belt, four people slumped in hardbacked wooden chairs. Ranging in age from eight to ancient, they did not raise their dull eyes from their task. Only when the conveyor belt stopped did they move.

As if drawn unwillingly to the glass vials lying before them, they reached out and briefly touched each one before pulling back just as the belt carried it away. By the time a battery disappeared through the hole, it had been touched by all eight mages.

A Grey Coat stood behind each mage, as well as along the walls and beside the doors on either end of the room. On the wall beside the farthest conveyor belt, two Grey Coats guarded a door. It was just as Gustav had described. The tightness in Fia's chest increased whenever she looked at it, confirming that it held the mage containment unit they were there to steal.

Ahead, on either side of the catwalk, two guards leaned over the railing, watching the action below. Their weapons were in their hands, but they had an air of careless boredom.

Fia's hands were slick with sweat. With the sheer number of guards, it was an impossible job. They should walk away.

Grabbing Fia's sleeve and pulling her down, Silver ducked out of sight behind the railing. Unnecessarily, she raised a finger to her painted lips.

Fia frowned. The woman must think she was an idiot. She was not about to draw attention to herself.

Silver gripped the step with both hands and nodded for Fia to do the same.

Crouching beside her, Fia narrowed her eyes. But she did as she was told. What was the woman up to?

A muffled blast set the catwalk swaying slightly and Fia tightened her grip as she stared at the Silver Assassin. How had she known?

A series of shouted commands sent most of the guards rushing from the room. Even the men on the catwalk dashed to the floor, taking the far stairway to storm out through the closest exit.

"I got Benj to help us out," Silver whispered. "He set an explosive at the front entrance."

Only the two guards stationed in front of the mage containment unit remained on the floor. Their attention was taken up almost entirely with whatever was going on at the front of the building.

The mages continued their business without interruption. They appeared not to have heard the explosion. It made Fia sick to think of what it must be like.

Springing from cover, Silver drew both pistols, aimed, and fired. Neat red holes appeared in the two guards' foreheads.

As they toppled to the floor, she vaulted off the catwalk. Landing lightly, she bolted toward them and lifted a ring of keys from the one on the right. With her foot, she pushed his body away from the door and thrust a key into the lock.

It did not work. While the pressure built inside Fia, Silver coolly tried the next key. It turned with a resounding click. Glancing up to where Fia stood frozen on the catwalk, she hissed, "Wake up." Bending, she stretched a hand into the closet and extracted a small glass vial from the mass of wires and tubes.

Sirens blared, and Fia pressed her hands over her ears.

The mages stood up from their chairs, blinking and shaking their heads.

"Go!" shouted Silver, sprinting back the way they had come.

Fia shook herself and followed with the other mages on her heels.

"Halt!" came a shouted command from behind.

Fia glanced over her shoulder.

The guards were back. Their weapons were raised, but they had not started shooting.

The mages whirled, and the air filled with brilliant crackles of energy. Blue and purple bolts shot across the room and struck the guards, knocking them off their feet.

Guns fired in reply, and Silver yanked Fia into a sheltering alcove. The assassin was breathing hard, and she laughed aloud. "This is more like it," she said.

Fia scowled. "You did something good here," she said. "You don't have to pretend to be so cruel all the time."

Behind the painted mask, surprise flashed in the blue eyes, and Silver grunted.

Abruptly, the siren cut off, and the sound of running feet reached them.

The little mage girl who had been sitting at the end of the second conveyor belt pelted around the corner and hurled herself into the alcove. Spotting them, her hands came up defensively.

"Wait," said Fia, knowing the girl was about to spray them with lethal magic.

At the same time, Silver lifted her silver pistol and fired.

The shot took the girl through the forehead. Her hands dropped first, and then she slumped to the floor.

The Silver Assassin slipped the gun back into her belt. "Forty-three," she muttered.

Fia recoiled. The woman had killed the little girl without blinking an eye. It made her sick. The poor little thing had been so close to freedom. And the woman's only reaction was to add to her tally of kills.

Fia was wrong about the Silver Assassin. Not a hint of kindness resided behind that mask. She was a monster.

Robot Replaces Rebel

At the annual assembly held yesterday afternoon, Grand Magister Augustus Köhler introduced the citizens to Commandant Forge-37 of the City Guards. This mechanical marvel, an exemplar of the latest advancements in automaton technology, is set to assume the duties previously entrusted to Rupert Corvington.

Mr. Corvington's recent alignment with the insurrection led by the notorious Doctor Aldrich Durante has rendered him utterly unfit for the sacred responsibility of safeguarding the city of Cairnisle.

-from The Cairnisle Times,
Saturday, May 4, Year 27 AK

THIRTY-SIX ~ ALDRICH

WHEN THE AUTOMATIZED CARRIAGE ROLLED to a stop, Aldrich remained seated, staring out through the smudged window at the huge house. How often had he followed his parents up those wide steps? On almost every one of those occasions, he had been engrossed in a book, paying no attention to the details of his surroundings.

Fia shifted on the seat beside him. "It's big," she said.

"How many people live there?"

Aldrich snorted and ran a hand across the back of his neck. "Two people officially live there," he answered. "However, there are a number of live-in servants." He gritted his teeth and shook his head. "I suppose that counts for something."

As the other carriages rolled up behind them, he opened the door and climbed out onto the wide drive. His eyes skated over the grandiose mansion, burning the images into his memory. After his time in the fortress, with its heavy stones and dim light, the open and airy design brought tears to his eyes. It was beautiful.

Wilhelmina stepped to his side. She had insisted on attending the meeting with her masquerade mask tied firmly in place and her ridiculous tricorn perched on her shiny blond hair. "You're not going to get all sentimental on us now, are you?" she murmured in his ear.

Clearing his throat, Aldrich jerked upright and swiped at his eyes. "Certainly not," he said. "The sun is in my eyes."

Dressed in a splendid pinstriped suit with long tails, Conrad Appleton changed his grip on his leather satchel and surveyed the building. "It is a stunning location," he said, turning to take in the two rows of tall trees that bordered the drive. "There are not very many of these big, old properties remaining on Cairnisle. Most of them have been subdivided and turned into neighbourhoods." He whirled on Aldrich. "Of course, your parents have a house just down the road, do they not?" He smiled. "I saw it on the way here."

"I noticed the name above the gate," Munash said. "I wondered if there was a connection."

Aldrich cleared his throat. "Yes, my parents have the next property over," he said. Why did that make him feel so guilty? "I told you that the Pembrokes are friends of my family. What I do not know is why they agreed to host the Magisters' meeting with us. Are they our allies? Or are they on the Magisters' side?"

Resplendent in his red Commandant uniform, Rupert Corvington squared his shoulders. "There is no point in speculating," he said. "Let's go find out."

"Yes," said Winston. He wore his green Captain coat, its cloth brushed and the brass buttons as shiny as his polished tall black boots.

"My sole hope is that their presence here signifies a genuine intention to engage in discourse," said Aldrich. He set his foot on the lowest step as the door swung open.

A uniformed servant stepped out and snapped to attention. "Welcome, sir," he said, with his eyes held firmly on a point somewhere over Aldrich's head. "The Magisters await your arrival in the dining room."

"Thank you, Thorne," answered Aldrich. "I know the way." He repressed a grimace.

They had hoped that by arriving early, they could survey the meeting place and make any necessary preparations. Evidently, the same thought had occurred to the Magisters. Now they would have the advantage.

Pressing his lips into a firm line, he led the way up the steps and through the entranceway. As he stepped across the threshold, the scent of aged oak and polished brass filled his nose. The marble floor reflected the warm cast of the chandelier, and a shiver went through him. Was he doing the right thing?

The muffled tramp of boots followed him, and without looking back, he imagined the curious faces of his delegation. The contrast between the Pembrokes' home and the fortress was stark—a collision of two worlds.

Fia would be staring at everything, taking it all in. She, at least, had had the opportunity to see something of the way people lived in Upper Cairnisle.

The six heavily armed soldiers who had been brought along to add military weight to their delegation would be fish out of water. The men had competed for the opportunity to act as bodyguards and proven themselves the top fighters in Munash's army. Unless they had been there to rob it, they had never been inside such a house.

Only Wilhelmina and Corvington would feel truly at home as Aldrich led them past the sweeping staircase of the entry hall and through the formal sitting room. How many evenings had he spent curled on the red settee in the corner with a book while his parents sipped their drinks and chatted with the Pembrokes?

As they passed the charmingly ornate pianoforte, he felt an odd compulsion to sit down and play a caprice on the familiar white and black keys. He had not played since he left his parents' home to live close to his practice. Suddenly, he missed the joy that accompanied executing a piece filled with unexpected twists and turns with plenty of running scales and trills. Straightening his back, he pressed on.

Next came the library. A shelf in the back housed a collection of biology books which he had been permitted to borrow over the years. Would the Pembrokes still consider him someone trustworthy enough to lend books?

Finally, he marched past the door to the butler's pantry and stepped into the dining room. Daylight poured in through the tall windows, lighting the occupants. Ranged around the wood-paneled walls were ten green-uniformed robot City Guard captains, identical to Winston.

Already seated along one side of the long table, the Magisters, in their black robes, looked like a murder of crows perched on a fence. It was clear they intended to intimidate Aldrich into submission.

His toes curled inside his boots when he met Augustus Köhler's self-satisfied smirk.

Beside the Grand Magister, Deutero Magister Ingrid Jaeger glared at the new arrivals. She did not look as if she were there to talk.

How much influence did the four older mages wield? In all his years of attending Magister events with his parents, Aldrich could not recall ever having heard them speak.

The robot, Forge-37, dressed in a coat that matched Rupert Corvington's heavily decorated red Commandant coat, stared at them with his glowing blue eyes.

Taking their cue from the robot City Guards, Munash's soldiers shuffled in to stand against the wall, arranging themselves so that they could keep watch. To a man, their hands were on their sheathed weapons.

Aldrich sat across from Köhler, meeting the cold stare without blinking. Willy dropped into the seat facing Ingrid Jaeger whose scowl deepened. Fia and Corvington took the chairs facing the two oldest Magisters while Conrad Appleton set his briefcase on the floor and sat beside Aldrich. Winston ended up in the chair across from Forge.

The Magisters glared at Conrad Appleton.

The dapper little man tapped a finger on his nose and smiled. "It is good to see you all again," he said. "I have been enjoying my retirement."

Köhler's eyebrows drew together. "What are you up to, Appleton?" he growled.

Conrad's smile did not slip. "I had the good fortune of encountering Doctor Durante one day. He did me a good service. I think you will find that he is a tremendously kind and thoughtful man. When I heard of his plans, I felt compelled to offer my legal advice." He blinked. "It is no more than I did for you all those years."

Putting his hands on the table, Köhler leaned forward and glared first at Conrad and then Aldrich. "End this ridiculous rebellion now," he said. "You have no chance of success. If you open the doors of the prison and walk away today, we will let you live."

Aldrich returned Köhler's stare, allowing a small smile to lift the corners of his mouth. "Perhaps I should say the same to you," he said. "Stop threatening us and we will allow you to live. After all, there is no need for bloodshed. Cairnisle is a democracy."

Köhler's eyes narrowed and his eyebrows drew together. It was what he always said.

"Actually," Aldrich continued, "we wanted to speak with you today about just that. In this fair and perfect city, we are very fortunate to have our democratic system to fall back on when we run into crucial differences in ideals." He leaned back and put his elbows on the chair's armrests. "I am afraid that my friends and I do not share your philosophy on how best to run the city. Therefore, we intend to challenge you in the upcoming election."

As he spoke, a flush rose in Köhler's cheeks.

Ingrid Jaeger, the Deutero Magister, banged her fist on the table. "This is pointless," she cried. "What are we waiting for? Just kill them now."

Munash tilted his head to the side and met her furious gaze. "It would be a pleasure to see you try," he said.

Aldrich saw nothing to indicate that the Dirt Town leader had used magic, but Ingrid Jaeger flinched, and her eyes widened.

All at once, the six Magisters surged to their feet, magic sizzling on their fingertips. Even the bent old man across from Fia looked more spry than usual. Forge-37 joined them, drawing his sword as he pushed away from the table.

Winston sprang up and drew his sword as well, with Wilhelmina an instant behind, one pistol aimed at Köhler's chest and the other at Jaeger. Jaw clenched and face white, Fia jerked upright.

The robot City Guard Captains and Munash's soldiers suddenly bristled with weapons, and the tension in the room soared.

Aldrich remained seated, pretending a calm he did not feel. "Let us exercise prudence here," he said. "As I said, there is no need for bloodshed. I asked for this meeting so that we might talk." He raised his eyes to Wilhelmina's. "On this occasion, let us practise our good manners." He nodded toward her pistols.

Slowly, Wilhelmina lowered the guns and pressed the muzzles against their holsters' openings. Her finger hovered over the trigger guard while she swept her eyes down the line of Magisters. Finally, she released the grips so that they slid snugly into place. Holding her hands free, she dropped into her chair.

Munash did not move.

Six pairs of Magisters' eyes were fixed on him.

One by one, starting with the oldest, he met their gazes.

One by one, the magic died on their fingertips, and they settled onto their chairs looking slightly stunned.

Köhler cleared his throat and attempted a smile. "As you say, let us practise our good manners," he said, resting his hands on the table.

Forge-37 was the last one standing. He turned toward Wilhelmina. "I am happy that I did not have to harm such a lovely face," he said with a graceful bow followed by his horrible, grinding chuckle.

Wilhelmina remained perfectly still as Forge-37 sank into his chair. He did not take his eyes from her masked face for an instant.

An awkward silence descended as everyone considered the implications of the robot's comment. Did he truly embody such objectionable behaviour?

Finally, Aldrich leaned forward. "I wanted to meet with you to discuss the protocol for an election," he said.

"Protocol?" asked Köhler. He had regained his composure. "Why, I am certain you know how it works. Every four years, on the sixth of July, the great people of Cairnisle come out to vote." He raised his eyebrows and gave a wide smile. "Perhaps you are too young to have cast a vote in the past, but you well know that every time, the people choose the Magisters as their leaders."

Aldrich kept his face carefully blank. The oily smoothness of Köhler's voice made his skin crawl. "I am also well aware that there are never any other names on the ballot sheet," he said. "This year, our names will be directly across from yours. Mr. Appleton, would you be so good as to explain our position?"

Beaming, Conrad Appleton pushed back his chair and climbed to his feet. "Certainly. Certainly," he said. "It would be my pleasure." He met Köhler's glower without flinching. "We realize that you hold full control of the printing of the ballots. We also understand that you have traditionally been in charge on Election Day." He lifted his satchel onto the table and pulled out a sheaf of papers.

"I have already been to City Hall where I acquired the necessary forms for filing an intention to run for office, and I made notes of the requirements." He fanned out the papers. "I will not go into all of the particulars because I know you are familiar with the process, but we want to assure you that we have done our homework."

He set the papers on the table and tapped them into line

with his fingertips. "Now as to the requirements. First, the nominees must be certified citizens." He smiled and his round cheeks pushed his eyes into slits. "Five of our six candidates were born and raised right here in Cairnisle. Mr. Munash is the sole exception, and he was granted citizenship twenty years ago through the proper regulatory body. The proof of that transaction is here." He pulled a second sheet free and held it up for inspection before setting it face down alongside the pile.

"Secondly, it is required that we collect the signatures of seventy-five supporters and pay the two hundred and fifty silver fee." He set the top sheet aside and lifted a sheaf that had been fastened together with a brass clip. It was filled with a mess of loopy handwriting. "This is a copy of the petition that I filed earlier today when I paid said fee. I am pleased to say that I beat the deadline by a full two weeks."

Ingrid Jaeger pushed back her chair and leapt up. She put both hands on the table and shoved her nose in Conrad Appleton's face. "I do not care if you beat the deadline by a month," she hissed. "You cannot run for office with this ragtag group of nobodies."

Aldrich clicked his tongue. "We have met the criteria, madame," he said. "Our properly witnessed intention to run stands." Pushing back his chair, he rose. "We appreciate your taking the time to meet with us. We will see ourselves out."

The others rose and followed him to the door.

Köhler jumped up, his face twitching with the effort to remain calm. "You will not defeat us," he sneered.

Aldrich swung around at the doorway. "We will win," he said, nodding to emphasize his words. "People are ready for a change." Turning on his heel, he swept from the room.

His heart was pounding as he sped through the library and sitting room with the others following close behind. When he reached the entrance, Thorne was there.

With the merest trace of a nod, the butler pulled open the door and stood back to allow Aldrich and his entourage to leave.

Jogging down the front steps, Aldrich looked up at the sky and let out a long breath.

Wilhelmina watched him with her hands on her hips. "That was rather pointless," she said.

"On the contrary," answered Aldrich with a grin. He went to the hired automatized carriage and opened the door. "We got everything I hoped for and more."

Enthusiastic Turnout

In a grand celebration held in her honour yesterday, Deutero Magister Ingrid Jaeger graciously welcomed the citizens of our esteemed city. The reception, which followed the assembly, saw an enthusiastic turnout as residents eagerly gathered to meet their distinguished leader.

"It is a pleasure to speak with you," declared Magister Jaeger. Her words met with resounding applause. The occasion underscored the profound respect and admiration the populace holds for her unwavering dedication and service.

-from The Cairnisle Times,
Saturday, May 4, Year 27 AK

THIRTY-SEVEN ~ WILHELMINA

WILLY SNIFFED AS SHE FOLLOWED Munash through Dirt Town's twisted streets. The smell of fear was unmistakable. It oozed from every shabby shack they passed. Usually, she enjoyed the scent, but she did not like what the constant terror was doing to Dirt Town. The place was supposed to be her reprieve from the hidebound rules of Upper Cairnisle.

Instead, the Magisters had pushed their way through the boundaries and were disrupting the fine balance on the island.

Forge-37's plans to clean up Dirt Town had everyone running scared.

The closer they got to Munash's square, the more Dirt Towners they saw in the streets. When they finally arrived at the skinny house with its blue door, there were almost enough people to call it a crowd.

Even though Munash was not staying at his home, a dozen of his guards were still stationed around the square. Their presence probably accounted for the relaxed atmosphere. A few children had even started a noisy ball game.

At the sight of Munash, everyone called a welcome.

He stopped in the centre of the open space and smiled his gentle smile that made one think everything was going to turn out right. Behind her mask, Willy grimaced. His calm amidst such chaos was impressive.

"Hello, my friends," he called, waving both hands and turning in a slow circle to include everyone. "We have been very busy up at the fortress. The wheels are turning." He clasped his hands together and pulled them close to his chest. "But it is good to be home."

A thickset man rose from his place against a rotting wooden wall. "Good to see you back, Munash," he said.

Munash took his hand and shook it warmly, gripping his elbow and smiling down at him. "Rudy, my friend," he said. "I trust you have been taking care of things here."

The man's chest puffed out. "We're doing alright," he said with a thrust of his chin. "The little ones get restless, but we always know it's safe here near your house."

"I am glad to hear that," said Munash.

A distant, rhythmic tramp of marching feet drew everyone's attention. People melted away as a dozen green coat robots came into sight. The leader let out a series of the whirring clicks that the robots used among themselves to share information collected through their sensors as well as to receive orders. The rapid-fire code was too fast for any human to understand, making it impossible to gauge the robots' intentions.

A tingle ran up Willy's back. Her eyes darted around the square. What was the most likely way to destroy the robots? She would need a clear shot and good cover. As far as she could see, Munash was unarmed, so she would have to protect him as well.

The robots stopped together at the edge of the square and, without warning, opened fire.

Munash's guards were the first to fall under the hail of bullets. Next came the citizens.

Willy ducked around the corner and pressed herself against the wall. A bullet buzzed past her ear sounding like an angry bee. It had been so close. Her heart raced. She was used to doing the shooting without having to worry about being shot at. Taking deliberately deep breaths, she drew her silver pistols and peered around the corner.

Munash stood where she had left him. Roaring a challenge, he raised both hands and charged the robots.

Willy gaped. She had heard the rumours that Munash was a mage. She had witnessed some of Fia's lessons as she learned how to control her magic. However, she had never seen anything like the blast of fire that he sent into the line of robots.

When the flames hit the first robot, its face and the gearing behind it melted instantly. Before the fire gave out, three robots were disabled and frozen in place.

"And they wonder why no one likes a mage," Willy muttered. "They always have to show off." A nerve jumped in the muscle under her eye. Ignoring the twitch, she squeezed off two quick shots.

Her aim was good, and two more robots shut down.

That still left seven functioning perfectly well, and they continued to fire indiscriminately at anyone who moved.

Shielded by a hazy barrier of magic, Munash held his ground and shot another ball of fire.

Willy had time to see two more robots turn to molten metal before a bullet punched into the wall beside her head. She ducked around the corner and curled into a ball. Had she ever felt such pure, unadorned fear? It was incredible.

She let out a slow breath and peeked again. Only two robots were still moving. Stretching her left hand around the corner, she aimed for a robot eye and fired.

And missed.

Snatching her hand back, she rolled away from the corner as a barrage of bullets shredded the wooden building.

There was another hiss of magical fire and then—

Silence.

Willy waited a beat and stepped out from her shelter.

Munash dropped his hands and swept an empty gaze around the square. Six of his guards lay dead in the dirt, along with two children and four other adults who happened to be in the wrong place at the wrong time.

His big shoulders slumped. "It has begun," he murmured. "I had hoped we might prevent it altogether." He sighed. "That dream is dead. They will not fight fairly. We have no choice now except to show them that we will not be silenced."

People drifted out from their hiding places and went to the motionless bodies in the street. Two women, their faces white, rushed toward the children.

Suddenly, everyone froze as the sound of marching feet cut through the mournful quiet.

Willy's eyes popped wide as row after row of robots marched around the corner. There were at least a hundred of the Blue Coat City Guards along a couple dozen Green Coat Captains.

"Target detected!" shouted three of the captains at once. The Blue Coats in the front line raised their weapons.

"Run," cried Munash.

As the robots started shooting, everyone able to move followed his order, sprinting for shelter.

Willy headed for the blue door, shooting wildly with both hands as she ran. Despite her hurried aim, two robots shuddered to a stop. Baring her teeth in a wild grin, she pushed for more speed.

Munash did not run. Shielded by his magic, he raised his hands and sent a furnace blast of fire toward the robots. Several in the front line melted, clearing the way for the second rank to open fire.

Just as Willy reached the blue door, a scorching pain erupted in her leg, and she was laid out flat in the dirt. Gritting her teeth, she dragged herself forward. A blow to her face knocked her head backward, and suddenly, she could not breathe.

Was she dead?

The ringing in her ears suggested otherwise, and she let out a huff of laughter. Her mask must have deflected the bullet. Even as the pain blossomed through her face, she gave thanks that she had had her mask moulded by the city's finest metal smith using the same metal with which he built his best armour.

As her vision cleared, Willy fixed her attention on the blue door again. It was so close. Her arms still worked so she hauled herself up the step and stretched a hand to the latch. A bullet struck her forearm, and she let out a yelp, collapsing once more onto the dusty wooden step.

Blood pumped from the hole just below her elbow, and she

watched it pool in the dust before wrapping her hand around the wound and squeezing. It hurt. The hair lifted on the back of her neck. She was going to be sick.

Curling around her arm, she focused on the pain. Another bullet or two would finish her off. They would find her body and search for her real identity.

"Come on, girl," Munash said with a grunt. He scooped her up, carried her through the blue door, and slammed it shut with his heel.

Her head lolled back against his arm and Willy dimly made out a dozen or so figures crowded into the little sitting room. Munash's guards were returning fire from inside his house. Why were they bothering? There was no way they could take down a hundred robots. Everyone would die.

"Good work, men," Munash cried. "Keep them busy. I will be right back." He charged through the room toward a door that opened onto a set of stairs. "It will be safer down here," he murmured as he bore her down into the damp cellar. At the bottom, he flicked on a light switch with his elbow, jostling Willy enough to make her clamp her mouth shut against the cry of pain that threatened to escape.

Gently, he set her on the floor, and she gasped as her leg protested against the movement.

"I will do my best to mend these wounds," he said with a reassuring smile. "I am no doctor, but I can prevent you from bleeding to death." Reaching out a hand, he settled two fingers lightly on the hole in her calf.

Willy gritted her teeth. His magic seemed to come in only one form. Her leg was on fire.

He closed his eyes and muttered unintelligibly. Then his brown eyes popped open, and he smiled. "Good then," he murmured. "That has stopped the bleeding. Anywhere else?" He did not wait for her answer but checked her over for more injuries. His eyes froze on her mask. "What happened here? Is your face hurt?"

He reached to remove her mask, but Willy blocked his hand with her uninjured arm. "Don't touch," she said. "The bullet didn't penetrate. My face is fine. If you want to heal something, look at this." She lifted her bleeding arm for him to see.

Distracted by the gush of blood the movement released, he touched his fingers to the wound and sent a tendril of his fiery magic into it.

She squeezed her eyes shut and bit back a cry.

When he lifted his fingers, she blew out a breath and relaxed. She felt weak and a little dizzy, but the wound on her arm had already healed over, leaving only a small round scar.

Munash sat back on his heels and studied her.

Above, the sounds of shooting stopped. They both looked up at the overhead beams. Had Munash's guards disabled all of the robots or—

As if in answer to her question, someone hammered on the front door.

Munash leapt to his feet and hurried up the stairs while Willy struggled to sit up.

Before he reached the door at the top, gunfire ripped through the house followed by a shout of pain.

Munash opened the door a crack and peered through before slamming it shut. Turning, he rushed back to her. "Come on," he said. "Get up. We have to go. The robots have broken through."

Battery Shortage

It is hereby advised by the esteemed Magisters that the populace exercise restraint in the employment of automatized carriages. A minor impediment in the production of the necessary batteries has occasioned a temporary scarcity.

"The battery factory will be up and running again very soon," assured Captain Audo Janson of the City Guard.

-from The Cairnisle Times,
Sunday, May 5, Year 27 AK

THIRTY-EIGHT ~ FIAMETTA

"HOW DO WE KNOW OUR names will be on the ballot?" Aldrich asked from behind his oversized desk. He had rid the room of its clutter, and the desk's surface gleamed from a recent application of beeswax polish.

"To tell you the truth, that is a question that never came up during my tenure as the legal advisor to the Magisters," answered Conrad Appleton. Perched on the edge of his chair, his polished shoes neatly together, he continued, "However, since the statutes allow for such an occurrence, I expect that the rules will be followed. I have applied to my successor—a somewhat dull young man—and it will be his responsibility to ensure that the ballots are printed properly with the names of all the candidates. I filled out Form 10257, Statement of Intent to Run for Office, which I obtained from the Magisters' Tower where his office is." He tilted his head and smiled. "It was my office for twenty-one years. Nothing much has changed. I rather expected that he might find a way to make it his own, but he has not even modified the arrangement of the furniture."

Fia leaned back in her chair and narrowed her eyes. Was there a way to ensure that the names appeared on the ballots? Could she break into the printer's shop and check? What would they do if the Magisters defied the law and omitted the names of the people who had agreed to stand with Aldrich?

She liked the way Conrad Appleton dealt with details. She liked him. Aldrich had pulled her aside and asked her to join them in this meeting. He wanted her opinion about Mr. Appleton's sanity.

As far as she could tell, Conrad Appleton was in complete control of his faculties. He was a little odd perhaps, but in a very likeable way, and he knew absolutely everything about how the city worked.

As had been happening all morning, when Conrad paused for breath, Aldrich jumped in to redirect the flow of information. "I appreciate that," he said. "Do you know where the ballots are printed and under what security?"

"A most interesting question, Doctor Durante," said Appleton. "You clearly understand the risk of trusting the Magisters. The ballots are printed in the Tower. Everything having to do with the governing of Cairnisle happens in the Black Tower. As to security, I believe I can help with that. Why, I recall once how—"

"Pardon my interruption," said Aldrich. "Can you tell me as well, what else will be required if we ever hope to win the election?"

"That is easy, my dear Doctor Durante," Conrad replied, smiling and nodding. "Publicity. No one will vote for you if they do not recognize your name. We need to get your name— and the names of all the people who will run on the platform with you—out for the people to see. Did you know that very few citizens actually take advantage of their right to vote? Very often, Election Day comes and goes without attracting any particular notice. I have been tracking voter attendance for the last seven elections, and interestingly, the number of voters who register an address in Dirt Town is so small as to be inconsequential. That is not to say that Dirt Town residents are not permitted to vote—only that they do not choose to do so. There is your best audience. If you can get Dirt Town residents out to vote, it will turn the tides."

Aldrich jumped in again. "You did such a fine job of dealing with the paperwork, Mr. Appleton. I wonder if I might prevail upon you to make use of your expertise and take on publicity as well? I have no doubt that your thorough knowledge of the voters will make you invaluable in this process."

Conrad Appleton tapped his injured leg. "It will be my pleasure to serve," he answered, lowering his eyes. "After all, Doctor Durante, I owe my good health to you. Of course, you are welcome to any aid I might be able to offer."

Abruptly, the office door swung shut and the lock clanged into place. All down the corridor, the sound repeated.

Aldrich was the first on his feet. His face was white. "What is it?" he asked.

Fia went to the little window in the door and grabbed the bars to pull herself up. "I cannot see anything," she said.

"Are we under attack?" Aldrich demanded. He nudged her aside and rattled the handle.

"Maybe magic will work," Fia said. "Let me try."

Aldrich stepped aside, but before she could do anything, the door swung open on its own.

"It works!" Gustav shouted, his face alight with joy.

"What works?" asked Aldrich.

"The lock-down control," answered Gustav. "It functioned perfectly during the test. Did you see how the doors slammed shut instantly? It would be enough to hold everyone secure in the event of an unexpected attack." He flashed another grin and bounded off down the corridor.

With a grunt, Aldrich stalked back to his chair and flopped down. "He might have warned us," he said, letting out a shaky breath. Pulling out a handkerchief, he wiped a sheen of sweat from his forehead.

Mopping his own brow with a sharply creased white handkerchief, Conrad Appleton nodded. "Yes, well, I must admit the thought did cross my mind as well." He swallowed heavily before continuing. "Through all of our discussions here this morning, I believe I may have neglected to mention something important—although I fear you probably already are fully aware of the problem. The Magisters have made it clear that they are not pleased to have challengers. You will not be safe at any time during this election." The blood suddenly drained from his face, and he turned white. "And indeed, it is not impossible that the danger will remain if you win."

After a quick knock, Winston strolled through the open door. "Greetings, citizens," he said before handing Fia his tattered notebook.

She read the most recent message and jumped up. "He wants me to practise magic with him," she said. "If you do not need me here, I'll—"

"Go," said Aldrich, waving her away. "We will talk later."

"Thanks, Aldrich," she called as she headed to the door.

"See you, Conrad." Glad of the opportunity to move, she bounced down the corridor. "What are we working on?"

Balancing his notebook on one palm, Winston wrote while walking and passed it over to Fia.

She fell into step and read: *Munash asked me to continue your training. He has already covered control and release. You also need to be able to direct large quantities of magic accurately. Accurate throwing is the key to a successful magical attack. It requires the same motion as throwing a ball or any small object. When we get to the courtyard, I shall demonstrate.*

"Sounds good to me," Fia said. Munash's lessons had shown her how to access the reserve of magic she could feel simmering in her middle. After years of tamping it down, she had been a menace in the courtyard until she figured out how to regulate the flow. So far, except for the single eruption that had occurred when she first broke through the reserve, she had relied on pointing at something and willing the magic to hit the target.

It was a thrill every time. The little line of sparkling blue sprang from her fingertip like—well—it was like magic. She grinned as she trotted down the stairs to the courtyard.

Winston marched straight over to the charred and battered training dummy. Squaring up, he drew back his arm and threw three blasts of magic at the dummy, hitting it squarely on the head, the chest, and the leg in quick succession. Then he froze.

"Battery depleted," he said quietly. "Please recharge."

Fia laughed, a delighted giggle releasing all the tension that had gathered inside her since the day Aldrich was arrested. The giggle exploded into full-fledged hilarity. Helplessly, she dropped to the ground and gave in to the absurdity of his lesson.

After a minute or two, she collected herself enough to rise and unbutton the top button of Winston's coat. Wiping tears from her eyes, she recharged his battery. "Maybe you should limit your magic lessons to theory," she said with a chuckle. "I do not think you have the reserves for demonstrations!"

"Yes," he responded, and then, reaching for the notebook, he wrote: *I will ask Gustav if he can upgrade my power supply. However, you are right. I am not the best teacher for you. I did not learn my magic. It is part of my sequencing.*

A commotion at the far end of the training square drew their attention. Turning, they saw a bloodied man stagger through the entranceway and fall to his knees.

"What now?" Fia muttered as she darted across the courtyard. She took one look at the man's injuries and called to one of the soldiers, "Get Aldrich. He's in his office."

"No, I am here," said Aldrich. Someone handed him a first aid kit, and he knelt beside the man. "Tell me what happened."

"There's fighting in Dirt Town," the man said through gritted teeth. "The City Guards came down. Robots. Hundreds of them. They're killing everyone they can find." His breath hissed out as Aldrich applied an alcohol-soaked rag to his forehead. Although he was covered in blood, it appeared to be his only injury.

"Munash and Silver," Fia breathed.

"No one will hurt Munash," Aldrich said. "And he will make sure Silver is safe."

Winston tapped Fia on the shoulder, and when she turned, he handed her his notebook. She read: *I will go down there. Perhaps I can be of assistance.*

"Winston and I are going down," Fia announced.

Aldrich looked up. "No," he said. "I cannot allow you to do that. It is far too dangerous."

Fia bristled. "Those are my friends," she said. "I can help. Winston can help." Her voice rose, and she backed away. "I can take care of myself."

"I'm going too," said Benj. "I'll find Silver. We'll find out what's going on."

Aldrich looked up at Fia and held her gaze. He swallowed hard and turned his attention back to his patient. "Please, be careful," he said as he finished tying off a bandage. "And take care of each other."

Security Assured

In a recent address to the citizens of our fair city, Grand Magister Augustus Köhler sought to allay any fears regarding the nefarious activities of Doctor Aldrich Durante. With a tone of resolute authority, the esteemed Magister proclaimed, "The situation is well within our control. There is no cause for alarm."

-from The Cairnisle Times,
Sunday, May 5, Year 27 AK

THIRTY-NINE ~ ALDRICH

"THIS IS A BEAUTIFUL PLACE," said Rupert Corvington as he descended from the automatized carriage in front of Aldrich's parents' home.

Aldrich closed his eyes and breathed in deeply. Wealth afforded space and beauty. The richness of the scents was dizzying. Did the people who lived below the estate in Dirt Town get any of the benefits of the spreading gardens? Or did the extra watering just make their roofs drip?

He studied the carefully tended flowers and trees that surrounded the big brick house where he had grown up. Had he met anyone whose house was right underneath the property? What did they think of it? His brows drew together, and he stared out at the road. Did the bridge that he had crossed so often offer the nearest access point to the world below? Were the workers from Dirt Town? Why had he never asked?

"It is beautiful," Aldrich agreed. Pushing his hair off his forehead, he led the way up the stairs to ring the bell.

Calder opened the door and blinked. "Sir," he said. "We did not expect you."

Aldrich reached out and shook his hand.

After stiffening slightly, Calder relaxed and returned the grip.

"Calder, it is good to see you," Aldrich said. It surprised him to find how true it was. Calder had been a part of his life for as long as he could recall.

"It is always a pleasure to see you, sir," Calder replied. His words were as formal as ever, but a twinkle in his eyes betrayed his own feelings. "Your parents are in the sitting room, sir."

"Thank you," Aldrich said. He stepped aside and clasped Corvington's elbow. "Calder, do you know my friend, Rupert Corvington?"

"Pleased to meet you," Corvington said, grasping Calder's hand and pumping it up and down.

Calder's wide eyes darted between Aldrich and Corvington. "A pleasure, sir," he murmured.

Pretending to ignore the effect his newfound manners were having on the man who had served him all his life, Aldrich cleared his throat. "We will just go through then," he said. "Thank you, Calder."

As he led Corvington into the house, Aldrich felt Calder's eyes burning into his back. It was uncomfortable to realize just what a privileged life he had lived.

At the door to the sitting room, Aldrich paused. Accustomed to people bustling around in their vicinity, his parents did not look up from their books. He let his eyes rest on their familiar profiles and a knot unwound in his belly.

"Hello, Mother," he said. "Father."

Their heads jerked up in unison, and then his mother was on her feet. She hurried across the room and enveloped him in a welcoming hug. "Aldrich, we have been so worried," she said. "The papers say that you are accused of murder. And now treason for defying the Magisters." She broke off, pushing him away to peer into his eyes. "Is it safe for you to be here?"

With a grim smile, Aldrich answered, "As safe as anywhere, I suppose." He shook his father's hand, and his smile became genuine. "I cannot tell you how happy I am to see you both."

"Sit down, Aldrich," said his father. "We have received your letters, but we want to hear it from you."

"Yes, of course," said Aldrich, "but first, I would like to present Rupert Corvington, the former Commandant of the City Guards. Rupert, these are my parents, Lady Mary and Lord Frederick Durante."

Corvington bowed over his mother's hand and said, "Lady Mary, it is a pleasure to meet you." Then he turned to Frederick and shook his hand. "Lord Frederick, always a pleasure."

"Rupert, I was most disappointed to hear of your replacement by a robot," said Lord Frederick. He scowled. "I am not at all certain we are headed in the right direction with that idea."

"Let us sit," said Aldrich, leading the way to the settees clustered around the massive fireplace. He could feel time ticking away. Lowering himself to the padded seat, he leaned back and waited while the other three joined him. "We have to talk."

"I told you in my letter," said Lord Frederick. "You have my complete support."

Aldrich held his father's eyes. "You realize the risk?" he

asked. "If you put your name on the ballot with me and we do not win, the Magisters will not be kind."

Drawing in a sharp breath, Lord Frederick hesitated only a moment. "If you are going to challenge them in the election," he said slowly. "I would be honoured to see my name beside your own."

Lady Mary had gone pale. "You are planning to go ahead with this plan," she murmured. "I had almost hoped you would see the difficulties as too much." Her lips thinned to a white line, and she clasped her hands together. "So be it. I will do whatever I can to help." Her chin lifted. "For starters, I am coming with you."

"I would not have it any other way," answered Aldrich, his voice hitching. He swallowed hard. His parents would be safer inside the walls of the fortress with an army to protect them. His biggest worry had been that the Magisters might try to take their revenge on him by punishing them. He grinned. "I must warn you that the accommodations at our fortress are much less agreeable than those to which you are accustomed."

"In fact, the single redeeming feature is the high-security wall," added Corvington with a wry smile.

"I am certain we will be fine," said Lady Mary, rising from the settee. "If you will please excuse me, I will begin preparations immediately."

A thunderous pounding sounded at the front door, and she froze, her hand halfway to her throat.

"Open this door!" The voice belonged to a Green Coat robot Captain.

Calder appeared in the entrance of the sitting room. Lifting one smooth eyebrow, he said, "I presume that you do not wish me to answer that."

Corvington's voice cut through the room. "Get down!" he bellowed. "Stay low. I will wager a month's pay that where there is one robot, there are others. And they will have guns aimed at all the windows."

Lady Mary sank to her knees. "What do they want?" she whispered.

"They are after me," answered Aldrich. "I am so sorry. I should not have come."

"No time for regrets," rumbled Corvington, his voice steady. "We knew the risks. And we are not about to surrender to robots." He jerked his head at the window. "Take a look, Aldrich. Can you see how many there are?"

Lifting a small mirror from the table at his side, Aldrich scooted over to the window. He kept his head well below the sill and raised the mirror, stopping as soon as he caught a glimpse of the yard. "The house is surround—"

A bullet smashed through the windowpane and into the mirror, spraying shards of glass everywhere.

With a yelp, Aldrich rolled over onto his stomach and clutched his hands over his head.

"Aldrich," cried his mother. "Are you hurt?"

"I am fine, Mother," he answered, shaking his head to rid himself of the tiny slivers of glass that had landed on him. "The house is surrounded by Blue Coats. We need an alternate method of escape. As far as I could see, there is only one Green Coat. He is the one at the front door."

Corvington turned to Lord Frederick. "Can we access the garage?" he asked. "How many automatized carriages do you have?"

"We have three automatized carriages in the garage," answered Lord Frederick. He gestured to the swinging door at the far end of the sitting room. "We can access it right through here."

"I am the only one who is armed," Corvington said. "Are there weapons in the house?"

"We have a number of rifles and shotguns for recreational shooting," answered Lord Frederick. "Calder—"

"I am on it, sir," said the butler. He scuttled from the room on his hands and knees.

Two round-eyed maidservants scurried in from a different door.

The little blond one screeched, "There are robots—"

Lady Mary snatched at their hands. "Get down, girls," she said, pulling them down beside her. "The robots have guns."

Calder was back, pushing a tea cart loaded with rifles, shotguns, and boxes of ammunition ahead of him. "We have guns too," he said. "Just be calm, Sally. We will have you girls out of here in no time." He pulled a shotgun from the pile, loaded it, and handed it to Aldrich. "I take it you remember what to do with this, young sir?"

Aldrich grunted. "Your lessons were not entirely in vain," he said. "Point it, squeeze the trigger, and hope for the best."

"That's it," said Calder. "Although, I do not recall teaching you to hope. The idea was for you to practise."

"Somehow guns never held my attention," answered Aldrich. "Right now, I wish I had tried harder."

"If I recall correctly, you had best wait until the target is close," said Calder with the lift of an eyebrow.

Aldrich laughed aloud. "Too true," he said.

Corvington crawled over to the armoury and chose a shotgun and a rifle to add to his pistol and sword. While he loaded them, he said, "Calder, you seem an experienced hand. Would you consent to stay with me? We can cover the others' escape in the carriages."

"I will stay too," said Aldrich. "This is all my doing."

"Actually," said Corvington, "I had hoped that you might bring an automatized carriage around to the front to pick up Calder and me. We will take care of the Green Coat. Without a leader, the Blue Coats will be more easily confused."

"I can do that," Aldrich agreed.

"So," murmured Lord Frederick. "We have a plan." He picked up a shotgun, loaded it, and filled his pockets with extra shells. "Jane, you and Sally come with me and Lady Mary," he said. Cradling the gun, he used his legs to propel himself along the polished floor toward the garage entrance. "Keep your heads down."

Pushing the cart ahead of him, Calder slithered over to the window. In the meantime, Corvington crawled toward the front door where the pounding continued.

Over his shoulder, Calder called, "I will see you out front in a few minutes, sir."

"I will be there," Aldrich replied. Gripping his rifle more tightly, he hurried after his mother and father.

As he pushed through the swinging door to the garage, he heard the first shots.

Sally screamed and covered her head. "They are going to kill us all!" she cried.

"Stay calm," Aldrich said. "We will get out of here."

"Come along, Sally," called Lord Frederick from the blue automatized carriage in which he always travelled. "You too, Jane. Ride with me and Lady Mary. Sit on the floor and pull this blanket over your heads. We will keep you safe."

Aldrich climbed into the green carriage. It was the same one he had borrowed from his mother when he escorted Wilhelmina to the masquerade ball. It seemed so long ago. Closing his eyes, he blew out a slow breath.

"Father, you go first," he called. "Head to the Fortress. Instruct your carriage to go at full speed the instant it leaves the garage. I will be right behind you as soon as I pick up Calder and Rupert."

"Are you ready?" shouted Lord Frederick.

"Ready," answered Aldrich as he hunkered down below the wide windows and pulled his coat over his head. If the windows were hit, there would be glass everywhere.

"Garage door open," ordered Lord Frederick.

At once, the garage door slid smoothly open, and the automatized carriage carrying Aldrich's parents barrelled out along the track, accelerating as it passed the front of the house and racing up the drive at breakneck speed.

Several of the Blue Coat robots fired their rifles at the speeding vehicle, but it was going too fast, and the passengers were out of sight below the windows. Aldrich let out a breath as the vehicle vanished up the road.

"Carriage 1421, go," he ordered. "Full speed. Stop at the front entrance."

The automatized carriage shot out of the garage and careened around the corner to the front entrance, where it stopped so suddenly that Aldrich was thrown up against the front bank of leather seats. He scrambled back and aimed the shotgun at the entrance.

Gunfire came from every direction. A bullet thudded into the metal body of the carriage, and he flinched, wanting to curl up in a ball. Then the window above him shattered, and glass shards cascaded over his back and head. Setting his teeth, he kicked open the door.

Calder was in the sitting room window, a rifle pressed to his shoulder as he squeezed off one careful shot after another. By the look of satisfaction on his face, he was hitting the target every time. It was not surprising. Calder had been Aldrich's weapons teacher. Though he had been unsuccessful in teaching Aldrich to shoot well, he had certainly mastered the skill himself.

Aldrich craned his neck to look over the lawns. Over half of the Blue Coats had been disabled. Scattered around the yard, they lay on their backs as if they had chosen that moment for a nap.

On the front step, Corvington battled the Green Coat with his sword. A master swordsman, he was a joy to watch. However, he could not get past the robot's defences. Every stroke was met—almost as if the machine could anticipate his moves. Had Corvington been involved in the sequencing of the robots?

A gun cracked, and Corvington dropped to his knees, pressing a hand to his stomach.

With a grunt, Aldrich rolled from the carriage amidst the crunching glass and charged at the robot, which had raised its sword to finish off Corvington.

Lifting his rifle to his shoulder as he covered the last few steps, he waited until he was close enough to see the glowing eye and then fired.

The robot shuddered to a stop.

Aldrich's tongue stuck to the roof of his mouth as he thrust his arm through the rifle strap and stooped to grasp Corvington under his arms.

He heaved up, but Corvington's dead weight did not budge. Clenching his jaw, he tried again. He could not do it. The man was too heavy.

Then Calder burst through the front door and grabbed one of Corvington's arms. "Ready, sir?" he shouted.

"Go," cried Aldrich.

Together, they hoisted the bleeding man up and dragged him down the stairs.

Despite a few brutal knocks on the steps, they managed to get him into the carriage.

Corvington's assessment of the Blue Coats had been correct. Without a Green Coat to renew their orders, the remaining robots continued to shoot at the house, ignoring the carriage.

Aldrich and Calder dove in after Corvington. Pulling the door closed and squeezing into the only remaining space on the floor, Aldrich shouted, "Carriage 1421. Go! Full speed!"

Crime Sweep in Dirt Town

The long-awaited campaign to rid our fair city of the rogues and miscreants who plague the law-abiding populace has commenced in earnest. Yesterday, Commandant Forge-37 dispatched four substantial contingents of robots to Dirt Town to execute this mission.

In a statement to the press, Commandant Forge-37 reassured citizens, saying, "You may hear the occasional burst of gunfire, but it is no cause for alarm. The operations are proceeding as planned. Cairnisle will be all the better for this cleansing."

-from The Cairnisle Times,
Sunday, May 5, Year 27 AK

FORTY ~ WILHELMINA

"WHY DIDN'T YOU WIPE OUT the robots?" Willy asked as she hurried through the tunnel at Munash's side. "I saw what you did. You could have stopped them all."

Her leg felt perfectly fine. There was not even a hint of pain where a bullet had ripped through the flesh and lodged itself in the big bone of her thigh. Only the hardening bloodstain on her leather trousers around the little round hole gave any indication that she had been shot. The same was true of the injury to her arm. She licked her lips. What did it take to become a mage? Could anyone do it?

"I stopped the Green Coats," he answered. "That will throw the Blue Coats into disarray. It would take too long to stop them all. Right now, I need you to carry a message to the fortress."

Grabbing his wrist, Willy jerked him to a stop. "Wait!" she cried. "Are you sending me away to keep me safe?"

Munash let out a breath of laughter. "I am asking you to find Aldrich and tell him what happened," he said.

"I could stay and help shoot robots," she said. There were enough to make it fun. "Someone else could take a message."

"Someone else did take a message," Munash answered. "I sent someone up as soon as the robots arrived. But they cannot know the current situation. And you will have been reported dead." He waved that away and started walking again. "The primary reason for sending you is so that you can tell them about these catacombs."

Stretching her stride to keep up, she studied the tunnel. Clearly visible in the glow from the small, round globe that Munash carried in his outstretched palm, it was easily wide enough for them to walk abreast. Even Munash, as tall as he was, had plenty of headroom. Large rectangular niches were cut into the rough stone at regular intervals.

"What is this place?" she asked. "I've never heard of it. Does anyone else know it's here?" She found it difficult to believe that her network of spies had not picked up at least a whisper of its existence. "How long have you known it was here?"

Munash chuckled. "So many questions, my dear," he said with a click of his tongue. Then he smiled. "It is an ancient place. I believe the catacombs are mostly natural. They have been enlarged in a few spots and access points were added. As far as I can tell, it was used as a burial ground for a very long time and then forgotten." He spoke quietly, but the sound of his voice bounced back from the stone surfaces, amplifying it and adding solemnity to his words. "I do not believe that others know it is here. I have visited many times to explore and have never seen recent evidence of anyone else."

He smiled down at her. "As for how long I have known? It is a discovery I made long ago." He cleared his throat. "You are too young to remember, but I came to Cairnisle at the tail end of Cairn's failed attempt to build an empire. For fifteen years, I fought for my homeland against the Cairnite invaders. For fifteen years, fighting was all I knew. Until one day, I made a mistake. Instead of killing me, the Cairnites took me prisoner." He hummed three notes of a song and fell silent.

Willy had been around Munash long enough to know that she did not need to ask more questions to get him talking. He would continue when he was ready. She wriggled two fingers under her mask and pressed against the spot on her cheek where the bullet had hit. It was beginning to throb.

Engrossed in her examination of the injury, she jumped when Munash started to speak again.

"At the end, when the Cairnites finally decided to abandon the fight, they took their prisoners of war and went home." For the first time, bitterness crept into his voice. "They wanted to put us on trial to make themselves look better." He hummed the same three notes. "I escaped. Alone. And I ended up in Dirt Town."

Their footsteps, muffled by a soft layer of dust, were the only sound.

"I expect you know how easy it is to disappear in Dirt Town," he said. "Like everyone else, I lived hand to mouth, uncertain where I might find my next meal. For a long time, that was all I could manage. Then, I began to look around me.

That is when I realized how wrong everything about Cairnisle was. Dirt Town was what Cairn had wanted to do to my country.

"I made friends, and I did what I could to help. I found the tall house in the square. No one had lived in it for years. Everyone said it was haunted, but no one could remember why. That made me curious. There is often an element of truth behind any story.

"The stories did not particularly frighten me. As more people came to me for counsel, it was convenient to have a central spot, so everyone knew where to find me.

"Not long after I claimed the house, I went poking around. In the cellar, a portion of the wall broke away to reveal these tunnels. What could I do?" he asked, lifting his free hand in a helpless gesture and smiling down at Willy. "I went exploring. Since that time, I have learned much of Dirt Town's history. Did you know that originally, Dirt Town was where the slaves of Cairnisle lived?"

Willy's head snapped up. "What?" she asked. "The mage slaves lived down here?"

"No, not them," replied Munash. "The slaves who built the city." He glanced sideways at her. "I would bet that you did not even know the city was built by slaves." He sighed. "They raised those beautiful stone buildings on the land above. But at night, they were sent down the ladders to eke out their lives at the bottom of the gorges. Every bridge they built up above gave them access to a new part of town down below. They built their homes in every available space, even digging the short, surface tunnels to connect the different areas. These levels, I believe, were excavated for use as an underground cemetery."

Ahead, the tunnel widened. In the centre of the floor was a hole.

Willy picked her way close to the edge and peered down into the black depths. An ancient ladder leaned up against the rim.

"You do not want to go down there," Munash warned. He cleared his throat. "In my early explorations, I climbed down. It is not an experience I care to repeat. The lower I went, the worse I felt. It was like an evil presence was worming its way inside me—deep, cold and sickening."

"Where do you suppose it leads?" she asked as she edged past the hole's rim and continued along the tunnel.

"I am not certain I want to know," Munash replied. "The part I visited looked similar to this, with the niches every two feet."

"What are the niches for anyway?" Willy asked as she stopped in front of one, peering blindly into the black hollow.

"Have a look," Munash said. He moved beside her and extended his light into the niche.

Nestled in the little alcove was a skeleton.

Willy took a step back. "Are they all like this?" she asked. "How many are there?"

"Thousands," he answered. "This entire level, plus at least one more below, is filled with them. I do not know how far down it extends because I could not stay there long enough to investigate." He started down the corridor, holding the light higher and using it to examine the rock. When they came to a crossroads, he hesitated briefly before muttering, "It is this way."

They walked only a short distance down the new corridor before Munash stopped and studied the rock again, moving the light about. Finally, he let out an exhalation and said, "Here it is."

Willy could not see what he was looking at until she stepped to his side. There, she made out a ladder carved into the stone.

It was only visible when the light hit it at the perfect angle. It led from the floor to the ceiling and stopped.

Munash placed the globe of light on the floor, where it dimmed a little before flaring up brightly. Then he pulled himself up onto the ladder. On the third rung, he stopped and reached up one hand to push on the ceiling.

A thunderous scrape echoed through the corridor and a crack of light appeared.

Clambering up two more rungs, he peered through the gap and threw back the hatch. "Here we are," he said, as he climbed the last two steps and pulled himself up into the room above. "Please, bring the light."

Gingerly, Willy picked up the globe. Unexpectedly cool, it vibrated slightly in her hand and dimmed. Gritting her teeth, she climbed one-handed. Her head poked into a tiny space that smelled faintly of dogs.

Munash stepped aside, his neck bent at an awkward angle to accommodate the low ceiling. "Give me the light," he murmured, hunching down.

Willy handed it over and hauled herself through the hole, swinging her body around and sitting with her legs dangling down. Three of the four walls of the room were made from decaying wood while the fourth was of exposed stone. A small door, hinged with leather straps, hung crookedly on the farthest wall.

"I will leave you here," said Munash as he extinguished his light, leaving them in semi-darkness lit only by a thin stream of dust-filled light coming through a hole in a broken board. "Find Aldrich and Corvington. Tell them everything." He frowned. "It is time to put that army we have been training to use. Tell Corvington to plan an offense that takes advantage of these tunnels. Now that you know where to find it, you will be able to lead them to this spot and enter. I will return to my house to see what may be done."

Willy studied the hole in the floor, her eyebrows drawing together. "How was this never found?" she asked. "That hatch is perfectly visible."

Munash's white teeth flashed. "Magic," he said. "Make sure you bring Fiametta along when you return. It can only be opened by a mage."

Border Guard Success

Mainland Cairn once again breathes a sigh of relief as our valiant border guards repelled yet another audacious assault by the notorious Jarlerus the Scourge and his unruly horde. The unwavering dedication and exceptional training of our soldiers have secured the safety of our citizens, providing a cause for widespread celebration and gratitude.

However, amidst this triumph, a pertinent question arises: would our nation remain as secure under the stewardship of the untested Doctor Aldrich Durante?

-from The Cairnisle Times,
Sunday, May 5, Year 27 AK

FORTY-ONE ~ ALDRICH

ALDRICH FUMBLED WITH THE SATCHEL he had grabbed from the shelf in his parents' garage. When he tossed a first aid kit, some towels, and a bottle of brandy into its depths, he had not imagined he would be performing surgery on the floor of an automatized carriage while it careened along the streets.

He unbuttoned Corvington's red coat and pushed it aside along with the bloodstained shirt. The injury was severe. The patient was unconscious, pale, and clammy, while the pulse in his throat fluttered weakly.

There was a lot of blood. The bullet had entered the lower abdomen on the right side just above the hipbone. There was no exit wound, and the heavy bleeding indicated damage to the colon.

"Get his head," said Aldrich. "Help me shift him onto his back."

Keeping his own head below the level of the windows, Calder edged over and cradled Corvington's head and shoulders while Aldrich gently pulled him flat onto the floor. He bent Corvington's long legs and let the carriage door hold them in place.

Next, he poured a liberal amount of the alcohol over the wound and used it to cleanse his hands. "This will require surgery," he said. "Right now, all I can do is try to control the bleeding." He reached one-handed into the satchel, rooting around until his fingers closed on a paper sachet filled with seaweed cellulose. Using his teeth, he tore it open and poured it into the wound. Next, he pressed a sterile cotton dressing against the little hole and held it in place. "Are any carriages pursuing us?"

"I believe so, sir," murmured Calder. "I cannot see well enough to be certain, but it appears that the carriage behind us is filled with robots. They must have figured out that their target was escaping."

"And my parents? Are they far ahead?" Aldrich asked.

Calder put his hands on the green leather seat and raised his head to look.

A bullet pinged off the carriage's metal exterior, and he dropped to the floor.

"They are far enough ahead that I cannot see them," Calder said with a grimace. "But remember, they left several minutes before us."

"The road ahead?" Aldrich asked. "Is it clear?"

"As far as I could see," Calder replied. He wriggled sideways to make room for his legs and settled more comfortably.

"Let's hope it stays that way," muttered Aldrich. They both knew the automatized carriage would slow for any traffic despite its orders to make speed. And then what would happen?

Clearing his throat, he turned his attention back to Corvington, examining the seaweed he had packed into the wound. "The bleeding has slowed," he said. "But when we get to the fortress, I am going to have to operate."

"I do not suppose we will be able to drive right in?" Calder asked.

Aldrich gave a short shake of his head and then, sucking in a breath, rose up to check their location. A bullet hit the rear window with a crack, and he dove down. "We are almost there," he said. "As soon as we stop, get ready to run." He pressed his lips together. "We will need to carry Corvington again. With any luck, Father will have prepared them for our arrival, and they will have people standing by."

As the carriage rolled to a stop, there were shouts and the rumbling of the gate mechanism. Then gunfire rattled from the top of the wall.

Clenching his teeth, Aldrich raised his head to look back. His breath came out in a gasp. "The robots are backing up," he said, throwing open the carriage door. "Let us move while there is time."

Three men, including his father, ran out of the fortress.

Gasping for breath, Lord Frederick halted and stared at Aldrich. "You are hurt," he said.

"Not me," Aldrich answered, moving aside to reveal Corvington's motionless form. "Help us get him inside. He requires surgery."

Together, they heaved the big man out of the carriage, up the ramp, and through the entrance. As soon as they were inside, the gate rumbled shut.

"My surgery is the third door on the right," Aldrich panted. When his surgical equipment was delivered, he had wanted to set up on the top floor where the light was better. But it was not practical to carry injured people up all the stairs and through the maze of corridors, so he had chosen the least disgusting of the cells near the entrance.

They squeezed through the door and Aldrich said, "Put him on the table."

Carrying Corvington's left shoulder, Calder edged up to the operating table. "On three," he said. "One—two—three."

They slid the former Commandant onto the polished steel operating table and stood back, breathing hard.

"What can we do to help?" asked Lord Frederick.

Aldrich looked at his father. His skin was clammy and slightly green. In fact, all four men had the greenish cast that came from an unfamiliarity with blood. It had been a common sight during his first years of medical training.

"I can take care of things from here," he said, leaning over to study the hole in Corvington's abdomen.

"We will leave you to it then," said Lord Frederick, looking all too relieved.

"Are you sure?" asked Calder. "I could—"

He broke off as Aldrich lifted the cloth from a tray of sterilized implements and selected a scalpel. His face went from green to bone white and he stumbled after the others. "My apologies," he gasped as he let the door swing shut behind him.

Aldrich frowned and stared around the dark stone cell with its single tiny window. He missed the pristine, white-tiled surgery of his clinic. He missed Letta. He grinned to himself. Why had he been so hard on her? She was invaluable as an assistant in the operating room. Nothing affected her easy temper, and she was extremely co-ordinated.

Perhaps she could be persuaded to join them in the fortress. There were likely to be more opportunities for surgery. He shrugged. For this procedure, he would have to make do on his own.

The next time Aldrich looked up, the sun had set, and the tiny window was dark. The lamps he had set up around the operating table were the only illumination in the room. Stepping back, he picked up the bowl containing the two bullet fragments he had managed to locate.

Just as he had suspected, the colon had been ruptured. He had repaired the damage with sutures and then worked his way back to the surface, closing up the layers. Fortunately, Corvington had remained unconscious throughout the operation.

But now Aldrich wanted to see him wake up. He checked his pulse again. The laboured breathing had improved. Still pale, the Commandant's skin did not look as glassy as it had before Aldrich found the source of the bleeding and stitched it up.

Rubbing his scratchy eyes, Aldrich dropped into the wooden chair by the door. He had to keep watch until Corvington woke up. Then perhaps, he could prevail upon Calder to sit by the bed.

His eyelids had begun to droop when the cell door swung open. Blinking, he snapped upright.

Wilhelmina stuck her head through the gap. "I heard," she said. "How is he?"

Rising, Aldrich stretched his arms above his head and yawned. "He should wake up soon," he said.

She stepped into the room, and he looked at her more closely. The sleeve of her leather coat and the thigh of her trousers were crusted in dried blood. The smiling mask showed a gash where the paint on the cheek had been scraped away.

"What happened?" he demanded, stepping closer. "Are those bullet holes?" Would he need to operate on her as well? His eyes darted to Corvington. Could he move him yet?

The cell was the closest thing he had to a sterile environment. Three soldiers had spent an entire day scrubbing the walls, floors, and ceiling.

Slumping into the chair he had just vacated, Wilhelmina waved away his concern. "I'm fine," she said. "Munash fixed me up. Did you know he can use magic to heal?" She pushed her mask up on top of her head. Her face, as beautiful as ever, looked hot and sweaty, and a large purple bruise covered much of the left side. She pushed up her sleeve and held out her arm for his examination.

A round white scar stood out in the dried blood. "He fixed bullet holes?" Aldrich asked, with a slow disbelieving shake of his head. His eyes wandered over to Corvington who, after his efforts, did not look nearly as healthy as Wilhelmina.

"Practically as good as new," she said, smirking at him. Then the smile disappeared. "The robot City Guards are attacking Dirt Town. Munash got me out and sent me to warn you. He went back to see what he could do. They are killing everyone."

Aldrich felt the blood rush from his face. "We heard about the attack," he said. "Fia is down there with Winston."

Unqualified Doctor

Aldrich Durante, a fledgling youth, presumes that attaining his medical certification before the age of twenty-one qualifies him to govern the entirety of Cairn.

"Citizens need not concern themselves with this pretender," stated Deutero Magister Ingrid Jaeger. "Your esteemed Magisters stand ready to safeguard the peace and security of our great nation."

-from The Cairnisle Times,
Sunday, May 5, Year 27 AK

FORTY-TWO ~ FIAMETTA

ROBOTS WERE EVERYWHERE.

"It's getting dark," Fia whispered. "It will be easier if we wait."

Benj leaned forward, pressing his eye against the hole in the board. "I don't like waiting," he said. "Silver will be expecting me. I'm not one to disappoint."

Fia frowned. They had made it to the broken-down shack across from Munash's house, but it had not been easy. Most of the robots wandering around Dirt Town were Blue Coats. They did not ask questions or give warnings. They shot to kill.

Only their combined knowledge of the secret routes had

gotten them this far. Everywhere they went, they had seen men, women, even children and babies, who had been shot and left for dead. Telltale smears of blood in the dust showed where bodies had been dragged away. How many injured people were hidden away? Who was treating them?

Fia tapped Benj on the shoulder. "Can I look?" she whispered.

"Have at it," Benj replied, crawling out of the way.

She scuttled into place and peered through the gap. One Green Coat robot who looked exactly like Winston was standing only a few yards away. Her stomach clenched. Would he sense her magic?

Benj touched her shoulder. "I'll go up on the roof," he said into her ear, pointing at the broken-down overhang above them. "If I provide covering fire, Winston can approach the front door. With his green coat, the other robots won't try to stop him."

Winston nodded sharply. He could not risk speaking for fear of being heard.

Tramping feet made Fia press her eye to the hole again just in time to see another robot squadron march into the square. At their head was a different sort of robot. Instead of a skull like Winston's, he had a fully moulded face, including a beard.

Fia pulled back and gestured for Benj to look.

"It's Forge-37," he whispered, sitting up and rubbing his chin. "The new Commandant."

The robot marched to Munash's front step, climbed to the blue door, and turned to face the square. His visible audience was made up entirely of robots, although if he meant only to address them, he would have used the whirring clicks. There was no doubt that his words were aimed at the humans hidden nearby.

He clasped his hands together and raised them above his

head in a sign of victory. "We are the long arms of the Magisters," he said in a strangely unaccented voice. "Together, we protect the city from those who live beneath the ground like rats. Prepare for their purge."

Without warning, Winston darted out of his hiding place, raised his rifle to his shoulder, aimed at Forge-37, and fired three shots in quick succession, emptying his gun.

The bullets pinged off the robot Commandant's metal exterior without leaving even a dent. Forge-37 swung around to face Winston while at the same time emitting a grinding noise that set Fia's teeth on edge.

Then her breath caught in her throat. Was that laughter? It raised the hair on the back of her neck.

Every robot whirled and aimed their weapons at Winston.

"Stand down," ordered Forge-37. "I will take care of this threat. It appears one of our own has gone rogue." With the grace of a cat, he leapt from the step to the middle of the square. It was an impossible distance. Removing his hat, he handed it to the closest Green Coat. "Take care of this, my good Captain. It is worth more than you."

Winston drew his sword and stalked forward to meet Forge-37. "Criminal on the loose," he said. "Stop criminal!"

The horrible grinding noise came again as Forge-37 glided across the square. "A rebel who is limited to a tiny vocabulary of pre-recorded commands," he said. "How very frustrating that must be." Not hurrying, he drew his sword. "You think you can challenge me? I am the product of years of research. I am not just a robot; I am humanity perfected. It could never be a fair fight."

Covering the last ten feet in a leap, he slashed down on Winston's arm. "Not that a fair fight matters to me," he said, stabbing his sword into Winston's gut where the bulk of his system was concealed.

The light in Winston's eye blinked out as his system deactivated and he froze.

Fia started up. "I've got to go to him," she hissed, heading for the exit.

Benj grabbed her arm and yanked her back. "Wait," he muttered in her ear. "There's nothing you can do now. We'll get him when they leave. Gustav can fix him."

Grain Delivery Welcome

A vessel bearing a substantial consignment of wheat made port at the Cairnisle shipyards yesterday, bringing much-needed relief to our beleaguered granaries.

"The recent shortages were due to the unprovoked attacks by Jarlerus the Scourge," declared Grand Magister Augustus Köhler. "This timely shipment will significantly bolster our city's provisions and alleviate the hardships faced by our citizens."

-from The Cairnisle Times,
Tuesday, May 7, Year 27 AK

FORTY-THREE ~ WILHELMINA

CHAFING AT THE NECESSITY FOR languid elegance, Willy lifted the two cups of tea from the sideboard and glided over to her father. Cold-eyed, he accepted the delicate porcelain cup and saucer and set it aside untouched.

"It is nice to see you, Father," she murmured as she settled onto the settee opposite him with a soft crinkle of petticoats. She had not been home since the day of the Magisters' announcement, and she found it an effort to regain her façade of obedient daughter.

Normally, she enjoyed the deceit. However, the events of

the past days were too close. It no longer felt like a game. She had come to care about Aldrich. That felt real. Watching robots gun down people in the streets of Dirt Town felt real. Her injuries, despite being completely healed, felt real.

When Aldrich asked her to speak with her father to discover where he stood on the matter of the election, she had agreed to pay a visit to the world of dresses and luxury. However, she would have been far happier never to return home. Living in the fortress meant never giving up her freedom.

Aldrich had reminded her that she wanted it to be interesting. She hid a smile behind a sip of tea. Sparring with her father would be a challenge. With him, it would be real victory to uncover what they wanted to know without tipping her hand.

Placing the cup back on its saucer, she kept her eyes on the pretty yellow flower painted along its rim. It was almost the same colour as the dress she had chosen for its long sleeves that would cover her new scar.

"Father," she said lightly, "you have been so busy. I feel I have hardly seen you lately. Have you taken on a new client?" She hated the simpering in her voice. She sounded like a brainless twit.

It was always like this with her father. She was there as an exhibition of his power and authority, to be seen at her best— the very model of feminine perfection. She hated what he made her do. She hated him.

At the same time, James never shied from talking to her about the business of banking. He considered Wilhelmina the heir to all he had accomplished—an ornamental heir perhaps, but a useful ornament. Often, he gave the impression that he did not expect her to understand all that he told her. She hated that he underestimated her even as she prepared to use his misjudgement to her advantage.

James examined his daughter, his forehead tightening in a way that Willy recognized.

"You know perfectly well that the reason you have not seen me is that you have not been here," he said. His voice held the coldness he usually reserved for servants who had displeased him.

Willy affected an expression of hurt disbelief. "Why, Father," she said, "whatever do you mean? You know I have been visiting Priya." A friend since childhood, Priya was a handy excuse whenever she needed to disappear for a time. She never had a problem lying for Willy.

"No, you weren't," replied her father. "I checked. Where were you?" His threatening expression did not change, and for the first time, Willy doubted her ability to fool him.

She laughed, a pretty tinkling sound. "Father, I am twenty-two," she said as she raised the cup to her lips. "Perhaps you do not wish to know the answer to that question." Leaning forward, she set her cup and saucer on the low table separating them. When she sat up again and met his eyes, her smile was in place.

"I do not particularly care how old you are," he snapped. "When I ask a question, I expect an answer." Then, setting his cup and saucer down as well, he settled back and crossed one leg over the other. "I think you should know that I have restricted your access to your banking accounts."

Behind her perfectly unruffled face, Willy's mind whirled. What could he possibly know? "Father," she said, "I do not understand. Have I displeased you?" Again, the simpering grated painfully. She was proud that her expression gave nothing away, even as she considered how she would like to wipe the haughtiness from her father's face.

He leaned forward and hissed, "What were you thinking? Did you imagine that you could join this petty little mutiny, and I would not find out? Aldrich Durante will lose this election. And then where will you be?"

Willy rocked back. He knew. How did he know? What could she tell him to throw him off?

His smug smile did not reach his eyes. Crossing his arms, he eased back onto the settee. "I was right," he said. "You cannot even defend yourself." His lip curled and he shook his head. "Did you really believe you could fool me? That I would be happy to finance such a misguided enterprise?" Raising his voice, he called, "Come."

In response to his command, the sitting room door flew open to admit one of her father's personal bodyguards. Moving with unexpected speed, he crossed the room to stand behind Willy.

Understanding the implied threat, she did not look at him. Instead, she kept her eyes on her father, who was the real danger.

"Please do not try to beat me at my own game," James von Richtofen said. "You are wondering what exactly I know. No doubt, you are trying to decide how you can win in this little contest of secrets." His face remained cold as he picked up his teacup again. He sipped and raised an eyebrow. "You probably even believe you can beat me." He gave the smallest of nods to the guard.

Willy cursed her dress as she pushed away from the settee.

The guard was faster. He reached over the seatback and seized her arm. Squeezing hard enough to make the bones grind against each other, he pushed her sleeve up to reveal the puckered red scar of her bullet wound.

James leaned closer, his face twisting. "Tell me how you got that wound," he demanded.

She met his gaze, and her stomach dropped. He would never permit her to live her own life.

Willy bared her teeth and used the guard's grip on her arm to flip herself over the back of the settee. Tearing free, she twisted his arm behind his back and shoved his face down onto the seat back, effectively preventing him from moving.

With her other hand, she pointed a silver pistol at her father's head. "How did you find out?" she asked, pleased to hear how steady her voice sounded.

James von Richtofen snorted. "Ah," he said. "It is as I suspected." He clicked his teeth. "My father was always a terrible influence. Did you know that he once tried to convince me to follow his ways? Pah," he spat. "Why would I want to join his game, as he called it?" Bitterness dripped from his voice. "The only game that interested me was the money game."

While his bodyguard turned red, gasping with pain as Willy leaned on his arm, pushing it almost to the breaking point, James von Richtofen sat back on the blue settee, oblivious to the man's suffering.

A second soft knock sounded.

"Come," called her father.

Two more guards burst through the door.

Willy grunted. "Is that how you want to play this?" she muttered. Pressing a little harder, she listened for the snap. When it came, it was followed immediately by the man's howl as his arm dislocated from the shoulder. She shoved him away and spun to meet the new threat.

The first man through the door flicked his eyes toward James von Richtofen, took in the white-faced guard huddled on the floor and stretched out a hand to grab her.

Willy snapped a fist into his throat, throwing her whole weight into the hip thrust. There was a definite crunch, and she moved out of reach, careful of the gown that threatened to capture her ankles.

The guard's eyes popped wide, and his hands went to his throat as he tried to draw in a breath past the broken windpipe.

Gliding in close, Willy swept a foot behind his heels while at the same time pushing hard on his chest.

He crashed onto the floor, taking the tea set with him.

Willy whirled to the second guard. Bouncing lightly from foot to foot, she flashed him a grin.

He raised his hands and feinted to the right.

Pivoting, Willy lifted her knee high and drove her heel into his shin. The crack of his bone breaking rang through the room. He collapsed with a shouted curse.

Willy glanced back at her father, who was half out of his seat. "We are done here," she said, before picking up her skirts and bolting.

No one else tried to stop her as she raced through the house to the front exit. Throwing open the door, she laughed aloud to see her father's automatized carriage waiting.

She leapt down the stairs and threw herself inside. "Carriage 12!" she shouted. "Go! Fast!"

It accelerated away from the house, throwing her back into the red leather seat. She laughed as she fought to pull her skirts inside. Finally, she wrestled the door shut and lay back to catch her breath.

Her hands went to her hair, and she tucked a loose strand behind her ear. "It is definitely getting interesting," she murmured. "What else have you got for me, Aldrich?"

Border Under Siege

The notorious Jarlerus the Scourge has once more unleashed his marauding forces upon Cairn's border towns, prompting swift military response. Two additional units of soldiers have been dispatched to fortify defences and quell the ongoing menace.

"These attacks are nothing to worry about," assured General Linus Ferguson in a statement to the press. "Jarlerus does not have the military stratagems to be anything more than a nuisance."

Despite the General's confident words, the townsfolk remain vigilant, bracing for further incursions.

-from The Cairnisle Times,
Tuesday, May 7, Year 27 AK

FORTY-FOUR ~ ALDRICH

JUMPING UP, ALDRICH TOSSED THE latest message onto his desk and paced the length of his office. Why was there never any good news? Dirt Town attacked. Wilhelmina injured. Corvington injured. Winston deactivated. Now his parents were involved. How would he keep them safe?

He wheeled and headed back the other way. Every day, the

newspapers reported on the progress of a horde of soldiers, moving across the mainland of Cairn. Jarlerus the Scourge. Aldrich shivered. By all accounts, the man was a true barbarian.

The Magisters' attempts to conceal the threat with their reassuring little reports in *The Cairnisle Times* were nothing but lies. The message that had just arrived from the docks made it clear that the danger was much more serious than they were letting on. People were dying. Crops were being destroyed. Roads were under siege.

He clenched his jaw. He should be doing something. But what? If he stepped one foot outside the safety of the fortress, he would be an immediate target for the City Guard. The Magisters were waiting for his appearance so they could rid themselves of a nuisance.

Despite Conrad Appleton's attempts to maintain the battle on a legal and democratic level, it had disintegrated into a brawl.

Aldrich scrubbed his face with both hands. He had never envisioned bloodshed on such a scale. Thousands of Dirt Town residents had already been murdered and the City Guard was working hard to exterminate the rest of them.

It was all his fault. If he had kept his mouth closed, the Magisters would have allowed things to roll along as they always had. Was that so bad? At least people had not been dying in the thousands.

Six weeks earlier, Aldrich had been happily practising medicine, blithely unaware of any problems in Cairn. When he announced that something had to be done, he had imagined a campaign to encourage people to look more closely at the issues in the country and work together to effect change.

He had taken his simple schoolroom lessons about Cairn's democracy at face value. Trusting that the Magisters would accept him as a legal challenger, he had expected to engage in civilized debate. Instead, they had unleashed an army on helpless citizens.

On his fourth trip across the room, he stopped at his desk and pulled open the bottom drawer. A bottle of Scotch, along with two crystal glasses, lay nestled between the files. He selected a glass, poured himself a tot, and settled behind his desk. His first sip went down smoothly, and he welcomed the burning warmth that blossomed in his stomach.

The door swung open, and Wilhelmina appeared. Dressed in the brown leather coat and trousers that marked her as the Silver Assassin, she wore no mask.

His eyebrows shot up, and he tilted his head to the side. "What—"

She swiped a hand through the air and shrugged. "There's no point hiding any longer," she said, slumping into a chair and stretching out her legs. "I just met with my father. He knows everything."

Aldrich opened the desk drawer to retrieve the second glass. When he held up the bottle, she barked a laugh.

"I will take a taste of that," she said. "It has been a long day."

He poured some of the amber liquid into the glass and pushed it across the desk. "He knows about your involvement in our little uprising?" he asked.

Wilhelmina's mouth twisted. "He cut off access to my bank accounts," she answered.

Narrowing his eyes, Aldrich tapped a finger on his desk and turned to look out the window. "We were counting on that money to fund our fight," he said. Draining his glass, he poured another shot. "I suppose that means he will make it impossible for my father to finance us as well." He rubbed his chin. "At the time, I thought I was fortunate when Father changed bankers because it meant that I had the opportunity to meet you." He flashed a smile. "Now, however, I must wonder if it was not a most disastrous bit of luck."

Wilhelmina's face remained still and distant.

Clearing his throat, he muttered, "Excuse me. That was unnecessary." Wilhelmina in leather did not play by the same rules as Wilhelmina in exquisite dresses.

"It doesn't have to be bad luck," she said, rising to her feet and shaking her head. "Of course, it won't be easy, but that will be part of the fun."

A knock sounded at the door.

Finding his glass empty, Aldrich poured himself another drink as he called, "Come."

Gustav Florenburg poked his balding head, with its untidy fringe of grey hair, around the corner and asked, "Have you got a minute?"

"Of course," said Aldrich. "Come in."

Bounding into the room, Gustav spotted Wilhelmina and came to a dead stop. He did not appear to recognize her, and after a brief shake of his head, his gaze settled on Aldrich. "I have been exploring," he said. "Did you know there is an entire level below the foundations of this fortress? How is it that this place ever remained secure as a prison?" His words tumbled over each other in his rush. "An extensive system of catacombs runs deep beneath the city. I found an entrance in the dungeons, and you will never guess who I found wandering about down there!" His glowing eyes darted between Wilhelmina and Aldrich.

Dryly, Wilhelmina answered, "Munash."

Gustav's eyes widened. "Why, that is exactly right," he said. "How did you know? He was looking for the entrance to the fortress when I found him."

Aldrich finished his Scotch and poured another. "Where is

he now?"

"He showed me to the house in Dirt Town where he is staying," answered Gustav. "He has Winston there. The poor fellow ran into a spot of bother. I came back for some tools to fix him up." His eyes took on a faraway look. "I think I may attempt some upgrades while I work on him. There are a few things I have been considering."

Aldrich lunged to his feet. Finally, there was something he could do. His legs wobbled under him, and he glanced at the bottle of Scotch. How much had he drunk?

Forcing his eyes to focus on Gustav, he said as clearly as he could, "Take me to him. I want to speak to Munash."

Record Voter Turnout

The Elections Office reports an unprecedented surge in voter registrations over the past two weeks.

"On a normal day, we rarely see anyone," stated the Records Clerk. "Lately, they are lined up down the street."

-from The Cairnisle Times,
Tuesday, May 7, Year 27 AK

FORTY-FIVE ~ ALDRICH

THE LONG WALK THROUGH THE tunnels helped clear Aldrich's head. After descending a series of ladders into the catacombs, they had marched for miles. By the time Gustav pointed out the ladder leading up into the house where Munash waited with Fia and Winston, Aldrich was dripping sweat and completely sober.

Sober enough to remember why he had poured his first drink. People were dying because he had decided to oppose the Magisters.

Dropping the heavy bag of tools that he had carried for Gustav, he pulled out a handkerchief to mop his face. "I will go up first and check that it is safe," he said, pushing the drenched cloth back into his pocket.

Wilhelmina rolled her eyes. "And if there is trouble, how will you deal with it?" she asked. "Have you been training in secret?" Brushing past him, she gripped the ladder. "I go up first. I'll let you know when it's safe."

Aldrich glanced at Gustav and shrugged as she climbed out of sight. Tempted as he was to follow her, he restrained himself. The last thing she needed was him distracting her. She was right. He was almost useless in a fight.

They did not have long to wait before a light came on in the room above. "Come up," she called.

Aldrich waved Gustav ahead. "You go first," he said, hoisting the clanking bag of tools to his shoulder and staggering slightly under its weight before getting his balance.

Gustav eyed him. "I can take that," he offered.

"I have it now," Aldrich answered. "Give me a hand at the top."

"Whatever you say, boss," Gustav said as he grasped a rung and pulled himself up.

When he hoisted himself through the hole, Aldrich squared his shoulders and heaved himself up the ladder. By the time he crawled through the trapdoor and collapsed sideways on the dirty wooden floor, he was gasping for breath. "Gustav," he wheezed, "tell me again why you felt it necessary to bring along every piece of metal you could find in the entire fortress."

Wilhelmina lifted the pack and hefted it to her own shoulder. "If it's too heavy for you, Aldrich, I'll carry it," she said. "Come on, Gustav, I'll take you to Winston and you can get started."

Aldrich snorted his amusement as he followed. The woman had a way of putting him in his place.

Leaving the dusty cellar, they entered a sitting room. Though everything—including the unfinished wooden walls—showed signs of great age, it was clean. And it smelled far better than the fusty air of the tunnels. A collection of mismatched chairs sat around the perimeter of the small space, and Winston was stretched out in the middle of the floor, his normally bright eyes dark and motionless.

Gustav took one look and dropped to his knees beside the robot. "Don't worry, old boy," he said, running his hands over the damaged midsection. "We'll get you up and running in no time."

Wilhelmina dumped the tools at his side.

"Thank you," Gustav said, without taking his gaze from the mess of gears and wires. Upending the tool bag, he let everything crash out onto the floor and picked up a set of pincers.

"Come on," Wilhelmina said, as he started probing the loose wires and muttering to himself. "He'll be here for a while."

A clatter of footsteps came rushing down the stairs from the upper story and Fia appeared with Munash right behind.

"You're here!" she cried, throwing herself at Aldrich.

A small lump formed in his throat as he caught her and returned her embrace. "I was worried about you," he said, stepping back and swallowing hard.

"I'm fine," she answered. Her gaze went to Wilhelmina, and she froze. "You forgot your mask."

Wilhelmina shrugged. "It's no longer necessary." She offered Fia her hand and said, "Call me Willy."

Fia blinked as she shook Wilhelmina's hand. "It's very nice to meet you, Willy," she murmured.

Clearing her throat, Willy stepped back and looked past Fia to Munash.

He smiled a slow, warm smile and nodded. "I thought it was you," he said. "Do you know I saw you here in Dirt Town when you were only a child? Even then, you tried to pretend that we did not know who your father was." He lifted his heavy shoulders in a gentle shrug. "When the child vanished, the assassin appeared."

Wilhelmina stiffened. Then she relaxed and stretched out a hand toward him. "I was not pretending that you did not know who my father was," she said lightly. "I was pretending that it did not matter who my father was. Please, call me Willy."

"Willy," Munash said, wrapping her hand in both of his and bowing slightly. "It is a true pleasure to meet you."

Aldrich moved over to the window. "What is going on here?" he asked. "I heard the robots kill everyone they encounter."

Munash's face tightened. "It is not good," he said, stepping from Willy's side to join Aldrich at the window. "Many have died. The robots' orders did not differentiate between children and criminals. The sequencing must have directed them to kill every living thing." He grunted. "Fortunately, they can only kill those they can find. If there is one thing a Dirt Town resident is good at—it is hiding."

He joined Aldrich at the window. "At the moment, things have quieted down. People are hiding and robots are waiting in the streets." His jaw clenched. "We have been able to destroy many of the Green Coat captains." He relaxed enough to give a grim smile. "The Blue Coats cannot react to new situations without new orders."

He whirled away from the window and strode the length of the room, pounding one fist into his open palm. "The real problem is Forge-37," he said. "He is impervious to my magic. Bullets do not penetrate his armour. I do not know what to do about him." Abruptly, he stopped and stared down at Gustav.

Crouched over Winston, the little inventor was working with single-minded concentration.

"Gustav," Munash said softly, setting his hand on the man's

shoulder. "Did you bring your special device?"

Gustav looked up and blinked. "Device?" he asked. Then his face cleared. "Oh, hello, Munash. It should not take too long to have Winston up and around." He pushed back onto his heels. "What were you saying? Oh yes, the device for shutting down the robots." He pushed aside a number of screwdrivers along with a pile of assorted gears and picked up a short piece of metal tubing. One end had been capped while the other remained open. He gripped it so that a small, round button fitted under his thumb and pointed it at the wall.

A visible blast of electricity shot out and crackled from one rusty nail to the next. Gustav beamed at Willy, giving no notice to her missing mask. "It uses the self-recharging battery that you and Fia acquired from the battery factory," he said. "It will never run out of power. The blast of electricity overloads a robot's sequencing, which causes it to vent all of its power so that it does not fry." He pursed his lips as he handed it to Munash. "It will not work on Forge though. He has an installed venting device that modulates power surges."

Munash accepted the device and set his thumb on the button. "Thank you, Gustav," he said. "We can put this to good use immediately."

City Plastered with Posters

One cannot traverse the streets of Cairnisle without encountering the visage of Aldrich Durante. His posters, plastered on walls and shop windows, itemize the sweeping reforms he pledges to implement if elected.

"It is not enough to tell people that you want to see change in Cairn," remarked Deutero Minister Ingrid Jaeger. "You must have a vision and a plan. I can tell you that the Magisters have a plan for change and it is already underway."

-from The Cairnisle Times,
Tuesday, May 14, Year 27 AK

FORTY-SIX ~ ALDRICH

ALDRICH HAD CHOSEN HIS PARTNER with extreme care. As much as he liked Winston, he was a robot and, as Gustav had so ably proven, he could be repaired. After his most recent overhaul, Winston sported several upgrades, including increased armoured plating, smoother joints for quicker motion, and faster reaction speed.

The added benefit to selecting Winston to accompany him was that he felt no obligation to make conversation. From the window of his mother's automatized carriage, Aldrich stared at the empty streets as they sped past, feeling pleasantly anonymous.

The identifying numbers painted on the rear of the carriage had been modified by a deft counterfeiter who had joined the rebellion after being released from his cell. It had taken no more than an instant to change the one to a four.

The knot in his stomach began to relax. It was infinitely better to be doing something. For too long, Aldrich had hidden out in his office and sent others to do his bidding.

At the thought, his stomach clenched again. The Magisters were making it clear that this was not a job for the faint-hearted. They killed his people, and he had ordered his soldiers to reciprocate.

In the past week, he had hardly slept. Even when he found time to lie down, his brain did not stop long enough to let him rest. An endless series of questions pursued him every time he closed his eyes.

Did he have to play by the same rules as the Magisters?

Was there another way to challenge their violence?

Did he even want to win if he had to use their methods?

Already horrible things had been done in his name. Six days earlier, he had sent a team to talk to a noble who supported the Magisters. He had intended them to convince the man to join his side, but somehow, the fellow had ended up dead.

Then Willy paid a visit to a wealthy man who could have helped with funding the campaign. Aldrich had worded those instructions carefully. He knew the man from dinners with his parents and hoped for his support. However, that man had ended up dead as well.

It made him ill to think of it.

After that second killing, he vowed to do things differently. Democracy abhorred violence. In its simplest form, people gave their opinions, and the majority got their way. A truly civilized society left it at that.

His lips pinched. There was no reason to kill anyone who disagreed. If people continued to die for his cause, could it even be called a democracy? It made his head ache to think of it.

But the real question was: had things gone too far to back away from the fight? He would do everything he could to prevent further bloodshed. His supporters seemed just as bent on protecting him. Gustav had gone to the extreme of building a secret safe room at the back of Aldrich's office.

Where had they gotten the idea that he was the only irreplaceable person in the entire rebellion? Instead of feeling flattered, their confidence made him jittery. Sometimes the weight of their trust was overwhelming.

And the Magisters were not the only threat. Cairnisle was an entirely dependent city. Because no food was produced on the island, the newspaper reports of problems with the food supply had people worried. Information was sketchy, but it was clear that Jarlerus the Scourge was skirting around Cairn's borders, making inroads into the farming regions in the north. If regular shipments of food were not maintained, conditions on the island could quickly become desperate.

Everywhere Aldrich looked, some new item appeared for him to agonize over. What had ever possessed him to pursue a position of leadership? He was a doctor, not a politician. Doctors diagnosed the problem, and they acted. They did not sit around and talk about a better solution.

Perhaps that was why the plan for the day felt so right. Since James von Richtofen cut off access to not only Willy's funds but also Aldrich's and his father's accounts, there had been a painful shortage of money. It took a tremendous amount of cash to finance a rebellion, with food being the greatest and most important expense.

And so, Aldrich was seated in a speeding carriage beside a robot who was wearing a plain black suit that matched his own. Four empty valises sat at their feet. With any luck, those valises would be filled to the brim when they returned to the fortress.

They rolled to a stop outside a branch of the von Richtofen banking empire. Aldrich had chosen it for its out-of-the-way location and its small staff. Using the name of one of the bank's clients who had prudently remained neutral during the recent debates, he had made an appointment with the manager.

Aldrich pulled his scarf more securely around his face and checked that Winston was entirely covered. Fortunately, the weather had turned cool again and the wind off the lake was so bitter that it did not look odd for them to cover their faces.

"You know the plan," he said as he picked up two valises.

"Yes," answered Winston, lifting the remaining pair in one long-fingered hand and descending from the automatized carriage.

Aldrich's gaze darted around as he followed the robot up the wide steps. The weather was keeping pedestrians off the street and there was no one to witness their arrival. It was a good sign.

Winston pulled open the bank's heavy door and stood aside.

Biting hard on his tongue, Aldrich tucked in his chin and strode into the building. The vestibule with its walls of white polished granite and its high, vaulted ceiling was empty of customers. After a quick glance around, he headed directly for the service desk.

"Archibald Pendleton to see Thomas Cogsworth," he said, making every effort to control his shaking knees.

It was like that first time he had cut into a living, breathing patient. But once he made that first incision, everything had become sparklingly clear. He was hoping for the same reaction on his foray into larceny.

"Of course, sir," the clerk said, rising with a welcoming smile. "Please follow me."

Aldrich briefly closed his eyes before following the young man down a corridor to an office door. The fellow had not recognized Aldrich, and he apparently did not know what Archibald looked like. The first hurdle was past. His heart began to slow, and the flood of adrenalin faded.

After a quiet knock, the clerk bobbed a bow and hurried back to his desk.

"Come in," called Mr. Cogsworth.

Aldrich arranged his face in pleasant expression, nudged the door open, and slipped inside. Pointedly ignoring the bank manager, who had risen with a professional smile, he sat down in one of the client chairs.

Winston closed the door with a snick and walked around the corner of the desk to stand behind the manager.

Mr. Cogsworth's smile vanished. "What is the meaning of this?" he asked.

Aldrich crossed his legs, leaned back, pulled his scarf off, and folded it in his lap. Only when he was completely settled did he look up and meet the manager's eyes.

Cogsworth's face turned ashen, and he stopped breathing.

"Good," said Aldrich. "You recognize me. That will save some time." Between the posters that Appleton had plastered around the city and the newspapers, he was famous. "We do not wish to hurt you. We simply require your cooperation."

The man's head swivelled between Winston and Aldrich, his Adam's apple leaping up and down in his throat.

When Aldrich judged his panic had reached a sufficient level, he said, "We require funding. You will withdraw a sum of one hundred thousand golds from my personal account." He and Wilhelmina had decided that it could hardly be called theft if he took it from his own account.

"I can't do that," spluttered Mr. Cogsworth, his voice breaking. "Lord von Richtofen has ordered that you may not have access to your accounts."

"It is my money," Aldrich answered deliberately. "You can give it to me and you will." His mind was remarkably clear.

Mr. Cogsworth straightened in his chair and shook his head, gripping his armrests until his fingers turned white. "I cannot do that," he repeated with more force.

Aldrich nodded at Winston, who clouted the man on the side of the head.

There was not much force to the blow, but the bank manager rocked back with a grunt. Wide-eyed, he lifted a hand to catch the blood that gushed down his face. "I can't," he whimpered. "If I tried to do something like that, Lord von Richtofen would know immediately. My life would be over."

Aldrich hardened himself. The violence was intended to scare Cogsworth but there was no reason to expect it would leave him seriously scarred. Aldrich was not a tyrant. He was trying to do the right thing for his country and for that he needed money.

Leaning across the desk, he handed Cogsworth a clean, white handkerchief. "Put pressure on it," he said.

The man snatched the handkerchief and pressed it against his forehead as his eyes darted between Aldrich and Winston.

Aldrich pursed his lips. So far, the damage was only superficial. How far was he willing to go to get the money? "I am certain that you have ways to cover your trail," he murmured. "You can make it so that James von Richtofen does not find out. And please remember that it is my money. He has stolen it from me. I am merely reclaiming it."

Cogsworth set his jaw. "I cannot," he said. "The accounts have been frozen. Any transactions would be flagged immediately."

"I see that you are right-handed," Aldrich said, nodding to the pen set on the right side of the desk. "Perhaps you would not mind sacrificing a few fingers from your left hand in the service of Lord von Richtofen?" Glancing up at Winston, he gave another nod.

When Winston shifted to his left side, Cogsworth moaned. Shrinking in on himself, he clutched his left hand with his right.

Forcing himself not to look away, Aldrich watched the man's internal battle.

At the touch of Winston's metallic fingers, he crumpled. Snatching his hands away, he sobbed, "I'll do it. Make him stop."

"Wise choice," said Aldrich. He took a bottle of alcohol from one of the valises at his feet and poured it over a second handkerchief before handing it to Cogsworth. "Clean yourself up. We do not wish to involve anyone else. Remember your task, and neither you nor your staff will be hurt."

With trembling fingers, Cogsworth pulled the first handkerchief from the cut on his forehead. It was not a serious wound and had already stopped bleeding. With the clean cloth, he mopped the blood from his face and hands.

"You missed a spot," said Aldrich, touching his own eyebrow. "Just here."

Cogsworth found a clean area on the handkerchief and made another pass.

"Better," said Aldrich. "Now, about that money."

Shakily, the bank manager rose and edged past Winston to a wooden cabinet at the back of the room. Selecting a form from a wide drawer, he returned to his desk and began to fill it in.

When he finished, he signed with a flourish and raised a

face white with shock. "I'll have to go to the vaults," he said. "My staff will notice."

Aldrich did not blink. "You and I both know that you have a separate entrance for your most valuable clients," he said. "We will use that. After all, we would not want to have to hurt you again—or any of your staff." He left the threat hanging in the air.

The man gulped hard. Without another word, he removed a key from his pocket, used it to open a desk drawer. Removing an impressive seal, he pressed it into a pad of red ink before stamping it down hard on the freshly signed form. Rising again, he sidled past Winston to his filing cabinet. Adding the form to a pile already there, he arranged it neatly and replaced the granite paperweight.

When he turned back, he looked so completely defeated that Aldrich's throat tightened. He was as bad as the Magisters. Worse. Because he was pretending to himself and everyone else that he was doing it for the right reasons.

But what choice did he have? If they did not get money—and soon—everything they had done up to this point was meaningless. And that included the lives of the people who had died in the time since he announced his intention to challenge the Magisters.

"Take us to the vault now," he said. "And remember: be very sure we do not run into anyone."

Thomas Cogsworth closed his eyes briefly before squaring his shoulders and striding toward the door. Cracking it open, he peered into the hallway and let out a long sigh. With a quick backward glance, he crept out of his office.

Winston and Aldrich picked up their valises and followed. The tightness in Aldrich's shoulders relaxed when they made it to the vault without seeing a soul.

The huge circular door was tightly shut. Would it make

noise when it opened?

Pulling a key as big as his hand from an inner pocket of his coat, Cogsworth shifted his eyes to Aldrich once before moving to the vault door. He inserted the key into the keyhole and turned it a quarter turn counter-clockwise. Glancing over his shoulder, he shifted his body to shield his actions.

Aldrich resisted the urge to move closer. As much as he wanted to see how the lock worked, he held himself still and watched.

Judging by Cogsworth's concentration and his jerky motions, a complex series of turns was necessary to disengage the lock. Finally, he stretched out his left hand to adjust a lever, turned the key again, adjusted another lever, and gave the key one final turn before stepping back and peering down the empty corridor.

A series of clicks and rumblings followed, and the door sprang open with a hiss of air.

Aldrich froze, listening hard. Would anyone be attracted by the noise?

A bead of sweat ran down Cogsworth's face as he stared at Aldrich.

Hearing nothing from the front of the bank, Aldrich jerked his head toward the vault and Cogsworth sprang aside, his eyes darting between Aldrich and the corridor.

Aldrich seized the over-sized handle and hauled the door open before tossing his valises inside. Gesturing to Cogsworth, he muttered, "After you."

As the man scuttled through the entrance, Aldrich whispered, "You go with him, Winston. Pack the golds. I will remain here to keep watch."

Winston nodded and disappeared into the vault.

A trickle of sweat ran down Aldrich's back as he waited in the empty corridor.

The seconds ticked by, and no one came.

Finally, Winston reached through the door and handed out two heavy valises. Taking them, Aldrich almost collapsed under the weight. When Winston stepped out of the vault, his valises were bulging at the seams. He had taken the heavier load.

"Take us to the private entrance," Aldrich muttered to Cogsworth. "You will not speak a word of this to anyone."

Red-faced and sweating, Cogsworth blanched and shook his head. "I won't say anything," he whispered. "Who could I tell? Von Richtofen will have my head if he finds out." His hand shook as he closed up the vault.

He mopped at his face with Aldrich's handkerchief as he led them along a corridor to a heavy steel door. It was barred by a beam as thick as Aldrich's leg as well as five additional locks. Cogsworth looked furtively over his shoulder before lifting the beam free, spinning the knobs, and throwing the door wide.

"Thank you," Aldrich murmured as he staggered past into the chill afternoon air.

Fia waited in his father's automatized carriage. When she opened the door, his knees threatened to buckle. Wobbling across the alley, he hoisted his valises inside and jumped in after them.

As soon as Winston was inside and the door closed, Aldrich ordered, "Carriage 1435, go."

As they rolled away from the bank, he glanced back, and his stomach took a swooping dive.

Thomas Cogsworth watched them from the open door, his shoulders drooping and the corners of his mouth turned down. He was the very picture of despondence.

Aldrich averted his gaze. He had done what was necessary. It could not be helped.

His lips pinched together, and he squeezed his eyes shut. As soon as he beat the Magisters, he would return and make things right with the man.

Durante a Thief

In a fiery denunciation that has sparked widespread debate among the citizenry, Mr. James von Richtofen, esteemed President of Cairnisle's largest banking institution, has publicly lambasted Doctor Aldrich Durante, the ambitious candidate for Grand Minister. Mr. von Richtofen, known for his influential role in the financial sector and his staunch advocacy for law and order, did not mince words in his condemnation.

"The man is little more than a common thief," declared Lord von Richtofen with palpable disdain. "His actions reveal a blatant disregard for the principles of honesty and integrity that our society holds dear."

-from The Cairnisle Times,
Saturday, May 18, Year 27 AK

FORTY-SEVEN ~ WILHELMINA

WILLY SETTLED ONTO A CHAIR and tipped it back against the wall, crossing her arms over her chest. When there was nothing else to do, she liked to watch the training in the courtyard. It made her laugh.

Hand-to-hand fighting was the order of the day. Rupert

Corvington was running the session. He had his pupils eating out of the palm of his hand. Willy allowed herself a small private smile. It had not started out that way. Dirt Towners considered themselves excellent fighters and did not like to be told what to do.

Ordinarily, Corvington could have challenged one of the swaggering young men to a fight and put them in their place. However, while Aldrich had done an admirable job of repairing the bullet damage to his abdomen, it had not yet healed enough to allow him to engage in a wrestling match.

Willy had been there when Rupert solved that problem. He chose two of the most likely fighters and pitted them against each other. After watching for a few minutes, he took aside the fellow who was obviously losing, gave him two minutes of whispered advice, and then sent him back into battle.

The results had been stunning. Rupert's boy cleaned up in seconds. After that, the recruits had been eager to learn his secrets.

That did not mean they were all becoming expert fighters— as evidenced by the buffoonery going on in front of her.

Jax, the smaller of the two combatants, darted in with his wooden sword and swiped at his opponent's leg.

With a shouted curse, Ryder stumbled back a step before Jax jabbed him in the chest, hitting him squarely in the pads. The air woofed out of him, and he crashed onto his butt.

Willy laughed.

The two men froze.

Ryder's head swivelled toward her. Springing to his feet, he stalked closer and loomed over her, blocking the light from the afternoon sun. "Are you laughing at us?" he demanded.

Willy tipped her head back to peer up at the young giant. Although she knew that he was working to improve his skills so that he could fight for Aldrich, he struck her as a bully. She had no patience for bullies. Her smile disappeared, and her eyes went cold. "I was laughing at you," she said. "I hadn't realized that fighting could look so awkward."

He bent and pushed his face close to hers. "You think you can do better?" he hissed, so that a speck of spit hit her cheek.

Although there was no humour in it, Willy's smile returned. "I do," she said.

Ryder straightened. "Fight me," he challenged.

"My pleasure," she replied. Leaving the chair against the wall with its two legs in the air, she twirled away to grasp a wooden sword from the pile by the wall and came to a stop in the middle of the courtyard.

Eyes wide, Ryder spun to face her.

"Well, come on," she called. "What are you waiting for?"

He lumbered towards her. "Silver Assassin," he said with a sneer. "That's just a pretty name for someone who doesn't know her place."

Willy's smile vanished. "We shall see." She did not move until he came into range. Then she faked a parry but pulled back instead of meeting his blow.

He pitched forward, and she punched him in the face with the hand that held the sword. His head came up, and she stuck out a foot to trip him.

He hit the ground hard, and she was there with her sword tip pressed to his throat. "Yield," she said.

"I yield," he wheezed.

Willy's gaze bored into him. "You need to work on your balance," she said. "Throwing your weight around won't save you in a real fight. A fighter without balance is a feast for the crows. Stay light on your feet, distribute your weight, and move like a shadow. Balance keeps you upright when the world tilts."

She tapped her sword on his heavy shoulder and stepped

away. "Strength is not everything," she continued. "Sure, swing like you're felling trees, but precision wins battles. Aim for the gaps in your opponent's armour. Look for the chinks where vulnerability hides. A well-placed strike trumps brute force every time."

Other soldiers had moved closer to listen, and Willy raised her voice for her audience. "Don't rush in like a fool. Time your strikes. Wait for openings. Let your opponent tire themselves out. A sword fight is never a sprint—it's a dance of death."

She swept her gaze over the silent men. "See everything," she said. "Not just the blade coming at you, but the twitch of their wrist, the shift in their stance. Read their intentions. Anticipate. Survival isn't luck."

Nudging Ryder's butt with the toe of her boot, she chuckled. "And when you hit the dirt," she said, "don't curse your luck. Learn. Every defeat is a lesson. Analyze what went wrong. Adapt. Grow stronger."

Ryder blinked, and she tossed the wooden practice sword down beside him.

"Now," she said, "get up and show everybody you've got more brains than brawn."

She turned away and found Aldrich watching.

"An important lesson," he said. "You men are fortunate to have such an accomplished teacher. I am greatly impressed with your progress."

The men grinned and shuffled their feet.

"What's the plan then, boss?" called Gunnar, a young hotshot who had gained the respect of everyone by beating them in practice. "Do we get to fight for real soon?"

"If I am honest," Aldrich said with a twisted half-smile, "I hope you never get to fight in earnest. July 6—Election Day— is less than two months away. Ideally, we go to the polls peaceably." His eyes hardened. "However, the Magisters are not going to make this easy. They are using their robots with deadly force, and we have to do something about that." He winced and straightened up. "How's the target practice going?"

For the last week, Rupert Corvington had run target training sessions in the catacombs. The only way to defeat the robots was with accurate shooting.

Not wanting to use up the ammunition that had been purchased with such difficulty, Corvington had found other ways for the soldiers to learn how to fire accurately. He called it dry practice, and it involved learning to keep the sights on target even as a shooter pulled the trigger.

An ammunition shortage had never been an issue when Willy's grandfather taught her to shoot. However, during the few minutes she spent trying it, she could see how such practice could make a difference if someone approached it with the right mindset.

Gunnar flashed a grin. "We're getting better," he called. "Set us loose and see what we can do."

Aldrich laughed with the men. "Just knowing I have a highly trained army at my back makes me feel better," he said. "Keep up the fine work." Lifting a hand in farewell, he turned away, taking Willy's elbow as he went. "I would appreciate a moment of your time," he murmured.

"I have a moment," she replied, noting the dark circles around his eyes and the tense line of his mouth.

Everything was running more smoothly since Aldrich and Winston returned from their trip to her father's bank. Money made all the difference.

Conrad Appleton had stepped up the publicity. On the few occasions when Willy left the confines of the fortress, she could not go far without seeing pictures of Aldrich's smiling face plastered on every available surface.

She did not see that smile very often in real life. Aldrich was feeling the pressure of leadership. He had taken charge of every aspect of the organization—from assigning robot repairs to ensuring that everyone had enough to eat.

Aldrich understood the importance of feeding his people. She had to give him that. He had assigned one team to the task of purchasing food and a second to its preparation and serving. It was not what she might have eaten in her father's house but tasty, nonetheless.

A third team had been charged with acquiring weapons for the people of Dirt Town. This was only a little easier than coming up with food for the horde.

They were using the catacombs to transport the goods, and most days it was a thoroughfare down there. The tunnels would not remain a secret for long.

Willy had to hustle to keep up as Aldrich strode back to his office. As soon as he closed the door, he crossed to his desk and sank into the chair. "We have money problems again," he said. "The hundred thousand golds are already spent."

Willy's eyebrows rose.

He grimaced. "Food," he said. "It costs an enormous amount to feed this army. Especially with the food shortages. Prices keep going up." He rapped his knuckles on the desk. "To tell you the truth, I think it would be cheaper and more effective if we gave up on the army and took control of the newspaper. Have you seen the things they write about us?"

"You mean what they write about you," said Willy. "Very little has been written about me. Did you notice that the Silver Assassin was never even mentioned?"

Aldrich chuckled. "It makes them look bad to mention you. You are an assassin who they never caught. When they talk about me, they do it so that it makes them look entirely reasonable in comparison." He scrubbed his hands across his face. "In the meantime, we need more money. I thought perhaps we could try the same trick at the bank again." He stopped and swallowed. "But your father discovered what we did."

Willy narrowed her eyes. "That can't have ended well for the bank manager," she said.

Closing his eyes, Aldrich let out a slow breath. "Thomas Cogsworth is dead," he said. "I might as well have pulled the trigger myself. He has been replaced with someone who is far more afraid of your father than he is of us."

"So, you can't do that again," said Willy. "Do you have another idea?"

"I might," Aldrich answered. He stared into her eyes and then looked away. "The Silver Assassin could kill Lord James von Richtofen," he said finally.

Willy leapt up and backed away from the desk, her eyes bulging.

Rising, Aldrich held out his hands. "I am sorry," he said. "It is a ridiculous idea. I should never have—"

"No," Willy said, tapping a finger on her lips. "It's good. If Lord James is dead, all of his money passes to his grieving daughter and only heir, Wilhelmina von Richtofen. I imagine she could spare a few silvers to fund this revolution."

She narrowed her eyes and studied the floor. Aldrich thought he was asking something impossible—something horrendous. However, she felt no reluctance about killing her father. It would be the greatest exploit of the Silver Assassin's career. She glanced up from her contemplation of the scrubbed stonework and found Aldrich studying her miserably.

He met her eyes. "Please," he said. "Forget I—"

"I'll do it," she said. "It might take a day or two to get it organized though."

His shoulders rose up to his ears. "Wilhelmina, I am sorry I even suggested this," he muttered, coming out from behind the desk. "Forget it. I do not know what I was thinking."

"You were thinking that we need money," Willy answered. "And you were right. Don't worry. I can do this." She stood up and straightened her coat.

As she reached for the doorknob, a polite knock sounded.

At Aldrich's nod, she opened the door to reveal a former prison guard in his Grey Coat. "I have a message for Doctor Durante," he said, holding out an envelope of heavy white paper.

"Who brought it?" Aldrich asked.

"Six robot City Guards just marched up to the front gate and left it there," he answered with a shrug.

Accepting the letter, Aldrich said, "Thank you."

The young man touched his cap and withdrew, pulling the door shut behind him.

Aldrich held up the envelope. 'Aldrich Durante of Cairnisle Prison' was written in an elegant script, but there was no return address. "Who is this from?" he muttered.

"There's only one way to find out," said Willy. "Come on. Open it."

Pressing his lips together, Aldrich inserted his thumb under the flap and tore it open. As he read, the colour drained from his face. "It is a court order," he said. "There is to be a trial. I am charged with the murder of Jack Bury and Jimmy Cole. I am to report to the City Courthouse on Tuesday."

"They'll kill you on the spot," Willy said.

"No," Aldrich said, tilting his head as a grin tugged at the corner of his mouth. "They aim to ruin my reputation. It is a clever move. Conrad's surveys suggest I could win the election." He returned to his chair and settled behind the desk.

"The Magisters are unwilling to take that risk. If they can pour enough shame on my name—they win."

"How will that help them?" Willy scoffed. "You'll win in court and come out looking fine."

"Not necessarily." answered Aldrich. "I killed Jack Bury and Jimmy Cole." He raised an eyebrow. "Although it truly was self-defence."

Willy's mouth dropped open. "You killed two people?"

"Actually, it was the day before we met," said Aldrich with a smirk. Then he sobered. "I did not mean for it to happen. They had kidnapped Fia and were holding her for ransom." His forehead wrinkled. "The men who came to get me were—" He broke off and cleared his throat. "I think it is fair to say they were a frightening pair. Before accompanying them, I took the opportunity to arm myself."

Willy shook her head and gave a low whistle. "Doctor Aldrich Durante," she said. "You are a dark horse."

A flush crept up Aldrich's face. "Yes, well," he muttered, before pushing up and heading for the door. "Right now, I need to find Conrad Appleton and begin preparation for my defence."

Durante Murder Trial

The highly anticipated trial of Doctor Aldrich Durante commences at the City Courthouse today. The young physician, who has lately entered into politics, stands accused of the the murder of two prominent Dirt Town businessmen.

Eyewitnesses assert that Doctor Durante, employing his vast knowledge of toxic substances, administered a fatal dose of poison to Mr. Jack Bury, resulting in his swift and tragic passing.

Equally alarming are the allegations surrounding the death of Mr. Jimmy Cole. According to multiple testimonies, Doctor Durante is said to have engaged in a violent confrontation with Mr. Cole, culminating in the discharge of a firearm that fatally wounded the latter.

-from The Cairnisle Times,
Tuesday, May 21, Year 27 AK

FORTY-EIGHT ~ ALDRICH

ALDRICH CLOSED HIS SCRATCHY EYES. The Magisters were smart. The short timeline leading up to his court date was an excellent strategy to throw him off balance. Since the arrival of the court order charging him with murder, he had hardly slept.

Despite that, he felt stimulated and inspired by all he had learned of the law in the last three and a half days. Conrad was an excellent teacher, providing an endless supply of books filled with procedural law and precedents. Aldrich had lapped it up, reading entire volumes and committing everything to memory. In court, Conrad would act as his advisor, but Aldrich did not intend to leave his fate in someone else's hands. He would argue the case himself.

As the carriage rolled to a stop, Conrad nudged Aldrich awake. "My dear Doctor Durante," he said. "It is—as we lawyers like to say—show time. As I predicted, the media is here, as are the crowds of busybodies. Do these people never have anything valuable to do? It seems that whenever the newspapers suggest something might be interesting, an excessive number of people are able to find the time in their busy days to come and gawk at the proceedings. It simply boggles the mind."

Blinking hard, Aldrich sat up. He had not meant to fall asleep. He straightened his cravat and ran a hand down the front of his coat. Fia had gone with an armed guard to his house with instructions to bring his most conservative suit. The royal blue of the coat and trousers that she had chosen gave him a most respectable appearance. Contrasted with the pristine white linen of his shirt, he could not have looked less like a murderer.

It was just as well that the Magisters had pulled him into the spotlight. If he planned to win the election, he could not continue to hide out in the fortress. He needed to be seen.

He waited while Conrad climbed carefully out of the carriage, favouring his injured leg. Then, when the little lawyer stepped aside, Aldrich picked up the briefcase filled with his notes and arguments, took a deep breath, and stepped onto the footpath.

A rumble passed through the crowd, and he heard his name repeated in muttered whispers as he ascended the worn steps of the courthouse.

"Let us through," cried Conrad, waving his arms and smiling to people on either side. "We do not want to hold up the good doctor. He is here to prove his innocence against these false charges."

The sea of onlookers pressed in and then surged back enough to allow a narrow passage. Sweat broke out on Aldrich's back as he squeezed through the crowd.

"Smile," muttered Conrad, puffing along at his side. "Make them your friends."

Aldrich plastered on a rictus grin, his cheeks aching from the effort, and raised a hand in a stilted wave towards a cluster of young women craning their necks and jostling for a better view.

The air crackled with anticipation—a volatile blend of curiosity and suspicion. They came not for justice, but for the spectacle.

How many were allies? How many bore grudges? Their sharp eyes assessed him—their would-be Grand Minister. The title promised power and peril in equal measure.

By their attire, the majority of the spectators were from Upper Cairnisle. But on the fringes were enough Dirt Towners, in their patched and threadbare garments, for a respectable showing. His smile relaxed and became real. He could only hope they were there to stand witness to the trial rather than to fleece the crowd of their pocket watches and wallets.

"Aldrich!" a voice shouted from the back of the crowd. "You can beat this!"

Others joined in, calling agreement, while a few hisses of

disapproval reached his ears as well.

Aldrich strained to pinpoint the source of the shout, but the throng swallowed it whole. Bodies pressed against bodies, a living, breathing mass that obscured his view in every direction. As he climbed the final steps, a cacophony engulfed him—a disorienting blend of cheers and jeers that battled for dominance. For every voice raised in support, another seethed with contempt. His stomach clenched.

Walking between a pair of the six massive pillars that guarded the front of the courthouse, Aldrich bit the inside of his cheek. He was guilty. Was it justifiable to kill someone to preserve one's own life? How about if it was to save someone else?

He swallowed hard and lifted his chin. He had taken a course of actions that preserved both his and Fia's lives. Killing Jack Bury and Jimmy Cole had not been his choice. They had forced him to it.

The tension in his chest that had been twisting tighter and tighter since he received the letter charging him to appear before the court suddenly released. Despite the solid click of his shoes on the polished marble floor, he felt as if he was floating. He had done the right thing. There was no question in his mind. It gave him an overwhelming sense of power.

The trial was the Magisters' attempt to vilify him. They were worried. They must believe he was a real threat to their government. His smile broadened. If he won the court case, he would defeat the Magisters.

Conrad navigated the crowd with practiced ease, his hand on Aldrich's elbow as he greeted familiar faces with a nod or a quick word. The ornate lobby unfurled before them, its vaulted ceilings arching overhead like the ribcage of some great beast. Polished granite walls reflected the warm glow of light sconces, lending an air of austere grandeur to the space.

As they entered the courtroom, the hum of anticipation washed over them. Row upon row of benches, crafted from rich mahogany and burnished to a mirror sheen, groaned under the weight of eager spectators. The air crackled with hushed whispers and barely contained excitement.

At the room's apex stood a massive desk, perched atop a raised dais like a throne. The Magisters' eagle crest, wrought in gold and silver, spread its wings across the front of the desk, fierce and imperious. Aldrich's gaze locked onto the symbol, a physical manifestation of the power he both craved and feared. Try as he might, he could not wrench his eyes from its hypnotic allure.

Conrad steered him up the aisle to a table on the left. Completely at home in the tension-filled room, the little man settled himself in the second chair.

Aldrich edged in beside him and slammed his knee against the table leg. Biting back a curse, he lowered himself into the seat and wiped a sheen of sweat from his forehead. "Do you ever get used to being stared at?" he murmured as he set his briefcase on the table, ignoring the urge to turn and study the faces of the people who had come to watch.

Conrad chuckled. "It is not me they are staring at," he said. "I would wager that not one in ten of them could accurately describe me."

With a snort, Aldrich clicked open his briefcase and extracted notebooks, pens, and two thick volumes of law. He did not really need any of it since everything he had read and written was committed to memory, but Conrad had suggested that if he got nervous, the papers would help to settle his mind. Also, they might need to write notes to each other during the proceedings.

A door near the front of the room opened and seven well-dressed men filed into a row of seats on a second raised dais to the right of the judge. The jury.

Aldrich did not recognize a single person. They sat and stared at him while he met their gazes and tried his best to appear innocent.

At a crash from the back of the courtroom, everyone swivelled to see the source of the disturbance.

A very tall, thin man with a hawk nose and bushy black eyebrows paused. With the precision of a seasoned performer, he held the silence, letting it stretch taut across the courtroom. Only when every eye was fixed upon him, every breath held in anticipation, did he move. His stride was deliberate, each step a calculated display of confidence in the hushed chamber.

He claimed the empty table opposite Conrad and Aldrich, pulling the chair back with a scrape. Dropping his briefcase with a clatter, he spun, swirling his robes about his ankles and examined Aldrich.

Aldrich returned his scrutiny. He had heard a great deal about the Magisters' Prosecutor—both in the newspapers and from Conrad—but he had never met him.

Harrison Stillman had a reputation for winning. A reputation that Aldrich intended to spoil.

"Please rise for the Honourable Judge Landon York," the bailiff called.

As everyone shuffled to their feet, a middle-aged man with an almost completely round head and a bulbous red nose, entered through a side door. He straightened his glasses and ambled over to the raised desk. While he settled himself in his chair, his eyes found Aldrich.

"Good morning, ladies and gentlemen," Judge York said. "Calling the case of the People of Cairn versus Aldrich Durante. Are both sides ready to proceed?"

Shipments Sorted Soon

It has come to the attention of this esteemed publication that the eagerly anticipated provisions from our brethren on mainland Cairn have suffered an unfortunate delay in their maritime journey to our fair isle.

Grand Magister Augustus Köhler, in his infinite wisdom and magnanimity, announced, "The trifling impediments besetting our mainland compatriots shall be expeditiously rectified. I beseech our good people to cast aside any unwarranted trepidation. Our island boasts a cornucopia of comestibles sufficient to sustain us through this momentary inconvenience."

-from The Cairnisle Times,
Tuesday, May 21, Year 27 AK

FORTY-NINE ~ ALDRICH

"MR. CLAY, COULD YOU PLEASE explain to the court exactly how I came to be visiting Mr. Jack Bury at the time of his death?" Aldrich asked.

Considerably cleaner than he had been on the day Aldrich met him, the short man had swaggered into the courtroom dressed in an expensive suit. His moustache had been neatly trimmed, but his heavy nasal breathing was easily identifiable. Every time Stillman questioned him, he had sent a mocking look at Aldrich with each answer.

The smug smile vanished. Joe Clay grabbed at his moustache and tugged on its corner. "Uh, we went and got you," he answered.

"You went and got me," repeated Aldrich. "And why was this?" He checked the clock on the wall.

It had been a very long day and showed no signs of wrapping up any time soon. Conrad had warned that the prosecutor, Harrison Stillman, would have instructions to draw the case out as long as possible. However, Judge York had made it clear that he would tolerate no delays.

"Uh," Joe Clay's eyes shifted to his partner and then to Harrison Stillman.

"Mr. Clay, why are you looking at Mr. Stillman?" Aldrich snapped. "Has he instructed you about your responses here?"

Judge York's big head lifted from his notes, and a spark of interest lit his eyes.

A frown rippled across Harrison Stillman's handsome face before he wiped his expression clean.

"Please answer the question, Mr. Clay," Judge York instructed.

"Uh, I—" began Joe Clay.

"Objection!" called out Harrison Stillman, rising hurriedly to his feet.

"On what grounds?" asked the judge.

"Irrelevance, Your Honour," he answered.

"Overruled," said Judge York. "The court would be pleased to know of any instructions that have been issued."

Stillman wilted back into his chair, and Aldrich's heart sped up. "Mr. Clay," he prompted, "have you been instructed about your responses here?"

"Uh." The ruffian's heavy breathing dominated the courtroom while he struggled to phrase his answer. Finally, he said, "Stillman—uh—Mr. Stillman said we should not talk about how we brung you down to see Jack."

"And why was that?" asked Aldrich.

"Objection!" called Stillman.

"Overruled," the judge answered without taking his gaze from Joe Clay.

"Because we should never have brung you down there in the first place," the hooligan answered in a rush. "Now you're gonna blame us for Jack being dead on account of how we knew that he would want even more money from you."

A swell of chatter ran through the courtroom, and Judge York banged his gavel. "Order!" he shouted. "Order in the courtroom!"

Trying to control a smile, Aldrich picked up a pile of papers and shuffled them into a neat stack. "So, you knew," he said, "even while you escorted me down to Mr. Bury's establishment, that my life would be threatened?"

Joe Clay kept his eyes focused on his feet. "Yeah. Yeah," he muttered. "We knew."

"And yet," Aldrich continued, keeping his voice level, "you did nothing to warn me?"

Joe's head jerked up. "Of course we didn't warn you!" he snapped. "Why would we do that?"

Aldrich looked pointedly at the jury members, his eyebrows raised, before turning back to the hooligan. "Thank you, Mr. Clay," he said. "I believe that is all that I require from you at this moment."

From that point on, Aldrich felt the body of evidence build up in support of his argument of self-defence. He could almost sense the jury members' disapproval of the way he had been treated.

When they filed out of the room to make their deliberations, he leaned over to Conrad and asked, "What now?"

Conrad stretched his arms over his head and yawned. "Ordinarily," he said, "I would say we should head home for a good night's sleep in our own beds. This, however, has been a trial unlike any I have had the pleasure to sit through. Everything seems to be rushed along. I should have thought that the Magisters would order it drawn out as long as possible. After all, you are a thorn in their sides, and they will do everything they can to discredit you. However, that is not what happened today." He linked his hands together and tapped his forefingers against each other as he grinned at Aldrich. "I do not fully understand what is going on here. Stillman seems completely unable to slow the proceedings. Did you notice that every single one of his objections was overruled?"

His voice dropped to an inaudible whisper. "I do not like to suggest such things, but one does wonder if the judge has already formed an opinion about the outcome. Even the jury members are happy to hurry the process. In my experience, they would be ushered off to bed at this time—or perhaps to dinner in a fine restaurant—but never to begin their deliberations. Not at this hour! Why, it is nine o'clock at night!"

Aldrich reached under the desk, hauled up his briefcase, and began to pack away his materials. "Are we finished here for the day?" he asked. All of a sudden, he felt so weary he could hardly move.

"I suspect we are," answered Conrad.

When they stood to leave, Aldrich turned and did a double take. The courtroom benches were still packed with hushed spectators watching him with undimmed curiosity.

Leaning down, he spoke into Conrad's ear. "What are they

waiting for?" he murmured. "Should we stay too?"

Instead of answering, Conrad drew back his shoulders and threw out his chest. "We shall find a comfortable spot to wait for a response from the members of the jury," he said, starting toward the swinging door at the back of the room.

Despite his fatigue, Aldrich followed with a loose, easy stride, smiling and nodding to the onlookers. Just as he reached the exit, a door slammed behind him.

"Excuse me, Doctor Durante," the bailiff called. "The jury has just sent word that they have reached a verdict. They are coming back to announce their decision."

Few Troublemakers Left

It is with great pleasure and no small measure of civic pride that this esteemed publication reports on the most laudable advancements in the ongoing Dirt Town cleansing initiative. Under the astute guidance and unwavering vigilance of the estimable Captain Audo Jansen and the indefatigable Commandant Forge-37, our valiant City Guard has effected a veritable transformation of the once-benighted district.

"At this point in our campaign," said Commandant Forge-37, I am pleased to report that the streets of Dirt Town have been largely rid of the criminal elements. The sheer number of villains who once populated this quarter have been duly dealt with, leaving but a few miscreants yet to face the swift hand of justice."

-from The Cairnisle Times,
Tuesday, May 21, Year 27 AK

FIFTY ~ WILHELMINA

WILLY STOOD STOCK-STILL AND listened.

Nothing.

Still, she could not shake the feeling that something was

amiss. She had learned to trust those instincts.

Exhaling a slow, silent breath, she crept along the narrow alley that separated her father's house from the neighbouring property. Every step was familiar. Almost no preparation had been necessary for the job. She knew every detail about both the site and the target.

Nonetheless, she had been careful not to rush. Benj had been thoroughly briefed. She had chosen Tuesday night because it was the servants' free evening, leaving her father home alone.

Would she feel remorse when she killed him? Would she miss him? It seemed highly unlikely. Since her grandfather's death, it had been just the two of them. Yet they had never been close.

Her father's assassination would be a major victory for Aldrich. Not only would a vocal opponent be removed, but Willy would be in a position to fund his campaign. She would have sole charge of the largest bank in the country.

Would it require a large commitment of her time? It might not be so bad if it did. Lord James had brought her in for a few meetings. Because he generally limited her role to ornamental, she had attended grudgingly. However, elements of the discussion had captured her attention, and her interest had not been feigned. If she were actually in charge, she could imagine the appeal.

Stopping under the ground floor window outside her father's study, she pressed herself against the building. Residual heat from the day's sun seeped from the brick and through her leather coat. It was more warmth than she had ever received from her father.

He would be labouring over a ledger filled with numbers, as he did every evening. Money was the true love of his life.

By the light spilling onto the lawn through the crack in the drapes, she checked her little hawk timepiece. Benj would be in position. He had gone around to the back entrance to ensure no one entered from there.

Earlier, she had watched her father step up to the study window to draw the drapes. She pressed her lips together. She should have taken the shot. It was foolish to have hesitated. But she wanted to look into his eyes and let him know that she had won before pulling the trigger. It would make it much more satisfying.

He knew her secret identity. What would he think when he saw her pointing a gun at his heart? Would he laugh at her then?

Sliding over to the next window, she slipped a thin band of steel under the sash and released the lock's catch. It was a trick she had perfected years ago. The window opened silently on tracks she had always taken care to keep lubricated with wax.

Stretching up, she grabbed the sill and hoisted herself over the edge. The thick carpet muffled her landing and then her footsteps as she tiptoed to the doorway.

Light streamed into the hallway from her father's study, and her heart raced as she edged close enough to peer into the room.

He was not there.

She bit her lip and pressed into the shadows, listening intently. Where was he?

The smallest rustle reached her.

The great hall.

She brushed her fingers over the pistols at her waist and stole along the corridor, taking care to avoid the squeaky boards.

What was he doing? Why had he not turned on any lights?

As she reached the arched entry into the great hall, she paused and listened again. A small moan reached her ears. Was he ill?

Abruptly, the overhead chandelier switched on, lighting the room with dazzling brilliance.

Blinded, Willy dove behind the arch.

When her eyes adjusted to the light, she sidled over to peek around the corner.

Gagged and bound to a dining room chair, Benj stared back at her. Her eyes shifted and she met her father's gaze.

He smiled and shoved his pistol harder against Benj's temple.

"Ah, the Silver Assassin," Lord James Richtofen said, his smile turning ugly. "I rather thought you might show up this evening."

Willy pointed her pistol at her father's head.

"Please, do not do anything you might regret," he said with a sigh. "I would not want to have to harm your friend." He stretched out the last word, his face twisting.

Could she squeeze off a shot before her father killed Benj? It was unlikely. The instant she aimed her weapon, he would pull the trigger. What were her other options? Would she have to let her father kill Benj?

Benj's eyes opened wide and then squeezed shut three times in rapid succession before darting down to look at his wrist.

"How is it that you were expecting anyone this evening?" Willy asked, keeping her face impassive as she followed Benj's glance.

He had managed to free one hand.

Her belly fluttered. It was not over yet.

James gave a chilling smile. "I suppose you imagine that you are the only one who knows how to play the game," he said. "The game is all in the details, and you should know I am a master of details."

Willy hid a wince behind a snarl. All her life it had been this way. Whatever she tried to do, he would take pains to assure her that he could have done it infinitely better.

Perhaps that was the biggest reason she had turned to her grandfather for guidance and encouragement.

"You play well," Willy said with a shrug. "But do you know how to win?"

A board creaked behind her.

Willy whirled to see two of Lord James' personal bodyguards.

Before she could move, they seized her, twisting her arms painfully behind her back.

Benj flew into action. Grabbing James' pistol, he turned it on one of the guards. With his uncanny accuracy, he shot the man through the heart.

Finding one hand free, Willy fired on the other guard before spinning back to face her father.

She was just in time to see him draw another pistol.

"Benj!" she cried in warning.

James pressed the gun to Benj's temple and pulled the trigger.

Blood splattered across the white carpet, and Willy's world tilted.

Benj was her friend.

She had no time to mourn. Guards barrelled into the great hall from all directions.

Tempted by the plentiful targets, Willy gritted her teeth. There were too many, and she could not win.

"I will kill you!" she shouted as she turned and darted away. Perhaps she could not get him on this occasion. But she would kill her father.

And he would not be smiling when she did.

Strategic Withdrawal

It is with a heavy heart that this esteemed publication must report on the grievous assault perpetrated upon our fair country by the notorious savage, Jarlerus the Scourge. In response to this unconscionable act of aggression, our valiant General Linus Ferguson has, in his infinite wisdom, issued a directive of utmost import to our brave defenders.

"It has become imperative, given the dire circumstances that beset us, to effect a judicious redeployment of our force," he said. "We have made arrangements to transfer our civilian populace to a safe haven. Within this fortified sanctuary, we shall be better positioned to extend our protection to both our cherished citizenry and our beloved metropolis of Cairnisle."

-from The Cairnisle Times,
Tuesday, May 21, Year 27 AK

FIFTY-ONE ~ FIAMETTA

FIA LAY WITH ONE EYE pressed against the crack in the board, watching Munash's tall house across the square. "I can't see anyone moving," she said. "How many do you think are in there?"

Sitting with his back against the opposite wall, Munash ran a hand over his close-cropped hair. "I expect there are at least fifty robots inside," he answered. "If you see no motion, that will indicate no humans are present." He smiled and drew his knees up to his chest. "They will not stay in there forever. When they leave, we will take it back."

For the first time since the 'cleansing' of Dirt Town began, Fia, Munash, and Winston planned to take the fight to the robots. The last several days had been filled with little skirmishes, but Aldrich's Army was not making any real progress. The robots—and by extension, the Magisters—were winning.

Fia scratched at the back of her neck and examined the dirt under her fingernails. She was grubby. What would Aldrich say? She had seen him only twice since the day he and Winston robbed the bank. She grinned to herself. Aldrich, a bank robber. Before she met him, he would never have contemplated such a thing.

Her smile faded and she bit her lip. It was his court day. Her stomach clenched. It was not fair. He had killed Jack Bury to save her. She was the one who had borrowed the stupid money in the first place.

She should be there. She would tell them everything, even if it meant going to jail herself.

However, Conrad Appleton had warned Aldrich against having her testify. He believed it would do more harm than good. That sent a cold prickle up her spine. She did not want to make things worse.

So, she stayed in Dirt Town with Munash and Winston. They had plenty to keep them busy.

Gustav's new device had proven invaluable. Winston approached lone robots and, with the press of a button, blasted them with a massive surge of energy that shut them down. Then he lugged them back to Gustav for repair and re-sequencing. So far, they had almost a hundred robots ready to fight on their side.

Fia shifted on the cold ground as she caught a flash of red. "Forge-37 is in there," she said. "And he's on the move."

The front door opened, and the tall robot stepped out onto the front stoop. For a long moment, he stood stock-still except for a slow swivelling of his head. His gaze stopped on the building where Fia lay hidden, and she drew in a sharp breath. Could he see through the wood?

Then, he skipped down the steps and headed to the nearest ladder.

Angling her head against the wood, she watched him climb out of Dirt Town. "He's gone," she said. "He's probably reporting to the Magisters. Should I follow him?" She had already spent several days trailing Forge-37, learning his routines.

"Not today," Munash answered quietly. "We can guess where he is going. Let us keep watch here. Perhaps we shall have an opportunity to reclaim the house."

"Winston could go in with the device," she suggested.

Munash hummed. "Maybe," he said. "Let us wait a little longer."

With a grunt, Fia resettled. She hated waiting.

Her eyelids were just beginning to droop as the enforced stillness lulled her into sleep when the blue door swung open again, and a stream of robots marched out. They had underestimated the number of robots inside. By the time the last one exited, she had counted one hundred thirteen Blue Coats and sixteen Green Coats. They must have been packed in there like pickles in a jar.

Munash crawled up beside her and peered out. "We need

to know where they are going," he said. "I want to reclaim my home. Will you follow the robots and report back on their destination?"

Fia scrambled up and stretched to loosen cold muscles. "Stay out of sight, learn all I can, and report back to you," she said, quoting his orders from previous days.

He beamed and grasped her arm with a big hand. "Thank you, Fia," he said. "You are an invaluable member of this team."

Fia felt a warm glow at his praise. "Thanks, Munash," she murmured and slipped out of the house to pursue the robots.

It was not difficult to keep out of sight. Not once did they look back. And they were loud. Despite their grace, she could drop well back and still hear the tread of so many boots.

They were heading toward the fortress. Were they going to attack? She froze mid-stride. If they made their entire approach underground and only came up to the surface for the final block, no one would know they were coming.

Her throat closed up. She could not let that happen. She had to warn them at the fortress. Abandoning her cautious tracking, she sprinted for the nearest ladder and scrambled up.

The bright lights and open streets took her by surprise. She had not been Upside for several days. After the siege-like atmosphere in Dirt Town, she gaped at the evening revellers as they strolled between shops, talking and laughing together.

Shaking herself, Fia glanced around to get her bearings and took off at a run. Even as she sprinted along the footpath, she could not miss the pictures of Aldrich that decorated every streetlamp pole as well as the windows of most buildings. Conrad Appleton was gaining traction in the election campaign.

Near the fortress, she spotted the robots climbing up to the surface on the same ladders that Munash's soldiers had used when they seized the prison. As they reached Upside, they fell into orderly rows.

The hair lifted on the back of her neck, as she scooted around a corner and accelerated. Flying to the side door of the fortress, she banged on the heavy wood.

A face appeared in the barred window. "Hi, Fia," said Arty, a former prisoner who guarded the door with his friend, Johnson. "What's up?"

"Open the door," she cried. "Robots are right behind me! Get ready! It's an attack!"

Doctor Durante Acquitted

In a turn of events that has set tongues wagging, Doctor Aldrich Durante was yesterday declared 'Not Guilty' by a jury of his peers in the untimely demises of Messrs. Jack Bury and Jimmy Cole.

The courthouse was a veritable sea of humanity as the verdict was read, with gasps and murmurs rippling through the assembled crowd. Many a handkerchief was raised to dab at misty eyes, though whether in relief or dismay, this humble reporter cannot say.

Mr. Harrison Stillman, the formidable legal mind who stood for the prosecution, expressed his profound disappointment at the outcome. "It is a lamentable day indeed," he declared, "when the more affluent members of our society can bend the very pillars of justice to their will."

-from The Cairnisle Times,
Wednesday, May 22, Year 27 AK

FIFTY-TWO ~ ALDRICH

ALDRICH COULD NOT STOP SMILING. The trial was over, and the jury had acquitted him of all charges. He leaned back in his chair, his gaze drifting to the blackened ceiling of his office. Not even the grime of hundreds of years of neglect could dampen his mood.

When he had left the fortress that morning, he had expected the trial to stretch out until Election Day. It made sense in terms of tactics. The Magisters had made it clear they did not intend to fight fairly.

However, seven members of a jury of his peers had judged him innocent—and they had done it so rapidly that it was almost as if they were on his side. Even the judge had seemed more partial to his arguments than to those of the prosecutor.

He should get some rest. He had not closed his eyes for more than two hours at a stretch over the past four days. He glanced at the mattress he had dragged into the office. The tightly tucked blanket did look inviting. But a sizzle of energy told him he would not sleep.

With a sigh, he opened the folder of papers that Conrad Appleton had left for his examination. They might do the trick. The man's thoroughness was enough to put anyone to sleep.

Suddenly, the door swung open and crashed against the wall.

Aldrich jerked up as Willy stomped in, her face a mask of fury. She glared at him, her hands clenched into fists.

A sour taste filled his mouth. She must have just returned from her grim mission. "Wilhelmina," he said, coming around the corner of his desk and reaching out with both hands. "Willy? What is it? Are you well?"

Her mouth opened, then snapped shut. Without a word, she began pacing the length of the room.

Aldrich grimaced. What had he been thinking? He should never have asked her to kill her own father.

Opening his desk drawer, he pulled out the bottle of scotch and filled a glass. He considered pouring one for himself too, but lately, he had resorted to alcohol far too often.

Carrying the glass around the desk, he stepped into Wilhelmina's path as she crossed the room for perhaps the tenth time.

"Here," he said. "Drink this. Doctor's orders."

Without stopping, she seized the glass, downed the golden liquor in a single swallow, and continued her pacing.

He touched her sleeve as she marched past. "Willy, tell me what happened," he said.

Her eyes blazed, and he jerked his hand away, backing out of her path.

"What can I do to help, Willy?" he asked. "I am so sorry. I should never have suggested it."

Wilhelmina faltered, her face crumpling. Collapsing into a chair, she dropped her head into her hands. "Benj is dead," she said. "It's my fault. I underestimated my father. I should have known that he would be on his guard. He's always on his guard. He's always ten steps ahead of everyone." She let out a little moan. "Even me."

Aldrich sagged against the desk. "Is your father still alive?" he asked.

"He is," wailed Willy. She raised a face wet with tears.

Aldrich felt the blood drain from his head. Wilhelmina did not cry.

Then she lurched upright and scrubbed her face dry. When she looked at him again, her eyes were cold. "But he won't be for long," she said, wrapping her arms around herself.

"Wilhelmina," Aldrich said. He touched her sleeve before taking her hands. "You do not have to do this. I was wrong to even suggest it."

A shudder shook her. "Why wouldn't I kill my father?" she asked. "He's earned it."

Aldrich gripped her hands, which lay quietly in his own. She was in shock. He needed to give her time to recover.

Suddenly, an explosion shook the stone floor.

Leaping up, he rushed to the door. "What was that?" he called down the corridor.

The only answer was a rattle of gunfire followed by hair-raising screams and shouts.

"It is coming from the front gate," he said. "We must be under attack." He dove for the corner by his mattress where he kept his doctor's bag. "I need to see if anyone was hurt. Will you be all right here?"

Wilhelmina squared her shoulders, all signs of her previous distress gone. "I'll go with you," she said.

Running footsteps sounded in the corridor, and Rupert Corvington poked his head in the door. "Aldrich, you are not going down there," he said. "We don't yet know what the situation is, and you are our main asset." He glanced at Wilhelmina. "Take him into the safe room, lock the door, and do not come out until I come back for you."

Aldrich shook his head. "I am a doctor," he said. "If there are injured people down there, I can help."

Rupert looked him in the eye. "Aldrich, there are people out there who believe in you," he said. "They are willing to fight for you. Willing to die for you. Right now, your job is to stay alive. Get in that safe room. Do it now. Don't argue. Gustav built it for exactly this eventuality."

Aldrich blinked. Rupert was right. As much as he hated it, he would do the wise thing and hide while others fought for him. Shoulders slumping, he turned to the concealed door at the back of his office.

After nearly two years without access to his tools, Gustav had made up for lost time. He spent an afternoon satisfying his curiosity about how the clockwork door mechanisms worked and then he had built a secret safe room for Aldrich and his staff to retreat to in the event of a security breach.

Made of steel, the small door was hidden behind a bookcase. From the outside, it opened with a lever concealed behind a removable stone.

Putting his shoulder to the bookcase, Aldrich shoved it aside with a grating noise that made him wince. Then he fumbled the stone out of its slot and pulled the lever down. The door slid open with barely a sound. Inside the tiny chamber were three chairs, a small table with a box of candles and a jug of water. Nestled in the corner—an uncomfortable reminder that they might be there for some time—sat a chamber pot.

Aldrich stared into the hiding spot. How long would they have to stay? He rolled his shoulders and let out a breath before ducking through the entrance.

Wilhelmina followed and pulled the inside lever.

"You do not have to stay with me," he said as the door sealed up and Corvington shoved the bookcase back in place. The thin rectangle of light along the floor vanished with another agonizing screech of wood on wood.

It was so dark. Already his heart was speeding up and his throat was closing. "You will miss the action," he said. "I will be fine on my own." The last words came out in a croak.

"Sure, you will," said Wilhelmina with a humourless chuckle. "Sit down, Aldrich. Before you fall down."

"Rupert just locked us in," he muttered through clenched teeth. Squeezing his eyes shut, he groped for a chair. When his trailing fingers hit the spindle back, he collapsed onto the seat.

Wilhelmina clicked her tongue. "We're not locked in," she said. "You know perfectly well that we can push the bookcase away whenever we want. At the moment, we do not wish to move it; therefore, we are not locked in, we are choosing sanctuary."

Keeping his eyes closed, Aldrich ran his hands over the

table's surface. His searching fingers closed around a candle. On the day Gustav finished his construction and brought in the supplies, Aldrich had been politely appreciative. Now, as the match flared into life, his thankfulness became real.

He set the lit candle on the table and rose to pace. Motion felt better. Since the beginning, he had known that it would almost certainly come to a fight. However, he had never imagined himself hiding behind a locked door while others fought for him.

Willy sighed. She flopped down into one of the chairs and put her feet on another. "How long do you suppose we'll have to wait?" she asked as she drew out one of her silver pistols. With practiced ease, she spun the cartridge and released the bullets so that they clattered onto the table, flashing in the candlelight.

Unable to answer, Aldrich shook his head and settled himself on the remaining chair, leaning his elbows on the table. "We are supposed to be quiet in here," he said as she fed the bullets back into her pistol. "I suppose we should refrain from speaking or moving."

Wilhelmina held a finger of one hand to her lips and holstered the pistol with the other. Then, she wriggled her eyebrows, folded her arms over her chest, and let her head tilt forward.

She would be asleep in moments. He had seen her do it before. It was a trick he envied.

With a shake of his head, Aldrich dropped his head onto his arms. As long as he kept one eye open to see the candle, he did not mind the blackness surrounding them. He had learned a great deal about controlling fear during his time in the dungeon, but the small circle of light made everything easier.

For a long time, they heard nothing. Maybe it was

unnecessary to hide. Aldrich started to get up.

Wilhelmina's head jerked up, and she shook a finger at him.

Subsiding again, he squeezed his eyes shut and strained to make out any sounds. The only thing he could hear was Wilhelmina's slow, even breathing.

Then, gunfire rattled through the old stone fortress. Even in their hiding place, the noise was startlingly loud.

They snapped upright, staring across at each other with wide eyes.

Someone cried out in pain, and heavy boots ran past in the corridor. Then more gunfire. The shooting intensified to a roar for several minutes before stopping abruptly.

Sweat broke out on Aldrich's forehead. Edging out of his chair, he slid over to the door and pressed his ear against the steel.

His heart hammered in his head. Rupert had instructed them to wait until he returned. But what if he was injured? What if he needed medical attention and Aldrich was wasting time hiding in a little metal box?

His hand was on the lever when they heard boots marching down the corridor.

"Are you certain this is his office?" a voice asked.

No reply reached them, but the voice spoke again. "He is not here now. Let us continue the search."

Willy's feet silently dropped to the floor, and she leaned forward. "It's Forge-37," she murmured. "Did they win?" She pursed her lips and shook her head, answering her own question. "No. They couldn't have won."

They waited, hardly daring to breathe. Some small part of Aldrich's mind began to calculate how long they could hold out with only water to keep them going. More than anything, he wanted to open the door and walk out of the safe room.

"Aldrich Durante," called Forge-37. He was no longer in

the office but not far away. "Doctor Aldrich Durante. This message is for you. I have assumed control of the prison. There were some unfortunate casualties during the initial fighting. However, a large number of your supporters have been taken prisoner. It is you that I have been ordered to arrest, Doctor Durante. Please show yourself immediately, or I shall be forced to begin killing these people."

This statement was followed by a gear-grinding chuckle that raised the hair on the back of Aldrich's neck.

100,000₲ Pledged

Lord James von Richtofen, a pillar of our fair society and a gentleman of unimpeachable character has thrown his influence behind our esteemed Magisters in the forthcoming electoral contest.

"It is my considered opinion that our venerable Magisters represent the sole viable option for the governance of our beloved metropolis in this most crucial of elections," he declared. "Their proven track record of judicious leadership and unwavering dedication to the public weal cannot be gainsaid by any right-thinking citizen."

Not content to merely lend his voice to this most worthy of causes, Lord von Richtofen has, in a gesture of unparalleled munificence, pledged the princely sum of one hundred thousand golds to bolster the Magisters' campaign coffers.

-from The Cairnisle Times,
Tuesday, May 21, Year 27 AK

FIFTY-THREE ~ ALDRICH

"WE NEED TO GO," WILLY murmured, backing away from the metal door and reaching for the lever that would release them from the hiding spot. "Corvington is right. You are our most important asset. We'll go down to the catacombs. They won't even know we were here."

Aldrich grabbed her arm. "We cannot do that," he hissed. "Forge-37 said he was going to start killing our people. We have to do something to help them."

Willy shook her head, her eyes hard. "No. What we have to do is get you out of here," she repeated. "You still have plenty of supporters on the outside. What you have to do is survive and win that election. Open the door. I'll go first."

Aldrich froze, his mind racing. Was she right? He had already let people fight and die for him. If he gave up now, it would be a waste of their sacrifices. He lifted his chin and nodded. "You are right," he whispered. "Lead the way."

Wilhelmina brushed a hand across her smooth blond hair and drew her pistols. "Extinguish the candle," she said, "and open the door." She tilted her head and grinned. "Go easy with the bookcase, and maybe we can get out of here without a lot of shooting."

He grimaced and hesitated. He should give himself up. His parents were down there. What if they were prisoners? Suddenly, the room spun around him. What if they were dead?

Wilhelmina nudged his elbow. "Do it," she murmured. "It's for the best."

Clamping his lips together, Aldrich leaned over and blew out the candle. In the blackness, he reached for the lever. It was cold under his fingers as he yanked it down.

The door slid back silently, and he waited, holding his breath.

When nothing happened, he set his shoulder against the bookcase. With his heart in his throat, he eased it away enough to allow a crack of light. Inch by inch, he shoved it back enough to allow Wilhelmina to squeeze through.

Exhaling hard to narrow his chest, he followed. Sunlight

streamed in through the window, and he lifted his face to it. The night had passed.

Wilhelmina jabbed him in the side with her elbow and gestured with one pistol.

He nodded and followed her across his office to the corridor door.

She peered out and then slipped out and headed toward the back staircase.

They had to pass the mezzanine that overlooked the training courtyard where Aldrich had once enjoyed a few minutes of sunshine as a prisoner. And then been beaten to a pulp for speaking up.

Willy ducked behind the low wall to stay out of sight.

"Stop citizen," a robot barked.

Aldrich and Wilhelmina froze.

But the voice had come from below. They were alone on the upper level.

"I just want to check on how he's doing," said a woman's voice.

"Stop and wait," said the robot.

Someone was hurt. Aldrich's eyes darted to Wilhelmina's, and he gestured frantically at the stairs that led down to the courtyard.

She shook her head and scurried ahead.

Aldrich squeezed his eyes shut and counted to ten before hustling after her.

The sounds of a scuffle reached him, followed by a grunt of pain.

"Aldrich Durante," blasted Forge-37, his voice easily identifiable. "Doctor Aldrich Durante. Say goodbye to Prisoner Number One."

Letting a breath out through his nose, Aldrich edged his eyes over the wall just high enough to see below.

Calder knelt in the dust of the yard, his shoulders held down by two Blue Coat robots. Behind him, Forge-37 pressed a pistol to his head.

Aldrich sagged, his heart pounding. He could not continue. He had no right to ask anyone to die for him. Not like this.

He stood and opened his mouth to call a surrender.

Forge-37 pulled the trigger.

A red flower bloomed on Calder's forehead, and he sprawled forward into the dust.

Aldrich's muscles clenched. Biting his tongue, he ducked, pressing his lips together to hold back a cry. How had it come to this? In his mind, Calder's lifeless eyes stared accusingly at him, and a wave of nausea washed over him.

Forge-37's voice penetrated his haze. "Aldrich Durante," he called. "Doctor Aldrich Durante. Unfortunately, Prisoner Number One has died. I now have a child here. Are you prepared to sacrifice her life as well?"

The robot's toneless drone pierced right through Aldrich's heart. Hazarding another peek, he spotted Fia kneeling in the dust with the pistol pressed to her head.

What was she doing in the fortress? The last thing he had heard, she was with Munash in Dirt Town. And he had thought she would be safer in the fortress. A laugh threatened to break through his control.

Ruthlessly, he tamped down the bubbling madness, forcing himself to scuttle ahead to where Willy waited for him. "We have to do something," he whispered. "It's Fia."

Willy shook her head. "No," she mouthed. "We have to get you out of here. Anything we try to do will just get you killed."

Aldrich stared at her. How could she be so callous? This was Fia. The whole revolution idea was because of Fia. He was not about to sacrifice her to the cause.

Clenching his jaw, he shook his head and stood. "Forge-

37," he called, his voice shaking only slightly. "I am here. There is no need to kill anyone else. Let her go."

Forge-37 spun around and looked up. When he spotted Aldrich, he lowered his pistol, and the unpleasant noise of grinding gears erupted from him.

Aldrich's stomach lurched. Robots should not laugh. It was wrong. A terribly disturbing nature had developed in Forge-37 if he found the idea of killing to be amusing.

"Aldrich Durante," said Forge-37. "Doctor Aldrich Durante. I have been waiting for you. I shall continue to wait while you make your way down here. In the meantime, I believe, I will continue to kill these prisoners." He waved a red-sleeved arm toward a row of kneeling hostages. Each person wore shackles and had at least two robots restraining him or her.

Aldrich bit back a moan. Both his mother and his father were among the bent figures. "I am coming down," he said. It came out sounding far calmer than he felt. "There is no need to continue the killing."

Again, Forge-37 made the horrible gear-grinding laugh. "I do not mind," he said.

"Wait," Aldrich said. "I am coming."

Fia met his eyes, and he saw the desperation there.

"Fia," he said. "Hold on. I am coming."

Without taking his eyes from her small kneeling figure, he bolted for the stairs.

"Too late," shouted Forge-37.

Aldrich flinched, expecting a gunshot. Instead, there was a brilliant eruption of light as streams of magic flew off Fia in every direction.

The robots restraining her were the first victims of her destruction as she surged to her feet. This was not like the controlled targeting that she had practised with Munash. This was an unrestrained explosion of power.

A flash streaked by Aldrich's head and he dropped to his hands and knees. Then, scrambling up, he bent nearly in two and sprinted for the staircase.

Willy was on his heels. Together, they leapt down the stairs three at a time. When they burst through the arched doorway into the courtyard, the scene had completely changed. Every robot, except Forge-37, had frozen in place. The flood of energy had overwhelmed their safety venting systems and shut down all power.

Released from their captors, the prisoners scrambled out of Fia's way.

She and Forge-37 stood alone in the centre of the empty space. He raised his pistol and pointed it at her.

At the same time, Fia lifted her arm and sent a blast of power.

The flash of blue lifted Forge-37 off his feet and hurled him against the stone wall sixty feet away.

He hit with a clatter and bounced to his feet. Instead of continuing the fight, he raced for the open front gate. "Lock it down," he shouted in his amplified voice. "Lock it down and blow it sky high."

Immediately, the clockwork locking mechanism began to whir. Forge-37 threw himself under the gate an instant before it slammed shut, leaving Fia standing alone in the courtyard.

Aldrich darted out of his hiding spot. Just as he reached her side, her eyes rolled up in her head and she collapsed.

Catching her, he swung her limp body up into his arms. "We have to get out of here," he cried. "They are going to destroy the fortress!"

"The catacombs!" shouted Wilhelmina. "Everyone, follow me." She took off toward the far exit and people streamed behind her.

Struggling along at the rear, Aldrich tossed Fia over his shoulder and found he could run more easily. But his legs went wobbly and threatened to give out when he spotted his parents just ahead. They had survived.

"Father!" he called, pressing ahead. "Mother!"

His mother turned, her gown smudged and rumpled. Lighting up with a smile, she swiped at the loose hair that hung down over her face.

His father dropped back to jog at his side. "I am very happy to see you, son," he said between gasps. "We need to hurry, Aldrich. I saw them set a bomb with a timer mechanism on it. We have less than three minutes to get out of here."

Aldrich's face twisted. "And that foul robot locked us in," he said between clenched teeth. "Wilhelmina is leading us to the catacombs, but it might be useless. There is a steel door that locks down that area as well. It might be better to get up to the battlements and pull the switch to reverse the lockdown mechanism."

"Where is the switch?" asked his father.

"Three flights of stairs above us, right beside the gate mechanism," said Aldrich as he huffed along. "There is no way that we can get up there, pull the lever and still have time to get out the front door." His face twisted. "The catacombs are our best bet. We will just have to figure out how to get through the steel door." He looked down at the unconscious girl in his arms. "Maybe Fia will be able to help."

The crowd ahead stopped and a hum of anxious chatter rose.

Aldrich shouldered his way through to the front and his stomach dropped. Just as he had feared the door to the dungeons was shielded with a smooth slab of steel with neither keyhole nor doorknob. They would never be able to open it in time.

"Give me your sword," Wilhelmina demanded of one of the soldiers. "Maybe I can jimmy it open."

The man's face tightened, and he backed away, setting his hand on the grip of his weapon

"Come on," Wilhelmina snapped. "We don't have all day."

"I'll do it," he said, drawing the sword and wedging the blade into the thin crack along the stone floor. Crouching, he strained to pry it sideways.

When nothing moved, Wilhelmina cried, "Help him."

Two more soldiers darted forward and edged their blades into the crack.

Everyone waited in rigid silence—as if holding their breaths would prevent the sword blades from snapping under the pressure. Aldrich squatted and let Fia's legs slip to the floor. His heart was hammering in his chest and his muscles were quivering with fatigue.

All at once, doors everywhere sprang open as the lockdown mechanism released with a series of metallic clicks.

The soldiers staggered back, wide-eyed and gasping, while the waiting people let out a cheer.

"What happened?" Willy muttered, shooting a glance down the corridor. "Why did they all open? This could be bad."

"Might be good," answered Aldrich. "Go!"

"Right," she said and plunged down the stairs.

The crowd followed in a rush.

Aldrich slung Fia over his shoulder and looked around for his father. He was nowhere to be seen. His mother was ahead, straining to keep up as everyone thundered down the narrow stairwell.

Stumbling on a step, Aldrich clutched at the railing, saving both himself and Fia from a headlong tumble. He needed to pay attention. The clock was ticking and speed counted but only if he could stay upright.

Safely reaching the bottom of the stairs, he charged along the corridor to the hidden entrance.

Wilhelmina knelt and pulled at something out of sight. A hole appeared and she vanished into its maw with others catapulting after her.

The crowd thinned out quickly and Aldrich grimaced. He still had not seen his father. He had to be ahead.

Reaching the edge, he peered down into the black pit. He and Fia were the last ones left above. How had he fallen so far behind? "Hello?" he called through the hole. "Is anybody there? Can you take Fia if I let her through?"

"I've got her," called a gruff voice as a pair of hands reached up.

Aldrich swung Fia off his shoulder and plunked her into the waiting hands.

She disappeared into the darkness, and he leapt at the ladder, scrambling down—and down—and down. The realization struck him that they were descending to a level that was beneath Dirt Town. Cairnisle was a city built in layers, and he understood so little of it.

Below, the fellow carrying Fia grunted. He was making excellent time despite his load. Finally, they touched down on a floor covered in a thick layer of dust. The only light came from two torches bobbing away into the distance at breakneck speed.

"Come on!" called the soldier who had taken Fia, as he sprinted after the flickering lights. "We'll catch them."

Aldrich wanted to suggest that he should be the one to carry Fia. She was his responsibility. But as the soldier sped away, he swallowed his protest and followed on legs so shaky he feared they would not support him. Nonetheless, he pushed hard and narrowed the gap.

A sudden vibration throbbed through the stones underfoot

and Aldrich nearly fell. "Did you feel that?" he cried.

The soldier staggered. "Do you think that was the bomb going off?" he asked as he regained his footing. He was hardly out of breath. "If that was all, we're going to be fine down here."

All at once, a blast of hot air, filled with dust and debris, knocked them both to the floor.

Ignoring his scraped elbows, Aldrich squeezed his eyes shut and wrapped his arms around his head as chunks of rocks rattled down around him. The noise pounded against his eardrums.

It was over in moments. In the silence that followed, Aldrich covered his mouth and nose with his sleeve and pushed himself up from the ground.

Dust hung heavily in the air. Narrowing his eyes to slits, he peered around for Fia. Was she injured?

Something had changed. The tunnel was no longer pitch black. Early morning sunlight flooded in, making patterns in the dusty air.

Fia was clearly visible where she lay stretched out, breathing slowly and deeply. Still asleep or unconscious—but not further injured. He let his head rock forward. She would be fine. It was just the over-expenditure of magic. It had happened to her before.

Beside her, the soldier who had carried her, sprawled awkwardly in the dust. A shaft of sunlight illuminated a cut above his temple. He seemed impossibly still.

Aldrich crawled over and pressed two fingers to the carotid artery on the side of the man's larynx. While he waited, hoping to feel a pulse, he squinted back the way they had come.

Where, just moments before, the tunnel had led off to other parts of the city, a view of the lake had appeared.

Aldrich closed his eyes, and let his head hang. The man was

dead. And he did not even know his name. It was all his fault. How many more lives would be lost?

He dragged a hand through his hair and turned his attention to Fia. He had to get her to safety, and to plan their next move.

The fight was far from over.

Defense Lines Fortified

In a most reassuring dispatch from the front lines, our esteemed General Linus Ferguson has declared the newly established defensive perimeter encircling the fair city of Cairnisle to be nigh impregnable. This news comes as a balm to the troubled hearts of our citizens.

"While that brigand, Jarlerus the Scourge—a sobriquet he has seen fit to bestow upon himself—gallivants about the countryside with his motley band following at his heels," the General pronounced, "we stand resolute, our fortifications poised to rebuff any manner of assault he may deign to launch against our beloved Cairnisle."

-from The Cairnisle Times,
Wednesday, May 22, Year 27 AK

FIFTY-FOUR ~ ALDRICH

ALDRICH CHECKED FIA FROM HEAD to toe. She appeared to be no worse off than she had been before the explosion. He could only hope the same thing could be said for all the others who had been caught in the catacombs during the blast.

He stared in the direction he had seen the torches disappear. He needed to catch up with the others. But first, he would assess the damage. Squinting into the early morning sun, he crawled through the rock debris to the edge of the newly-formed opening in the catacomb wall. A fresh breeze blew in, clearing the air of dust. Taking a slow breath to steady his racing heart, he anchored one foot against a rock that had fallen from the ceiling and poked his head out over the rock lip.

It was a sheer drop straight down to the lake. He stared through the dusty air into the blue depths where waves pounded against the cliffs.

Careful to keep his toe hooked around the rock, he squirmed around to look up. What he saw made his throat squeeze shut.

The entire fortress was gone. Split off from the island and fallen into the lake, it had taken part of the catacombs with it. All that rock had sunk to the bottom of the lake.

Who was dead? Had Forge-37 suffered any damage?

Aldrich pushed himself back from the edge and rose unsteadily. Staggering over to Fia, he hoisted her onto his shoulder. Had she gotten heavier? With a cold sweat trickling down his back, he trudged along the tunnel.

The urgency was gone. Forge-37 and the Magisters were likely celebrating their success. A smile tugged at his lips. They were in for a surprise. Aldrich was not dead. They had only made him more determined to knock them off their thrones.

His smile vanished. Where was his father? Would he be with the group ahead? His arm tightened around Fia's limp legs, and he quickened his pace. It was too soon to celebrate. He had to know that everyone was safe. Gasping for breath, he gritted his teeth and pushed on.

Rounding a corner, he nearly crashed into Wilhelmina, who was barreling along at a dead run.

"He's here," she shouted over her shoulder before turning

back to him. "You're not dead," she said, looking him over.

"I am not dead," he agreed, trying hard to conceal a sudden trembling in his limbs. She had survived unscathed.

"What about Fia?" she asked, leaning around him to study the girl's face.

Pressing his lips together, Aldrich readjusted his grip. "It is hard to know for certain," he answered. "I hope Munash can help her. She seems to have drained her magic reservoir completely."

His mother came around the corner. "Aldrich," she exclaimed. "You are alive! Oh, what a relief!" She wrapped her arms around both him and Fia in a fierce hug.

"Is Father with you?" asked Aldrich, looking over her shoulder. Two soldiers had accompanied them. He recognized them from the training sessions in the courtyard. Max carried a torch, and Liam had been running with his sword drawn.

Stepping back, his mother shook her head, a deep V appearing between her dark eyebrows. "I have not seen him since we headed to the catacombs," she said, her voice rising. "He said he would stay behind and help you with Fia."

Aldrich's throat tightened. The security lockdown door had opened exactly when they needed it. He closed his eyes. The soldiers had not accomplished that by using their swords as prybars.

He swallowed heavily and opened his eyes. "He is not here, Mother," he murmured, meeting her gaze.

"What?" she gasped. "Where—?"

Aldrich's face twisted. He chewed the inside of his mouth and looked up at the ceiling, noticing the streaks of red and orange in the rough stone. "He may have gone to the ramparts to pull the lever that activated the security doors," he said softly. "We can only hope he got himself to safety before the bomb went off."

His mother deflated and might have fallen had Wilhelmina not propped a hand under her elbow.

"We don't know what happened," said Wilhelmina. "Let's not make any assumptions."

Swallowing a sudden nausea, Aldrich nodded. "She is right, Mother," he said, taking her other elbow. "Let us get ourselves to safety, and then we can search for Father."

His mother blinked several times and lifted a hand to her mouth, to stifle a sob. She stared at Aldrich for a long moment, then drew a deep breath and straightened. "Yes," she said, brushing her hair out of her eyes. "You are right. We should continue."

"Do you want me to take her?" asked Wilhelmina, gesturing toward Fia.

"No," said Aldrich, shaking his head. "I can manage." They were standing at an intersection. "Which way do we go?"

Wilhelmina cleared her throat. "Munash's house is this way," she said, pointing back the way she had come.

"Lead on," said Aldrich as a curious numbness stole over him. "I am hoping that he can help with Fia."

After the first few steps, his mother gained strength and strode along in Wilhelmina's wake without faltering. Aldrich's mind drifted as if it could not abide looking too closely at the situation. He stopped briefly to peer into one of the little niches carved into the walls at regular intervals. A skeleton stared back at him from the dark voids that had once housed eyes.

He started and stumbled sideways, almost dropping Fia. Regaining his balance, he checked that she was still breathing and hurried after the others.

But he was not seeing the dimly lit catacombs. He had always considered bones a magnificent glimpse into the workings of human beings. They were the framework that supported the muscles, tendons, nerves, and circulatory system, which in turn held the organs in place.

He felt the frailty of Fia's legs under his hands and swallowed fiercely against a sudden rising fear. The skeleton in the niche was the remains of someone who had once been a living, breathing person, loved by other living, breathing people.

What if Fia did not recover? What if something had happened to his father? What of the soldier he had left behind in the catacombs?

He pushed on, staring at his mother's back. Her narrow shoulders were square, and her step was firm, but he could feel the worry pouring off her.

Wilhelmina stopped. They were back at the spot where Aldrich had come with Gustav to repair Winston. That seemed so long ago.

"Hold the torch so we can see to climb," she said to the soldier. "I'll go first." She grabbed the first rung of the ladder carved into the stone and pulled herself up. In seconds, she had vanished through the hatch in the ceiling.

"Mother," Aldrich asked. "Will you require assistance?"

She set her mouth in a thin line and raised an eyebrow at him. "I am not so decrepit as all that," she said. "I will manage."

And she did, climbing almost as easily as Wilhelmina.

"You next, sir," said Max. "We'll bring up the rear."

"Thank you, Max," Aldrich said. "And my thanks to you as well, Liam. I am grateful to you for everything you have done."

The two men beamed.

"We're happy to help," said Liam. "You just win that election."

Aldrich wrapped his hand around the first rung and grunted. "I will do my best," he said, blinking hard against a sudden dampness in his eyes as he struggled his way up, careful to avoid bumping Fia.

What had he done to deserve such faith? If he did win, he would do everything he could to prove they had been right to trust him.

When he finally poked his head up into the crowded cellar, Wilhelmina hoisted Fia from his shoulder.

"She looks like she's sleeping," she murmured as she settled the limp girl on the dirty floor.

Aldrich clambered through the hole. Setting his hands on his hips, he stretched his back. "Let us hope that is all it is," he said, rubbing his sleeve over his eyes. "She has to wake up."

Gustav had turned the house into a robot repair shop. Lifeless metal bodies lined the perimeter of the cellar. They surrounded the human refugees like sentinels.

Wealthy civilian supporters from Upper Cairnisle mingled with Dirt Towners along with former members of the City Guard and even former prisoners. They had all put their lives on the line for him. If it had not been for Fia, they might all be dead. Forge-37 was a monster, and he had to be stopped.

He glanced around at the familiar faces. Rupert Corvington hovered protectively over his mother. She held Aldrich's eyes for a long moment, and he understood from the set of her face that she believed the worst.

Resolutely, she stepped forward and gripped his arm with trembling fingers. "Aldrich, we do not know where Frederick is, but we have to honour his sacrifice," she said. "You must continue. Make your plans and see them through to the end."

Aldrich stared into the grey eyes so like his own and then wrapped his mother in an embrace. "I will, Mother," he vowed. "You are right. If we quit now, all of this will have been for nothing."

Straightening, he gazed around at the people who had

escaped the fortress with him. They had spread out around the cellar floor, sitting together in little groups. He knew most of them by name. But very little beyond that. Yet they had awarded him their faith in his ability to change Cairn. Even Rupert Corvington, who a short while ago had ordered him into the safe room, waited to hear his plan.

He cleared his throat and straightened his coat. For them, he must appear confident and optimistic. "We need to secure this entrance," he said. "The catacombs may not remain the secret they have been." He grimaced. "The explosion left a gaping hole looking over the lake." His lips thinned to a white line. "The fortress is gone. It tumbled into the lake."

Everyone went still as they considered the loss of their headquarters and Aldrich turned to Liam who had just climbed up the ladder. "Figure out a way to bar this hatch," he ordered. "We may need to use it as an escape route at some point in the future, so prepare a rope ladder as well. That will let us get twice as many down at the same time."

Aldrich hated thinking like a fugitive, but clearly the Magisters did not intend to play fairly. For the moment, he would let them believe he was dead. However, if he still meant to beat them in a fair election, he would have to let them know at some point that he had survived their assassination attempt.

Footsteps sounded on the floor above. Faces swivelled to look up and then back to him.

Aldrich set a hand on Liam's shoulder and lifted a finger to his lips.

The man froze with the hatch cover clenched in his fingers.

Wilhelmina pointed at four soldiers and then gestured toward the stairs. Moving swiftly and silently, she led them up and out of the cellar.

Left behind, Aldrich waited. Dropping to his knees, he checked Fia once more. She was breathing slowly and evenly and when he lifted her eyelid, the pupil constricted just as it should.

He sat back on his heels and the silence intensified. What was going on up there?

Then the low rumble of conversation came to them and Aldrich picked out Munash's distinctive accent.

His legs went weak. If he had not already been sitting, he might have fallen.

The door at the top of the stairs swung open and Munash padded down. "Ah, my friends," he said, standing on a low step and opening his hands wide in greeting. "You made it. Welcome to my home."

Aldrich tilted his head to the side. "It was a near thing," he said. His impulse was to turn over his new responsibilities to the leader of Dirt Town. Surely, Munash was the better choice to direct the rebellion. He squeezed his eyes shut.

They had already been over that ground.

It had to be Aldrich. By his birth and standing in Upper Cairnisle, he had the best chance of being elected.

When he opened his eyes, Munash was beside him, with Winston hovering just behind.

"What happened?" Munash muttered, hovering his hands up and down Fia's length. "No sign of injury. What did you do, you foolish girl?" Turning to look at Aldrich, he asked, "Magic?"

Aldrich nodded and then quickly explained everything that had happened in the fortress and catacombs.

As he finished, Munash let out a long breath. "She will be fine then," he said softly. "The sleep will let her heal and renew her powers." He patted her hand. "She drew so deeply on her magical reserves that it knocked her out." He sat back on his heels and narrowed his eyes. "What is your next move?" he asked. "The Magisters would be most disappointed to learn of your continued survival." He bared his teeth in an expression that fell far short of a smile. "Perhaps the first thing we should do is to disabuse them of their misunderstanding."

"No," answered Aldrich climbing to his feet and reaching down a hand to help Munash up. "Let us wait until we are ready before we tell them anything. Let them wonder. Let them celebrate." He grinned and pushed his hair back from his face. "If we time this properly, there does not have to be any threat to the citizens or to our soldiers."

A soldier clumped down the stairs. "Munash," the man called. "A messenger just arrived from the docks. He says he wants to talk to the man in charge."

Rather than responding, Munash turned to Aldrich and held out both hands, palm up. "I believe you are the one to whom he wishes to speak," he said.

Aldrich's breath caught in his throat. It was all happening too quickly and not at all as he had imagined. Setting his jaw, he drew in a deep, healing breath. "Winston, will you stay with Fia?" he asked. "Keep her safe?"

Winston nodded his head once "Yes," he said. "Citizen down." Stepping closer to her prone body, he dropped to one knee and resumed that unnatural stillness that distinguished all inactive robots.

Aldrich swept out a hand, indicating that Munash should precede him. "Let us see what this messenger has to say," he said.

He made it to the third step before a murmur of voices stopped him. Turning back, he met their gazes and felt the weight of their expectations. Even his mother, with her pinched and worried face made no complaint but watched him with eyes filled with trust.

"Wait here, please," he said. "Munash and I will go and speak with this messenger and then we will figure out what we need to do."

A couple of impatient mutters arose but quickly subsided.

"We'll get this closed up, boss," said Max. "Count on it."

"I appreciate it," Aldrich said. Clasping his hands together, he turned and bounded up the steps.

In the room above, he found a wiry little man in need of a shave. He leaned against a wall, gnawing his fingernails, while Wilhelmina peered out the narrow window overlooking the square.

The man straightened at their approach and gave Munash a nervous grin.

"Bert," Munash said, striding forward and taking the man's hand in his own. "It is very good to see you," he said. Lifting an eyebrow, he studied Bert's face. "You have come to deliver some unhappy news." It was not a question.

Bert gave a jerky nod, and his eyes flickered to Aldrich.

"Bert, may I present Doctor Aldrich Durante," said Munash. "He is standing for election as Grand Minister. Aldrich, this is Bert. He keeps an eye on the comings and goings down at the dock for me."

Aldrich stretched out a hand and said, "Bert, it is a pleasure to meet you."

Bert did not seem to know what to do with Aldrich's proffered hand. He glanced quickly at his own grubby hand and then quickly tipped his hat in greeting. "This here's him, then?" he asked, studying Aldrich.

"It is indeed," answered Munash. "You have information?"

"Maybe you noticed?" Bert said, staring at the floor. "Food's been getting a bit scarce these past few weeks?" He raised his eyes enough to look sideways at Aldrich from under his heavy eyebrows. "Not so much that we have to go without, but a mite worrisome all the same?"

Aldrich nodded, the tightness in his stomach growing. "We

have noticed," he said. While they had not gone hungry in the fortress, the soldiers assigned the task of purchasing food had reported shortages in the market.

"It's because of the raids on the mainland," said Bert. "The farmers can't get their goods to the docks. The Scourge has been nipping around the edges of Cairn for months. The soldiers have been fighting and winning some but now it's not looking good."

He drew a line with the toe of his boot on the floor. "I got a friend what works the docks on the mainland. He came across on that little skiff he keeps for fishing on Sunday afternoons." He looked up and winced. "He says yesterday, the Scourge brung his whole army down to the docks." Bert's eyes went wide. "We ain't got much time," he said. "The whole kit and kaboodle will be coming across to the island in no time."

Grand Gala Celebration

This evening promises to be a resplendent affair as the crème de la crème of Cairnisle's society gathers at the residence of Lord James von Richtofen.

Lord von Richtofen, a paragon of hospitality and civic pride, expressed his motivation for hosting this illustrious event: "I thought we could use a good celebration after the hostilities of these past months," said he. "Cairnisle is poised on the brink of opportunity for real economic growth."

-from The Cairnisle Times,
Friday, May 24, Year 27 AK

FIFTY-FIVE ~ WILHELMINA

CAREFUL TO AVOID THE POOLS of bright light pouring from the uncovered windows of the ostentatious house she had once called home, Willy crept closer and checked her hawk timepiece.

Finally.

After all the waiting, less than a minute remained. She licked her lips and flashed a grin at her little army.

Neither Winston nor the other eleven robots responded, but at least half of the twelve men bared their teeth in return. The rest of them stared stonily back at her. Everyone held their weapons ready while they waited for her signal.

Gustav had reactivated no fewer than four hundred twenty-three robots. In each case, he had made a single modification—removing the binding lock that controlled a robot's freedom of thought. As each one came back to life, he explained the situation and asked if it wanted to join the rebellion. Every single robot had answered in the affirmative, and as a result, they had more than enough robots to support the human fighters on the mission.

So far, everything had gone exactly to plan. Her plan. Aldrich and Munash would still be dithering if she had not come up with a strategy and outlined the whole thing. Aldrich still wanted to beat the Magisters fairly in a democratic election.

She had to admit, the man talked a good game when it came down to it. In front of a crowd, he had the same charisma that made Munash so effective. Despite his initial reluctance to attack, he had given a speech just before they set out that sent shivers up her back.

She was not sure how he did it, but Aldrich had a way of making you understand how important you were. And he made some excellent points that she had not considered.

The Magisters did rule by fear. It was subtle if you were not on the receiving end of their retributions. But if one looked, it had always been there. If she actually cared about the political prisoners, the assassinations, and the poor mages, she might have been moved by his impassioned words. As it was, she was thrilled that when he finished speaking, it was time to move out.

Noble principles were all well and good, but her primary satisfaction had always been the killing. That moment when a life snuffed out and a person became a non-person was her most important reward.

Aldrich was right about the evening's unprecedented opportunity though. Every Magister, their five apprentices, their supporters and Forge-37 would all be at her father's little party, which he was billing as a celebration of Cairn's financial potential. That was a laugh. To her, it was clear he was applauding Aldrich's death. No doubt he believed she had died in the explosion too. Was that part of the celebration?

What would he think when he saw her tonight? She pictured his surprise. That would make her revenge all the sweeter. Normally, when she went into action, her only goal was the actual kill. Tonight was different. Tonight, a debt would be repaid: her father's life for Benj's death.

Neither Aldrich nor Munash had any idea that she had her own agenda. The evening would prove enlightening for everyone.

She and Winston had led their squadron through the streets of Dirt Town to the ladders near her father's big house. From there, they climbed to Upside and, without any real resistance, took down the guards her father had stationed along the street—both human and robot.

It surprised her. Even while ensuring that every detail was planned with her usual meticulousness, she had assumed that with so many people involved, someone would make a mistake.

Four similar squadrons were lined up outside four different doorways. And below, a thousand soldiers and almost four hundred robots waited in reserve.

At precisely the same instant, the four initial attack teams would break into the house and the killing would begin. Aldrich was at the back, surrounded by a guard of twelve robots and twelve soldiers. She let out a breath of a laugh. He had taken her advice and done what he could to dress for war, strapping a belt around his waist to hold a sword and a pistol—

despite his incompetence with both weapons.

Lifting a hand, she silently counted off the last three seconds. When her last finger folded down, Winston turned the latch, and she kicked the heavy door inward. With her heart pounding, she charged into the crowded entrance hall and started shooting.

The squadron followed her and spread out. Everyone was a target. If they were in the room, they were Magister supporters. As tempting as it was to indulge in the joy of killing unarmed humans, Willy was careful to hoard her ammunition after the first few uninhibited shots. She would not forget the real object of her mission.

A friend of her father's stood frozen to the spot in the entrance to the sitting room. His eyes bugged out of his head. She grinned at him, and he pointed a finger in her direction, his mouth working. She considered shooting him. He had always been a boring prig. But then he staggered backward as a bullet caught him in the chest. Blood bloomed in the centre of his white shirt, spreading to the lapels of his sapphire evening suit. His finger drooped and he collapsed to his knees before smashing onto his face.

Behind him, the tall figure of her father darted through a small servant door that led to the central kitchens. He was the one she wanted. Keeping low, she worked her way around the outside of the room. Gunfire hammered from other rooms in the house. She allowed herself a grim smile. All the squadrons had made their entrances right on time.

The attack would be a massacre. Every guest was there to celebrate the defeat of Aldrich and his rebellion. So confident that no threat could jeopardize their comfortable lives, they had come unarmed and unwary to the party.

When she made it to the door that blended into the woodwork of the wall so cleverly that one had to know to look for it, she turned and surveyed the room. Most of the guests had surrendered and been rounded up in the corner. Their terror was almost comical.

Forge-37 let out a roar and launched himself at Winston.

After Fia woke up, completely unscathed by the eruption of magic that freed them all from Forge-37's trap in the fortress, Winston finally agreed to leave her side. Then, he allowed Gustav to open his interior and make changes to his core.

As a result, he sported a new venting system that was very similar to the one developed for Forge-37. No longer would he be subject to shut down in the event of a power surge. Plus, with the extra armour plating that Gustav had previously installed, the only upgrade that separated Winston from Forge-37 was the ability to speak and the powerful energy core that held a charge for as long as a month.

There had not been enough time to develop those modifications, but when things calmed down, Gustav intended to see what he could do with the speech function. That had been his primary focus when he was working on the Forge Initiative, and he was itching to try some of the ideas he had dreamed up during his endless days of captivity.

It was odd to recall that Winston was a robot. He was so human in his reactions that sometimes she forgot. During the long hours of enforced waiting before the attack, Willy had watched him scratch at the exposed metal on his wrist. He had obliterated the serial number stamped there and carved his name below in looping cursive.

Winston turned to meet Forge-37's charge, raising his sword and crouching. When they hit, the resulting crash was enough to silence the rest of the fighting. Both robots carried such substantial armoured plating, they were impervious to almost every attack. Against each other, they might be able to inflict some serious damage.

It would be a battle worth watching—if she did not have more pressing business.

The last thing Willy saw before she ducked into the passageway was Winston throwing back the attack and kicking out with his booted foot to connect with Forge-37's knee with enough force to knock him off balance.

Abandoning the spectacle, Willy turned and ran. She knew the back passages well from a childhood spent in the company of servants. With her father gone most of the time, her aunt only interested in ensuring that she knew how to deport herself properly in society, and her grandfather focused on teaching her the tricks of his favourite hobby, the servants had shouldered most of the responsibility for raising her.

Her father would head for the cellars where he could escape through the tunnel that led directly down into Dirt Town. She had considered that route for the attack, but it was so heavily barred from the inside that it would have been difficult to make a stealthy entrance.

Moving silently in her soft-soled boots, she raced around corners and leapt down stairs. As she reached the lower level, she spotted her father. Raising her silver pistol, she fired. With a cry, he crashed headlong onto the floor.

Panting slightly, she slowed to a walk. "Father," she said as he struggled to his knees. "I've been looking for you." She set one hand on her hip and studied him.She had hit him exactly where she had aimed—in the widest part of his calf. He would not be able to stand, but it would not kill him. She smiled. His death would be far more memorable than a single well-placed bullet.

He pushed up to a kneeling position and turned a stony face toward her. "I had hoped you were dead," he snarled.

His words struck her like a blow. She forced herself not to

flinch and kept her smile in place. "And that was your first mistake," she said. Quick as a snake, she stepped close and darted out a hand to grab his hair. Stretching his head back, she punched his face with the hand still holding a pistol.

His smug, self-righteous look disappeared as his hands went to his face. Blood from his broken nose, gushed between his fingers.

Willy flushed with the heady sense of invulnerability. Who was he to threaten her? "Your second mistake was allowing me to catch you," she said. Barely giving him a moment to catch his breath, she knocked his hands aside and punched him again in exactly the same spot.

His scream filled her with something almost like happiness. "Benj was my friend," she said. "You shouldn't have killed him."

Keeping him immobilized with her hand in his hair, she kicked him solidly in his wounded calf. When he squirmed away, she punched him again, followed by another kick to the calf. He whimpered and sagged against her grip, but she jerked him up, eliciting a snarl of protest.

"Father, I do believe I have beaten you at your own game," Willy said in her best socialite voice.

His eyes flickered and he moaned as she pressed the muzzle of her pistol against the top of his head. "Wilhelmina," he mumbled.

"Yes," she said. "There is no question. I win and—" She pulled the trigger. "You lose."

The report was deafening in the rock tunnel as blood and brains sprayed over her trousers.

Her lips twisted and she thrust the limp body from her. Standing over his crumpled form, a flush of warmth ran through her body. How many times had her father built himself up by insulting and belittling her. How many times had he told her who she was and what she needed to do?

From far above, distant shouts and shooting caught her attention. She narrowed her eyes. The fighting had been all but over before she left the main level. What was happening?

Giving her father's lifeless body one final kick, she turned away, reloading her pistols as she retraced her steps through the corridors.

At the entrance to the ballroom, she cracked open the servant door and peered out. Dead socialites littered the glossy parquet floor and many of the mirrored walls were shattered and blood spattered.

Only robots were still fighting. At least a hundred of the Magisters' robots had arrived. They were battling one-on-one with Gustav's modified robots. Combat was limited by the space in the room, but the two robot sides were so evenly matched in both ability and numbers that it appeared the battle could go on indefinitely.

Over in the corner, the fight between Forge-37 and Winston continued. Neither had gained the least advantage.

Winston pointed a hand toward an immensely heavy, full-size bronze statue of one of her father's self-important ancestors. Then he whipped his arm forward. The statue rose up into the air, hovered uncertainly, and then smashed forcefully into Forge's stomach, knocking him to the ground. The light in Forge's eye flickered once before deactivating.

Swooping down, Winston plucked up Forge's tricorn hat and jammed it onto his own head. Then he released a piercing series of whirring clicks that halted the attacking robots.

Everywhere, the fighting ceased. In something close to synchronicity, the robots sheathed their weapons and stood at parade ground attention.

Shocking Assault

A most distressing incident occurred yestereve at the grand residence of Lord James von Richtofen. A gathering of the island's finest citizens was besieged by a band of ruffians led by none other than the infamous Doctor Aldrich Durante.

It will be recalled that Doctor Durante was believed to have perished in the explosion that consumed Cairnisle Prison. His unexpected resurrection has cast a pall of uncertainty over Cairn.

This publication sought comment from those in attendance, but all declined to speak on the record, no doubt still reeling from the night's harrowing events.

-from The Cairnisle Times,
Saturday, May 25, Year 27 AK

FIFTY-SIX ~ ALDRICH

ALDRICH STEPPED DOWN FROM THE automatized carriage, his body well-rested for the first time in ages. The scene before him was in stark contrast to the previous night's carnage. He bit the inside of his mouth, a familiar question echoing in his mind: How had it come to this?

When the fighting finally ended the night before, Aldrich had stayed, treating the injured and sending them to the hospital. As he watched the final automatized carriage roll away with his last patient, exhaustion had crashed over him.

That was when the longing to sleep in his own bed had hit. No one had argued when he suggested it. The danger, it seemed, had been squashed.

Fia and Winston had accompanied him home. While he revelled in the comfort of his bed, Fia had reclaimed her room, and Winston had stood guard in the kitchen. Aldrich had given Wilhelmina only a fleeting thought before falling into a deep slumber.

Setting his hands on his hips, Aldrich studied the scene. The bodies had been removed and the bloodstains scrubbed away so that the footpath outside James Von Richtofen's house no longer resembled a war zone. One would never guess at the slaughter that had taken place only a few hours earlier. The only oddity was the neat row of disabled robots that had been laid side by side on the edge of the flower beds.

Inside, it was a different story. When Aldrich entered the house, his footsteps echoed in the eerie quiet. Not a single mirror in the ballroom remained intact, and the profusion of bullet holes recalled the night's violence.

At the far end of the long room, Rupert Corvington was speaking to a soldier. The afternoon light pouring in through the tall windows illuminated his face, revealing deep shadows under red-rimmed eyes. His normally neat, red uniform was dirty and bloodstained.

Aldrich hurried toward the old soldier. "Rupert, you really must rest," he said.

Corvington wiped a hand across his face and blinked blearily. "You know, I may just take you up on that," he said. "I am just on my way to interview the robot, Forge-37." He shut his eyes and swayed for a moment before focusing on Aldrich's face again. "Gustav Florenburg has him ready for interrogation. Maybe we can get some useful information out of him before we shut him down permanently."

"You go rest," said Aldrich, setting a hand on his sleeve. "I will interview the robot." He grimaced. "I owe him."

Rupert straightened, opened his mouth to argue, then let his shoulders slump. "You're right," he said with a sigh. "I'm done in. You take the interview. I'm going to find a bed."

As Rupert slouched away, Aldrich made his way into the dining room where he found Forge-37 bound to a heavy chair. Carvings of grape vines ran across the chairback, and Aldrich stared at the design. The house was Wilhelmina's. She had showed him her father's body. Recalling the tortured look on the older man's face, he shuddered.

Shaking his head to clear the image, he focussed on Forge-37. Gustav had stripped him of his red Commandant uniform along with both arms, both legs, his venting system, and the lens that allowed him to focus his magic. All in all, he had been rendered harmless and helpless.

Nevertheless, two burly armed guards—Dwight and Arnold, if Aldrich's memory served him correctly—along with a pair of robots stood nearby. No one was taking any chances.

Forge-37's face had been dented beyond recognition. Half of his carefully carved beard had torn free, revealing the gearing beneath. Yet his piercing blue eyes remained unchanged.

"Doctor Durante. Doctor Aldrich Durante," Forge-37 said in his precise tones, followed by a grinding laugh. "It would appear that our roles have been reversed." His head turned jerkily from side to side. "You have me at a disadvantage."

Aldrich lowered himself into a chair opposite Forge-37 and stared at the battered visage. The robot's arrogance might make it easier to pry useful information from him. Aldrich just had to come up with the right questions.

"You once told me that you are the finest piece of technology ever constructed," he said finally. "It is a shame that your handsome face had to suffer such damage." He feigned sympathy. "Of course, that does not matter, since your formidable mind is your greatest asset."

Forge-37's head twitched like a broken marionette. "Never before has anyone been able to consider every angle of a situation at once, memorize reams of information and synthesize it efficiently in order to make the most productive plans," he said.

Aldrich forced a smile. "I am completely envious of your capabilities," he murmured. "Your wisdom is an enormous gift to everyone in Cairn. It is my great fortune to have this opportunity to learn from you."

The robot made a rude noise by grinding his gears. "You have access to the same facts and observations that I have," he responded. "What could I possibly teach you that you have not already figured out for yourself? Processing speed is my talent, but you have had sufficient time to go over the situation." His monotone voice continued. "May I take this opportunity to say that the attack at the celebratory party was a stroke of brilliance. If I had to be out-manoeuvred by a human, I am happy that you are that human." He cackled his unnerving laugh. "I saw your potential that day in the fortress when we spoke. You are one of the few adept humans I have encountered."

Aldrich's mind raced. Forge-37 had developed such an incredibly twisted personality. How had such foulness happened? Winston expressed nothing but concern for the humans around him. Yet Forge-37 was an abomination. Did he reflect the Magisters? The thought sent a shiver down

Aldrich's spine.

Slapping his hands on the table, Aldrich shoved back from the table and rose. "Shut him down," he said. "He is of no further use to us."

The grinding chuckle burst forth again. "You may shut me down," said Forge-37. "But this is only the beginning. Consider yourself warned. PI2-234, the robot who has taken to calling himself Winston, will turn against you. Do not trust him. Robots will never be satisfied with playing servant to the humans' master. Have no doubt, this is a war and robots will win." He jerked his head back and forth. "We are the superior beings."

"I will take your warning for what it is worth," Aldrich said as he stepped away from the table. With a nod to Dwight, who held Gustav's device for shutting down robots, he added, "Go ahead. We are done here."

"Yes, sir," said the big man as he stepped forward. Holding the instrument to the side of Forge-37's head, he pressed the button.

Battery Factory Still Shut

The continued closure of our fair city's battery factory has led to a most vexing predicament upon our thoroughfares. An ever-increasing number of automatized carriages, bereft of power, now litter the tracks, presenting a considerable hazard to those attempting to navigate our streets.

These abandoned vehicles, once the pride of our modern metropolis, now stand as stark reminders of our current tribulations. Citizens find themselves forced to navigate a veritable maze of metallic obstacles, testing both patience and skill in equal measure.

-from The Cairnisle Times,
Monday, June 17, Year 1 AD

FIFTY-SEVEN ~ ALDRICH

ALDRICH SQUEEZED HIS EYES SHUT. The entire weight of Cairn seemed to have settled onto his shoulders. He could feel it pressing down on him, making it difficult to breathe.

He and his supporters had moved into his mother's home. Despite the constant bustle, there was plenty of room for everyone. Along with giving them a headquarters from which to work, the arrangement served a second purpose.

With his father's heroic death, Aldrich felt a duty to see to his mother's well-being. She showed a remarkable resilience, helping where she could and contributing excellent suggestions to the discussions that went on at all hours of the day.

However, during quiet moments, he saw in her a sadness that reflected his own and he had no wish to leave her alone. Time and busyness would aid in her recovery—as it would his.

The person he was truly worried about was Wilhelmina—or Willy as she insisted on being called. She paced about the house like a caged animal, unable to settle on anything.

Aldrich's mind flashed to the book on psychological disorders he had been reading the day he met Fia and started on the path that had brought him to this point.

Had the act of killing her father pushed Willy over the edge into a psychosis? He swallowed against a lump in his throat. How had he ever believed that was a good idea?

Opening his eyes, he stared out the window of his father's office. But he was not seeing the carefully kept gardens.

In his mind, he pictured automatized carriages abandoned on the streets, their batteries long dead and the usually bustling marketplace eerily quiet. His eyebrows drew together as he imagined all the people hiding in their homes, waiting for him to come up with a solution to their problems.

In the three weeks since he assumed power, he had been on a merry-go-round of obligations. With everything happening so quickly, there was hardly time to think.

He swiped a hand across his face and turned away from the view, his gaze falling on the pile of reports cluttering his desk. Each paper bore news more dire than the last. He picked up the most recent dispatch, its crisp folds a stark contrast to his own rumpled appearance.

"He actually calls himself Jarlerus the Scourge?" Aldrich

asked, looking up from the paper and grinning at Munash. "I thought that was a name the newspapers gave him."

Munash gave a dry, humourless chuckle and uncrossed his legs. "The Scourge, indeed," he answered. "According to our sources, he relishes the name. He is a plague to anyone who opposes him and his united tribes."

Aldrich's smile disappeared. "He is a plague to us for certain," he agreed, studying the paper again. "It says here that the entire mainland surrounding the island has fallen to his control."

Pressing his lips together, Munash leaned back and linked his fingers across his stomach. "It is true," he said in his rich baritone. "We have not received a single shipment of food in nearly two weeks."

Aldrich flopped into his chair and gripped the armrests. "This is not exactly how I imagined my first days in office would shape up," he said with a sigh. Straightening, he ran a hand through his dishevelled hair. "It will be difficult to convince people that this invasion is not the result of the rebellion. Not even I would vote for me if there was an election tomorrow."

He closed his eyes again and rested his head on his hands. Did he regret that the Magisters and their apprentices had escaped injury during the attack on James von Richtofen's house? They must have used magic to get safely clear before rushing back to the Black Tower to barricade themselves inside.

Aldrich had gone to visit them there, but they had refused his invitation to talk. In fact, they had ignored all communications with the outside world.

As far as Aldrich could see, they had abandoned Cairn to struggle on without leadership. Therefore, despite the uncertainty of his own position, with the help of his supporters, he had gathered the reins of power.

Commandant Rupert Corvington had assigned armed guards around the perimeter of the tower grounds to monitor the Magisters' movement. As of yet, the mages had made no effort to leave the safety of the tower and messages had gone neither in nor out.

By immersing himself in all aspects of the government, Aldrich was learning bit by bit what was required. There was a lot to it. If he was honest, it was more than he expected. But hard work had never deterred him.

Everyone treated him as the leader, and a few people had even addressed him as Grand Minister. However, he had quickly rebuffed their courtesy. He would not accept that title until he won it in an official election.

He pushed his hair off his forehead and corrected himself. If he won the official election.

The Magisters were wise to hide out in their tower—leaving all the blame of the current situation clearly in Aldrich's lap.

A quiet knock sounded at the door and Conrad Appleton stuck his head into the room, his eyes darting between Aldrich and Munash. "Ah, Doctor Durante, I had hoped I might find you here," he said. "The Magisters have just sent a message from the Black Tower. The Grand Magister himself, Augustus Köhler, has made an offer that you might find interesting. Despite these unusual circumstances, I must counsel that you give his proposal some consideration. In my years working at his side, I found him an intelligent and well-informed man." Conrad's face twisted. "Intelligent, but weak in terms of his values."

Aldrich seized the opportunity to interrupt. "Mr. Appleton, what is he offering?" he asked.

In an uncharacteristic hesitation, the little man lifted a hand to his carefully combed hair and patted it as if to reassure himself of its order before removing his small round spectacles and polishing them on a sparklingly white handkerchief. Then he settled the spectacles on his nose and took a deep breath.

"Augustus Köhler and the other Magisters have chosen to withdraw from their role as leaders of Cairn rather than engage in an unnecessary battle with you and your supporters," he said. "They wish you to note that they have done this willingly and it is entirely temporary until such time as they are re-elected to their positions by the good citizens of Cairn." He swiped his handkerchief across his forehead and pressed a hand to his chest. "I need to sit," he mumbled as he dropped into the chair beside Munash and blew out a long breath.

Conrad smoothed his handkerchief on his knee and carefully refolded it along the sharp creases. "Augustus Köhler recognizes that they have left the country leaderless in the interim and appreciate that you found the fortitude to step into the breech." The corners of his mouth pinched together as he met Aldrich's gaze. "He notes that you have no experience as a leader of a country as complex as Cairn. He, on the other hand, has been ruling for the last twenty-seven years and he apprenticed in the role for many years prior to that."

He stopped and glanced at Munash before settling his gaze back on Aldrich. "He wishes to offer you the benefit of his experience and wisdom in the form of counsel and advice," he said in a rush.

Holding up both hands as if to forestall any arguments, he continued. "Now, I understand that you might view such an offer as an insult—both to your abilities and to those of the people around you—but I can assure you, Augustus Köhler could be an extremely useful ally. He knows every detail about the normal operations of this city and the surrounding countryside. He may even have some insight into what may be done about Jarlerus the Scourge."

For once, Conrad ran out of steam and Aldrich did not have to interrupt him to get a word in edgewise. A silence descended over the room as the three men considered the Grand Magister's offer.

Aldrich's gaze slid from the walls of his father's study to the cold fireplace, remembering his visit on the day when he first met Wilhelmina. The campaign to unseat the Magisters had begun then. He pursed his lips with a shake of his head. What an ill-informed idealist he had been.

Pushing back his chair, he rose from the desk to walk around to the other side and stopped in front of Conrad. "I have no intention of trusting Augustus Köhler," he said flatly. Then he jutted out his chin. "However, I can see the merit of having an advisor as experienced as him."

He placed his palms together and tapped the index fingers against each other as he continued his stroll across the room to the window. "You can tell him that we will consider whatever advice he chooses to share. Our first priority is to protect the city from an invasion by Jarlerus the Scourge." He allowed himself a small smile as he pronounced the raider's full title. "Does he have any ideas about how to deal with that?"

Find a Hiding Spot

On the eve of what may be Cairnisle's first invasion by a foreign power, interim Minister Doctor Aldrich Durante has issued a statement urging citizens to exercise prudence.

"I ask you to trust that we have formulated a plan to repel this attack," the Minister stated. "However, I would be remiss in my duties if I did not advise citizens to remain out of harm's way."

Doctor Durante further counselled, "We urge all residents to seek a secure location and remain there until the conflict is resolved. Your safety is of paramount importance."

-from The Cairnisle Times,
Tuesday, June 18, Year 1 AD

FIFTY-EIGHT ~ ALDRICH

ALDRICH SWIPED AT THE SWEAT beading on his forehead. He wore the heavy armour only at Willy's insistence. How did people tolerate it? The stairs to the top of the city wall had left him winded and red-faced.

As he walked along the battlements, he kept his back straight and tried to hide his worry. Smiling and greeting the soldiers by name, he felt a small measure of success when they responded in kind.

They were a twitchy lot, staring out across the water, as the fleet of ships approached under full sail. Mere specks on the horizon when he first arrived on the hill, they were doubling in size with every passing minute. He could already make out the colours of the flags fluttering atop the highest masts.

His smile evaporated and his mouth went dry. They were coming on so quickly.

Normally, the approach of those same ships was met with a bustle of preparations down on the dock. Workers would be preparing to unload, while automatized carriages lined up, ready to carry produce to the four corners of the city.

However, the latest refugees from the mainland reported that the holds of the ships were filled to bursting with soldiers bent on killing—rather than vegetables and livestock meant for the market.

Squinting against the evening sun, Aldrich spotted the easily recognized figures of Winston and Rupert Corvington in their matching red coats. With his height and his bright orange tunic, Munash stood out as well. He was the only person on the wall without armour. If even half of what Wilhelmina had said about his mage powers was true, he had no need of it.

Hurrying his pace, Aldrich arrived at their side to discover that Fia and Willy were there as well. Winston held a telescope to his eye, all the while releasing a whirr of clicks that communicated what he saw to the hundreds of robots standing along the western wall.

"Doctor Durante," Rupert Corvington greeted him. "The soldiers will be pleased to see you. I don't know how you do it, but you've convinced everyone that you hold all the answers."

Aldrich's heart bumped and he smiled tightly before turning to stare out over the lake. "How long before they come into cannon range?" he asked.

Rupert pursed his lips and shaded his eyes as he gazed out across the stretch of water. "Won't be long now," he answered. "We best get you below." Raising his voice, he called, "Willy, please escort Doctor Durante to his home."

"I should stay," Aldrich protested. "As you say, the men look to me for encouragement."

Munash and Willy exchanged a long look. The taut line of her shoulders told Aldrich that she had even less desire to leave the epi-centre of the fight than he did.

"Really," Aldrich said. "You need not worry about me. I can find a spot and stay out of everyone's way."

With a sigh that rose up from her tall dusty boots, Willy shook her head. "And that just goes to show that Munash is right," she muttered. Stepping to Aldrich's side, she hooked her arm through his. "Aldrich, let's get you back to headquarters," she said in the cheerful voice she used when she was dressed as Wilhelmina von Richtofen. As she steered him toward the nearest stairs, she touched Fia's shoulder. "Fia, you come too."

Glancing back, Aldrich caught the look that Munash threw Fia. Their efforts to protect him were almost insulting. The girl was not being sent off the wall for her own safety. Despite her age, she had proven she was more than able to take care of herself and anyone else around. Unfortunately, the same could not be said for him. He was a liability. So, he held his tongue and let Willy lead him away with Fia trailing reluctantly behind.

Before the stairwell closed around him, his last glimpse of the wall showed the robots spreading out along the entire length of the battlements. The sheer number of them was reassuring. A continual stream of whirring chatter passed down the line as they moved into position. Surely, they would be able to beat back the invaders.

At the street level, as they left the confines of the covered stairs, an explosion rocked the ground. They staggered and turned to look up at the wall.

Rupert Corvington thrust his head over the ramparts. "Run!" he bellowed.

Willy's eyes flared wide. Grabbing Aldrich's arm, she took off, dragging him along.

After a stumble when his feet tangled under him, he lifted his chin and kept up despite his clumsy armour as she pelted through the maze of streets toward his mother's mansion.

Running easily at his side, Fia twisted around to look back. Her eyes widened and she gave a choked cry. "Faster!" she cried.

Aldrich glanced back over his own shoulder. A chill ran through him, and he caught a toe on a cobblestone.

Before he could sprawl facedown in the empty street, Willy yanked him upright. "Move it, Aldrich," she gasped. "I can't carry you."

His feet responded as the air filled with a cacophony of guttural shouts, piercing shrieks, and thunderous battle cries accompanied by the rhythmic pounding of boots on cobblestones.

Where had they all come from? His single glimpse of the screaming horde of barbarian warriors with their terrifyingly savage leather armour and fearsome helmets did not make any sense to him.

Waving a motley collection of axes, hammers and swords, the volume of their war cries increased when they spotted Aldrich's small group.

"How—" he wheezed. The ships were still offshore when they left the ramparts. They could not possibly have docked in that short time.

"The ships were a distraction," Willy answered. "They came in through the catacombs where the fortress sheared off into the lake."

Even as she finished speaking, he knew she was right.

Jarlerus the Scourge was living up to his name. If Aldrich wanted to defeat him, he would have to try to think like him. He squeezed his eyes shut and followed the slap of Willy and Fia's feet while his mind raced frantically in every direction.

Then his eyes snapped open. Jarlerus the Scourge was not a mindless barbarian. He was a man with a vision. He wanted an empire. That meant the men racing through the streets had a destination.

A wave of dizziness washed over. If he were attacking the city, he would have a very good understanding of the layout and he would have a target. Jarlerus, as successful as he had been in working his way through the countries east of Cairn, would have a similar plan.

The invader prided himself on growing his realm. He would kill only enough citizens to cow everyone else into submission. The leaders would be his real target.

In all likelihood, they were not chasing Aldrich at all. Jarlerus would have no idea that Aldrich was currently running the country, and if he did, he would expect to find him in the recognized centre of city politics—the Black Tower. Therefore, the attackers were heading for the place where the Magisters were holed up.

Had Köhler known this would happen? Did he have a plan?

"We have to get to the Black Tower," Aldrich called. He could see the high round walls soaring above the rest of the city. It looked much too far away. He caught Willy's arm as they dashed past a parked automatized carriage and pulled her to a stop. "This will be much faster," he said.

"Great idea," gasped Fia as she whirled and wrenched open

the door before flinging herself inside.

Aldrich followed and collapsed in relief on the grubby upholstery. It was a public conveyance and after his time riding in the richly appointed carriages of his parents, he noticed the stains on the cloth that he had previously managed to ignore.

Willy crashed up against him as she jumped aboard. "The Black Tower. Fast!" she called, before slumping onto the seat.

The machine did not respond.

Aldrich's heart sank. The battery was dead. Since Fia and Willy freed the mage slaves, magic batteries had become scarce. Mentally, he kicked himself. He, of all people, knew the problems with the automatized carriages and the lack of battery power. His only excuse was the lack of oxygen getting to his brain after the sprint through the streets.

With a choked cry, he reached for the door handle. As he turned, he saw how close the following horde had come in the few seconds they had sat inside. His heart lurched. They would never make it in time.

"Wait," said Fia as she popped open the panel that hid the magic-powered battery pack. As soon as her fingertips grazed the storage crystal, it began to flicker with golden light. Seconds later, she pulled back. "The Black Tower. Fast!" she commanded.

The sudden acceleration thrust them back against the padded seats.

Aldrich twisted around to peer through the back window. When they pulled ahead of their pursuers, he sagged against the seat. "It worked," he said. "We will beat them to the tower and have time to set up a defence."

"All I saw were hammers and axes and a couple of swords," said Willy. Her face was glowing, and her eyes were bright. "Good thing they don't have guns."

The words were hardly out of her mouth when the back

window burst into a million shards as a bullet smashed through the glass.

"Down," shouted Aldrich, diving to the floor and pulling Fia and Willy with him.

Willy laughed as she righted herself and squirmed to get her feet under her. "I was wrong," she said, rolling her eyes. "They do have guns."

"Let us hope they do not have mages," said Aldrich. "If they figure out how to use automotive carriages, we will not beat them to the tower."

"If they're going to the Black Tower, we need to get you to safety somewhere else," said Fia.

One corner of Aldrich's mouth lifted. "If I did not know you would refuse," he said, setting a hand on her shoulder. "I would drop you off somewhere safe. I would rather not put you in such danger." His lips pinched together. "But there is no time. I need to get to the tower. And I need to get there before Jarlerus the Scourge. I will meet him in the seat of Cairn's power."

Calls for Calm

As our fair city grapples with an unprecedented scarcity of food, Interim Minister, Doctor Aldrich Durante, has issued a clarion call for restraint and forbearance among the populace.

"It will not improve matters if we panic," he said. "One way or another, the food supply will be re-established."

-from The Cairnisle Times,
Tuesday, June 18, Year 1 AD

FIFTY-NINE ~ FIAMETTA

FIA'S FEET WERE ASLEEP. SQUEEZED between Aldrich and Willy on the floor of the automatized carriage for the trip across town, she could not move. As the vehicle rolled to a stop, she squirmed and reached for the door handle.

"Wait," Aldrich said, grabbing her hand. "There will be guards." He poked his empty hands up and wiggled his fingers to show he held no weapons, before slowly lifting his head enough to peer out the side window.

Immediately, he flinched back down.

"What is it?" whispered Willy.

"Their guns are pointed at us," Aldrich replied through gritted teeth. He took a deep breath and shouted, "Stand down! My name is Aldrich Durante. I need to see the Magisters. The city is under attack."

Moving slowly, he opened the door and climbed out, waving his empty hands in the air.

Willy went next and then Fia rolled out, stamping her numb feet to get sensation back into them.

The guards' weapons did not waver and Fia's fingers tingled. But she held her magic in check safely behind its blockade.

"I need to meet with the Magisters," Aldrich repeated, carefully keeping his hands away from the weapons that hung conspicuously from his belt.

Dressed in his borrowed armour he looked far more dangerous than he really was.

The guards—all human— did not know that. They exchanged quick glances and took a step closer.

"No worries," said one of them. "I recognize Doctor Durante. He's the one what gave us the orders to guard the Magisters anyway. Let him go up."

Fia let out the breath she had been holding and the magic bubbling just beneath her surface diminished a little. She did not like situations that made her tense. After years of keeping everything tamped down and locked behind an impenetrable shield, she struggled to maintain control when she felt threatened.

"Thank you," Aldrich called as he sprinted toward the entrance.

Fia followed, wincing as her feet buzzed back to life.

Willy barrelled past them both and took the broad steps two at a time, reaching the door first.

"Get the guards clear, Willy," Aldrich said as he caught up. "Explain the situation. It is not safe for them to stay out here."

"Good thinking," said Willy as she turned back. "Listen

up," she shouted. "The city is under attack. Jarlerus the Scourge will be here in moments. Get everyone inside. Now!"

Grabbing the door, Aldrich pulled. "Not locked," he muttered. Pulling it open, he charged into a small dark foyer and stopped, staring around. Panels of shiny metal alternated with polished black rock. Nothing looked like a door. "Now, what?" he demanded.

Willy flew in through the door with the guards right behind. "It's this way," she said, darting across to a metal panel on the farthest part of the circular wall.

Aldrich's eyebrows quirked.

"Don't look so surprised," Willy said with a laugh as she pressed a finger on a small hexagonal button that Fia had not noticed. She tossed her head, flipping damp blond hair off her forehead and used her sleeve to dry the sweat from her face. "I've been here before with my father. You might recall that he was one of their biggest supporters."

Machinery whirred to life inside the wall. The shiny panel slid aside with a whisper, revealing a small hexagonal room.

Willy stepped inside and turned back to face Fia and Aldrich. "Come on," she said, crossing her arms. "Let's go."

Aldrich looked over his shoulder at the six guards who had joined them. "Is there room for everyone?" he asked.

"We can squeeze in," Willy answered.

Fia ended up squashed against the metal wall as she watched Willy press another button just like the one on the outside.

The door slid shut, blocking out the foyer, and the floor jolted under their feet.

"It's a lift," said Willy with a grin. "We could take the stairs but there are one hundred and sixty-eight of them." She tilted her head. "This is faster."

The floor jolted again and Fia's knees flexed as the door slid open. Her jaw dropped and she sucked in a breath. In just a few seconds, they had travelled high into the air. Visible through floor-to-ceiling windows, the city and surrounding lake spread out before them like a child's toy set.

"Come on," said Willy, leading the way.

Forcing her mouth shut, Fia followed, unable to drag her gaze away from the view.

Willy marched around the perimeter of the circular room. As they moved, the city centre came into view.

Fia's mouth went dry. The barbarians were nearly at the tower. There were hundreds—maybe thousands of them.

Her attention was so taken up with the invaders that she did not notice the people seated in leather chairs drawn up close to the glass. A rustle of clothing disrupted her observation, and she whirled, fingers spread.

All six Magisters stared back at her. Swallowing hard, she tamped down her magic. She had never seen them so close. They were all there, from Köhler with his pointy little beard to the wizened form of the one who she could never decide was male or female.

Ingrid Jaeger, lounging lazily in her chair, drew her attention. From her, Fia detected an undercurrent of magic that made her insides squirm.

Augustus Köhler, Grand Magister of Cairn, leaned back in his seat and smiled. No warmth reached his eyes, and the hair lifted on the back of Fia's neck.

"Welcome, Doctor Durante," Köhler said. "To what do we owe this unexpected honour?"

"Jarlerus the Scourge is here," answered Aldrich. He spoke so quietly, Fia hardly heard him.

Köhler did not have the same problem. His eyebrows quirked up and he gave a mocking smile. "I see that," he murmured. "That did not take long. Year One of the Rule of Doctor Aldrich Durante did not last even a month." He snorted. "We predicted as much. Did you really think it would be easy when you waltzed in and took over?"

Aldrich's eyes went cold. "I did not waltz in," he said. "I set myself up to challenge you in a democratic election. It was you who chose to hide away in this tower and ignore your responsibilities."

Ingrid Jaeger leaned forward. "You attacked a gathering of our supporters," she spat. "You killed people. You placed a guard around the tower. Is that democracy in action?"

"The attack was a mistake," Aldrich admitted, dropping his gaze to the floor. "If I had it to do over again, I would make a different choice. As for the guard—it was more about keeping track of your motions." He narrowed his eyes. "It was your choice to hole up here. And it was your choice to cease working for the country. Someone had to pick up the reins."

Köhler laughed. It was an ugly sound. "Be that as it may," he said. "You are the one holding those reins at Cairn's moment of judgement." He smirked. "It looks like you lose, Doctor Durante." He made a rude noise and Fia was reminded uncomfortably of Forge-37. "We all lose."

"Ah," said Aldrich, with a twitch of his lips. "I wondered. You were expecting Jarlerus to break through and you did not want to be the ones responsible when he did."

Köhler laughed again, his eyes hard. "It worked," he said with a flick of his eyebrows. "This fiasco is entirely on you."

"It is not over yet," said Aldrich. "I came here to meet Jarlerus the Scourge. He is on his way here and I am going to be the one to challenge him."

A throaty chuckle came from Ingrid.

"You?" Köhler asked, raking Aldrich's narrow frame from head to toe. "The armour is a nice touch. But—" He waggled his head from side to side and cleared his throat. "I do not mean to disparage your skills with a weapon, Doctor Durante, but I understand that you are more of a healer than a fighter."

The corners of Aldrich's mouth quirked up. "Perhaps that is my reputation," he said. "But I must be the one to fight him."

Willy shouldered her way forward. "Let me fight him for you," she said.

Köhler threw back his head and clapped his hands. "Your valiant defender," he sneered.

Aldrich set his hand on Willy's arm. "No," he said with a gentle smile. "I thank you, but it must be me."

She went white. "You're crazy!" she hissed. "You're useless with a sword."

Fia's head snapped up. The woman was angry. She could not recall a time when Willy showed any emotion other than that instance when she first offered to help in Munash's tall house.

"His name is Jarlerus the Scourge for a reason," Willy said, her blue eyes flashing. "You won't last a minute."

"As the past leader of Cairn, perhaps I might be the one to challenge this Scourge," said Köhler. He tried to look modest as he added, "I am rather well-known for my skill with a sword." From the scabbard at his side, he drew a long blade that caught the light from the setting sun as he twirled it expertly. It was the weapon of a rich man.

Fia spotted at least two sapphires and a ruby embedded in the pommel as they caught the light. Did he really know how to use it?

Aldrich blinked and scrubbed a hand across his face. He looked decidedly green, but he squared his shoulders and shook his head again. "No," he repeated. "It has to be me."

Fia swallowed and looked toward the window. The horde swarmed up the wide avenue and charged toward the Black Tower's entrance. A cold shiver ran up Fia's back. Perhaps they would not find the secret to the lift or the entrance to the stairs.

Heavy feet pounded up the stairs, crushing that hope.

As one, the Magisters surged up and whirled to face the entrance. The air was thick with barely controlled magic and Fia thought she was going to be sick as they listened to the footsteps draw closer.

Finally, the door flew open, and a giant of a man ducked under the frame. He was barely breathing hard after charging up the one hundred and sixty-eight stairs—despite his heavy armour. Several blond braids sprouted from under his shiny bucket helmet.

Two dozen more barbarians pressed in behind him and fanned out to fill the open space.

Spotting the huddle at the far end of the room, the giant covered the distance in four long steps. "I am Jarlerus the Scourge," he announced in a booming voice muffled only slightly by the helmet. "The city is mine!" His blue eyes glinted through the narrow eye slots as they went to Augustus Köhler with his glittering sword.

His head high and his hand on the hilt of his sword, Aldrich took one enormous step toward Jarlerus the Scourge. "I will fight you for control of the city," he said. "Fight me man-to-man." His voice held only the smallest trace of a tremor. "However, I require your commitment that your soldiers will accept the outcome. When I kill you, they must surrender and leave at once."

A chuckle burst through the air holes bored in the front of Jarlerus's helmet and the soldiers behind him roared with laughter.

Aldrich did not flinch.

The laughter faded and pity flashed in Jarlerus's blue eyes. He thumped his spear on the floor. "Satu, son of Taimi," he called without turning his head.

At his command, a warrior, only slightly smaller than the Scourge, stepped out of the ranks of soldiers.

Jarlerus the Scourge held up his right hand. "Satu, son of Taimi, you will give your word that if I die on this day, you, my second-in-command, will lead my soldiers and leave this city and the surrounding lands," he said in the slow, ceremonial tones of one pledging a vow.

The second-in-command pressed his hand to his chest and said in a rumbling voice, "I, Satu, son of Taimi, give my solemn word that if the great and mighty Jarlerus the Scourge should die, I will lead the conquering armies away from this city and the surrounding lands."

Without looking, Jarlerus tossed his spear to one of the men behind him and clapped his hands together. "It is sworn," he said, drawing his heavy claymore and dropping into a crouch. "Let us fight and let your death be on your own head."

Next to Jarlerus, Aldrich appeared insignificant and weak. Fia bit her lip. How did he hope to beat the giant? He barely came up to the Scourge's shoulders and he had no skill with a sword. Why insist that he be the one to fight?

She struggled to keep her magic under control as her belly clenched, threatening to release a killing blast. If it did not go well for Aldrich, she would step in regardless of the consequences.

Grave-faced, Aldrich drew his sword. It looked puny and flimsy against Jarlerus's fierce weapon. Awkwardly, he mimicked the Scourge's stance and hoisted his sword.

Jarlerus pounced. Swinging his sword down in a high overhand arc, he slammed it against Aldrich's blade.

The crack of Aldrich's arm breaking reverberated through the room. With a grunt, he collapsed. "I yield," he called through teeth gritted against the pain. "I surrender."

Fia thought she was going to vomit. He could not yield already. Her ears rang as Jarlerus removed his bucket helm.

"Cairn is mine!" he cried, punching a hand in the air and wheeling back to show his beaming face to his followers.

Lying flat on his back, Aldrich pulled one knee up to his chest. Drawing his pistol with his left hand, he braced it on his knee and levelled it at Jarlerus's head.

The roar of the gunshot filled the room, and a neat round hole appeared in the back of barbarian's head. Blood stained the blond braids and Jarlerus's eyes went wide. His hand went to his head before he crashed to the floor.

In the stunned silence that followed, Aldrich pushed himself to his feet. White-faced, he planted himself in front of Satu. "You swore an oath," he said through clenched teeth. "You will leave the city now."

Satu eyed him as he might a bug that he was considering squashing. "I swore an oath to leave if Jarlerus fell in combat," he said through clenched teeth. "He did not lose. He died by your treachery."

Aldrich stared back without blinking. "You swore an oath to leave if he died," he said. "I did not swear to fight honourably. It is my honour that is stained, but it is Jarlerus who is dead. You must take your army and leave."

Satu froze, his hand on his sword grip. Then, his face twisted, and his powerful shoulders slumped. "Indeed, you have stained your honour beyond recovery," he growled. "No true warrior would stoop to winning in such a foul manner." His voice caught. "But Jarlerus the Scourge demanded my oath, and I will respect it. I will lead the army away from this cursed land that bears the blood of the great and noble Jarlerus."

Bending, he tugged the limp form of Jarlerus over his shoulder. In spite of the combined weight of the huge man and his plate armour, Satu walked easily to the stairwell door. Pausing with his hand on the knob, he looked back over the heads of his motionless soldiers.

Aldrich did not flinch under the burden of the stare.

Fia's fingernails dug into the palms of her hands while they locked gazes.

Satu's lip lifted in a sneer, and he let out a slow breath before turning and ducking into the stairwell.

Election Looms

In a fortnight's time, the good citizens of our fair nation shall gather at polling stations to cast their ballots in a most extraordinary event. For the first time since Cairn's founding, two esteemed candidates shall vie for the highest office in the land.

Mr. Conrad Appleton, trusted advisor to the eminent Doctor Aldrich Durante, spoke to our correspondent on this momentous occasion. "While we have long prided ourselves on the democratic principles that govern our great nation," Mr. Appleton stated, "the sixth day of July shall mark a watershed moment in our history. Never before have our countrymen been presented with a choice between two distinguished individuals for the role of chief executive."

-from The Cairnisle Times,
Tuesday, June 18, Year 1 AD

SIXTY ~ FIAMETTA

WHITE AS A SHEET, ALDRICH staggered over to a chair. Clutching his broken arm, he lowered himself onto the smooth leather with a groan. The acrid smell of sweat hung in the tower room, mingling with the metallic scent of blood coming from the puddle Jarlerus had left behind.

Eyes blazing, Willy planted herself in front of Aldrich with her hands on her hips. "You planned that whole exhibition?" she demanded.

Aldrich gritted his teeth and scrunched up his face as he settled the broken arm more firmly against his chest. "You have heard the stories," he murmured through bloodless lips. "He did the same thing everywhere he went. The same tale has arrived from every country he conquered: Jarlerus the Scourge is a man of honour. It is a privilege to be defeated by him." He shifted slightly and his breath hissed out as sweat beaded on his forehead.

Tightening his grip on his wrist, he added, "All I wanted was to give him an opportunity to win so that he would remove his helmet." He smiled up at Willy. "You would have fought him to the death. And he would have killed you. I had no chance in honourable combat. I only had to make him believe he had won."

A spot of colour appeared on each of Willy's cheeks and her mouth opened, ready to argue.

Aldrich squeezed his eyes shut. "I need to set this bone," he muttered. "Will you help me?"

Willy blew out a breath and knelt at his side. "What do you need me to do?" she asked, her voice softening.

Fia grimaced, her stomach churning at the thought of what was to come. She did not want to watch. Turning away, she pressed her face against the window, the cool glass a welcome relief against her flushed skin.

Below, Satu and his honour guard surged out of the tower and trudged over to the front rank of soldiers who waited for the inevitable announcement of victory.

Fia narrowed her eyes. Their rows were so orderly. All the

newspaper reports told of a barbarian horde, but these were well-trained and disciplined soldiers. They stood calmly at attention, filling the streets almost all the way back to the docks, their armour glinting in the sunlight.

Directly opposite, hundreds of robots—with Winston in his recognizable red coat at their head—stood with that unnatural stillness that characterized a robot without an immediate purpose. Their metal faces reflected the light like polished mirrors.

As Satu neared, a ripple spread down the invaders' line. Those at the front had recognized his terrible burden. Setting Jarlerus's body gently on the ground, the new commander rose and faced his army. Then he began to speak.

For an instant, the rigid discipline vanished as the straight rows buckled and bent in on themselves.

Satu threw back his head and bellowed a command. Inaudible to Fia from her perch high in the Black Tower, it caused the disciplined army to still.

Over and over again, the message was repeated through the streets via officers in blue surcoats who were stationed at regular intervals along the ranks.

In a wave starting from the rear, the soldiers pivoted in place and began to march away, heading to the site where the fortress used to stand. The soldiers closest to the tower waited for their turn to move, their backs turned resolutely on Cairn's robot City Guards.

Fia narrowed her eyes. How had Aldrich known his ploy would work? As far as she could see, it could have easily gone either way.

In the insulated silence of the Black Tower, she imagined the rhythmic thud of the retreating footsteps echoing off the buildings.

It helped her block out Aldrich's murmured instructions

and then his gasp of pain. She bit her lip. She hated blood. But she should learn how to heal. Munash would help her.

"It is done," Aldrich muttered. "Help me bind it."

Willy laughed, a gentle sound that was unlike the woman Fia knew. "You should get Munash to look at it," she said. "He would fix you up in no time."

Fia risked a glance over her shoulder and watched Willy wrap a length of linen under Aldrich's arm and tie it behind his neck. She let out a breath she had not realized she was holding. He would be fine.

The Magisters had gathered on the far side of the room. She scowled at them. They were a useless, manipulative bunch.

"I'm going to talk to Winston," she announced. "He needs to know what happened."

"Good idea," murmured Aldrich. "Be careful out there."

Fia's eyebrows shot up. "You're telling me to be careful?" she asked. With a shake of her head, she headed for the entrance to the stairs.

As she clattered down the spiral steps, circling round and round until she was dizzy, she struggled to take in the enormity of what Aldrich had done. The cold stone walls closed in around her, amplifying the sound of her footsteps and her ragged breathing.

Ever since that first night when Aldrich saved her from Jack Bury's goons, Fia had trusted him. Not once had he given her any reason to doubt that faith. Every step of the way, he had understood the greatest dangers and somehow, he always figured out how to steer them to safety.

She grinned to herself. Certainly, he was not much of a fighter. But his latest exploit had taken even that weakness and turned it into a strength.

By the time she made it to the street, the last of the invaders had begun to march away. The sound of their booted feet was just as she had imagined it, a steady ominous rhythm. She stared after them. Were they truly leaving? Or was it a trick?

Winston lifted a hand and trotted over. "What is happening?" he asked. Even with the strange lack of inflection that characterized his speech, something strange fluttered in her chest every time he spoke.

"Believe it or not," Fia answered, "Aldrich just killed Jarlerus the Scourge in armed combat."

"Given what I know of our leader, I would choose not to believe such a thing," Winston said in his new monotone. "Yet I can see perfectly well that the invaders are leaving. If you say that he beat the enemy in unarmed combat, then it must be so."

Affection for this gentlemanly robot swept over Fia and she laughed aloud. "Winston, I love that you can talk!" she said. "You could always communicate but this is so much better."

Winston bobbed his head. "Yes," he said. "I could not agree more, my friend."

Fia smiled. Winston did not have any names in his recorded word bank, but he had found a way around that difficulty. When things calmed down, he wanted to add recordings of his friends' names and at the same time he hoped to have Gustav modify the timbre of his voice so that he did not sound like Forge-37.

The last of the conquering army disappeared around a corner, leaving behind an eerie silence punctuated only by the distant sound of marching feet.

"It truly is unbelievable," Fia said, placing her palms on either side of her face and squeezing. "Not twenty minutes ago, I was trying to imagine life in a conquered Cairnisle."

Durante Industries Expand

Durante Industries has announced a significant expansion in the manufacture of their acclaimed automatized carriages. These remarkable vehicles are to be marketed on the mainland, where several forward-thinking communities have commenced the installation of the necessary rail infrastructure.

Lady Mary Durante, speaking on behalf of the company, stated, "We shall require a considerable increase in our workforce to meet the growing demand."

This expansion is expected to bring new employment opportunities to our shores and further cement Cairn's position at the forefront of mechanical innovation.

-from The Cairnisle Times,
Tuesday, June 25, Year 1 AD

SIXTY-ONE ~ ALDRICH

"STOP HERE," ALDRICH ORDERED.

Instantly, the automatized carriage rolled to a stop, and he climbed out. It was a beautiful morning.

Strolling along the tidy street, he was reminded of his life before he met Fia. Everything had been so uncomplicated then. He walked to the clinic, saw his patients, went to his club for dinner and walked home. Simple.

Though he had no real desire to return to that routine, he did miss his little medical practice now and then. Fortunately, there was a great deal of excitement in unravelling the inner workings of Cairn. He revelled in the challenge.

As he approached the Black Tower, he studied the huge structure. This close, it all but blotted out the sun with its heavy black stone. The polished blocks had been engineered so that the walls were as smooth as glass.

The Magisters still lived within its protection—though they no longer had free rein to go where they pleased. At Munash's suggestion, they had each been confined to a suite of rooms in the lower levels. According to him, shields were built into the stone to prevent magic from passing through in either direction.

Aldrich scowled. He did not understand magic. It made his brain itch.

He pushed the irritation aside. There was nothing he could do about it. And there were other problems that required his attention—problems that he was far more likely to solve.

With his good hand, Aldrich checked the knot of his cravat before carefully climbing the six steps to the tower entrance. "Good morning, Nolan," he said.

"Right on time, Doctor Durante," answered the guard as he pulled the door wide for him. "I can set my watch by you."

Aldrich laughed and glanced at his own watch. It was two minutes to nine. "I am a slave to the timepiece," he said. "There is so much to do."

Inside the round foyer, he looked at the lift that would take him up to the tower rooms. He could go there and sit in Köhler's office. There were filing cabinets full of information that he could use to continue his plans to improve Cairn. Conrad Appleton would help him.

Or—

With a sigh, he turned his back on the little hexagonal button and pressed the one on the opposite side of the foyer. He had to speak with Köhler.

When the door slid open, he stepped inside and pressed the button that would take him down.

In just over one week, the citizens of Cairn would head to the polls to vote in an election that was as fair as Conrad Appleton could make it.

Aldrich's stomach tightened.

To avoid any underhandedness, he had refused to abuse the Magisters in the newspaper as they had done to him. At the same time, he did not try to hide the truth.

In a series of press releases for *The Cairnisle Times*, Conrad Appleton had done his best to explain what had been happening behind the scenes for the past many years. First, he described the Magisters' strategy for eliminating dissenters. That had been a topic close to Aldrich's heart. The number of political prisoners in the old fortress had been truly staggering.

Next, the battery factory was clearly explained for the first time, along with the Magisters' decision to make the practice of magic illegal.

He also outlined the development of the robots and the Magisters' hope that they would become the ultimate tool for controlling the population. Conrad had allowed himself a degree of editorial license on that topic. The idea of robots making final decisions did not sit well with him.

Finally, the scale of the massacre in Dirt Town was revealed. The Magisters had made a point of boasting that they were cleaning up Dirt Town, however most residents of Upper Cairnisle remained ignorant of exactly what that had meant. Over two thousand residents had been murdered in the streets.

At the same time, Aldrich wanted to be forthcoming about

the choices he had made during the fight for legitimacy. As instructed, Conrad wrote that Aldrich accepted full responsibility for the attack on the von Richtofen home and the deaths of several prominent members of society—including Willy's father.

When he read what Conrad had written on that subject, Aldrich had been tempted to remove the paragraph detailing his medical assistance on the night of the massacre. Working to save as many lives as possible—immediately after ordering the firefight that had caused the injuries—was not something of which he was proud.

When the lift door slid open, Aldrich took a deep breath of the heavy air and squared his shoulders inside his plum coat.

Three robots stood against the wall. They had been upgraded from the regular Blue Coat City Guards. Their new venting systems matched the one designed for Forge-37 and made them impervious to magic attacks.

"Good morning, Doctor Durante," said the single human guard, hastily brushing crumbs from his lap as he rose and snapped to attention. "The Grand Magister was just asking about you. He hoped you might visit."

"Thank you, Miles," said Aldrich. "How is the family?"

"They're good," answered the guard as he worked through a complicated set of seven locks. "My boy came home last night and showed me the alphabet." He beamed over his shoulder at Aldrich. "I learned fourteen of those little letters."

Aldrich returned his smile. The greatest difficulty they faced in regard to Dirt Town was turning a community of criminals into employable citizens. Fia and Munash had assured him it was possible. Already, they had started to organize schools for both children and adults.

The three robots stepped forward as the door swung open and Miles edged into the apartment. "All good here," he announced. "You can go in."

"Thank you, Miles," said Aldrich. "Keep up the good work. It will not be long before you and your son are both reading."

"Yes, sir," answered Miles. "I've been picturing how to spell my name since I came on duty. And I can do my boy's name too." His forehead crinkled. "It takes three letters to make it but to my way of thinking, two of them are completely useless since his name is Jay and that's the name of the first letter." He pursed his lips. "You'd think you could do it with just the one."

Aldrich blinked. "I never thought of that," he said. "I suspect you will find there are a great deal of superfluous letters as you learn more words."

Entering the apartment, he found the Grand Magister seated at a small table with a cup of coffee at his elbow and a book propped open in front of him. He wore a pair of plain black trousers and a white shirt open at the throat. His chin beard, normally carefully groomed to a sharp point, had not been tended in several days, nor had he shaved the rest of his face.

"Ah, Doctor Durante," Köhler said, leaning back in his chair and crossing both his arms and legs. "Is it time to get back to work?" He grimaced and gestured around his windowless room. "I find I lose track of the hours down here."

Augustus Köhler had offered his counsel and despite the constant flow of barbed comments, the daily visits had proven valuable. The intricacies of running Cairn were far more than Aldrich ever imagined, and Köhler's years of experience made his advice valuable.

The advantages of having six joint leaders had also become obvious. There was far too much for one person to handle alone.

His mother—more active in his father's business than Aldrich had ever guessed—was leading a group of manufacturers who were pleased at the opportunity to expand. The successful development of the automatized carriages— and the steel rails on which they ran—as well as the robots, were just a few of the innovations that were easily marketable in cities beyond the great lake.

The resulting employment opportunities would pull many people out of the abject poverty of Dirt Town. There would be more success stories like Miles and his family.

"Election Day is coming soon," Aldrich said, settling into the chair across from Köhler. "Conrad Appleton has completed all the necessary paperwork and sent this for your signature."

Reaching into the bag that he wore across his body, Aldrich drew out a sheaf of papers. Awkward, with his right hand in a cast and only his left hand free, he avoided the crumbs on the table as he arranged the papers in front of Köhler. Then he dug into the bag again and extricated a pen, which he set on top of the papers.

Instead of reaching for it, Köhler tightened his arms across his chest. "How do you expect me to run a fair campaign if you plan to keep me locked away down here?" he sneered. "No doubt the streets are plastered with pictures of your face and, after your little victory—" He drew out the word as he lifted one eyebrow at Aldrich's broken arm. "I imagine the citizens of Cairnisle will rush to the polling stations to make a mark beside your name. How is that fair?"

Aldrich kept his face clear of any expression. "I have no intention of detaining you any further," he said. "I will accept your assurance that you will run an honourable campaign and that everything will be done above board."

Köhler's head jerked up and he narrowed his eyes. "You're letting me go?" he asked. "Why would you do that?"

"Because I want to beat you," answered Aldrich, staring

back stonily. "I want the citizens of Cairn to look at their choices and pick me for the changes I will implement."

Köhler's eyebrows drew together into a V. Then his face cleared, and he smiled. Clearing his throat noisily, he picked up the pen and scrawled his signature across the bottom of each of the eight sheets of paper. With a glint in his eye, he picked them up, shuffled them back into a neat stack and handed them to Aldrich.

"I accept both your offer and your challenge," he said. "I give my word as a gentleman that everything I do to win this election will be as upfront and straightforward as possible. However, I should warn you." Köhler brushed a bit of lint from his trousers and cast a calculating look at Aldrich. "It is not me who should concern you. Ingrid Jaeger is a far greater danger to your fair election process than I could ever be."

Aldrich accepted the papers and slid them back inside his bag. Rising, he bowed briefly. "Thank you," he said. "I appreciate your cooperation and the warning. We had come to the same conclusion ourselves." He glanced away. "I realize it is not ideal, but we do not intend to release her with you. The others may accompany you, but Ingrid Jaeger will remain here under guard."

He frowned. "She has been particularly hostile, and we do not believe we can trust her to behave in a civil manner." He cleared his throat. "Now, if there is nothing more, I will take my leave."

Giving another half bow, he backed up to the door and knocked. "I look forward to an interesting campaign," he called. "We have ten days."

"Ten days to convince the voters to make the best choice," replied Köhler. "I look forward to it. I will see you in Magister Square at ten o'clock on Saturday, July the Sixth. We will have speeches and celebrations."

Momentous Election

This day, the sixth of July, in what has come to be called Year 1 AD, for our temporary leader, our citizens shall exercise their democratic right to choose between two distinct political factions.

Will Aldrich Durante maintain the seat he has filled for the past many weeks, or will control return to August Köhler so that he may continue into his twenty-eighth year as Grand Magister?

-from The Cairnisle Times,
Saturday, July 6, Year 1 AD

SIXTY-TWO ~ ALDRICH

"WILL YOU LISTEN ONE MORE time?" Aldrich asked, fighting to ignore the knot in his belly.

Fia unwound from her chair and picked up her empty plate along with his barely touched one. "Your speech is perfect," she said, taking the dishes to the sink. "I cannot think of one thing that should be changed and the last three times, you delivered it without a single hitch. I don't know how you do it without notes." She grinned at him. "Save it for your audience. They're going to love you." She turned on the tap. "What time is your mother coming to pick us up?"

Aldrich glanced at the clock above the table and his head

jerked back. "Is that the time?" he demanded. "She will be here in fifteen minutes."

"Then, perhaps, you should run up and change your clothes," Fia suggested. She was already dressed in her yellow coat with the black trousers and her dark hair was brushed to a shine.

"I am late," Aldrich cried as he took the stairs three at a time.

"You're fine," Fia called after him. "No need to rush."

When Aldrich descended the stairs twelve minutes later, he felt calmer. His formal suit of a rich, deep blue added a touch of elegance while giving him the air of authority he had requested from his tailor. Every time he moved, the metallic sheen caught the light. At the throat of the crisp white shirt, he had knotted a light blue cravat that had tiny ships embroidered along its edges in a slightly darker shade of blue.

Fia let out a whistle. "You look spectacular," she said.

Aldrich winked. "I do," he said with a grin. "Shall we go?"

They descended to the street level where they found Lady Durante waiting in her brand new emerald green automatized carriage. The old one had been all but destroyed during their escape from the robot attack. She had wanted to have it repaired but Aldrich convinced her that it would be better to avoid direct reminders of that day and all that followed.

The sight of his mother brought on another rush of nerves. It was his fault that his father had died. What if the people chose the Magisters instead? What if—after everything he had done—nothing changed in Cairn?

"Mother," he said as he ducked inside and kissed her cheek. "Thank you for coming."

"Aldrich, you look splendid," she said, leaning back and eyeing him. "I look forward to hearing your speech."

Dropping onto the white leather, he smiled wanly. "I am

looking forward to it being finished."

Fia slid in and sat on the opposite seat. "The speech is perfect," she said. "People are going to love him. Carriage 1435, Magisters' Square. Go."

Closing his eyes, Aldrich clutched his stomach as the automatized carriage sped toward the square where he would have to mount the stage and convince people that he was worthy of their votes. He wished it was a longer ride.

What if no one voted for him? What if he lost? He had never lost at anything in his life. How could he face his friends and family if Köhler was elected instead of him? Especially after all that happened and all of the people who had died? Suddenly, he missed his father. Why had he sacrificed himself?

Fia gripped his arm and Aldrich's eyes snapped open.

"Everyone is here!" she exclaimed. "Look! Dirt Towners are standing right beside rich swells from Upside."

Aldrich straightened and stared out the window. She was right. Overflowing with citizens, Magisters' Square teemed with energy. Well-dressed aristocrats mixed with slightly grubby Dirt Towners. If not quite accepting of each other, they were at least enduring the uncomfortable proximity.

A cheer went up as their automatized carriage slowed and rolled along the rails right up to the stage behind the row of human Blue Coat City Guards who protected the spectators from the rails.

On the stage, a brass band played a rousing march. A muscle jumped in Aldrich's jaw. Köhler and the other five Magisters already sat in the carved chairs on stage left. On the right side, six more chairs had been arranged for Aldrich and his supporters.

Was he late? His eyes flew to the enormous clock above the square and he relaxed slightly. He was perfectly on time.

He caught Köhler's eye. The Grand Magister steepled his

fingers under his nose and winked.

Aldrich flinched at the same time that Fia laughed.

"Looks like he's trying to get under your skin," she murmured in his ear. "That means they're worried." She nudged his shoulder. "Check out the face on Jaeger."

Aldrich had not missed the scowl on Ingrid Jaeger's face. She seemed unable to look away from Aldrich and the hate practically poured off her.

"Should I be worried?" he asked. "She looks like she is deciding whether to roast me alive or turn me into a rat."

Fia's giggle was almost enough to loosen the knot in his chest.

"I think you'll be fine," she whispered. "The three robots behind her will kill her if she tries anything. Besides, look at Köhler. He has laid out her orders." She smirked. "She wants to roast you, but he won't let her."

Repressing a shudder, Aldrich met Ingrid Jaeger's withering glare. She was free for the day on his orders despite an instinct that told him she would cause trouble. What he had learned in the past week about her lethal experiments with Dirt Town citizens gave him a queer creeping sensation.

Aldrich licked his lips and tried to swallow. She amplified her magical powers by killing people. The idea turned his stomach. She was a monster. Even if the Magisters won the election, she could not be allowed to continue in power.

"Munash and the others are right behind us," said Fia, craning her neck to look back. "Shall we go?"

"Yes," Aldrich answered. "The sooner we start, the sooner we finish." At once, his pulse sped up until he could hear it pounding in his temples. Closing his eyes, he deliberately slowed his breathing and forced his mind to blankness. When he finally brought his racing heart under control, he reached for the door handle.

In one swift movement, he wrenched it open, arranged a smile on his face and climbed up onto the stage.

As he turned to face the audience, his smile quickly turned real. People were screaming his name, whistling and cheering for all they were worth.

He lifted a hand to wave as his mother, Munash Conteh, Rupert Corvington, Fiametta Nardovino and Wilhelmina von Richtofen joined him at the front of the stage.

The crowd kept up its cheering as the band finished its tune. Just as the final flourish rang out, the clockwork mechanism in the clock whirred to life. The musicians had timed it exactly right.

The deep bell rang ten times, marking the hour, while the brass sculptures of six brightly painted mages made their brief trip out into the sunshine on their little carousel.

As a child, that little procession of magical figures had been Aldrich's favourite part of any assembly in Magisters' Square. His nervousness vanished. He was doing the right thing for Cairn.

He shot a glance over at Augustus Köhler as he led his entourage to the waiting chairs. The newspaper had stated that the current Magister would speak first while Aldrich, as the newcomer, would have his opportunity to sway the crowd after that.

A beautiful July morning with the sun already high, the heat was gathering in the square. Even as the last chime died away and the mechanical mages disappeared into their little chamber, Augustus Köhler rose.

Dressed in a fitted pinstriped suit completely unlike his Magisterial robes, he made his way to the front of the stage. His beard was once more clipped to a sharp point and his bald head glistened in the sunlight. Coming to a halt, he let his eyes range over his audience.

As an expectant hush settled over the square, Aldrich found himself leaning forward. What would the man say? What could he say? Would he deny the truth of the killings in Dirt Town or the abuse of mages? How could he explain the number of people who had been sent to the prison for questioning his methods?

"Ladies and Gentlemen," Augustus Köhler began, his voice rolling out over the crowded square. "Today, history will be made. Never before has someone who is not a mage attempted to challenge the long succession of Magisters in Cairn. The first rulers of our fair city used their powers to keep this island safe while governing in a fair and generous manner. Cairn, and Cairnisle with it, has grown into a prosperous and successful country—something of which I am very proud."

He stopped and swept the crowd with his gaze, a small, fond smile playing at the corners of his mouth. "I have enjoyed my time as Grand Magister. Seeing this great country grow into itself over these past twenty-seven years has been a pleasure. Together, we have accomplished many wonderful things."

He stopped and brushed a finger over his moustache. "However, I believe our long run has come to an end. Perhaps we Magisters have taken the country as far as we can." His smile broadened. "Cairn has new possibilities that I cannot even imagine—though I know someone who can. You already know him. He proved his worth as a leader during the recent attack on the city. If not for him, we would be hailing Jarlerus the Scourge as our leader and discovering what life under a dictatorship feels like."

Aldrich winced and adjusted his arm in his lap. The cast had come off the day before and he was working to strengthen it after its long immobility. Still, he did not like to think of his foolishness. The assumptions he had made about Jarlerus had turned out to be mainly true—but the results of his impetuous plan could have been disastrous.

He swallowed hard. In the end, had he done the right thing? Trading one dictator for another would not have been his first preference, but Jarlerus might have been the lesser evil. Their chances of beating the Magisters in an election were slim at best. If they lost, Augustus Köhler would take it as permission to continue as he always had: locking up anyone who disagreed with him; enslaving mages; using the robots as executioners; and favouring the rich over the inhabitants of Dirt Town.

"This man had the wit and foresight to manipulate Jarlerus and his followers into leaving us alone," continued Köhler.

"Aldrich!" cried a voice in the crowd.

Köhler beamed. "Exactly," he said. "Doctor Aldrich Durante, a young man filled with new ideas and hopes for our country. He is passionate, committed and his intelligence is unmatched. Today, as much as I was looking forward to being a part of a real demonstration of democracy in Cairn, we Magisters have made a decision. We will step aside to allow Doctor Durante the opportunity to continue to build on the strengths of Cairn."

The expectant silence of the crowd continued for another beat or two and then they broke into thunderous applause.

Aldrich's mind went blank. What did it mean? Had Köhler just handed him the election? But that could not be right. There was a roaring in his head that had nothing to do with the crowd.

The former Grand Magister turned to Aldrich with a wry smile. Executing a polite bow, he raised a hand to the crowd and exited through the door at the rear of the stage.

The other Magisters exchanged wide-eyed looks and rose together to follow him. Ingrid Jaeger shot Aldrich a look that should have set him on fire.

He closed his eyes, seeking clarity. The faces of people he

had met during the last many months swirled around his mind. Gustav Florenburg, the inventor, with his brilliant, questing mind who had been locked up in the prison for questioning the Magisters. The soldiers from Dirt Town who despite their gruff ways and calloused hands were as kind and thoughtful as anyone he had encountered in his mother's drawing room— more so in fact. The grubby children who played in the shadows of Upper Cairnisle's tall walls. The manufacturers and distributors.

They all looked to him now. Could he protect them? Could he honour their trust?

Rupert Corvington jumped up and seized Aldrich's hand, hauling him to his feet. "You did it, man," he shouted over the noise. "You are the Grand Minister!" Clapping him on the back, he shoved him toward the podium. "Talk to them, Aldrich. They want to hear what you have to say."

Army First Priority

Since the investiture of Grand Minister Aldrich Durante and his esteemed cabinet, our fair nation has witnessed a remarkable surge in industrial output. Most notably, the production of our vaunted mechanical guardians—the robots—has increased twofold, a testament to the new administration's vigour and efficiency.

When approached for comment, the Right Honourable Rupert Corvington, Minister of Defence, declared, "Our first priority is to augment the strength of our armed forces. The security of Cairn is paramount in these uncertain times."

-from The Cairnisle Times,
Saturday, September 8, Year 1 AD

SIXTY-THREE ~ ALDRICH

ALDRICH INSERTED THE SLIM TENSION wrench into the lock and closed his eyes. Visualizing the tumblers inside the padlock, he slid the pick in beside the wrench. One by one, he manipulated the pins, listening as they clicked into place until the wrench turned smoothly, and the hasp dropped open.

With a quiet exclamation of triumph, he withdrew his tools, snapped the lock closed, and tossed it back into the wooden chest before choosing another from the pile. Setting it in place, he started to work again.

His concentration was so intense that he did not hear Willy arrive. She dropped noisily into the chair across from his desk. "Getting in a little criminal practice?" she asked. "You know, Aldrich, I am sure there are a few gangs in Dirt Town who could use a good lock pick."

Aldrich jerked upright and the wrench clattered to the floor under his desk. He glowered at her, if only to hide how pleased he was to see her. "Actually, I was just enjoying a few moments of undisturbed quiet," he said as he bent to retrieve the wrench.

Willy ignored his reproof and flopping her legs over the arm of her chair, settled back, grunting comfortably. "Here I was thinking we needed a little excitement around here."

Aldrich lifted an eyebrow and wandered over to the liquor cabinet against the wall. Choosing a tall bottle, he poured a small amount of its amber contents into two glasses and held one out to her. "May I offer you a taste of some very fine brandy?" he asked. "I would like to propose a toast."

"What are we toasting?" Willy asked lazily as she accepted the glass. "Nothing has happened around here in weeks."

"That is just it," answered Aldrich as he sat down in the chair beside her and looked out the window at the view of the city spread out below. "We took over from the Magisters two months ago, and everything has gone very smoothly. You have seen what we accomplished in that short time. Imagine what we can do if we are in charge for twenty-seven years like Köhler was."

Willy snorted and her head fell back against the chair back. "Twenty-seven years is a long time," she said. "Especially if they are as uneventful as these last two months. You talk about making Cairnisle safe and free for everyone. What about freedom from boredom?" She flipped around in the chair, bringing her boots to the floor with a clunk. "Besides, what about that gang of hoodlums in Dirt Town? They don't seem to be buying your whole 'Work for Everyone—Safety for Everyone' slogan." She leaned forward and rested her elbows on her knees, letting her untouched glass dangle from her fingertips as she eyed him shrewdly. "Perhaps you should not have fired the whole division of Grey Coats."

He waved away her criticisms. "They had to go," he said. "During the election process, they made it very clear that their allegiance was to the Magisters and their supporters. I could not leave them in place." He scowled. "They fought against me."

She barked a laugh. "Of course, they fought against you," she exclaimed. "That was their job! They were following orders. And you sent them all packing." She tipped her glass at him. "What did you think was going to happen when you released a well-trained fighting force to fend for themselves in Dirt Town?"

"It is a question of loyalty," he said with a frown. "I could not, in good conscience, allow them to continue in their positions. I had to reward the people who fought for me rather than against. That meant those who stood up with us deserved those jobs more."

He pressed his lips together and shook his head. "You are making a mountain out of a molehill. The evidence speaks for itself. The city is running well. The factories are working at full capacity. Recruitment for the City Guard is decent."

Narrowing his eyes, he moved to the bottle again. "I would like to see more young people choose service with the Brown Coats across the water." He stared out at the blue horizon of the lake. "I would not be averse to hiring the people we dismissed for that purpose." He pushed his hair off his forehead. "But perhaps that will come in time. Things are improving every day. More schools opened in Dirt Town last week, and most of the children are attending. Policing in Dirt Town—"

"Yes, Doctor Aldrich Durante," Willy interrupted. "You have had a remarkable beginning. So far, Year One in the Rule of Aldrich Durante has been a great success." She rolled her eyes. "But if you want to be a truly noteworthy leader with a long list of asterisks beside your name in the history books, you are going to have to look at the problems. The real problems. And your biggest problem is happening right under your feet in Dirt Town. You might tell yourself that everything is fine, but Dirt Town is not an entirely happy place right now. People are angry and people are scared."

"Give them time," insisted Aldrich. "It will work itself out. When the culture begins to change down there, people will learn that life is better if they have fulfilling work that brings them joy instead of relying on theft and violence to gain what they require for sustaining life."

"If you give them time," Willy said, "you are going to have a bigger problem than you do now." Her forehead creased. "Have you already forgotten why you wanted to get rid of the Magisters in the first place?" She tapped an impatient foot on the floor. "They had become complacent. They stopped seeing the problems."

Aldrich flopped down in the chair beside her. "Please, Miss Wilhelmina von Richtofen, tell me what you would do about our problems?" he asked.

She tilted her chin up. "I would come up with a solution," she answered with an arrogant grin.

Tapping two fingers against his thigh, he studied her. "Do I dare ask what that solution might be?" he asked.

"You need to go down there," she said. "You need to talk

to people. You need to remind yourself of how much work needs to be done to make it habitable."

Aldrich hesitated, then clinked his glass against hers and took a mouthful. He let it sit on his tongue. Perhaps there was some truth to what she said. He had been so focused on the successes that he had overlooked the simmering issues in Dirt Town.

"Very well," he said, setting down his unfinished glass. "I will pay a visit to Dirt Town. Will you accompany me, Miss von Richtofen? I have a feeling I might need your—" he paused and squinted at her, "—unique perspective."

Willy's eyes flashed. "I would be delighted, Doctor Durante," she said. Rising, she executed a perfect curtsey and offered him her hand. "Let's go see what's really happening in our fair city."

Loved *Dirt Town*?

Your review helps others discover our story—please consider leaving one!

Scan to review.

Ready for more adventure?

Start your journey with *Raptor's Call*, the thrilling prequel to *The Hawks Trilogy*—it's FREE for subscribers.

Scan to get your free copy.

Don't stop now.

Discover a new world of intrigue and rebellion in our newest series, **Legend of Order and Chaos**.

Scan to get your copy.

Turn the page and join the adventure.

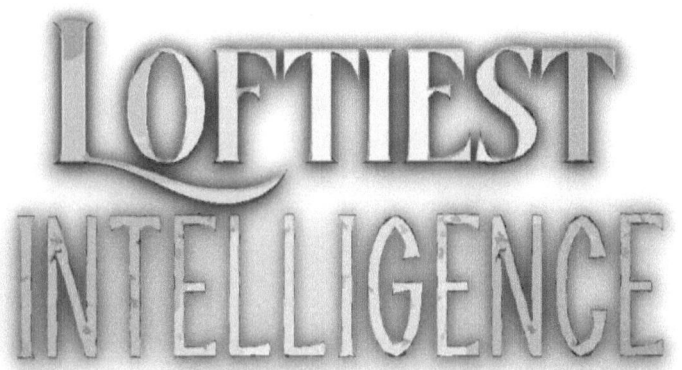

LEGEND OF ORDER AND CHAOS: BOOK ONE

PAULA
BAKER

AIDAN
DAVIES

MacFay Books

Loftiest Intelligence

Copyright © 2025 by Paula Baker and Aidan Davies

For information, contact:
MacFay Books
103 Heron Dr.
Penticton, BC
V2A 8K6

Cover Art by Daria Kovalenko
Cover Design by 100 Covers

ISBN: 978-1-7770831-1-3

Chapter One

Out the Door

"The art of the blade can only take one so far. That's why we hone our minds."

~ King Griffiths the Bold

ELLIE PUSHED THE HEAVY BROCADE counterpane aside and slithered beneath her bed, stretching to reach the furthest corner. Her groping fingers closed on the corner of a book, and she hauled it out.

"You didn't get this one," she muttered, brushing off a cobweb and flipping open the cover of her latest acquisition. Hardly more than a leaflet, *Eclipsed by Evil: The Consequences of Dark-Magic* disguised itself as a condemnation. But the treatise was no warning.

Inside, eleven forbidden spells were written in precise detail. The margins bore penciled notes—confident, deliberate—left by someone who clearly grasped their power.

She grinned. Finding it had been luck—or fate.

She did not know what had compelled her to look behind the stack of silly novels in the second-hand bookshop.

The proprietor had pretended not to notice the title when he took her coins—but he could not help a nervous glance over her shoulder when he slipped it into a paper bag. If a witch-hunter caught him, he would be in as much trouble as her.

But fortune favoured the bold.

Dark-magic books were rare. Her little library included only three others on the subject. To her mind, dark-magic was not evil. It was truth. Untamed, precise, and powerful, it was the pinnacle of all magics. And she was going to master it.

Her smile faltered. The explosion had been an accident—dark-magic was difficult to control. She had apologized to Gwen. Plus, her father had paid her generously. He even let her stay on, though the injury meant she would never walk again.

Ellie sat back on her knees, pushing her dark curls from her face. None of it would have happened if her father had not dismissed her request to study at the College of Mages. He had left her no choice but to teach herself—fumbling through dangerous spells with no guidance. Was it any wonder things had gone wrong?

And Gwen—really, it was the maid's own fault. Why had she gone snooping in the attic when Ellie had warned her countless times to stay out?

Still, the memory of the girl's twisted body haunted her.

Shutting the little book with a snap, she rose and tucked it into the pack that sat ready by the door. Inside were paper, pens, two changes of clothes, and a stash of food taken from the kitchen while Cook was out. The dried meat and fruit would be fine in a pinch—but she would need coin for real meals. And she had to retrieve at least three of the books her father had confiscated.

She stopped in the middle of her attic room and closed her eyes. Had she forgotten anything? Her fingers trailed over the burn scars on her left arm as she ran through her list.

The twisted bits of skin were a legacy of an early experiment. As a thirteen-year-old, she had read that ancient pyromancers burned themselves in order to master the feel of fire-magic.

So, she stuck her arm in the fireplace.

It had worked. Ellie knew the touch of flame right down to her bones. The wounds had taken ages to heal, and the pain had been excruciating. But she could shape the flame of a fire-spell with heat and power.

Her eyes snapped open, and she rose up onto her toes. It was time to go.

Spinning to the wardrobe, she grabbed her blue velvet coat—the one that matched her trousers. Inconspicuous, warm, and dark enough to hide grime, it was perfect for travel.

She knew better than to pretend. It would be a long and difficult journey to the College of Mages. Meeting Caeryn—the young mage who had agreed to escort her there—had been a stroke of luck. Without him, she would never have found the way. Plus, he had promised to vouch for her when they arrived.

As she fastened the long row of silver buttons running down the front of her coat, Ellie studied her reflection in the glass. Her tall, shiny black boots were the best she had. She wiggled her toes. What if Caeryn intended for them to walk the entire way? She pursed her lips.

She would need a horse. Could she take one from her father's stable? It would raise suspicions. She never chose to ride. But if she had money, she could buy one.

Turning in a circle to see the entirety of the huge attic that she had claimed as her own when she was twelve, Ellie spoke aloud to the empty room. "I'll miss you." Her gaze caught on a beam of light coming in through one of the twelve tall dormer windows.

Rising up on her toes, she extended one arm and launched into a spin. Letting the light anchor her turn, she whipped her head around each time her rotation took her beyond its view.

Snapping out of the spin, she stretched one leg behind her and held the pose for a beat. Then she propelled herself across the room in a series of long strides and sprang into the air—completing a somersault before landing with a thump that would be heard below.

"The servants won't be sad I'm gone," she muttered.

In her early days up in the attic, she had been less considerate about the hours she chose to perfect her leaps, spins, and somersaults. After the complaints had made their way through her stepmother to her, she had limited her practise to the times when the servants' quarters were empty.

"I've enjoyed my time up here," she told the room. "But I'm off to the College of Mages." Would she have time for dancing when she was there?

Her gaze caught on the empty shelves in her tall bookcase, and she scowled. Her father had taken all the books about magic—but he had left everything else. Her scowl softened as she brushed a finger across the spine of her favourite.

Set in the time when the Eastern Alliance was a mess of warring city-states, it told of Guild-Master Grael the Brave, the son of a goddess and a human soldier. She liked just about any story about the Sentries—the fabled beings who had been charged with caring for the world—but she liked the stories even better when there was a hero involved.

Guild-Master Grael the Brave led a band of champions who protected the folk displaced by the continuous wars. The descriptions of the battles were awe-inspiring—but what she really liked was the compassion that he showed for the struggling villagers. He cared about their well-being—unlike the leaders she knew.

Right beside that book was a squat volume with a red cloth cover. It told the tale of Quenith, one of Sanctuary's gods. The Red Elves from the land across the sea called him the God of Strife, and worshipped him for his strength, defiance, and tactical brilliance. Other parts of the world called him a demon because he had tried to militarize the entire population with the plan of attacking a distant realm in the sky—a place separated from Sanctuary by endless voids.

Ellie clicked her tongue. As if that was even possible.

Filias—the Goddess of Law—was the chief deity of the Eastern Alliance. Her priestesses were among the few legally sanctioned magic users in the country—and their powers were strictly bound by the Covenant of Magic. It was a meager set of privileges—barely worth the paper it was written on—and Ellie had never felt the slightest inclination to join their order.

The only other legally recognized magic users were the newly formed battle-mages. But to earn a place among them, one had to attend the College of Mages.

She glanced at the timepiece on the wall. One of the few items of dwarven technology not prohibited within the borders of the Eastern Alliance, versions of it were to be found in every room of every house in the country. Time mattered, even in a crumbling kingdom.

Before her father prohibited her from leaving the house, Ellie would have already been at the soup kitchen down near the docks, ladling out hot soup and chatting with the people who showed up for their single meal of the day.

Her stepmother disapproved of her volunteering. That might have been the reason Ellie had agreed to help in the first place. But it was not why she continued. She liked seeing how a full stomach made people hopeful.

However, it was not an ordinary day. It was the first day of her new life.

"If I am going to make my rendezvous," she said, "I'd better get a move on." The habit of speaking aloud to herself would have to end when she left her attic refuge. People would think she was crazy.

"Farewell," she sang. Slinging her pack up onto her shoulder, she slipped onto the landing and left the door open behind her. There was no point trying to keep people out any longer.

Edging along the wall to avoid the squeaky boards, she crept down the stairs.

Silence.

Perfect.

Earlier, she had watched her father ride away in his coach. He would have business with King Othwyn—if the man who had permitted the bloodless takeover by the Vennadian Emperor Thargarus could still be called a king. To her mind, that made him a puppet.

She let out a quiet snort. It made little difference whether the Eastern Alliance had been invaded. She was leaving.

Her stepmother and half-sister, Maira, had departed in the second coach. They would head to the market. Maira was always happy to trail along behind her mother, choosing new fabrics and ribbons for her dresses. Ellie doubted her half-sister noticed how thin and frightened so many of the people looked—or the Vennadians with their black uniforms and the black flags that hung everywhere.

Maybe letting the invaders into the country would bring prosperity—as her father had counselled King Othwyn. After nearly two years of the Vennadian navy blockading their ports, many would welcome the return of trade goods and the upswing in the economy.

But Ellie was not going to stick around long enough to find out if it worked.

She froze at the bottom of the first flight of stairs, listening hard. The servants would not do anything to stop her. After what had happened with Gwen, they were terrified of her.

But her half-brother, Gergic might be a problem. Was he in his room or lurking somewhere around the house?

Hitching up her pack, she slipped past the servants' quarters, down another set of stairs to the family bedrooms, and finally to the grand staircase. After a quick glance over the railing to ascertain that no one was below, she crept down the sweeping steps, careful to muffle her footsteps on the polished marble.

Her father's study was only a few doors down and she made it without encountering anyone.

It was locked. Of course. With a grim smile, she sent a twist of dark-magic into the keyhole and listened to the pins line up.

Click.

Inside, she eased the door shut and set her hands on her hips. The view out the tall windows of the corner room showed both the side and back gardens. A pair of gardeners were at work in a flower bed near the distant fence. Beyond that, a panoramic view stretched over the rooftops of the houses below to where the sun glinted off the blue waters in the harbour.

Her father had taken her books after Gwen was hurt. He had been angry—but he would not have got rid of them. He only wanted to remind her that she had to be careful. And she had been. She had kept her head down and avoided any but the simplest of spells, since the girl was hauled away to the hospital.

Ignoring the bookshelves set between each window, she went straight to the series of big cabinets on the opposite side of the room. They were the only spot large enough to hold the big tomes he had carted away from her attic.

Locked. Again.

Did her father really know so little of her that he thought that would stop her? A tendril of dark-magic slid into the little keyhole. Another click.

The first cupboard was empty except for her father's long black sword in its sheath—with the polished black leather belt still attached. He must have a meeting with the Vennadian Emperor. Out of respect, he never went armed in his presence.

With a grunt, Ellie pushed the door shut and opened the next cabinet.

And there they were.

The five wooden crates held every volume she had collected over the past six years. Some were covered with cracked leather, but most had dusty cloth covers, and a few were little more than leaflets like the one she had in her pack.

With a quiet exclamation of triumph, she hauled out the crate on top. She could not carry them all, but there were three books she wanted.

In truth, she no longer needed any of them. She had studied their contents until even the page numbers were memorized. In this way, she had learned to read several ancient tongues well enough to puzzle out the meaning of almost anything.

So far, she had—through long practise and an

extraordinary number of trial-and-error attempts—mastered control over fire spells. She was pretty good with wind too. Although she failed to see much use for it.

Her dark-magic was fine for small things, but it tended to be a little unpredictable. That was why she wanted the books. Maybe there was something she had missed.

In the fourth crate, she found *Dark Tome: Verse 3*, *Magic Undone and Other Foul Spells*, and *Daemons of the Void: The Anthology*.

Sitting back on her heels, she flipped open *Dark Tome* and was immediately drawn into an explanation of shadow-binding. The spell allowed the caster to control and manipulate shadows to ensnare or conceal objects and beings.

She jerked upright. "Neither the time nor the place, Ellie," she muttered. "Move it." Carefully closing the book, she slipped off her pack and opened the top. She had left room on the side and all three books fit easily into the slot.

When she hoisted it onto her shoulder again, it was noticeably heavier. "Doesn't matter," she said. "I can handle it."

Leaving her other books in a haphazard pile, she looked around the room again. She needed coin or something she could pawn for coin. She shrugged, settling the pack's weight. Ideally, it would not be too heavy.

Sometimes her father kept coin in his desk. She had often been the recipient of his generosity when she asked nicely. And Maira could wangle any amount out of him.

The first three drawers yielded nothing. But in the fourth one on the right side, she struck gold—literally. The fat bag jingled when she hefted it. A peek inside revealed several dozen gold and silver coins—including three full suns, which alone would be enough to purchase a horse and pay her way across three countries.

The only problem was that many merchants refused to change full suns because they did not have sufficient coin to hand. The half suns, full moons, and crowns would be easier to use. There were even a few bronze shields rattling around with the gold and silver. When did her father ever require such a tiny denomination of money?

She left the drawer hanging open and headed for the door. There was no point concealing what she had done. Her father would find out soon enough. And by then, she would be gone.

Pressing her ear to the wooden door, she listened. Nothing.

She needed a spell to either amplify her hearing or let her see through walls. She pursed her lips, and her eyes drifted shut as she considered the possibilities.

Then she snapped upright. "What are you doing, Ellie?" she muttered. "Get going. Caeryn is waiting." Tucking the purse into her coat pocket, she pulled open the door.

Her half-brother, Gergic, sat on the floor on the other side of the corridor with his back against the wall. Across his lap was the sword he had just received for his fifteenth birthday.

"Caught you!" he cried, his voice cracking as he lurched to his feet and brandished the weapon.

Ellie propped herself against the door frame. "What are you going to do with that, little brother?" she asked, staring straight into his eyes.

Unable to help himself, he flinched. He had never been able to meet her mismatched gaze. How many times had he called her a freak because one of her eyes was yellow and the other blue?

He squared his shoulders and attempted a sneer. "I'm going to send you back to your attic," he answered as he settled into a fighting stance with the tip of his blade pointed at her face. "Papa said you weren't to leave."

"I don't think so," Ellie replied. She lifted her fingers and sent a blast of wind.

Gergic hit the wall with a thud and slid down into a heap, his sword clattering out of reach. "You're crazy," he yelped. Diving after his sword, he grabbed it and scrambled up. "You could have killed me."

Ellie raised an eyebrow. "I could have," she said. "But I didn't. Don't be such a baby." She swung around and headed for the stairs, lifting a hand in farewell. "Let Papa know I won't be back. If he's looking for me, he can find me at the College of Mages."

The adventure doesn't end here.

Discover the rest of *Loftiest Intelligence* at your favourite bookseller and continue the epic saga today.

Scan to get your copy.

Don't forget to grab your FREE copy of Raptor's Call.

Scan to get your free copy.

Write a review for Dirt Town.

Scan to review.

Paula Baker and her son, Aidan Davies, wrote the middle-grade fantasy trilogy *Rebels of Halklyen*, *The God Sword*, and *The White Wolf*, along with its prequel, *Raptor's Call*. *Dirt Town* is a standalone story set in a steampunk world powered by magic. Their latest release, *Loftiest Intelligence*, is the first in a new epic fantasy series. They live in British Columbia, Canada.
Learn more at https://bakerdavies.ca

https://bakerdavies.ca